TAXI

TAXI

Manjula Padmanabhan

hachette
INDIA

First published in 2023 by Hachette India
(Registered name: Hachette Book Publishing India Pvt. Ltd)
An Hachette UK company
www.hachetteindia.com

1

Section break icon from Freepik

Hardback edition (2023) ISBN 978-93-5731-244-8
Ebook edition (2023) ISBN 978-93-5731-243-1
Paperback edition (2024) ISBN 978-93-5731-495-4

Hachette Book Publishing India Pvt. Ltd
4th & 5th Floors, Corporate Centre,
Plot No. 94, Sector 44, Gurugram – 122003, India

Typeset in Arno Pro 11.5/14.5 and Arial 10/14.5 pt
by Manipal Technologies Limited, Manipal

Printed and bound in India
by Manipal Technologies Limited

MIX
Paper from responsible sources
FSC™ C043100

To all those who have enabled me to remain a non-driver

1

There are jinxes,
Big and small
They are nasty,
One and all.

– JINXES, BIG & SMALL

The girl's nose was bleeding as she settled into the back seat. It was 3 a.m. Maddy could see her in the rear-view mirror, attempting to pinch off the flow with her bare fingers. Not succeeding.

Their eyes met in the mirror.

'Tissue?' suggested Maddy, tapping the box that lay on the divider between the two front seats. She started the car, shattering the sleepy silence of the colony.

'Ogay,' said the young woman through her blocked nose, taking a tissue.

'Lean your head back,' advised Maddy. She remembered from when she used to have nose bleeds. In school. More than thirty years ago now. Switching to Hindi, she said, 'When you get home, wrap an ice cube in a hankie and hold it against your nose.'

'Ogay,' said the girl. She held the tissue to her nose.

As the car passed under a street lamp, Maddy saw the light glisten on the girl's wet cheeks. She may have been as young as seventeen, passing for twenty with her make-up, her glittering shoes, her beaded silk dress.

As they approached the colony's gates, Maddy slowed down, giving the security guard a chance to look in. Maddy was tall and light-skinned with strong features: straight nose, clear brow, full mouth. Combined with her close-cropped hair and grey jacket, her appearance convinced the guard that there was nothing to see here. He suppressed a yawn as he waved her out.

The girl hadn't said a word on the outbound journey. In this, she was unlike the majority of Maddy's clients. Most of them preferred to sit in front and talk.

This girl had entered the back seat without speaking. Maddy knew her from previous rides. A night-shifter.

The first time she'd ferried a night-shifter, Maddy hadn't recognized the implications of the flashy clothes, the time of night. Two years later, now, she knew without question. She asked for double the amount of a normal full-day fare. Three thousand rupees for the first four hours and five hundred for every extra hour thereafter. The girls never protested. They always sat in the back, always in silence.

From the back seat, there came the sound of soft sobs. Maddy glanced in the mirror and realized that the girl's face was swollen. Her hair was disordered. This was a first. No passenger so far had returned to the car visibly damaged. Maddy struggled to maintain the barrier that curtained her professional self off from her regular self.

Maddy allowed the silence to last through four traffic intersections before drawing in a breath and asking, in a careful voice, 'What happened? Did he… hit you?'

In the mirror, the girl jerked upright.

Maddy was about to ask again when the girl forestalled her. 'Mind your own business!' she snapped. Her accent had a nasal twang. Perhaps she'd grown up in one of the many small towns that clung like ticks on a lean-legged dog along the highways leading into and out of the capital city.

Nothing more was said for the rest of the journey.

The girl was returning to an address across the river, far to the east. Maddy had collected her from and dropped her back at other addresses before this. But tonight, she was going to a colony called Sunshine Housing Estate. Maddy suspected that this was her actual home whereas the other places were temporary rentals. This colony had gated entrances too, but within its low-slung walls was a jumble of three- and four-storey flats. They were stacked tight as egg crates on either side of the narrow lanes.

The girl directed Maddy with terse commands: 'Third gate to the right. Right again. Next left, next—' Street lamps were in short supply. Maddy could sense her Hyundai flinching in the narrow alleys, as if it could sense the threat to its glossy black exterior.

'Corner building,' said the girl.

In the early days, Maddy had felt a shrinking distaste as the time neared for her passengers to count out their notes for her. If they sat in front, she used to look away. If they sat behind her, she faced forward, waiting for them to make the first move.

The discomfort vanished quickly. The majority of her clients paid at the outset, often in an envelope. They had become regulars, most of them. If a first-timer asked Maddy how she preferred payment, she told them what the others did.

Tonight, however, the girl slid out, slammed the door and clip-clopped away.

Maddy was too startled to react.

She called after the young woman's retreating back.

'Hey! Miss ...' Her voice boomed in the night.

The girl plunged into the unlit entrance of her building without a backward glance.

Maddy sat still.

This had only happened once before. A passenger had spent her entire trip, both coming and going, giggling and snuffling, with her cell phone held so close to her mouth she was practically chewing on it. In the end, it had seemed entirely in character when she jumped out and sprinted away without a backward glance.

On that occasion, Maddy had waited a few minutes, then shrugged and gone her way.

But tonight?

She gazed at her mirror ornament swinging gently back and forth in the air stream from the air conditioner vent. It was a jaunty little thing, a metallic green-gold version of the nimbu mirchi evil-eye deflector favoured by taxi drivers.

Tonight, she couldn't afford to shrug.

She angled her head to look up at the building through her windscreen. A light came on in a window on the third floor.

Turning the engine off and opening her door, she stepped into the dense heat of the night.

She had the key fob in one hand, a slender torch attached to its ring. Up three floors she went, with only the finger of light to guide her. Each narrow landing had two doors on it. On the third floor, a line of brightness showed under one of the doors. Turning towards it and finding no doorbell, Maddy banged directly on the painted plywood.

Immediately, a shadow obscured the line of brightness.

The door was flung open, and there stood the girl. 'Stob noise,' she mumbled in English. In the harsh light of a naked bulb directly over the door, the young face looked misshapen. A purple brinjal had bloomed under the left eye. Both nostrils were plugged with thick screws of tissue paper, looking like tusks.

She caught Maddy's wrist, pulled her in and shut the door. 'I can't bay,' she said. Fresh tears were now streaking down her cheeks. She jerked the paper tusks out of her nose and repeated, clearly now, 'He don't pay me. I have no money. Nothing.'

Maddy took in a deep breath.

The girl was standing like a stray dog on the pavement outside a restaurant. Ears lowered, back rounded, trembling.

Maddy wanted to slap her.

Reaching with both her hands for the younger woman's shoulders, she said, 'Stand straight! Come on. Straighten up. Now look me in the face.'

The girl raised her head, startled.

'You want me to say that I understand? But I don't. All right? I need the money too. Come on.' She turned the girl around so that she was facing away, towards the other room in the apartment. 'You can do it—'

But the girl swung around.

Her face was transformed into a demon mask of rage. It was almost comical. Her eyelids flared, her eyes became two angry, bulging orbs, the corners of her mouth were bent downwards into ugly hooks as she struggled to form words.

'You... you...' Words failed her. Two bright gouts of blood flushed from her nose.

She switched to Hindi. 'You dare touch me! Miserable filth! Cunt-dirt.' Even in full flood, she remembered to pitch her voice low. 'You fuck off now, FUCK OFF!'

Maddy stood her ground. She towered over the girl. 'Give me even one rupee of what you owe me, and I'll go,' she said. Her voice was calm.

The girl was panting.

She was still wearing her beaded dress and heels. Whirling around now, she grabbed her small black pocketbook from where it lay on the table and emptied its contents. Coins and make-up and a single crisp blue note flew out of it. She snatched up the hundred-rupee note, crumpled it and threw it in Maddy's face.

Then she spat a thick gob of blood and snot onto the bare cement floor between them. In a low voice, as if reciting verses from memory, she began to intone a litany of filthy terms. 'Whore-shit, mother-cunt, pig-turd...'

Maddy had caught the note before it fell. She turned and walked out.

She got to her car with the girl's ugly words still rattling inside her mind. She pressed the ignition switch and waited for the plush comfort of her seat and the stream of chilled air to steady her.

She felt sorry for that young woman struggling to survive in a harsh world, using the only resource she had, her body. But she felt sorry for herself, too. She needed the cash. Not having it was going to be a problem.

It was 4.30 a.m. by the time she got home.

She rented an apartment in South Delhi. It was a luxury, this modest two-storey unit in the calm, well-ordered housing complex of the Asiad Village. A luxury she could not afford.

She entered the darkened interior, poured herself a glass of cold water from the fridge, then went upstairs to her bedroom, turned on the air conditioner and changed into a caftan.

She lit a cigarette, sitting cross-legged on her bed in the darkness.

Thinking.

A cock crowed in the distance.

She lay down and soon fell asleep.

2

A faint hope
Needs soap
Jasmine tea
And hemp rope.

– JINXES, BIG & SMALL

The front door boomed open. Maddy shot upright in bed, tangled in the sheets. From downstairs came the thump of a walking stick.

'Hooooo!' A cracked voice called from inside the house. 'O-hOOOO!'

Maddy got to her feet but was disorientated. *What time is it…* She bent to squint at the clock by her bedside. *Not quite eight*. No time to get dressed. She'd have to go down as she was – unwashed, unbrushed, in her caftan.

'Where are you, madame?' the voice continued. 'Get up, get up—' Then, as an aside, 'Sleeps all day! Huh. Lazy bitch. No wonder she can't pay!'

Maddy called down as she hurried out onto the landing. 'Yes,' she said, her voice bull-frogged, clotted with sleep. Clearing her throat, she tried again. 'I'm here, Mrs Bansal.'

'What is *here*?' croaked the landlady, turning arthritically, trying to crane her neck back. '*I* am here – but you? Stuck in bed! Lazy sow!'

The woman wore a stiff organza sari that swaddled her diminutive body like the twigs of a bird's nest. From above, her head, poking up from the centre of the nest looked absurdly like an angry fledgling, with its bare skin, sharp beak and two tiny black eyes contained within swollen, purple eye-sockets.

Maddy hurried down the single flight of stairs barefoot. 'Mrs Bansal,' she said, clearing her throat again, 'Ten o'clock is what you said.'

The older woman, no longer angling her head to look up, looked around now for a chair to sit on. With both hands, she held on to the rounded handle of a thick, black cane. 'Stupid little cunt,' she muttered to herself, 'that's all they are these days. Young women. Filthy whores. Making me wait.'

The apartment, tiny and compact, had been designed to house the international athletes of the 1982 Asiad. The central well of the unit rose high, with two small bedrooms tucked into the mezzanine. There was a bathroom on that level with the kitchen right beneath. Generous windows let in light and air.

Mrs Bansal had lowered herself into one of the three chairs by the round table that occupied the middle of the ground floor.

Maddy said, as she towered over the shrivelled figure, 'It's not yet eight.'

'Eight or eighty – who cares! Where's my money?' cawed the old lady. 'That's all I care about.'

'I was going to get it this morning—'

The landlady's beak jerked up. The glittering black pinpoints stabbed out of their mauve pouches. 'Too late, too late!' the cracked voice cawed in triumph. 'I gave you all the chances! Three months, three months!'

Maddy looked down at the woman, expressionless. The need to pee was occupying front and centre of her thoughts.

'I *told* you to have it ready for me today,' continued the crone-fledgling. 'I *warned* you! But you? Coming home at all hours! Snoring in your filthy bed. Oh, yes...' The fleshless lips drew back now in a snarl that might have been a smile, exposing a barricade of grey teeth, too uniform to be her own. 'You think I don't know your secrets, huh! But I *do*! I *know*. I found out. Filthy business. Whoever heard of a woman private taxi driver! Huh. A whore with a car.'

There was a crash from the front door as Lata, the maid, came in. She held a packet of milk in one hand. A polythene bag containing bread and eggs dangled from the wrist of the other hand, which also held the front door key.

Her eyes flared with alarm at the sight of the landlady.

Mrs Bansal swivelled her beak towards the newcomer. 'Ho! You. Girl. Where's the tea? Bring water first. Lazy bitch! Is this the time to show up for work? Quickly now.' She turned back to her tenant. 'Okay. Where was I? Yes – *whoring*...'

3

The niggling doubt
Staggers out
With long black tail
And hairy snout.

– JINXES, BIG & SMALL

Traffic was jammed solid at the intersection of Ring Road and the Mehrauli turn-off. Bystanders had gathered like flies, drawn to the site of an accident.

Scorched air jittered above the hot metal skins of the stalled vehicles. The machines parped, snorted and bellowed. Men stood up from their two-wheelers, and passengers inside a DTC bus lengthened their necks in the direction of the scene.

Urchins darted from car to car holding up polythene-wrapped copies of *Elle* and *Cosmopolitan*. 'Muddum! Muddum!' they called to any women they saw. 'Ellie–Cojum? Ellie–Cojum?' Sweat from the children's matchstick limbs dripped down the plastic-wrapped covers on which dewy-skinned models exposed their perfect teeth and swelling cleavages to the world.

Maddy gestured towards the clamour. 'This is my landlady's tribe,' she said to her passenger. 'Her blood relatives. I'm the one that's different! Just by noticing it, just by hating it, I'm the one out of place.' She was dressed in an oversized men's T-shirt, dark blue with an all-over print of green alligators. She wore black slacks and black sneakers of the kind that had a high ankle cuff and elaborate laces.

'Some day in the future, when I've morphed into her, I'll be stuck in traffic and won't notice a thing.'

'Huh,' snorted her passenger, Malli, short for Mallika. She had straight, thick white hair that she wore short. She was dressed in a pleated white skirt with a fitted black chiffon blouse, and red shoes. '*Morphed into her*! You wish!'

Maddy looked puzzled. 'What d'you mean?'

Malli was a dear friend. She employed Maddy whenever her own driver was on leave. Today she was en route to the airport. She was as petite as her friend was tall, as carefully groomed and overtly feminine as the other was not.

'Your landlady will suck you dry long before you can morph!' said Malli.

Maddy's lips twitched in a wry smile. 'Oh. Ha.'

'How much does she want now?'

Maddy shrugged. 'I've been sending her my rent money but not the so-called "maintenance charge". Three K extra. I told her that I'll pay it, sure, okay, okay – but it's been tight. I've been paying the rent but not the extra.'

She paused, as they both watched the buzzing gawkers. 'A month goes by. Two months. Then the other day, the phone rings. I pick it up, and it's her on the line—' imitating her landlady's harsh squawk "*—I'll have you arrested, Mrs Ma-DAME! Yes! I'll throw you out! Yes!*" I say, "Mrs Bansal, I'll have twelve thousand for you next week." She doesn't miss a beat. "*Twenty thousand!*" she shrieks. "*For making me wait! In cash! June first!*"'

Maddy sighed. 'That was two weeks ago. Since then, I've been getting daily phone calls. Threats. Curses. Reminders that I have nothing in writing. No legal rights.'

She looked out towards the clotted cars. The police had arrived with an ambulance. They were shoving the audience back, making space.

'And?'

'I tell her that I'll have it for her today, this morning. Yesterday, I went to the bank, broke one of my FDs. But I was still short by two thou'. I thought I'd be still okay because I had a night-shift passenger. I should've got around five K, cash in hand. Except I didn't. Shitty little—' she suppressed the word '—night-shifter makes me wait four hours then runs out on me without paying. I even went up to her flat to demand the money. She calls me filthy names and throws a C-note in my face.'

Maddy frowned at the memory. 'Okay, I tell myself, okay; there's still time to get to the bank in the morning, break another FD and be back in time for Mrs Dung Beetle.'

The knot of traffic had begun to dissolve.

'But no. That's too easy. Instead, what happens? Dung Beetle comes to the house early. *Two hours* early. I tell her I'm going to the bank but no-o-o. She won't listen.' Maddy shook her head. 'She's done, she tells me. I've had my chances—'

The car directly in front of Maddy's jerked forward. She immediately shifted into gear and jerked forward too, only to stop again, having moved a couple of inches.

'She wants me out. Tells me that she knows about my taxi business. Calls me a ...' she broke off to shriek, '*AHH!* Idiot wants to DIE!' She jammed the heel of her palm down on the horn, hard. 'AAARRHhhh! KANGAROO!' She yelled, thumping the windshield with the flat of her palm as a pedestrian, having dashed across the road between her car and the one in front, hopped up onto her front bumper before speeding off to the left.

'Ahh,' said Maddy, shutting her eyes tight. 'Ahh. Sorry. I shouldn't—'

Now the traffic really was moving.

For several minutes, neither of them spoke as they sped forward.

Then, 'That's the sort of thing that really gets me going,' said Maddy, meaning the pedestrian. 'I feel angry. All the time. Maddened. There's this kind of *boiling* just under my skin. The rubbish on the streets, the beggars at the traffic intersections. There's a pregnant mother now, just at the turn-off towards the Asiad Village. She's not in her senses. She'll have her baby on the street, and everyone will probably just hurry on past her, hurry, hurry, hurry… don't look, don't think. The water shortages, the power cuts. The rudeness. I can't shut any of it off! And all the time, I feel this *fury*, I want to *kick*! I want to kick my landlady, kick that stupid little... whatever... last night – I want to *kick* and *kick* and *kick*—'

She broke off, shaking her head.

Malli said, 'Maybe you need a break?'

'Heh!' said Maddy, smiling. 'A break? No. I need a reset. Brain reset. I'm finding it harder and harder to hold it in. The problem is me. I don't suit the world I'm in. I feel like a balloon filled with tiny glass splinters. Ready to burst in the face of anyone who dares cross my path.' She gave a ragged laugh. 'Listen to me! I sound dangerous.'

'These are dangerous times,' murmured Malli. 'You're just reflecting what's out there.'

'Like Mrs Bansal,' said Maddy. 'See what I mean? I've become her already! Every second word she says is a curse.'

They were still on the Outer Ring Road, now passing by the Munirka Furniture Market.

Malli gestured to the side of the road. 'See – there? A parking spot. Why don't we stop? Come on. I forgot to tell you that the flight's delayed. We have time for a smoke.'

'Okay,' said Maddy, acting on the impulse. She pulled into the space.

Malli brought out a packet of Silk Cut, still wrapped in cellophane.

'I have my own,' said Maddy. She reached into the glove compartment as she lowered her window. Instantly, the roar of the traffic, like a bull's thick head stinking of heat and grime, thrust itself in.

Directly in front of the car's well-polished nose, on the raised pavement, a labourer covered in grey dust was hauling a sack of cement onto a handcart.

Maddy lit her cigarette and inhaled sharply. 'Wah. That feels so good.' She breathed out slowly, the smoke curling in languid tendrils around her face. 'Hoo! Thank god for tobacco! Hoo.'

She closed her eyes, pausing a moment before returning to the topic of her anger. 'Mind you, it's not that I'm complaining. About the anger, I mean. It's like eating a green chilli on an empty stomach. It keeps me bright and hot. All day long.'

Malli clicked her tongue. 'Come on. You *are* complaining.' From her handbag, she brought out a round silver container as plump and smooth as a ball of dough. It had a lid that fit tight. A narrow flange extended forward, offering a means of lifting the lid. Malli flipped it up, revealing that it was a tiny purse ashtray. Beneath the flange was a shallow depression that functioned as a support for the cigarette. She tapped the ash into the receptacle.

'No! Why? I'm enjoying it. It's been some months now. Coming on slowly. I never used to curse. Never. But now? I wake up cursing. It's like some people wake up and take a dump. That's what my brain does! Wakes me up and takes a dump at the world,' said the older of the two friends, laughing.

'Real cursing or the "kangaroo" type?'

Maddy shrugged, saying, 'How does it matter?'

'I read somewhere that *real* cursing releases stress. But kangaroo-wallah curses do nothing at all—' Malli gave a sympathetic smile. 'Sorry!'

Maddy frowned, then shook her head. 'I dunno. Kangaroo-wallah, I suppose. I mean, I wake up *angry*. Like I've become this muscular predator. This panther, stalking the placidly grazing herds of antelope...'

She chuckled at herself.

'It's funny to hear myself say this out loud. I've not mentioned it to anyone before. Who would I tell? My brothers? No! My parents? Forget it. They'd never understand. My other customers? My landlady? Hah! She'd evict me for sure then! I never hear other people talking like this – no one *I* meet. My regular customers are like … I don't know what word to use—'

Malli sat forward. 'Wait, wait. Back up. Your Mrs Bansal … did you say she *knows*? About the taxi business? And she wants you out because of it?'

Maddy paused, inhaling.

At that moment, glancing up, she noticed for the first time the labourer bent over directly in front of the car.

He had the angular build of a goat. He wore a threadbare vest over striped shorts with a red rag tied around his temples. His deep bronze skin was obscured by pale grey powder except where rivulets of sweat had formed dark lines, as if deliberately pencilled in. He straightened up, and his gaze came to rest upon the two women in their car.

There he had remained, standing beside his handcart, staring at the women.

Through the glass of her windshield, Maddy looked up directly into the man's face. She caught his eye and saw his expression. But he did not look away. He seemed to be in a trance. She held his gaze for a full minute before snapping the contact. She realized there was no meaning to it. It was not a communication.

Turning to Malli, she said, 'See that man over there, that labourer? I want to go and kick him too.'

'Tch!' said Malli, shaking her head reflexively. 'Stop it.'

'But just *look* at him! Look at him staring at us! As if the difference between him and us is so great that we're just things to him. Not people. He wouldn't even stare at animals in that way.'

Malli shook her head.

'I know, I know,' continued Maddy. 'You and I are not allowed to talk like this. It's considered tasteless. But *why*? That's my point. Aren't we ignoring the fact that he's also a man? If he were the same class as us and one of us said that we wanted to go beat him up because he's ogling us, that would be fine, wouldn't it?'

Malli flexed the corners of her mouth. 'Let it go. It's not our fight. Not today.'

'Just agree with me that it's a class issue,' said Maddy. 'If a labourer looks at us with hot eyes, our response is different than if a rich man does the same thing – yes or no?'

'If a rich man does it, we take him to court and paint his face as black as we can. If the labourer does it, we tell ourselves that he's a migrant far from his family and deserving of our deepest sympathy,' said Malli. She stubbed her cigarette out inside her ashtray and snapped the lid shut. 'We don't throw him under the same bus as a man who should know better.'

'But my question is about the nature of the *heat*,' persisted Maddy. 'Is that the same?'

'How can we ever know? What scale is there with which we can compare one man's heat against another's?'

They both looked outside once more. The labourer was sitting on one of his loaded sacks now, oblivious of them. Smoking a bidi.

Maddy nodded thoughtfully. 'Now that's a good question,' she said. 'I bet no one has an answer to it.' She pressed the window switch, tossed her cigarette stub out and adjusted herself in her seat.

'There are times when I think that just to think such questions is to stray from the straight and narrow path,' she said as she pressed the ignition. 'I wonder if there's something wrong with me for wanting to explore the dark alleys of speculation.'

'Never!' said Malli. 'I never believe that I'm the one who is at fault.'

'And I always do,' said Maddy, smiling.

4

The fighting chance
Came from France
Broke a leg
And couldn't dance.

– JINXES, BIG & SMALL

Maddy did not go home directly from the airport. She liked to buy fruit from a small stall in Greater Kailash II's M-Block Market. She had just picked out some oranges, apples and a bunch of bananas when she felt her phone buzzing in the pocket of her jeans.

An unfamiliar number. A client? She had a hundred-rupee note ready in her hand for the fruit vendor and held the phone to her ear with the other hand.

'Hello?' she said.

'Ms Sen?' It was a man's voice. 'Thank you for taking my call. My name's Chetak … Chetak Mehta. Do you have a moment?' His accent was clipped at the edges like a well-trimmed British hedge.

'I'm sorry,' said Maddy, watching as the fruit seller counted out change. He had already bagged the fruit, using the nylon tote that she'd handed to him. 'Do I know you?'

'No,' said the man. 'Just hear me out, okay? I'm on your side—'

'What?'

'Please listen carefully,' said the man. 'Your landlady, Mrs Bansal, has sent a bailiff to your house. They're emptying it out—'

'WHAT?' Maddy stopped dead, with the change clutched in her hand and the fruit seller holding the bag of fruit out towards her.

'I'm standing opposite your front gate. It's going on right now. They're dumping the contents of your entire house out on the road.'

'WHAT'RE YOU SAYING!' shouted Maddy, careless of the gaping face of the woman beside her, also trying to buy fruit. 'Who are you – what are you—' The change dropped from her hand as she grabbed the bag from the fruit vendor and began jogging towards her car.

'My name's Chetak Mehta,' said the man patiently. 'Look, you're out on the road somewhere—'

Maddy swung her head this way and that, trying to see if anyone was standing within sight of her, laughing at her, some man, some fool trying to mess with her. 'WHERE ARE YOU!' she said, yelling into the phone. Changing her mind, she said, 'No, forget it. I'm ending this call.'

She'd reached her car. Yanking open the door, she slid inside, slung the fruit and the cell phone into the passenger seat as she stabbed at the ignition switch with her finger. In her mind, she was airborne, riding a bolt of lightning towards her home. In reality, however, the car was completely unresponsive. No twinkling lights, no friendly welcoming *ding*.

The phone rang again. Same number.

She tapped 'reject', then sat staring at the darkened dashboard.

She was panting, her mind blank.

Wait, she thought. *Wait.*

The call was rubbish. *Of course, it was!* A crank call. How could she be taken in by some stranger calling with a completely ridiculous message? What had he said? Something about a what – a bailiff? *Bailiff!* How did they think up these things?

She forced herself to relax. Her hands dropped to her lap. As soon as she did that, the car's lifelessness suddenly made sense. Of course! She was holding the fob in her hand. It was a safety feature: the ignition button wouldn't work unless the key was inserted in its slot. She pushed it in, pressed the button again, and the great black machine purred to life. *Ding!* it said, smiling. *Ding.*

The phone rang again. She rejected the call again.

She started to pull out of her parking spot.

The phone buzzed, this time with an incoming message. Same number.

The words *MAIN ROAD BLOCKED* flashed briefly before she could dismiss the message.

Tapeworm, she thought. *TAPEWORM! How dare he?*

Anxiety flared anew, but she thought, *Crank call. It's a crank call.*

She was ten minutes away from home. It was a Sunday afternoon.

The phone buzzed again. *I'M WEARING BLACK* flashed the notification. He knew that she was seeing only the stub. *Shut up, stink bug!* she thought. *Shut up, shut UP*. She'd block the number the moment she got home.

Five minutes later, she had turned onto August Kranti Marg. There were three traffic stops before the main right turn that led directly towards the Village. *Quieten your breath,* she said to herself. *No need for panic, no need at all.* It was all a giant, childish lie. A madman had got hold of her number and was harassing her. For no reason. Just because he could.

Traffic was moving languidly but steadily.

In less than ten minutes, she was at the lights beside her turn-off.

Then she leaned into the turn and was facing the entrance gate of the Village.

Her heart began to pound.

The main access road into the colony was indeed blocked solid.

There was a sentry post at the entrance gate. It was mostly ineffectual, but today, all three sentries – slender young men wearing tan brown uniforms – were facing inwards, away from the main road and towards the long column of honking, growling cars waiting to move forward.

The phone buzzed. *TURN TOWARDS SHAHPUR JAT*

'*Stink bug*!' she whispered out loud, her voice catching in her throat. 'I *hate* you. How d'you know where I am? *Trashy, trashy, trash-TRASH*! HOW! Why!' She was starting to sob. The road forked awkwardly, but she did still have time to peel away to the right.

TURN AWAY IF YOU…

She took the turn. Tears were streaming freely now. If someone had asked her why she was weeping, she wouldn't have known what to say. Other cars had also made the same decision and peeled away, so it wasn't a smooth transition. But at least she and they were all moving.

She continued pressing forward, until there came a bend in the road towards the right. The phone buzzed again with an incoming message. She ignored it, moving forward. When a parking opportunity opened up on the left of the road, she stopped.

The phone buzzed yet again.

She didn't look at it or pick it up. She wanted to wait until the whirling sensation in her head had quietened down. She continued to tell herself that it must be a crank caller. That some supremely malicious person had found a way to fist her all the way to her gut. Maybe he'd heard Mrs Bansal talking about the irritating female tenant, maybe he'd decided to play a silly joke. Maybe he was sitting in a car himself, caught in a random traffic jam along the main access road into the Asiad Village.

There was a yawning cavern in place of her stomach, however. She heard Mrs Bansal's voice saying, 'I want you out. Now,' followed by a string of curse words. 'You think I'm a weak old lady who won't throw you out – but you're wrong! I'm a weak old lady with big, big friends. I'll kick you out; see if I don't.'

Maddy picked up the phone. Two more messages had come in, but she didn't look at them. She went to the missed call list and clicked on the number that was listed as 'three missed calls'.

The phone rang only once.

The stranger's voice: 'Hello again.'

Maddy sat with her eyes shut. Tears were still falling but more slowly.

'I know you won't believe me,' said the man, 'but I am truly sorry.'

Maddy said nothing. She was thinking to herself that the man's smooth, UK-educated accent made it that much harder to dismiss him.

The caller paused, as if to give her a chance to say something. When she remained mute, he said, 'Where are you?'

She drew in a deep breath. 'Why ask? You already know.'

'Not really,' he said. 'Just guessing.'

He's lying, she thought. 'Okay, never mind. I'm in Shahpur Jat. Parked.' She could feel the sobs starting up again but breathed in, holding down the spasm in her throat. 'I don't know how to loop back into the Asiad Village.'

He paused again. 'Are you… do you have somewhere to go? A friend's home?'

Maddy was silent. 'Why should I believe anything you say to me?' she said, finally. 'I don't believe you. I need to see for myself.'

'Yes, I understand,' said the man. 'That's why I sent the photograph. With one of my messages.'

'I haven't looked,' she said, wanting to scream, wanting to wail. 'I… don't understand any of this. How…' She began to sob audibly. 'I don't believe it! I DON'T!'

He waited politely.

When she was no longer heaving, she said, 'Who ARE you? Why did you call me?'

'Once again, I don't expect you to believe me. But I,' he paused, 'would like to help.'

'I don't understand. I don't want to be helped by strangers.' *Strange men*, she thought. 'I have no reason to trust you. Why were you right there? How could you know what my landlady was going to do?'

'It's not entirely mysterious. I'm a lawyer,' said the man. 'I can explain everything. It might be easier if we talked face to face, but I'll understand if you're not ready for that. Do you have somewhere to go?'

She didn't want to answer him. 'I don't know. I can't think clearly. What about my—'

She looked at the photograph he'd sent of the front of her home. She wanted to vomit at the sight. All her possessions lay jumbled in the open street of the colony. Chairs and tables lay overturned with their spindly legs stuck obscenely up in the air. Curtains, cushions, books, art, and smashed crockery were spread out in every direction.

'I...I mean, I have to do something about all my STUFF. I can't just—'

She wanted to scream but didn't.

'It's no longer on the road. That's what I wanted to tell you. I brought two moving vans with me. All your stuff has gone into them.'

Maddy snapped the call off.

A moment later, her cell phone buzzed again.

STAY WHERE YOU ARE, said the message. *I'LL FIND YOU.*

Leaning forward with her head on the steering wheel, she sobbed like a little girl.

5

A cool head is
Sometimes dead.

– JINXES, BIG & SMALL

A man tapped on the passenger-side window. Maddy had caught a glimpse of him in her rear-view mirror as he approached the car. He looked familiar, though she didn't think she'd met him before. Tall. Dark grey trousers. Black shirt.

Chetak.

She had moved from her original parking spot by the side of the road to a patch of open earth bordered on three sides by oleander hedges. On the fourth side was a tea stall, a grain store and a paan shop. Her window was open, letting in the stench of garbage and stale urine.

She released the lock on the passenger door but kept her face turned away, her right hand against her left cheek, her palm outward, as if warding off a blow.

Chetak opened the door and slid into the seat.

She waited with her face averted.

'I can explain,' he said as he pulled the door close.

She said nothing.

'I'm a lawyer,' he said, 'as I mentioned earlier.'

She continued to look away.

'I heard two other lawyers saying your name. In court.'

'Why did you know it? My name, I mean.'

'I... I knew of you,' said Chetak. 'Through one of your clients.'

'Who?'

'Mrs Gamadia,' he said. 'She's a relative. Mother's cousin.'

Maddy remembered her. A talkative elderly woman. Always paid in advance. Sometimes she asked to go on a long drive with no particular destination in mind. They'd park along the highway and have a smoke together. 'Okay.'

'I was thinking of getting in touch with you,' said Chetak. 'I know someone who—'

'Look. Until half an hour ago, I'd never even heard of you,' she said, still not looking at him. 'Yet you happened to be in front of my house while my...' She breathed in sharply. 'While my landlady was throwing me out.' Her voice caught in her throat. She swallowed hard. 'You say you heard my name through your relative. Okay, she gave you my number. Okay, you heard my name being mentioned in court. But so what? How does that lead to you getting involved in my personal affairs?' *Meanwhile,* she thought, *I have no home, no furniture, no clothes. Only my car.*

'I can explain,' said Chetak again.

She shook her head angrily, saying nothing.

'The landlady was just a coincidence. I was going to contact you anyway.'

'Yes, but *why*?' she demanded. 'Your relative must have told you that I only accept female clients?'

'Because I...' He paused. 'Because there's an offer I want to make. On behalf of someone else.'

'What offer?'

'A job offer.'

She almost laughed. 'Oh, please! I'm self-employed. Why would I want a job?'

'Steady income. Plus accommodation.'

'*What?*'

'It's part of the deal. A self-contained suite.'

'Do you know what this "deal" sounds like?'

'Yes, I know what it sounds like,' said Chetak, 'but it's not that. At all.'

'What next! A nice hotel somewhere? Hourly rates?'

'It's a private home. In Hauz Khas.'

'Don't be ridiculous,' she said.

'We can go there right now,' he said. 'It's—'

'Stop it!'

'I've sent your things into storage—'

'I don't *understand*!' she said, suddenly and loudly. 'Why are you doing this! Who are you—' She held her hand up. 'No! Not your name. I mean...' She whipped around to stare at him, looking at him full in the face for the first time. He was clean-shaven, with toffee-brown skin, a beaky nose and thick black hair. 'I mean, who are you *really*? And why is any of this happening?'

He had positioned himself as if to maintain the greatest possible distance between the two of them. His back was against the door, his arm curled around the headrest. 'I already know that nothing I say will make sense. Until you see for yourself that it's not a scam.'

'See what?'

He had large, heavy-lidded eyes and was gazing at her with an expression of cool self-possession. 'The house.' He was a lawyer, after all. Making life-changing statements was part of his professional toolkit. 'Not the building but the people in it. The other people living there. Interesting people.'

She was staring hard at him. 'What people?' She was trying not to breathe hard. 'I don't understand,' she said, then silently cursed herself. *He's already told me that it won't make sense. I've just proved his point.* 'I don't know why any of this is happening.'

'It's very difficult, I know,' he said. 'You'll have to trust me.'

'And how *can* I!' she exclaimed. 'I'd have to be mad.'

He dropped his gaze now. He seemed about to say something. Then didn't.

It's an elaborate act, she thought. *It's all carefully rehearsed. Nothing he says or does is unplanned.*

'If it helps, I could tell you,' said Chetak, looking up and away from her, 'who else lives in that house—'

'I don't care who lives where!' snapped Maddy. 'I want to know why there's a complete stranger in my car telling me what to do with my life!'

'The house and the people in it are part of the explanation,' said Chetak. 'If you agree to come there, you'll find it easier to believe me.'

'Suppose I don't?'

'Then I'll get the keys to the storage locker, hand them to you and say goodbye,' he said. He looked so reasonable, so unflappable. 'You won't hear from us again.'

'Us?' she said.

'Like I said, I'm acting on someone else's behalf.' He looked at her. 'This isn't about me. It's about someone else. A woman.'

She didn't know what to think. She looked away, trying to compose herself.

'I could tell you to get out of my car,' she said. When he said nothing, she continued, 'But you know I won't. Because ...' she paused, trying to understand her own motivation, 'because you made a plan. You plotted all your moves.' She looked at him. 'Including offering me the choice to walk away. It's all one big charade though, isn't it? You know I won't walk away because you think I can't afford to.'

'Well,' he said, shrugging slightly, 'I wouldn't call it a charade.'

'It doesn't matter what you call it,' she said, leaning forward to turn on the car, 'that's what it is. The choice you're offering me is an illusion.' The vehicle hummed to life, and she began to reverse. 'How did you get here? What about your car?'

'I sent it off with the driver,' said Chetak.

Maddy glanced at him. His face gave nothing away. 'You were so sure?'

'I wasn't sure,' he said. 'Just hopeful.'

'So, who is the woman?' asked Maddy. She had just eased into the late afternoon traffic streaming south along Khel Gaon Marg.

'I don't think you know her,' said Chetak.

'Does she have a name?'

'It's Laine. Verity Laine,' said Chetak.

'*Verity?*' said Maddy. 'That's an odd name.'

'She's English.'

'Why do I get the feeling that you don't want to talk about her?'

'Look, I realize the whole situation must sound extremely unusual. But then,' he took a deep breath, 'so are you. Unusual people bring on unusual situations. You must have noticed that by now?' Then he pointed ahead. 'Turn right at the traffic light, please.'

'We're all unusual in our own ways,' said Maddy.

'Maybe so,' said Chetak, 'but some of us are more overtly unusual, let's put it that way. First right turn, please,' he said. 'Then left again—'

'I've been here before,' she said, frowning. 'We're somewhere near Mayfair Gardens?'

'Near but not quite there,' said Chetak. 'On Google Maps, it looks empty. A sort of grassy field. Go straight. There's a dead end and a gate in the wall. That's the one.'

6

There's a secret,
Large and dark
Hiding in
The public park.

– JINXES, BIG & SMALL

On the gatepost, written in curly but slightly faded script lettering was the name 'Garden Villa'. Chetak got out and pushed open the wrought-iron gate. Getting back in, he directed Maddy to drive on towards the back.

At first sight, the house looked like a modern two-storey building. White bougainvillea cascaded down its front. A trellis-work fence bordered the right side of the driveway. On the other side of the fence was a well-tended lawn. The glossy leaves of a tall rubber plant poked up from above the fence.

But the property extended much farther back than its front entrance suggested.

Not only was it double the length than was typical, but the rear did not match the front end at all. By the time they reached the parking area at the back, Maddy felt as if she'd driven through a time warp.

The back of the building looked as if the architect had put together a sampler of eighteenth-century stonework styles. The ground-floor entrance was a white marble archway with a brass-studded wooden door inset within it. Between where Maddy had parked the car and the entrance was a decrepit marble fountain, currently filled with twigs and dried leaves. Behind the car, the property extended towards a yard and a two-storey servants' quarter. A pair of elderly neem trees lent their shadows to the scene.

'We'll go in from the side,' said Chetak. They began walking back in the direction they had come, towards the gate. It took them a good five minutes, with the sun beating down overhead. Maddy noticed that the wall to their left was textured with a recurring design. In places, it was perforated, like a stonework jali. There was only darkness behind it – nothing to be seen.

When the stonework gave way to a plain white wall, Chetak quickened his pace. Maddy saw that he did so to be able to open the only door on this side of the building when they reached it.

They entered a small, air-conditioned wood-panelled space. Its floor was tiled in white marble octagons alternating with black squares. A khaki-clad security guard sat at a miniature table with spindly legs, a guest book open on top of it. The man rose as they entered, preparing to offer a pen to Maddy, but Chetak forestalled him with a wave of his hand.

Maddy said, with an edge of suspicion, 'You won't sign me in?'

'I'll do it later,' said Chetak, turning towards the only other visible door. It was at right angles to the entrance, with a horizontal viewing pane in its wooden surface. Behind this door was a shallow two-person elevator. He invited Maddy to step inside.

The overhead light in the elevator flicked on as she entered. There was a mirror on the back wall. Seeing her reflection, Maddy said, 'Does it matter that I look a mess?' She was still in her alligator T-shirt and jeans. She hadn't brushed her hair since morning.

'No,' said Chetak, then winced. 'Ha. Trick question!'

Maddy's mouth twitched, but she didn't reply. Briefly, they shared the framed view of themselves in the mirror, two tall people occupying a limited space. She swivelled away, feeling like a wild bird that has knowingly stepped into a cage.

He pressed the topmost of three numbered buttons on the panel. The lift jerked as they progressed past the first floor and onto the second. There, it stopped with another jerk. Chetak drew back the grille and held it in place with his elbow as he pushed open the wooden outer door.

'Please,' he said to Maddy.

She stepped through into a space similar to the lift lobby downstairs. In the place of the security guard was a beautiful red and ochre Moroccan rug wall hanging. But on the right, instead of the panelled wall was a vast hall. Light poured in through tall, frosted windows. Coloured pressed-glass panes in the skylights cast blue, green and orange trapezoids onto the white marble floor. Two easy chairs and an upholstered sofa with rosewood arms and legs commandeered the middle of the space. There was a pressed-glass pane in the door to the right of the lift.

'One moment,' said Chetak as he turned to knock on the door.

But a woman's voice, high and sweet, called to him before his knuckles made contact.

'Chetak!' it said, 'is that you?'

A silhouette appeared behind the glass, and in the next moment, the door opened, and a woman leaned out.

She looked, thought Maddy, like a marble statue come to life. It wasn't so much that she was pale as that she had classic features: a pretty nose, neat brow and firm chin. Her short blonde hair was going grey, framing her face in soft curls.

Her mouth curved up in a smile as she said, 'Oh! Hello Ms …'

'Madam Sen,' said Chetak, supplying the name.

'—*Madam* Sen,' she finished, with her right hand extended. She had come out now and was standing outside the room, dressed in a white shirt and dark brown slacks. 'I'm so glad to meet you.' There was a slight pause. 'That... that really *is* your first name? Madam?'

Maddy had leaned forward to shake the woman's hand. 'Yes,' she said, 'I changed it legally.' She was feeling extremely awkward. Her gaze flickered towards Chetak, who had remained standing by the door that he hadn't knocked upon. 'In the US. Many years ago.'

'Well, then,' said the other woman, still holding Maddy's hand, 'that sounds like a story! My name, by the way, is Verity. Verity Laine.' Her accent, though clearly British, had rounded edges. As if it had been gently sandpapered by the length of time she'd spent in India.

'Oh!' said Chetak now, 'sorry, I should've—'

Verity shook her head, saying, 'No, no, it's done now, and anyway, let's take this inside, shall we? Chit? Will you be joining us?'

'No,' he said, stepping back. 'I'll go down, sign her in and then I'll… you know…' he tilted his head, 'I'll be downstairs.'

7

A kingdom! A kingdom!
My horse, for a kingdom!

– JINXES, BIG & SMALL

It was a study, lined with books and wall posters. Small Afghan rugs glowed against the white marble floor. There were two desks. One was piled high with papers and took up much of the right side of the room. The other was a stripped-down writing desk at the farther end. It faced out towards French windows and the deep veranda beyond, with a back view of the bougainvillea that poured down from the terrace above.

'Shall we sit?' said Verity, waving towards the low settee on the left. There was a matching easy chair beside it. 'I was going make myself some tea. Would you like a cup?'

But Maddy was standing still, unable to make any more decisions on this already tumultuous day. She was holding her handbag against her belly with both arms, like a child clutching a favourite toy. She wanted to *stop*. To do nothing. To curl up in her own room, on her own bed, to think. Except, of course, she couldn't. She no longer had a room to call her own.

'Please,' she said, 'I'd like to… to… wash my face first.'

'Oh, of course,' said Verity, moving forward, pointing to a door on the left, hidden behind a theatre poster from the *Phantom of the Opera*. 'There's a light switch on the right, as you enter,' she said.

Maddy went in, closed the door and leaned against it, not bothering to turn on the light. Tears began coursing down her face once more. She rarely cried. Being brought to this brink twice on the same day was deeply humiliating for her. The suddenness with which she'd been thrown out of her home was perfectly balanced by the bizarre way in which she'd been offered a solution.

She, who was used to being self-reliant and forward-thinking, felt as if she'd been kidnapped and thrown into the prison cell of someone else's life. Someone with no control over her own fate. Specifically, a woman. Born into subordination, with only binary choices: EITHER she enters a pit of vipers OR she marries an ogre with three heads.

Think! she screamed to herself. *Don't give in! Whatever this condition is, it's temporary. It has to be.*

She breathed in, opened her eyes and looked around at the small washroom. The hand basin was in front of the door. The toilet was to the right. Looking around, she found the light switch and turned it on. Along with the overhead light, a tiny ventilation fan above the toilet began whirring. The walls were pale yellow, and the floor was tiled in one-inch squares, yellow and white, in a deliberately irregular pattern.

As she washed her face, the feeling that she was in the grip of unnamed and unfamiliar forces returned to her. This gushing tap, for instance, suggested a full tank of water overhead. It was not something that 'everyone' had. Even in the smart, well-designed Asiad Village apartments, the water supply was irregular.

As for this little washroom? It, too, hinted at an invisible hive of power that could pull together the resources to provide such conveniences in a way that made the result seem effortless. Even though it couldn't be. There was no fuzz of dust anywhere. The taps and basin were shining. The wastepaper basket was lined with a plastic bag, currently empty. She knew, from her own experience of living alone, that this seemingly simple effect required invisible hands to be at work every day, all year long.

Who owned this house, this huge estate tucked into the back pocket of a well-heeled residential colony? Such properties bore the hallmarks of dirty privilege. The kind that's earned by dishonest means.

Or else it was inherited. Suggesting merely another level of privilege. Not necessarily dirty but certainly exclusive.

It seemed unlikely to her that Verity could be the owner. She did not bear the stigmata of high privilege. Her clothes were simple in an unglamorous way. She wore no make-up or jewellery. She wasn't wrapped in a fine veil of scent, her hair did not appear to be carefully styled, her nails were neat but not painted. And yet. Just to live in a place like this assumed connections to power. Without an understanding of those connections, any association with her would bristle with uncertainty. It was impossible to consider living under such conditions.

Maddy shook her head to clear her thoughts as she wiped her face dry. Her mind was made up. Squaring her shoulders, she opened the door to the washroom and stepped out.

'I'm sorry,' she said as she looked around and located the other woman, already seated in the armchair by the settee. 'I'm sorry, Verity. I've decided that I can't do this. Whatever it is. I can't stay. I really must go.'

Verity's expression, as she looked up, was unsurprised. She nodded slightly and then looked down again at the little tray on which she had arranged cups and a small saucer of ginger nut biscuits. 'Yes,' she said, 'I had a feeling that's what you'd decide.' The tray was perched on top of a spindle-legged table that exactly fit the tray's dimensions. 'I think I understand.'

Then, as the sound of a kettle hissing made itself heard, she said, 'Would you like to leave at once? Or shall we have tea before you go?' She looked up again and smiled.

Maddy opened her mouth to say, *No tea! I'll go!* The words that came out, however, were, 'Yes, thanks. I'll have the tea.'

8

Being a-lert
Is sweet and pert
Being a-larmed
Might get you harmed.

– JINXES, BIG & SMALL

When they had both settled down with their respective cups of tea, Verity said, 'Tell me, Maddy, what exactly has Chit told you?' She corrected herself, 'Chetak, I mean. He hates being called Chit!'

'Very little,' said Maddy. 'He mentioned a proposal of some sort. Connected to driving. That's what I understood, anyway.'

'Would you like to know more?' Verity's face, when seen full frontal, reminded Maddy of the full moon. It was round and pale. The grey-blue eyes were calm, but there was something else in the expression. Wistfulness?

'I was wondering the same thing,' said Maddy. 'What do you know about me?' She felt awkward. 'I don't understand why I'm here. There was something *off* about the timing. I don't know whether you know what just happened to me today? Did Chetak tell you?'

She felt better as she spoke. She didn't wait for a response. 'It's not just that we've never met before. It's that I've never heard of any of you. Not Chetak, not you, not…' she glanced around the room, 'not this house and whoever else might be in it. You've all just dropped out of the sky and into my life. Yet you know enough about me to want to make some kind of offer. I find that *weird*.'

'I understand,' said Verity. 'And I can explain. But the explanation involves saying something about what I – or *we*, I should say – would like from you.' She paused. 'Shall I go on?'

Maddy nodded.

'I know three things about you,' said Verity, 'One, you operate an informal taxi service. Two, you're doing it without a licence or a meter. And three, you're a woman in this line of work.' She allowed herself a faint smile. 'That makes you, if you don't mind my saying so, extremely unusual. Would you agree? It's unusual?'

Maddy took a sip of her tea, realized that it was too hot and put her cup back down on its saucer. 'Unusual, yes,' she admitted. 'Women can get commercial licences to drive three-wheelers in some states, but here in Delhi? I've not seen them.' She glanced at Verity. 'I looked into getting a licence to drive a cab as an independent operator, but I found it kind of restrictive. You have to belong to existing networks of female taxi drivers because it's a potentially dangerous job. You're expected to ply exclusively at airports and train stations.

'And the other women I met while waiting to be processed—' She broke off, shaking her head. 'I don't know. They formed a group. And I didn't want to be part of a group. I wanted to operate on my own terms, in my own car and with clients who might actually be friends or friends of friends. The whole nature of cab driving is that it's not exclusive. Whereas I wanted, quite frankly, to *be* exclusive.

'I believe I don't need a licence so long as I work for people who understand the nature of the contract. They're paying me in the way that anyone might pay a friend for doing something that's difficult for them to do for themselves. I don't advertise, I don't solicit clients, I don't make myself available to just anyone. It's like a consultancy. An exclusive service for a very select group of people.'

She thought about the girl of the night before. 'Sometimes, things go wrong. A client gets out without paying. It happened just last night. And there's nothing I can do about it – I mean, I can't go to court or anything. But it doesn't happen very often.' She shrugged. 'Women are usually honest, at least with one another. Most of my clients really appreciate the service.'

Verity said, 'But you're vulnerable. Aren't you? Someone could report you, alleging that you're running a clandestine service. Just to be mean.'

Maddy shook her head. 'That's true for anyone. Everyone has some kind of Achilles' heel that someone else can exploit.'

Verity sat a little straighter. 'It depends,' she said, 'on a person's perceived vulnerability. Single women, for instance.' Her pale eyes looked like searchlights as they bored into Maddy's. 'Single women are assumed to be targets of one sort or another. So that's what we become. Even when we're not especially weak or unprotected.'

'"We"?' asked Maddy. 'Why d'you assume that I'm single? I haven't told you that.'

Verity laughed. 'Touché! Good point – you've even named yourself "Madam" to maybe signal that you have a man in your life!' She changed tack. 'How *did* you do that, by the way? Register "Madam" as a first name?'

'It wasn't difficult in the US,' said Maddy. 'I changed it while I was living there.' *When I was married*, she thought, *a long time ago.*

'Oh, I see,' said Verity. There was still a question in her eyes. 'And was there a reason for that? For choosing a title as a first name?'

'Not really,' said Maddy, shifting in her seat. 'It was a sort of nickname. In school. And then it stuck. No one ever actually says it like that – it's always Maddy or variations like Mads or Moody! You know how people love to make up names.'

She was smiling at the memory. Then her smile faded. 'It was my husband's nickname for me. We were married young. And then he... died,' she said. Her voice was matter-of-fact.

'Oh!' said Verity. 'I'm sorry.'

Maddy shook her head. 'No, no, it's all right. It's been several years. I had already changed my name. It was one of our little jokes.' She shook her head again. 'Not everyone finds it funny, though. My landlady, for instance.' She glanced at Verity. 'She thinks "Madam" is simply fake. That I'm hiding something she wants to know. One more thing that's wrong or unnatural about me. She calls me Ma*dame* – with an emphasis. To make it clear that she means, you know...' A sudden blackness engulfed her. She had managed to forget, for a few moments, the pit that had opened under her feet.

Verity was watching her.

'Did Chetak tell you what happened this morning?' Maddy asked again.

'Yes,' said Verity. 'He called me from the site. I don't know how he managed to be there at the time it was going on – something about overhearing lawyers in court – but it was your name that stuck in his ears. We had already been talking about you, you see.' There it was again: a flash of emotion, like a heat print left on cold glass, fading too quickly to be recognized. 'He'd told me he was going to reach out to you, but before he could do that, he heard the lawyers talking. He asked me then. If it would be all right to warn you. He had your number because of his... aunt, was it? Great aunt? Anyway. I said yes.'

Leave now, thought Maddy. *Leave, leave!* She looked around. 'May I smoke in here?'

Verity got to her feet. 'Not inside, no! But on the veranda? Would that be all right? Chit goes there—' Then she smiled. 'Of course, I disapprove!'

'Yes,' said Maddy, rising quickly. 'Everyone disapproves.' *And I don't care,* she thought.

9

A crashing bore
And a crowing hen:
Two bad choices,
Everywhen.

– JINXES, BIG & SMALL

A blast of heat greeted them as they stepped onto the veranda. 'God!' exclaimed Maddy.

'It's easy to forget, isn't it?' said Verity. She stood a little distance away. 'I *must* find some way to turn off the air conditioning.'

Maddy coaxed a cigarette out of her morning's pack. 'What?'

'The air conditioning,' said Verity. 'The whole house is ducted – well, this part of it – in such a way that turning off one particular room is very difficult. Impossible, actually.'

'Why do you want to?'

Verity didn't answer right away. She was looking up at the bougainvillea, the flowers out of sight above the tangled mass of brown limbs. It had been trained to flow over a bamboo trellis that curved down from the overhead terrace and forward over the front end of the veranda. 'We're living in the tropics,' she said. 'Living in an air-conditioned bubble is all very well, you know? But the reality is the heat.' She stopped abruptly, as if she felt she'd already said too much.

Maddy was enjoying the mild rush of her first puff. She released a thin stream of smoke from her nostrils, enjoying everything about it. Including the fact of still being a smoker in a world that hated smokers.

'Maddy,' said Verity, 'do you have someplace to go? I mean today. Tonight.'

I have my car, thought Maddy. Out loud, she said, 'I have friends at whose houses I could crash.'

'All right, then,' said Verity. 'I'd like to make an offer. Why don't you stay here overnight? There's a spare room – I mean, my study is my spare room. We can set up a bed in there. I can get you some clothes to wear for now.' When Maddy said nothing, she continued, 'I want to tell you what the proposal is. It's a crazy idea. But I get the feeling that you're no stranger to crazy ideas.'

Correct, thought Maddy, *but you don't have the right to tell me so*. She said, 'If it's clear that by staying the night I'm not agreeing to anything else, then… yes.' As she said yes, she felt as if a gong had boomed deep within her spirit. She could feel its reverberations in the back of her teeth, at the roots of her eyelashes. Like in a fairy tale, this was the first step into the enchanted – or was it accursed? – castle.

'Understood,' said Verity. 'Would you like to finish your cigarette first, or shall I tell you right away?'

'I'll finish my cigarette,' said Maddy. She held it between her teeth as she fished inside her handbag, using both hands. She located her own pocket ashtray, companion to the one that Malli used. Opening it, she tapped the ash, then looked up. She felt extraordinarily calm. It was the nicotine, of course. So what? She was a smoker. 'Actually, no. Go ahead. Tell me now, please.'

Verity smiled, but the melancholy or pain or whatever it was had also risen to the surface with the smile. 'I don't drive, and I don't own a car. My friends used to say that I must get a car and a driver, but I never wanted one. I got around on my bicycle or I used public transport or I accepted lifts from my friends. But things have changed. I can't manage like that any more. Without a car, that is. Which is why, when Chit mentioned that his mother's cousin – or whatever – had taken a ride with a woman driver, my ears pricked up.

'It seemed so logical: women are often good and reliable drivers. So why not as chauffeurs? A woman driver would keep the vehicle clean, be on time, run errands without stopping to… whatever – get into fights! Go drinking with our buddies! Yet I've never heard of anyone here, with a woman chauff—' she paused to feminize the word, 'chauffeuse maybe? A woman employed to be a private driver. The idea absolutely thrilled me. I felt, if ever I could accept having a driver, then that's what I'd like.'

She had turned her full-moon face towards Maddy with an expression of mute supplication. She didn't want to beg, and yet, that's what she was doing. 'I could accept a woman as my driver. I could accept *you* as my driver.'

It was a warm and genuine compliment. Maddy twitched her shoulders in mild embarrassment. 'You've not even had a ride with me yet,' she said.

Verity now sighed. 'All right. But there's a second part to this story.'

She drew in a breath before continuing, as if bracing for a blow. 'I would not be your only employer – or, let me say it like this: there's another person in the picture. A man. A rather well-known man, who lives in this house. He occupies the whole of the ground floor and half of the first. We would pay you separately, him and me. Between us, you'd have an excellent salary, all expenses found. Plus, you'd be staying here, too, in this house.

'But I… well… this is the crazy part, I suppose.' She was struggling to find the right words. 'This rather well-known man asked me not to name him just yet. Not until you decide if you want to accept the role. He wanted to know if you'd be willing to perform your task as a… a...' she stopped and took in another deep breath before saying, 'as a man.'

She looked Maddy square in the face. 'That's about the size of it. I know it sounds bizarre. If you want to run out of here screaming, I wouldn't blame you.'

Maddy shook her head and shrugged. 'Bizarre? No. Not really. Why?' she said. 'This city's so hostile towards women. You have to wonder why more women don't, you know...' she shrugged again, 'give it a try.'

10

A lingering threat
Is what you get
When waiting for
A better bet.

– JINXES, BIG & SMALL

They decided not to discuss the idea further for the moment. It was not yet six, but once they were back inside Verity suggested setting up the study for Maddy's use right away.

'And dinner – I'll get you something from downstairs,' said Verity.

'Oh, no,' said Maddy. 'I can run out and get something for myself; in fact, there's some fruit in the car—'

Verity made a quick movement with her head, something between assent and denial. 'No, no, there's a running kitchen. There's always plenty to eat. I'll send someone off to rescue that fruit.'

Maddy began to protest, but Verity interrupted her with an embarrassed smile. 'Please, we need, if possible, to keep you out of sight. At least until you've made a decision.'

'What about the man at the desk downstairs?' asked Maddy. 'He saw me.'

'Bahadur? He keeps to himself.' She got up. 'I'll ask Chit to bring the fruit in. Would you mind giving me the key, please – it's called a fob these days, isn't it! It's a modern car, I'm sure?' Her manner was that of someone batting away mosquitoes in quick jerks.

'A Hyundai,' said Maddy. 'Elantra.'

'Really? I think Chit has the same model.'

'A great car,' said Maddy, getting out her fob. 'I'm really happy with mine.'

'Any special requirements for dinner?' asked Verity. 'There's usually four or five of us at the table. Veg and non-veg are both equally easy.'

'I eat everything,' answered Maddy. Tiredness was overwhelming her. She wanted to lie down. Blot out consciousness. She handed over the fob.

'Thanks,' said Verity. 'I'll give it to Chit. More plausible if he does it rather than me.' She got to the door of the room. 'Oh, and what about a charger? For your phone? You'll want one, won't you?'

'I always carry mine,' said Maddy, patting her handbag.

'Okay then,' said Verity. 'I'll be back. There's more tea if you want – coffee and biscuits – back there,' she pointed, 'behind that screen.'

She stepped out, then immediately stepped back in to say, 'And the Wi-Fi password! You'll want that, too. It's on the little desk, the one by the screen.' She left once more.

Maddy looked around. *What the HELL have I got myself into?* she wondered. It was like an Enid Blyton adventure. Complete with tea and biscuits. *But this is real life,* she thought. *There's no safety net.* She wrapped her arms around herself. *And what about my house? My stuff? And...* She winced and squeezed her eyes shut. *Can't. Can't think about it now.*

The presence of so many books was calming. She got up, from where she sat on the settee, to look at the shelves surrounding her. The closest one featured the colourful spines of large-format picture books. *Children's World of Animals. Big, Better, Best: Word Hunt. All The Places You've Never Been! Butterfly Maniac. Algorithms for Fun and Fortune.*

On the farther shelf, the books were smaller, packed even tighter, two rows on each shelf, with paperbacks. She went over to look at them. Novels and short story collections. Maugham. Collette. The Alexandria Quartet. Paul Gallico. Authors from the fifties and sixties. These were all titles that she herself had known and loved. The spines were creased in the way of books that are well-beloved. And poetry! So much poetry. A whole shelf devoted just to it. The English poets that she had 'by-hearted' all through school and college.

She reached to pick out a volume, then drew back her hand. *No*, she thought. *Better not! Or else, like Persephone, I might be forced to stay.* She smiled at her foolishness. There was nothing to keep her here. Nothing at all. She could leave at any time. In the middle of the night, if she wanted. *Of course, at this moment, I don't even have my fob with me! What'll I do or say if she doesn't give it back to me?*

She returned to the settee. *Why do I trust her?* she asked herself. *Surely not just because she's British! Is that all there is to it? Her cultured accent, her genteel manner. It could all be a front. But for what?*

She reached for her phone and was surprised to notice that it was vibrating silently. Malli. As she swiped the front of the phone, she saw now that there were dozens of missed calls and messages. She had muted the thing while waiting for Chetak to find her in Shahpur Jat.

'Maddy!' her friend's voice shrilled. 'WHERE ARE YOU?'

'I—' said Maddy.

'I've been calling non-stop!' Malli's voice was frantic with the accumulated load of worry. 'Bindu—' her house help 'called me as soon as I landed in Bombay, screaming and crying that your landlady's goons had carried away your entire house in two giant moving vans… Your girl Lata literally ran for her life while the milk was boiling over – she even forgot her phone. What the hell – what the HELL, MADDY! I thought you must be dead – or bleeding in some ditch—'

'No, no, I'm okay,' said Maddy, 'but it's true about—'

'OKAY?' shrilled Malli. 'You're OKAY? You're sitting quietly somewhere while your house is being destroyed – and you can't even call or… OH MY GOD, MADDY. My GOD. This is too much now. Too much. Where ARE you? Why didn't you go straight to my home? Why didn't you call?'

'Because you were in the air!' said Maddy. She jumped to her feet, feeling simultaneously agitated and far removed from her friend's frenzy. *I was in shock,* thought Maddy. *I didn't think about Lata. I should have. But I didn't.* 'I'd stopped to buy some fruit. And I got a call—'

'Lata couldn't call! She'd lost her phone—'

'—from a stranger,' continued Maddy. 'Telling me that my landlady was evicting—'

'Wait, WAIT!' shrieked Malli. 'What're you telling me – you're just standing around with your thumb in your bum while your HOUSE IS BEING RANSACKED? What're you doing NOW! Have you lost your mind? You've got to run to the police – file an FIR. Please tell me that's where you are right now—'

Maddy was panting with the stress of listening to her friend.

'Malli,' she said, 'Malli, please listen to me before you say anything more. I'm in a safe place – or, anyway, I think it is – but… but I can't take any action just now. I'm in shock. Please, just listen to me. I'm all right, I'm not alone and I'll call Bindu, but I can't—' she saw Verity's shadow on the glass panel of the door, 'I can't talk now. I just can't.'

She disconnected as Verity re-entered the room, holding the fob aloft. 'Success!' she said, 'The fruit's being washed and… Oh! What's the matter?'

Maddy didn't realize that she was clutching her head with the phone held out in front of her. 'I… oh… nothing—' She put her hand down. 'A friend called… saying that my house help… oh my God, I'm such a *monster*! I completely forgot about Lata—'

'You've got to slow down,' said Verity. 'You're having a delayed reaction to an assault. Because that's what it is. An assault on your property.' She handed the fob to Maddy. 'I've asked Chit – *Chetak*! – to join us. He'll know what to do—'

'You don't understand! I should've called… I didn't even *think*—'

'Yes, yes, but it's behind you now. Can't undo what you *didn't* do earlier. Sit down, please. Just sit.' She was standing close to Maddy, not touching her but holding her hands out, as if trying to contain the hectic energy pouring out of the other woman.

There was a knock on the door. 'Come,' said Verity, looking around.

Chetak entered bearing a basket of oranges, apples and bananas. 'I thought I'd… Sorry! Is this a bad moment?' He stood in the doorway, as if poised to leave again.

'Please,' said Maddy. She was sitting once more, her eyes shut. The phone was on her lap, both hands held to her head. 'I just… I need to…' She didn't know how to continue, so she stopped.

Verity stepped away. 'She needs space,' she said. Taking the basket of fruit, she placed it on the seat of the easy chair. 'We'll be right outside,' she said to Maddy, 'whenever you're ready.' Then she ushered Chetak out of the room without looking around again.

11

Here's a furious
Argument:
Which is better?
Aix or Ghent?

– JINXES, BIG & SMALL

Some hours later, Maddy was once more alone in the study after Verity had helped her settle in for the night. The settee had been converted into a bed. She'd showered and changed into a borrowed caftan. She'd asked for soup and sandwiches for dinner and had eaten it on her own in the study.

She had turned off all the lights and was sitting on the bed, facing the French windows. Only a glimmer of light from the garden filtered in through the bougainvillea. Verity had requested that she smoke outside the room, on the veranda. It was dusty under the creeper's luxuriant growth, however, which was why there were no chairs placed under it.

Maddy had talked with Malli once more and at length. They were both calmer. Bindu and Lata had both been reassured that Maddy was alive and well. They knew now that the things in the house had been removed for safe keeping by friends, not goons. In the morning was when Maddy would look into what legal steps lay ahead.

But when she had tried to explain the offer that had been made, Malli told her that it was madness to even begin to consider such a hare-brained scheme. 'Listen to me,' she said, 'just listen to me. Everything you describe stinks like a public toilet that has never been cleaned. The novelty of a woman employed to drive a private car – okay, a little unusual – is one thing. To ask you to dress up as a man? *That* is where the madness begins!'

'No,' said Maddy. 'I don't think so. I really don't—'

'What sort of people will even make such a suggestion? Don't you see how twisted that is?'

'There's no such thing as a lady chauffeur here in Delhi. I don't even know if there are any in India,' said Maddy. She felt compelled to argue despite the fatigue clogging her brain.

'So that's what I'm saying! Why even do something that there's no existing model of!'

'Because it's... I mean... why am *I* a driver, after all?' returned Maddy. 'Because it's something I'm good at, something I can do. Yet this city's conventions make it difficult or impossible for me to just *be* that simple thing – a woman who happens to be a driver.'

'All right, all right. So that's what I'm saying, na? It's one thing to want a lady driver for another woman. But if they insist that you must dress up as a guy, then... what else will they force you to do!'

'They're not insisting!' protested Maddy. 'It's my choice. My own car is still here with me. My clothes have already been washed and ironed. She explicitly told me, "'You're free to leave."'

'Oh my GOD! That's how they catch you, don't you understand? These are very clever people. Make no mistake. They have guessed that you're the type who thinks, *Ah! I can leave whenever I want! So... I'll stay!* Can't you see that?'

'I can understand your point,' said Maddy. Her tone was subdued.

'Then why aren't you leaving right now! Get out of there right now. Go to my house. I'll be back in two days. Or sooner if you need me.'

'No.'

'But WHY! That's what I don't understand. You have no idea who these people are! Why d'you trust them?'

'I don't know!' said Maddy. 'And I don't trust them. Not really. Even as I say this, I'm thinking that the room might be bugged or my phone might be bugged while I sleep or… or... I don't *know*! But I'm tired, and I don't want to leave.'

'Just stop thinking.' Malli's voice was growing shrill once more. 'Get up, go to your car and leave. Now. NOW.'

It was clear, however, that Maddy was not going to leave. Malli made her final pitch. 'Just promise me one thing: wait for me to come before you sign anything. I'll come straight there from the airport. They might pressure you to sign-sign-sign, but you have to stand firm.'

'Okay, yes, I promise,' said Maddy. 'I believe they'll understand—'

'Haha,' said Malli. 'We'll see how happy they are when they find out that you're not a complete maniac, ready to sign over your life just because they say please and thank you in BBC accents. And that's another thing, you know? This idea that you're doing them some big favour by becoming a transvestite—'

'No!'

'—believe me, the moment your duty's over, they'll just kick you out and forget that you ever existed. That's how the super-rich behave. Have you even asked yourself what will happen if you fall sick? If you have an accident on the road? And you're taken straight to the men's ward?'

'Oh. My. *God!*' said Maddy, who had not, in fact, considered this point.

'You've not thought anything through. I know what you're like. Even after everything that's happened in your life, you're still chasing after rainbows. Don't be fooled! By their nice manners and their pretty, pretty words! That's only so long as they need something from you. Once their use for you is over, that's when you'll see their true colours.'

The call ended with Malli's voice ringing in Maddy's ears.

Particularly that last statement.

Reaching into her purse, Maddy drew out a strip of Calmpose. She hardly ever took painkillers or sedatives, but of late, she'd had trouble sleeping. She pressed out one small white tablet now, knowing that it would knock her out in less than a minute.

That's what she needed.

Oblivion.

12

A sneaking suspicion
Slithered by
Smooth and green,
Sleek and sly.

– JINXES, BIG & SMALL

Maddy awoke feeling calm and rested. It took her several moments to recollect where she was, and why, before sitting up.

It was still dark outside.

She got up and went onto the veranda, which was continuous with the whole breadth of the second floor. She guessed that Verity's bedroom also opened onto this space, but a solid cane partition divided one side from the other. The morning air was so fresh that she decided against polluting it with a cigarette.

Back in the study, she tidied the bed, made herself some tea and picked out a book of verse called *Favourite Poems.*

She smiled as she leafed through the pages, recalling poems that she'd loved as a child. Then she put the book down and asked herself whether that was why she was unwilling to leave this strange house and these even stranger people. *Am I responding to some rarefied code, a schoolgirl's version of the Masonic handshake?* she wondered. *Are stray bits of poetry and a few familiar books enough to cement a deep bond between me and a complete stranger?*

Was it real, was it solid?

Or was it just another *A Crown of Feathers*? In Isaac Bashevis Singer's wise and melancholic story of that name, the perils of believing in prophetic visions are epitomized by a crown of feathers hidden inside a pillow.

What about the wealth that was powering the discreet opulence of this lifestyle and this house? All right, some famous man was living downstairs. Fine. Verity had murmured something about minor royalty and succession drama. Fine. But what of Verity? How did she maintain herself in this place? Or in this country? Foreigners usually did not remain here indefinitely. Who was she *really*?

It was unlikely that any of these questions would be answered in a hurry.

At seven, there was a knock on the door.

'Ready for breakfast?' asked Verity.

'Yes,' Maddy called out, 'in a minute!' She threw on her freshly laundered clothes from the day before and emerged, hastily raking her hair with her fingers.

'Good morning!' said Verity. 'Did you sleep well?'

'Very,' said Maddy a little sheepishly. 'I had help. I took a pill.'

Then she looked up and exclaimed suddenly, 'Oh! It's a *mirror*!' What had seemed like one immense room the day before was, she now saw, an illusion: the floor-to-ceiling mirror behind the potted palms effectively doubled the length of the space. A cleverly placed bamboo screen behind the palms prevented people from seeing reflections of themselves.

Verity laughed. 'Yes! It's a shock to realize that, isn't it?'

Breakfast had been laid out on a sideboard beside the door to the study. 'Chetak said he'll be joining us in fifteen minutes,' said Verity, helping herself to toast and scrambled eggs. She had explained that she normally ate in the formal dining room on the ground floor. The only reason they were eating upstairs now was to keep Maddy out of sight until she'd made her decision, either way.

Maddy served herself cubes of cut papaya from a bowl. 'Surely it's very early for Chetak to be visiting?'

'He lives close by,' said Verity as she settled down on the settee. 'But he's always in and out. He works for, you know,' she tilted her head, 'the man downstairs.'

'Ah,' said Maddy. She remembered her conversation with Malli.

Sitting down on the armchair facing the tall windows, she said, 'Last night, I spoke to my friend again. The one who'd called earlier. She can't believe that I would consider your offer. About taking on a job dressed as a man.'

Verity was dressed in a pale pink chikankari kurta, with a white salwar. She nodded as she said, 'She's probably right: it *is* a crazy idea but...' She had an impish smile as she took a bite of toast. 'If I could do it myself, I would!'

Maddy stared at her uncertainly. 'Dress as a man, you mean?'

Verity gave a slight chuckle. 'No. It's not the gender thing but the *other* one. Wanting to be on the other side of the class divide. Do you see?' She glanced at Maddy. 'I can't tell whether you think I'm just mad or that you understand what I mean.'

'I don't know either,' said Maddy truthfully. 'I'm not sure I agree about even wanting to. I mean,' she chose her words carefully, 'wouldn't it only ever be fake? Play-acting at being underprivileged, like a specialized kind of tourism?'

Verity nodded. 'That's a complex point you've made, Maddy. And a good one. But the fact is, even with the best of motives, it's one of the barriers that I could never cross. Not here, with my light hair and eyes.' She gave Maddy an appraising glance. 'Maybe you, too, I'm guessing? Might find it difficult, yes?'

Maddy said, 'We-e-ll. Being a woman driver is hard enough. Just figuring out where to find a toilet when I'm going to spend hours parked outside someone's house at night is an issue. Doing that while pretending to be a man, in a super-macho city like Delhi? That's a whole other level!'

'According to Chit,' said Verity, 'if you want to get this right, you need to spend some time up on the terrace, in the sun. Darkening your skin. He thinks you're too light-skinned to pass as a driver.'

Maddy frowned. 'Really?' She thought it was an odd remark. Mildly insulting.

A loud clanking groan sounded from the lift shaft.

'That's him now,' said Verity.

There was a thump, followed by a rattle, then the wooden door was flung open. Chetak bustled out. He was carrying a stack of black folders tied with string and had a satchel hanging from his right shoulder. Over his left arm was what appeared to be a dark blue suit, weighted down at one end by a wooden hanger.

'Ah, thank goodness for air conditioning,' he exclaimed. 'Good morning, Verity, and hello again, Maddy. Look! I have a uniform for you to try on.'

He put his burden down on the second armchair.

'Join us for breakfast?' asked Verity, pointing at the sideboard.

'No, no, thanks,' he said. 'Three things I wanted to do before I go to court. One was to drop off this uniform.' He held up the hanger so that the material hung freely, revealing a smart-looking suit in dark blue material. It had an edging of red along the collar and at the cuffs.

'Secondly, a phone for Maddy. If you take on this job, you'll need to have a work phone, right?' He held it up, then handed it to Maddy. 'I always have a spare one set up for emergencies. A very basic Nokia with all the usual functions – messaging, roaming, voice recording—'

'Voice recording?' asked Maddy, puzzled, as she took the phone from him.

Chetak shrugged. 'People leave voice messages when they're too busy to text?'

'Oh!' said Maddy, not entirely convinced. 'Guess I've never done that.'

'The third thing is with regard to your flat, Maddy,' said Chetak. 'You need to tell me what you want to do.' He draped the uniform on the back of the armchair as he spoke. 'Or, if you'd like, I can advise you.'

'I'm sorry, what?'

'The unconscionable summary eviction carried out yesterday,' said Chetak, tugging on his lapels as if he were speaking in court, 'has to be answered with a decisive counteraction. The other party has grievously damaged your property and rendered you literally homeless, causing you severe mental distress. We will show that the other party carried out this eviction with full knowledge that the action was illegal and unwarranted, without giving due notice of their actions… Shall I continue?' He glanced towards Maddy, a smile in his eyes.

Maddy did not return the smile. 'I don't know what you mean by "we",' she said. 'You're not part of this. What is it? A suit? A petition? I… I mean, you're going ahead as if you and I are somehow *partners*! But we're not! I don't even know that I want to move against Mrs Bansal; I don't have the financial means to do any of that…'

She stopped, flustered and miserable. 'I wish you wouldn't do things without consulting me first.'

Unruffled, Chetak inclined his head. 'I am consulting *for* you, Madam,' he said, forgetting that the title was actually her first name. 'That's what this is. A consultation. The first-person plural "we" in connection with a client's case is a common legal convention. Something we lawyers use to give the impression that "we" are both on the same side. It's a little disorienting, but you'll get used to it.'

'I'm *sorry*,' said Maddy, 'I don't think I can—'

Verity cut in, 'Wait, please. I think he's being funny. Are you being funny, Chit? Because this might not be the right time.'

'I'm not being funny,' said Chetak. He was no longer smiling. 'You *must* respond to your landlady's illegal action in a timely fashion.'

'Yes, but...' Maddy glanced towards Verity, then back at Chetak. 'I don't want to be rushed into anything! I'm still very uncertain about why I'm even here!'

'Maddy,' said Chetak, leaning on the armchair's back, 'what I'm talking about has nothing to do with Verity's proposal. I'm talking about your home. Your rights as a tenant. Whatever you decide about Verity's proposal, you've still got to fight for your home. People like your Mrs Bansal are vicious, heartless bullies. They push people like you around because they know you'll be squeamish about pushing back—'

Maddy, desperate to stop the flow of words, said, 'But you're *also* pushing me!'

'Yes,' said Chetak with cool aplomb. 'I am. But not for the same reason.'

Maddy said, 'Oh, really! It's for my own good, is it?'

'Frankly, yes,' he said. 'Let me add, though, that it's for my own satisfaction, too. I'm sick of watching the Mrs Bansals of this world get away with their petty crimes. All the time.' He straightened up. 'I've got to be on my way. I'll need to know if you want to be advised by me or not—'

'Just a minute,' cut in Verity. She looked at both of them as she spoke. 'What I suggest is, Maddy, why don't you drop Chetak off at court? I mean, drive him there in your car. You can talk along the way. Then, take your time coming back here. Visit your friends. Or be by yourself. What you need is to get away from here. You have our numbers. Come back when you're sure of what you want to do.'

Her pale eyes were penetrating, the pupils like pinpoints. She seemed to see straight into Maddy's confused brain.

'Okay,' said Chetak. 'Verity's right. You need time to think.' He began to collect his files and papers but left the uniform draped on the chair. 'We'll take my car so that I'm sure I have what I need with me. I'll drive on the way out, then you take the car, go wherever you want and come back to fetch me after five. That'll give us plenty of time to talk.'

Maddy glanced at Verity. 'I… I…' she stammered, unable to make up her mind.

Verity nodded, 'Just go on, Maddy. Whatever you decide, it'll be the right decision.'

'Okay,' said Maddy. 'I'll get my handbag.'

13

A passing fancy
Went to sea
Caught a fish
And ate for free.

– JINXES, BIG & SMALL

Maddy sat alone at a table in the coffee shop of the BelMondo, a new five-star hotel in Vasant Enclave. The serving staff, male and female, were dressed as farmers from the Punjab. Both sexes wore pink turbans and embroidered waistcoats.

Maddy wondered at the audacity of the designer who had chosen to go down such an extravagantly cross-gender path. Then she thought, *What about me? That's what I'm planning to do, after all. Is it as crazy as Malli seems to think?*

She shook her head at herself.

It had been five years since she'd moved back to the city of her birth. She and her two older brothers had spent their early childhood in the US. Their parents had tried to live in both countries for a while before choosing the US. Eventually, all three children had taken US citizenship.

In high school, Maddy opted for linguistics. In college, she took Spanish and earned an MA. That's where she met Liman, her husband-to-be. A soft-spoken Lebanese man with an MBA and an interest in Sufi music.

They had both wanted to pursue careers in academia, but when the politics got too much for them, they decided to get married and travel instead. He got a bank job in Dubai, where they both settled. She worked as a UN interpreter and travelled back and forth to Geneva.

They'd been happy.

She stirred the foam in her coffee cup.

It had been so sudden, his death.

The car had overheated while he was out on the highway. It blew up and burned its single occupant to a cinder. Such a clean, spare death. Rather like the man himself. He left no shadows, no complaints. The fragrance of his sweet, uncomplicated personality was all that he had left her.

Eight years had passed since then. Lim's parents had died many years before their marriage. Her parents were both alive, retired, living in Florida. She had gone back to them initially. She had thought it would be possible to pick up the traces of her former life. But she'd been wrong.

She drank down the remains of her coffee, went to the counter to pay for it, then to the hotel's shopping mall. She knew they had a Fabindia outlet. She bought three tent-like dresses and three midi-length kurtas in bright, feminine colours, with embroidery at the edges and matching churidars. Two pairs of plain white cotton pyjamas. Three silk dupattas.

There was a Skechers outlet, too, at which she bought a pair of sneakers and a pair of Hawaiian flats, with thick white soles and rainbow-stripe straps.

In the washroom at the mall, she changed into the brightest of her new outfits. When she emerged from the toilet stall and saw herself transformed in the mirror, she smiled at her reflection. The kurta was deep scarlet with a bold pattern of swirling indigo leaves printed on it. Her height combined with the length of the garment resulted in a shock of colour in the otherwise grey-and-chrome room.

There was an attendant present, a woman with an ironed-in disgruntled expression on her face. She glanced up, surprised at the sudden brightness, and smiled. The smile transformed her face. Now the woman pointed to the lower edge of the suit and said, 'See – the tag is there.'

The door swung open, and a family breezed in, laughing and chattering – a mother with teenage girls. Maddy reached down to tear the paper label off, leaving the annoying plastic barb dangling in place. She glanced around to thank the attendant before hurrying out of the washroom, still stuffing her old clothes into the voluminous Fabindia courtesy bag.

While waiting for the valet to bring Chetak's car to her from the underground parking, she thought about the combination of control and trust that Chetak had displayed by inviting her to drive his car. It had been a spur-of-the-moment decision; she was sure of that. Verity had assumed that Maddy would want to be in her own vehicle. By offering his, Chetak was signalling his willingness to be a part of this extraordinary scheme, and with the same move, disarming her.

To be in his car was to surrender to his zone of influence while giving Maddy unsupervised access to his personal vehicle. It felt like an astonishing intimacy to share with a virtual stranger, but maybe it wasn't that at all. Maddy smiled to herself as the silver-grey Elantra glided into view. Maybe it was just another clever move, a higher order of manipulation.

She tucked a tip into the palm of the valet as he held the door open for her. She flung her purchases over to the passenger's side and settled behind the wheel. How convenient that they both just happened to have the same make of car! Almost identical, except that his had a few custom features: a superior music system, for instance. The front seats were upholstered in real leather.

It was 11 a.m. on a weekday. Traffic flowing into the city was relatively calm. She drove along the Inner Ring Road, then up

Aurobindo Marg and towards Jor Bagh. She found parking easily, right outside a small eatery. She bought herself a sandwich and brought it back to the car as she changed into her new shoes. She flexed her feet inside them, enjoying the sensation of newness.

There was a knock on her window. She looked up to see a young boy in a striped T-shirt, holding up a wad of poison-pink parking ticket coupons. She rolled down her window and nodded when the boy said, 'Twenty.' She accepted the coupon and rolled the window up again.

All these interactions, she thought. *All these interactions will be different if I'm not wearing a bright red kurta. If I'm wearing a driver's uniform. If my hair is even shorter. And if I give off that vibe. That guy-to-guy vibe.*

The way the boy had looked at her right now, for instance. It was the slightest flicker of a glance, a Malcolm-Gladwell-BLINK moment. A judgment had been made, an assessment. Neither good nor bad… that wasn't the point. *The point is, if I'm a man, it'll be different,* she thought. *I'll have to be prepared for that. I'll have to know what the correct responses are. Or pretend to know.*

What pool of experience could she draw upon? What kind of person would help her? Another driver, an employed chauffeur? But then, he'd have to be in on the plot, wouldn't he? He'd have to be trusted with a secret. A rare and unusual secret. Juicy beyond the average person's wildest dreams. Or… maybe not. Maybe drivers and others like them entertained ideas of this kind all the time. *Who am I,* she thought, *to decide what the dreams of a driver might be?*

She looked around, outside the windows of the Elantra. There were three other cars, all white, lined up alongside hers. None of them had drivers inside them. They were smaller than the type of vehicle that typically had chauffeurs. They were more likely to be owner driven. They had the modest dimensions of cars belonging to women who used them as tools of their trade as mothers and housewives. They needed to be small, dependable and easily manoeuvrable in order to get their owners through the daily round of chores built around a family's schedules.

Her own car and the one she was in now were giants by contrast. Extensions of the gracious home, the air-conditioned office, the boardroom. They radiated privilege. They dominated the spaces they entered. When they were driven by women, those women became honorary men. People like the parking attendant didn't mess with such women.

She looked around at the interior of the car. Unlike her own, there was almost nothing personal in it. No mirror ornament, for instance. She had a Ghostbusters decal on the rear window while this car had none. There were bottles of Bisleri water in the side pockets of the rear doors, no magazines, no pamphlets stowed away in there, no personal trash whatsoever. Hers had reusable grocery bags, takeaway menus from the fast food joints she often went to and the occasional candy wrapper.

No doubt this car was kept spooky clean by Chetak's driver. But even so, it was sterile.

The air freshener, therefore, became more significant than it might otherwise have been. It was the model of a dragon in flight, made of glass. The dragon's mouth was open, suggesting that the faint aroma of lemon and something else – she couldn't place it – came from its mouth.

She smiled as she leaned forward to check. Yes, it was as she suspected. The base of the unit had a tiny emblem emblazoned on it. Belonging to the *Game of Thrones* universe. A dragon rampant.

House of Targaryen, huh! she thought. *Interesting!*

14

The perfect storm
Is not the norm.

– JINXES, BIG & SMALL

At ten minutes to five in the evening, Maddy headed towards the quiet lane near the High Court, where Chetak had got down from the car in the morning. They had agreed that this was where she would collect him when he was ready to go home.

As she neared the rendezvous point, her phone beeped with a message from Chetak. He was on the main road, he said, at the corner of such-and-such. Then she looked up, and there he was, still in his black robes.

As she pulled over to where he stood, he gestured to her to remain in the driver's seat. Opening the passenger door, he got in, saying, 'You can turn in here,' meaning the lane they were next to.

She had already understood the point. It was to avoid being noticed as they changed positions. She began to turn as soon as he was in. She sensed that he was staring at her, perhaps because of her clothes. She glanced in his direction. 'Well, yes,' she said. 'I decided that I needed to establish a clearly feminine persona. Entirely distinct from the masculine image that I might…' she paused, '*might* need to cultivate.'

'Yes,' he confirmed, 'I see.' He was holding his files and folders to his chest, as if undecided where to put them down.

'Please don't assume that I've made any decisions yet,' she said. 'It's just to keep my options open.'

'Understood.'

'I was thinking we could go to Pandara Park,' she said, 'to exchange places.'

'Good plan,' he said.

They were there in less than ten minutes. He tossed his stuff on the back seat as he exited the car and hurried around to her side. He held the door open for her as she got out, then slid into place behind the wheel while she went around and folded herself into the passenger's seat.

He got back on the road, nosing his way into traffic. When he had decided which path to take towards Hauz Khas, he said, 'So, is there anything you'd like to talk about now?'

Earlier that day, on their way to the court, as soon as they were in the car, she had said, 'I'm sorry, but I don't want to talk about anything just now. Not the house. Not the eviction. Not even the proposal.' He had nodded without comment. They had completed the journey in silence, except for a brief exchange about logistics.

Now she said, 'Yes. I've had time to think about some of the things I want to know – or I should say, *would like* to know. Verity mentioned a famous man who doesn't want to be named until I've decided what I want to do. Fair enough. But what about Verity herself? I feel she's withholding something. Perhaps something I need to know? After all, if they're both going to employ me, I need to have *some* idea of who I'm working for.'

Chetak nodded as if he understood what she meant but said, 'I'm sorry. Did she say that it would be a joint employment?' When Maddy directed a questioning glance at him, he said, 'That she and this... um... famous man would *both* be your employers?'

Maddy, watching as he negotiated the six-way roundabout going south, said, 'Yes. I had the impression that working for him and as a male driver was entirely his idea. She began to like it after he'd brought it up.'

Chetak nodded without comment, then said, 'How about her? Did you ask her about herself? Why she's here, how long she's been in India?'

Maddy said, 'No. Last night, I needed time. I still need time. I don't know what I'm looking at, what I'm getting into.' She took in a deep breath. 'When I talk to her, she seems so…' she hunted for a word '…*normal.* Sensible. I keep thinking of, you know, Mary Poppins. Or maybe I mean Julie Andrews. I keep having to remind myself that on the contrary, whatever she looks like, she's asked a stranger to work for her as a cross-dressing chauffeur!' She turned her head towards Chetak. 'Do you know what I'm saying? Personally, I don't think it's such a big deal. But Verity seems to think it's highly eccentric. And my best friend, the only person with whom I've spoken about where I am and what I'm planning to do, thinks it's completely insane. She thinks I'm mad to even consider such a scheme.'

Maddy paused, waiting for Chetak to respond. When he didn't, she said, 'Aren't you going to say anything?'

Now they were at a traffic light, heading towards Aurobindo Marg. He glanced in her direction, then back at the road. 'I'm thinking about what you said just now – that you don't think it's such a big deal.' He was choosing his words carefully. 'I think you know perfectly well that it *is* a big deal. But you want to do it anyway.'

'Huh?'

'I'm trying to examine the situation as honestly as I can. The problem, as I see it, is that you *want* to do it, don't you? You want to try your hand as a cross-dressing chauffeur,' he said. 'Or else, you'd have backed away by now. Because there are risks involved. The streets of Delhi are not a stage set for some kind of Elizabethan farce. But you haven't backed away. Why not? *That's* what you need to ask yourself.'

He stopped as if he wanted to say more but had chosen not to. The light changed. He moved forward, leaning to his left and into the six-lane avenue. 'Excuse me for putting it this way, but I think your own motivation is what you need to examine.'

Maddy was looking straight ahead, wondering what to feel. Was he telling the truth? Had he put his finger on the nature of her own confusion? Or was he subtly goading her by telling her that she was a daredevil?

She shifted in her seat.

'Okay,' she said. 'Okay, let me try another tack.' She paused before blurting her question out. 'What's in it for you?'

He shook his head. 'No,' he said. 'Don't go down that path. It's about you, not me. My involvement is secondary—'

'Even though you're the one who reeled me in?' she cut in. 'You say you heard about me from your aunt and that you mentioned me to Verity because she talked about a chauffeur. But your involvement now goes beyond simple happenstance—'

'It's true,' he said. 'I'm not a disinterested bystander. And if you do take up the proposal, you will certainly know much more than you do now. But *this* decision, the one directly in front of all of us now, is purely *yours*. Yours alone.'

She gave an exasperated gasp. 'I need a cigarette. I have my own—' She pre-empted an offer from him as she dug into her handbag. 'Is it okay? To smoke in your car?' She fished out her pack. 'I've not had one all day.'

'Yes, it's okay,' he said. 'May I take one of yours? Haven't had any all day today either.'

They were at the traffic lights close to the Air Force Museum. Some distance away was the intersection that went under the Inner Ring Road overpass.

Maddy lit her cigarette and said, inhaling, 'Change of subject then. I want to talk about what it'll be like if I *do* take on the proposal. Wait. Yes, I know you're going to say that I need to discuss this with Verity.

That it's her decision. But I want to talk about it now. With you. Call it a dress rehearsal if you want.' She exhaled. 'May I go ahead?'

'Of course,' said Chetak, lighting his own cigarette.

'I think my greatest problem will be other drivers,' said Maddy. 'I can't believe they'll be fooled. The moment I open my mouth... I mean, I can pitch my voice low, but what'll I say? What conversation will I have with them?'

'Oh, I don't believe that'll be a problem,' said Chetak. The light changed to amber. 'Drivers don't automatically start jabbering with one another. You can avoid contact with others.'

He sat up, preparing to surge forward in the middle of three lanes. The two cars ahead of him were already moving. 'Corporate drivers can be a snooty lot,' he said, following the car in front. He shifted gear and picked up speed. 'Being in a uniform will help—'

As they swept forward, they heard a screech of brakes. On the right, a flash of white. 'Ahh!' cried Maddy. Had there been a thud? She swung around in her seat, straining against the belt, twisting around to see through the gap between the two front seats. 'Oh my god, my god… a child—'

But their momentum had already carried them too far forward. Whatever had happened was behind them, did not involve them, and they still had the light. They had to keep moving. Shrieks and car horns sounded behind them, fading with distance.

Chetak stayed his course, saying softly, 'Shit. Shit. Shit…'

Maddy gasped several times in quick succession, her hand to her mouth, followed by a sudden sharp yelp of pain. '*Ouch*! My cigarette!' Then she was digging in her handbag for her pocket ashtray.

During this time, Chetak had gone on straight ahead, speeding past the entrance to AIIMS, and the row of open-fronted medical supply stores that lined the left side of the avenue.

By the time he began easing towards the left, Maddy had found the ashtray and snapped it open. She jammed the glowing tip into it repeatedly, her eyes shut, as if trying to stub out the scene of the accident from memory. When she was able to look up again, Chetak had slotted the Elantra into a spot in front of an impromptu flower stall and come to a complete halt.

They sat in silence, listening to the faint ticking sounds of the vehicle as it cooled. The late afternoon shoppers drifted in clumps of three and four directly in front of them. Meanwhile, the trauma of an anonymous street accident continued to twitch in their minds.

'Sorry,' said Chetak. 'There was nothing else to do. I had to keep moving.'

'Yes,' said Maddy. 'I know.' Then she paused and added, 'Or... I don't know. I might have frozen up. I don't know. I just... *don't know*. It's never happened before. An accident right in front of me. Behind me.'

'Thirty seconds earlier, it would have been us,' said Chetak. 'Jamming on the brakes. Shit. Shit.' He shook his head, as if trying to dislodge the image. 'I barely saw it – a sort of blur in my side mirror. Did you? See it, I mean?' He continued to shake his head. 'And *thud*. You're done. The driver, I mean. There's no recovery from that kind of accident. You're *done*!' Then he shrugged. 'Well, I mean. Depending on who you are. Who the victims are. The whole circus unfolds.'

There was silence as they both processed his words. Then Maddy asked, 'What happens? I mean, right away?'

'The police arrive or – no – the first people to get there are bystanders. They pour out of the empty air, fall out of the sky, thick clouds of them. Back there right now, the intersection must be seething. Then the police arrive. Someone calls an ambulance.'

'AIIMS is right there,' said Maddy, using the familiar acronym for the All India Institute of Medical Sciences.

'They'll still call an ambulance. The owners of the car will be written up right away. God save them if they don't have their papers or if they try to get away. The crowd would beat them to a pulp. The sympathy is always with the victim. Whatever plans the driver may have had for his life, they'd be gone now.'

Maddy was silent for a beat. 'So,' she said, 'if that had been us back there?'

Chetak looked away. His cigarette was still lit. He took a drag on it before answering. 'It'd be a mess. I don't know. I'd have to call in a few favours, I suppose.' He swung his head towards her. 'What about you? Never been in any accidents?'

'As a private taxi driver, you mean?' She shook her head. 'No. Maybe I've just been lucky. Or maybe I'm just a jolly good driver!' A smile flickered on and off. 'But I was thinking about what it'd be like, if, you know…' she trailed off, 'if I was a chauffeur.' She glanced at him. 'What would I do? Would I be treated differently to the owner of the car? Would I be dragged off to police custody?' She grimaced as she spoke. 'What would they do to me – the police? I mean, once they found out, that I'm…' She gestured with her hands, pointing to herself. 'That I'm not what they think I am?'

Chetak gave a soft chuckle. 'Oh my god! Chaos. They wouldn't know whether to beat you up or rape you!' He flinched even as the words came out of his mouth. 'Shit, sorry.'

'Tch,' said Maddy, shaking her head. 'No. Don't apologize. That's the world we're in. I'd rather face towards it than away.'

'Let's not get ahead of ourselves,' said Chetak. 'You've not even decided yet whether you're going to do this… thing.'

'But these are some of the issues that I've been thinking about,' she persisted. 'What would happen to me in case of an accident? If I'm alone in the car?'

'You wouldn't be alone, don't you see?' said Chetak. 'You'd no longer be a private operator. You'd be an employee. You wouldn't be in your own car. You'd be in a car that belongs to someone else. Not just anyone either—' He stopped abruptly.

Maddy frowned. 'You mean Verity?'

Chetak was looking away. 'No, no,' he said. 'She doesn't have a car.'

'Then what? What do you mean?'

Chetak opened his door, stubbed his cigarette out on the road and closed the door again before he answered. He turned towards Maddy and said, 'You need to know more about the situation before you make any decisions, Maddy. I've said enough. For the rest, you need to ask Verity.' He pressed the ignition button. The car growled softly. 'We need to get back.'

15

A lucky break
Is fun to take
With sparkling wine
And carrot cake.

– JINXES, BIG & SMALL

'Wait,' said Maddy as Chetak drove in through an unfamiliar gate, 'there's more than one front entrance?'

'Actually,' said Chetak, 'this *is* the main one. A part of the garden wall forms the cul-de-sac you saw at the end of the lane yesterday.'

The car's wheels hissed on the gravelled driveway. The path curved around a patch of greenery shaped like a teardrop. The narrow end pointed towards the gate. Chetak circled around the patch, passing another car that was parked directly by the door into the building. He parked facing out, towards the gate.

That other car was a Jaguar, black and gleaming. It projected an air of ownership over the entire property. Its driver was standing beside it, a tall, thin man, with a peaked cap upon his head.

As Chetak and Maddy got out and walked towards the house, the driver acknowledged Chetak. He returned the nod while continuing to walk towards the door. As they neared it, the driver moved aside very slightly, as if to suggest that he knew he wasn't expected to open that door.

Instead, Chetak, using a key to let himself in, pushed the door open and stood aside to allow Maddy to walk in first. 'After you,' he said.

In the hallway, which was broader than the lift lobby on the other side, there was a polished teak door facing the one they had just passed through. On their right was a stairwell. 'The lift on the other side is for staff – like you and me!' Chetak laughed. 'Just joking. The building has several entrances. This side has only the stairs, no lift.'

From behind the teak door, there came the sound of a man's voice. '—listen to me – no, no – that's not what I'm saying—' they heard. It was an older man's voice.

Gravelly. With an accent that Maddy could not place.

She had already started up the stairs, however, and a moment later, the voice had moved out of range.

There were two doors on the first-floor landing, with numbers beside each. *Do they go to separate rooms or separate apartments?* wondered Maddy as she continued up to the next floor. Chetak followed close behind. When they were on the final flight up to the second floor, he'd caught up.

The landing had a skylight overhead. Thin-leaved ferns were lined up in dark red pots on either side of the passage, as if standing to attention. Verity's high, clear voice was audible. She seemed to be on the phone. Maddy turned towards Chetak, unsure whether or not to proceed, but he said, 'Go on in. She's expecting us.'

Maddy heard Verity say, 'Look, they're here now,' a moment before she leaned out of her front door, her face animated. 'Bye,' she said into the phone, disengaging as she looked up in greeting. 'Sorry! Hello! I was just on the phone, come in.'

There was an air of lively distraction about her. 'My goodness,' she said to Maddy, 'all in red!' She was smiling, her face pink with exhilaration. 'You look wonderful. I'm glad. Come in.'

She walked ahead, drawing the two of them in with her. Now they were in the counterpart of the mirror lobby on the other side of the house. It looked like a living room but with a wide-screen TV along one wall and a stack of audio equipment alongside it. There were glass-fronted cabinets filled with cassette tapes. Several hundred of them. The floor was bare white marble with carpets, as in the study. A door with a pressed-glass panel led from this room into what must be Verity's bedroom.

The centre of the room was dominated by three leather-upholstered armchairs, each one different yet similar in size and comfortable solidity. They brought to mind three grown siblings of a cultured family. No sofa. The tall windows were curtained with fine, plain white mulmul. A single tall vase nodded with feathery white ferns. It was cool inside the room, and the single overhead fan was turned off.

Walking forward, Maddy said, 'Thanks. Yes, well… I… I needed clothes right away. So that's where I started. I bought what I'm wearing and a couple of other things and… shoes… and…' She faltered to a stop. The other two were gazing at her with what may have been an air of expectancy. Or was it something else? Was it amusement? Were they secretly laughing at her little show of independence and self-will?

She couldn't know. 'Like you suggested, Verity, I thought about it. I took all afternoon. I couldn't decide. In my mind, I know that it will be smarter to walk away.' She looked up now, meeting Verity's eyes head-on. There was an edge of defiance in her voice and stance. 'But in my heart, I know I want to go ahead. So that's what I'm going to do. I'll… I'm accepting your offer. I'm saying *yes*.'

Verity, who might have been expected to exclaim with pleasure, instead grew solemn. 'My dear – please don't mind me calling you that, I can't help myself – what can I say? I think that's extremely brave of you.' She blinked hard a couple of times. 'I mean, *I've* spent the day telling myself that you surely would decide *not* to. That I was wrong to ask. Particularly at a time when you've just had a terrible shock – lost your house, I mean. I can't imagine it – a punch to the guts.'

Chetak looked as if he wanted to interject, but before he could, Maddy said, 'No, please. I think we could waste a lot of time on hand-wringing, but the thing is, I've decided now. I've thought about it. I want to move ahead. And that's part of why I bought these clothes, you see.'

She had been holding her parcels and her handbag. 'May I put these down, please?' She went ahead and did so anyway, dropping them onto the nearest leather chair. 'I was thinking that I'll have to play two roles. One as me and one as the driver. Or else, it'll become entirely too bizarre and impossible. Just entering and exiting this house will become a crazy charade, in full view of the other household staff. It simply would not work at all.'

She was talking as if to herself, voicing the thoughts that she'd been entertaining intermittently all through the day. 'I need to be two distinct people. Myself as I am now,' she spread her hands and indicated herself, her clothes, her entire persona, 'as well as the uniformed driver, who comes and goes, on and off duty. Do you see?' She turned and looked at the other two. 'It has to be that way. Since I'll be living here – because that's what you said, Chetak, right from the start – that I would be living here?'

'Yes, yes,' said Verity at once. 'Of course. Even if you hadn't lost your home, that was the idea if you took on the position.' She turned her head to look at Chetak, then back to Maddy. 'Because, otherwise, you'd be seen coming in and out of your home as a uniformed driver, and the neighbours – never mind your landlady – would surely find that most peculiar!' She grinned suddenly, the skin of her face stretching and turning pink.

'You'd have to find a telephone booth to change into, like Superman!' said Chetak, smiling, too, but an edge of uncertainty clung to him.

'But I see your point, Maddy, of course, I do. It was always going to be the most complicated part of the plan – how you would manage the transition without being immediately found out.'

'Only a limited number of people,' said Chetak, 'should ever be in on the idea.'

'Yes,' said Maddy, nodding vigorously. 'In order to maintain the illusion.'

'It has to be a secret from the other staff, you mean?' asked Verity, turning to Chetak. 'I don't know about that. It'll be so very difficult… I mean, I don't know. Don't you think Suresh or Jyoti, either of them, could keep a secret?'

Chetak shook his head decisively. 'No. No, it wouldn't work.' He glanced at Maddy. 'He's the cook downstairs. And his wife. It's not a question of *can* they keep a secret. It's the *type* of secret. It's because it concerns someone whom they would consider one of them: a staff member. A driver. It wouldn't make sense to them that a driver was *also* a resident in the house. And a woman at that. I mean, frankly, they'd find that idea just... perverse.'

He looked at Verity, and she returned his gaze, frowning. 'Ah, yes. Of course.'

'And once they know, they are bound to share that information with all the others. With Bahadur and the other man, Prem, who alternates with him, and Ravi, the regular driver, and the gardener.' He shook his head more vehemently. 'Before you know it, it will be on the evening news!'

Maddy asked, 'Because of who *he* is, you mean? The mystery man downstairs?'

Both Chetak and Verity nodded.

'All right then,' said Maddy. 'That just confirms what I had felt instinctively. That it's got to be a secret.'

'Okay,' said Verity, looking uncertain. 'Gosh. It's going to be tough.'

'Moving along,' said Chetak, 'I have a question.' He turned to Maddy. 'Any thoughts about a name?'

'Yes, actually,' she said, smiling. 'I was thinking of Madan.'

Verity was nodding, but she was still thinking about the earlier theme. 'That's a good name. But keeping your identity a secret from the other staff is going to be really tricky.'

Chetak said, 'Including staying here. Staying in the house, I mean. A live-in driver is unheard of.'

'Oh. come on, Chit… Chetak! Surely that's up to the employer – where the driver lives?' said Verity. 'I mean, it's no one else's business.' Then she gave her head a quick double-shake. 'Or wait. I'm forgetting a very important part of all this. We can't do anything at all unless we've discussed it with...' she tilted her head, 'our mystery man.'

Chetak had been leaning on the back of one of the chairs, but he straightened up now. 'Speaking of whom,' he said, 'I should go down.'

He looked towards Verity and said, 'Will you follow? The two of you?'

Verity started to speak, but Maddy stepped in. 'Why don't I go down in uniform? You left it here, didn't you, Chetak, the one you brought in the morning? So then, let's get started with this program. I'll get changed. And if you wouldn't mind, Verity, I'd prefer it if you would stay upstairs with me, please. I'll need your help getting ready.'

Chetak turned to leave, then stopped at the door, swivelling around. 'What about shoes? Men's shoes?'

Verity smiled. 'I have a pair that one of my guests left behind.' She looked rueful. 'I'm sorry. Once I start thinking about a plan, I can't stop.'

16

See the happy accident!
Smiling sweetly, Heaven sent!

– JINXES, BIG & SMALL

Maddy stepped into Verity's bathroom to change. The mirror above the wash basin showed her from the chest up.

The uniform was the way she'd seen it in the morning, on a hanger, now dangling from the shower-curtain rail.

It consisted only of a top and bottom. There was no undergarment. The top looked like a safari jacket, except for the piping and the dark material it was made of. She removed her long red kurta, then undid the buttons on the uniform's jacket and slipped it off the hanger. She put it on, did up the buttons and turned to look at her reflection. The shoulders were perhaps half an inch too broad for her, drooping slightly. The chest fit reasonably well but could not conceal the shape of her breasts.

Reaching under the back of the jacket, she undid the clasp of her bra. It was a familiar manoeuvre that she'd learnt in boarding school, removing a bra from underneath a top. Once it was no longer fastened at the back, she could easily slip the shoulder straps off on either side by reaching up through the arms of the jacket. Then the bra could be drawn out by reaching in through the neckline of the uniform's jacket.

Turning back to the mirror she thought, *Much better*.

She'd never been big-breasted, not even as a short, chubby preteen. She'd grown out lean and tall, with broad shoulders and a small waist. In school, she'd endured much ribbing for the flatness of her chest. She was always cast as the male lead in school plays, with a pencilled-on moustache and blue eyeshadow smoothed onto the sides of her face to simulate a grown man's five o'clock shadow. In the West, as soon as she had her own money to spend, she'd bought herself lightly padded bras and had worn them ever since, just to give herself the semblance of a womanly figure.

And here she was now, worrying that she wasn't, after all, quite flat enough to pass as a man! She gave herself a wry smile. Even without the bra, there was the shadow of a swell under the two breast pockets of the jacket. She twisted her torso from side to side to see if there was a jiggle. Which there was, but worse than that was the chafing; without a bra, her nipples would be in a state of constant stimulation.

From outside, Verity called, 'How's it going in there?'

'Not great,' answered Maddy. 'Just a minute.' She shook the pants off the hanger and stepped into them, without bothering to remove her sandals. The waist was loose, of course. It was bound to be. But the hips were almost tight. She had a firm and shapely behind that was *not* happy to be confined within a man's trousers. The open-toed sandals absolutely did not suit the cuffs of the trouser legs. 'Coming out now,' she called, gathering up her clothes.

She stepped out, saying, 'I can't see myself full-length in there, so it's hard to judge.'

Verity said, 'Hmm. Well. I'd say it's not all that bad.' There was a shadow crease between her brows as she concentrated. 'The clothes are doing all the heavy lifting. You're wearing a man's uniform and so... you look like a man. Even though your face is not at all masculine. If you were standing beside a car dressed like that, no one would look twice. It's like that party trick with the six face cards. You know the one? Well, I'll show you someday, but the point is, we form impressions based on familiar reference points. Someone in a uniform standing by the front door of a car is a driver. And a man.

That's just how we're trained to think.' Now she pointed towards the sandals on Maddy's feet. 'Shall I bring out the shoes?'

Maddy was starting to unbutton the jacket. 'Yes, I'll wear the shoes, but before that, I'll need to do something drastic about the chafing,' she said, pointing towards her chest. 'It's already driving me crazy. Do you happen to have a long strip of cloth?'

'Something like a chunni, you mean?' asked Verity. 'I have a white one. Chiffon.' She'd already spun around to go to her bedroom.

'That'll be perfect,' said Maddy. She shrugged off the jacket and turned around, away from Verity, forgetting that behind her was the door to the bathroom. It had a full-length mirror on it. She was reflected in it, bare from the waist up.

Verity returned, holding the length of white chiffon floating from between her hands. 'Oh! Sorry,' she said, halting where she was, some steps away. 'D'you want to be alone?'

'It's all right,' said Maddy as she turned towards her, her hands outstretched to receive the cloth. 'I got used to being undressed with other people around in the US.' She turned back towards the mirror. 'Also, I've done this before, I mean, for plays, in school – what I'm about to do now.'

She folded the chunni lengthwise a couple of times so that it formed a narrow strip. 'It used to work quite well.' She placed the middle of the strip firmly against her chest, pulling the ends away behind her. 'I can do it on my own but haven't for quite a while—'

Verity came forward, quickly picking up the slack from Maddy's hands. 'Let me help,' she said. 'I've done this, too, in the past. The venerable art of breast-binding—'

'Also in the service of school plays?' smiled Maddy, still facing the mirror as Verity passed the trailing lengths of white chiffon forward. 'Thanks, yes, it's long enough that I can cross it again and pass the sides back to you.' She grunted softly. 'Ooh, yes, you can pull it quite tight, it doesn't hurt—'

'And tuck it in,' said Verity as she folded the soft cloth into the material that was already crossed over behind the other woman's back. 'Sure it's not too tight?'

'Sure,' said Maddy as she adjusted the folds so that they were smooth rather than bunched.

'A couple of pins, just to be safe? We don't want you unravelling!'

'Maybe let's not do that today?' said Maddy. 'I mean since this is a trial run? Or will we spend a long time downstairs?'

She bent to pick up the jacket from where she'd let it drop and slid it on once more.

Verity paused. 'Everything depends,' she said, speaking slowly. In the mirror, Maddy saw the pensive expression again, with its suggestion of something withheld.

'Maybe he'll immediately think it's all too ridiculous. Or maybe he won't.' Her eyes met with Maddy's in the mirror. 'So far, he's been intrigued about the idea. He believes it can't possibly work. He's got old-fashioned ideas about women! Can't believe that one of us could truly function as a chauffeur.'

She watched in the mirror as Maddy buttoned the collar. 'Turn around now, please?'

She was nodding even before Maddy had turned to face her. 'There. That's MUCH better! You know what it is? You're not hunching your shoulders forward as most of us do, automatically, when we're not wearing a bra. Now that you're all squared away, your shoulders are back. You're standing more like a man! What do you think? How does it feel?'

'Pretty good,' said Maddy as she turned and turned again, looking at herself in the mirror as well as back at Verity. 'Snug and secure. It's really quite comfortable.'

'Yes,' said Verity, reaching forward to straighten one of the pocket flaps. 'Now there's no sign at all. No telltale bulge. Not even the slightest jiggle.' She stepped back to get a fuller view. 'How about the shoes? They're in my room.'

'Yes,' said Maddy, turning back towards her reflection in the mirror. She began to run her fingers through her short hair, pushing it all back. *Brylcreem is what you need, my dear,* she thought, smiling. It was hilariously bizarre. She really was looking remarkably like a young man. A neat guy, pleasant-looking, of medium height and moderate build. And wearing ladies' sandals! *What a scream,* she thought, *what a glorious scream.*

'There's a cap, too,' called Verity from inside her room, where she could be heard opening and closing a cupboard door. 'I'll bring it out.'

17

Quiet moments
Come and go
'Tween the loud ones
To and fro.

– JINXES, BIG & SMALL

'We'll go down this way,' said Verity, pointing back towards the door through which Maddy and Chetak had entered. 'It's more direct.'

'Are there really so many different ways of getting around this building?' Maddy asked.

Verity chuckled drily. 'Oh, my, yes. It's riddled with back staircases. Originally built by some princeling, like I said. You know the story,' they were approaching the first-floor landing, 'original owner dies, heirs tear one another apart. In this case, the two remaining widows eventually split the old building in half, back to front. The front section got modernized and got sold to... to... an unrelated party. The back section remains in the nineteenth century. To this day.'

They were on the final flight down. 'Did you see it? The back of the building, the day you arrived? Chit likes to park there, then walks around to the elevator.'

'I remember something ornate,' said Maddy. It was only one day ago, but already, a month seemed to have passed.

'I can tell you more later, but anyway, to answer your initial question, yes, there are many ways in and out. Here we are now.'

They were downstairs, at the teak door. 'I'll just give Chit a call.' Her cell phone was already in her hand as she speed-dialled a single digit.

The sound of a phone ringing was audible on the other side of the door, and in the next instant, Chetak came out. He looked first at Verity, saying, 'Ah! Hello again.' Then he raised his head to look at Maddy. 'My heavens,' he said. 'We've not met! Have we? Wow.' He was speaking in hushed tones and broke into a broad grin. 'Quite a transformation. Bravo. Come right in.'

To Verity, he said, 'Why don't you go ahead? He's waiting for you. I'll…' he nodded towards Maddy, 'I'll interview the new chauffeur before bringing him in.'

Verity turned to go, then looked back around at Maddy. 'Are you all right with that, Maddy? I think Chit… Chetak's right. It'll work better that way.'

Maddy nodded in answer to Verity's question, then leaned towards her, speaking in a conspiratorial whisper. 'So we're on? Meaning, I'll enter the room and you'll introduce me as Madan?'

'I… well… yes,' said Verity, clearly pleased with this idea. 'We'll do that. You're Madan, and you've been brought in by Chetak for a job interview.'

'Okay, fine, but wait,' said Maddy. 'We need to have, you know, some way of signalling that one of us wants to stop. A word or a sign of some sort.'

'Safe word,' supplied Chetak. 'That's what you mean, right? Yes. I like that idea.'

'All right then,' said Verity. 'The safe word – *words,* rather – are "kindred spirit". From *Anne of Green Gables.*' She looked at Maddy. 'You know it, don't you? It was a favourite of mine. Right. I'm going in. The library, Chit, okay? You both wait just outside, and then I'll call you in, okay?'

'Okay,' said Chetak and Maddy together.

The hallway was octagonal, with the same black-and-white flooring as the lift lobby on the other side of the building. There was a bell-jar chandelier overhead, and the walls were covered in deep red wallpaper with a floral design. There was a gilt-framed mirror and spindly-legged side table on the wall beside the teak door. Between the mirror and the stairs was one more door, painted white.

'Nervous?' asked Chetak.

'A little, yes,' said Maddy. 'It would help to know whom I'm going to meet.'

'Not really,' said Chetak. 'Might make you even more nervous.'

'Isn't it possible I already know him?' asked Maddy, unimpressed.

'Oh, I'm sure you know *who* he is. No question of that. But if you knew him personally, you'd know this house,' said Chetak. 'He's extremely sociable.'

'So, fine!' exclaimed Maddy, keeping her voice low. 'We might have met somewhere else!'

Chetak had something else on his mind, however. 'Look,' he said, 'I'm going to say something I shouldn't.' He turned towards her, his expression serious. 'I'm not happy with this male-impersonator idea. Particularly after this afternoon's ride. I've seen how foolhardy it can be. You're putting yourself at risk.'

He sucked in his breath as she stared at him, saying nothing. 'It's not too late to back out. No one will hold it against you. You can say that you're only willing to drive Verity around in your own car. Nothing will change. Especially not Verity. She likes you. She wants to help you. You can still live here.'

But they heard a door open a short distance away. 'Chetak?' Verity called. 'Would you bring your… young man in, please?'

Chetak looked a question in Maddy's direction. But she had made up her mind. 'I'm doing it,' she said.

He nodded his acceptance and went ahead of her through the teak door, saying, 'This way.' They entered a formal drawing room, fussy with gilded furniture and a grey-veined marble floor.

Crossing the room, they approached a half-open door, showing a darkened interior. Verity was standing just inside the entrance, music playing softly behind her. When she saw them, she moved back inside and out of sight.

Once again, Chetak moved ahead of Maddy. Pushing the door open, he entered, then turned towards her and said in Hindi, 'Come.'

18

Why can't the Golden Mean be kind?
If it were, I wouldn't mind.

– JINXES, BIG & SMALL

It was an intimate room, with floor-to-ceiling bookshelves lining three walls. The black floor and dim lighting created the impression of a boudoir that doubled as a study.

Verity stood on the far side of the room. Two carved mahogany armchairs sat up at attention on one side of her. There was an Afghan rug on the floor and a tiny love seat upholstered in red brocade on the other side of the rug. Beside Verity, with his back to the door, was a man with white curling hair. He turned just as the newcomers entered, a broad, stocky figure in late middle age, wearing a dark suit, the white shirt open at the neck. In his hand was a whisky glass, tinkling with ice and winking in the way of lead crystal.

He was indeed a famous personality.

Shorter than he looks on TV, was Maddy's first thought. She remained near the entrance as Chetak shut the door behind her. She kept her gaze neutral, looking in the man's direction but aiming for a spot just behind his left shoulder. Her pose, with both elbows slightly out at the sides, hands crossed, holding the cap that Verity had given her, was that of someone feeling ill at ease.

'This is Madan,' said Chetak, coming around from behind. He held his hand out, as if he might steer her forward but didn't touch her. 'Madan Lal Singh.' He paused before gesturing towards the man. 'And this is...' he paused very slightly, 'Russi sir.'

The broad features, with the pink-white complexion and heavy-lidded eyes behind square-frame spectacles, appeared often in the newspapers and on opinion shows on TV. A highly respected Supreme Court lawyer, known as much for his erudition and quick wit as for his willingness to fight the good fight.

'Oh!' he said, and his eyebrows popped high. He was momentarily speechless.

'Well… I…' Then he smiled, nodding. 'Madan Lal Singh! Yes. I must say… that's good. Very good.'

Maddy knew the accent now: Anglo-Parsi. In person, and directed towards her, the voice had a honeyed warmth, a musical fullness. It was like listening to a wind instrument created to play human speech.

She did not lose her composure, however. Maintaining her unsmiling, neutral gaze, she said in a low voice, 'Ji.' It was the perfect response to a potential employer's first greeting.

Now the man's smile deepened. Leaning forward he said, 'Ah… Madan? May I call you that? Are you comfortable with English? Yes? Good, good. Tell me a bit about yourself, Madan. How many years have you been driving?'

'Ji, sir,' said Maddy, inclining her head. She spoke in a subdued, deferential tone. 'Twenty years, sir. First in USA, then Dubai. Now in Delhi, for three years, sir. Private taxi service, sir. Only for ladies.' Without making a great show of it, she affected an Indian-inflected accent.

'Private taxi service? You never worked for a salary?'

Maddy said, 'Sir, in USA, I worked as Uber driver.'

'Yes, okay,' said the man. 'Meaning you have experience as a chauffeur. You have also worked for other people as a driver. Not only private. You know what I'm saying?'

'Sir, yes, sir,' said Maddy. She shifted her position slightly, relaxing into her role. The other two people in the room faded from view.

The conversation was being conducted at two separate levels, one make-believe and the other real-world. In the make-believe conversation, an older man with white hair was interviewing a well-built, tall young man for the position of a driver. In the real-world conversation, Maddy was telling a powerful senior lawyer about herself and her qualifications to take the job of a woman playing the role of a male chauffeur. 'Sir, you want to know, can I only work for myself? Or can I take orders? Sir, I can do it. I can take orders.'

'Very good,' said the man. His voice had gone soft. 'Very good.' His smile was warm, appreciation tinged with respect. His whole face was wreathed in the creases of a lifetime filled with mirth, his eyes twinkling. This was a man who loved to be entertained. 'And what about cars? What cars have you driven? How do we know you're a safe driver?'

Maddy felt a strong desire to giggle bubbling up within her. A reckless, heady sensation. 'Sir,' she said, 'I have good experience with all cars. Let me give you test drive, sir? Just now, we can go – all – Verity madam, Chetak sir also. In sir's car.'

The man beamed at the prospect. 'Yes!' he said, putting down his glass and looking towards the other two. 'Excellent idea. Let's do it – let's go for a spin!'

But there was a sharp rap on the door, and it opened without anyone asking for permission to enter. Maddy turned to see a wiry figure in the doorway, silhouetted against the light from the drawing room. 'Sahib… dinner?' he said.

It had to be the cook, Suresh. There was a petulant edge to the voice.

The two words he had uttered were layered with rebukes: *I have made a rich, substantial meal, ready to be served; yet these worthless sahib-dogs have not signalled their willingness to sit down; what about the two females upstairs; did anyone tell me if they, too, will sit for dinner;*

nevertheless, I have made enough for them, too; not that they deserve it, the hussies; and these people will waste another half hour dilly-dallying; my night routine will be delayed…

He'd never voiced any of these words out aloud, not even to his wife. He never had to. It was all conveyed in the tone of his voice and those two words.

'Oh!' said Verity, as if startled to be recalled to the mundane business of food and meals. 'Oh! Yes. Of course! Sorry, Suresh. We're just coming. Russi?' She had turned towards the man. 'Let's delay the ride until afterwards, shall we?'

'Ji,' said Suresh, hearing the only words that mattered to him in this context. He backed away from the door and shut himself out of view once more.

'I don't know,' began Russi, 'can't we just…' the high spirits that had animated him just moments ago had crashed to the ground, 'take a spin? What d'you say, Chetak? Don't we have time?'

But the younger man broke the spell entirely. 'Kindred spirit,' he said, looking pointedly towards Maddy. 'Let's wait on the drive.'

19

One fell swoop
Blew the coop.

– JINXES, BIG & SMALL

Maddy excused herself from dinner, and Verity escorted her back upstairs. She changed out of her uniform in Verity's room as Verity talked animatedly.

'He liked you!' she said. 'There's no question about it. You're in. And you were brilliant. Really.' Her face was bright. 'Are you sure you wouldn't like to have dinner with us downstairs, once you've changed? You'll get to meet the ladies.'

'What ladies?' asked Maddy as she slipped back into her sandals. The shoes she'd worn for the introduction had been uncomfortable. Too loose, rather than too tight. It took an effort of will to not be distracted by the fear of stumbling or tripping, even when she wasn't actually moving.

'The other two tenants in our side of the villa,' said Verity. 'They're both women of a certain age, as we used to say in the past. They're only slightly older than me, mind you! But they're characters. Each in her own special way.' She glanced over at Maddy. 'I imagine they might be like some of your regular clients perhaps. Women who aren't attached to men, for one reason or another. It seems to affect some women more than others.'

This remark hung suspended in the air like a wisp of smoke, reminding Maddy that it had been too long since her last cigarette. 'Thanks, but no, really,' she said. She collected her things as she spoke.

'I should go back to the other side. Down the way we came? And around the back of the building?'

'Oh, *no*,' said Verity, shaking her head vehemently and moving forward. 'There's a passage right here. I mean, from this room to the other side. Through the Looking Glass – literally,' she said, pointing to the panelling on the wall between this room and the mirror lobby on the other side.

Maddy hesitated. There was nothing to be seen. 'There's a door here?' she said, going up to the wall. A vertical strip of wood that defined the edge of one of the panels looked marginally thicker than it needed to be.

'Push it sideways,' said Verity.

'Oh!' said Maddy as it slid smoothly to the right, revealing a dark, unfathomable space. Verity, who was standing beside her, reached into the unexpected cavity and flicked on an overhead light.

A long, narrow chamber was revealed. They both stepped into it. At its far end was a plain white door with a handle. Close beside them was a sliding door similar to the one from Verity's room. Maddy slid it back to find herself looking out into the mirror lobby of the other side of the house. There were the palms, the armchairs and the sofas, except that now she was looking at their backs.

'Will you be okay?' asked Verity. 'I need to go back down to dinner. I'll send some up to you, shall I? It'll be kept on the breakfast table. I'll tell Jyoti to cover it so that you can come out and get it whenever you want.'

As Maddy crossed through, closing the door behind her, she heard Verity do the same inside her room. *What an odd place*, thought Maddy. Wall-sized mirrors, secret exits, stairs and lifts.

Once she was in Verity's study, she looked around, feeling a sense of familiarity. After just one night! The towel and hand towel that she had used the night before were where she had left them, on the side table. The flip-flops were there, too, but now she had her own pair.

She put down the things she was carrying and went out onto the veranda. She'd brought her cigarettes with her. Just as she lit up, the phone rang. It was Malli.

'Why aren't you here?' she asked at once, no preamble. 'I got home five minutes ago. The first thing I asked Bindu was, "Where is Madam-Madam?"' The double name was amongst the small jokes between them.

'I'm still here. In Hauz Khas,' said Maddy. She felt her hair roots tingling from the cigarette. 'Malli, I'm going to do it. I'm going to be a chauffeur.' As the words came out of her mouth, she felt a bolt of exhilaration. What a rush, what a rush! 'It's going to be a crazy-wild ride. I'm going to love it.'

'Oh my god!' said Malli. 'I told you not to do anything until I got back! Stupid woman. Just get out of there!'

'No,' said Maddy. 'I'm going to do it. I'm committed.'

'What, you've signed in blood? You've filled out in triplicate? Don't be a fool! Get out of there. Before they bewitch you any further—'

'No, I think you should come here. Come over and meet them. Her, rather. Verity. Once you meet her, you might feel differently. She's quite special.'

'Yeah, yeah,' sneered Malli on the phone. 'They're all quite special, these foreigners!'

A ripple of irritation ran up and down Maddy's spine. 'Today, I finally met the man whose house this is,' she said. 'The one who needs me to be a chauffeur-man.' She felt a reluctance to say Russi's name.

'Some greasy Mafia don? Some smooth-talking industrialist who wants to acquire a sexy chauffeur?'

'No!' said Maddy. She felt an absurd desire to protect her new-found friends. 'He's… well…' She said the famous name, feeling awkward and false as the syllables issued from her mouth.

'Oh my *GOD*!' exclaimed Malli again. 'These aren't people to mess around with! Don't you understand? You're out of your league, missy. Get out of there!' Her voice went quiet as she pleaded now. 'I'm begging you. Please. Come away from there. This is not going to end well. You know in your heart it won't! Listen to me!'

The ripple of irritation was growing. 'Malli,' said Maddy, 'please don't. Don't try and talk me out of it. Please. You're making me nervous, and when I'm nervous, I won't budge. You know what I'm like. Let's leave it now. Leave it. But come see me in the morning. We'll talk then.'

'Okay, bye,' said Malli, ending the call abruptly.

Maddy put her phone away in her pocket, standing in the darkness of the veranda. With only the bright tip of her cigarette for company, she allowed the sound of her friend's disappointment and anger to wash over her.

There are no clear paths, she thought, *except the one we choose for ourselves.*

Finishing her cigarette, she dropped it on the floor and stubbed it out carefully with the toe of her sandal. Then she picked up the stub and went back into the room.

Verity messaged to say that she was turning in for the night. She hoped that Maddy had whatever she needed. Maddy responded: *Yes, thanks!*

She ate the dinner that had been delivered upstairs, used the washroom in the study and made her bed for the night. As on the night before, she drew up the small table that had served as a nightstand to hold her cell phone and watch. Then she slipped under the sheets and fell asleep.

20

The gentle reminder
Wears us down
Makes us weep
And whine and frown.

– JINXES, BIG & SMALL

Maddy woke up in the darkened study thinking she'd heard a scream. She got up and walked around the room. The air conditioning dampened sounds from outside.

What could it have been? A moth blundering into her dreams? She opened the pressed-glass door and leaned out into the mirror lobby. She sensed invisible boundaries being crossed as she stepped out, but she ignored them. No one had forbidden her from moving around.

She carried the penlight torch from her key fob in hand. She didn't need to switch it on. A faint illumination came in via the tall windows. She went up towards them, then gasped softly as a dark form lunged towards her on the right: her own reflection in the mirror.

The windows had tall brass tower bolts that looked bright and well-polished but were too stiff to shift. Fearing a loud clank if she forced one of them down, she turned towards her reflection.

She lit her face with the penlight torch under her chin, giving herself a ghoulish leer. *Halloween stories!* she thought, remembering her childhood in the US. Moving along the mirror, she came to the sliding door that she'd used earlier that evening.

She stepped into the tween room, playing the bright oval of her torch's beam here and there. The walls and ceiling were bare. On the floor was a long, thin Persian rug. At the far end was the white door. She paused a moment before going up to it to try its handle. It was well-oiled and turned easily.

The door swung outwards, revealing a vast inner world – an inner courtyard between the two warring sections of the building. The front half, where Maddy stood, was all straight lines and concrete. Facing her, on the other side of the courtyard, open to the sky, were the carved stone arches and jalis of a vanished era. The moon was low in the sky, but even so, the marble pillars and fretwork were plainly visible.

She stepped out onto the ledge beyond the door. From it, a cast-iron fire escape spiralled down. Maddy leaned over, looking through the iron lacework. It paused at the first floor before continuing down to the tiled floor of the courtyard.

Across the breadth of the empty space, there was a jharoka on the same level at which she stood on the second floor of the other side. Framed within the graceful arch, with its matched curves, sat a still, doll-like figure.

In the light of a tiny diya flickering on the sill in front of her, the figure's pale skin and hair had an ethereal quality. She was dressed in the style of a miniature painting, all in white, with a dupatta on her head and draped around her shoulders.

Her eyes were dark pools at this distance, so it was impossible to know where she was looking. After a few moments of hesitation, Maddy lifted her right hand and waved.

With a dreamlike inevitability, the woman waved back.

Then, not knowing what else to do, Maddy slowly backed away and turned and closed the white door behind her.

21

The dark night
Of the soul
Is the early morning
Of the mole.

– JINXES, BIG & SMALL

The barber had brought his portable hairdressing station with him. It was already set up on the veranda outside the study. Before he arrived, Maddy had gone over to Verity's room and changed into her uniform. When she appeared via the study and onto the veranda, it was as Madan.

She saw that the barber had placed a white plastic chair so that it was facing out, towards the sunlight. His portable table was positioned in front of the chair. Its hinged lid was open. The top of the storage compartment was covered with a folded blue plastic sheet. The underside of the lid contained a mirror that was propped upright. Maddy could see herself, the dark blue of her suit and a part of her chin reflected in the mirror.

Verity, who had accompanied her onto the veranda, said, 'This is John. Russi's barber.' Then to the man, she said in English, 'John, good morning! This is our new driver. Madan.'

The barber looked up when Verity addressed him. His skin was the colour of polished ebony, chiselled by time. His hair was a white cock's comb that reared up from the crown of his head. He wore a cream-coloured shirt and grey pants. Both hung loose on his frame.

His slippers were two flattened scraps of black leather, placed on the dusty floor of the veranda by the door to the study.

He had pale grey eyes, like a pair of moonstones, each with its black pinpoint. He turned the two moonstones towards Maddy now, his ebony features registering no reaction as he surveyed her. It was a casual yet measuring glance, the kind he might give any client needing a haircut.

She was a good head taller than him. As he gestured towards the chair, inviting her to sit down, he turned to Verity and said, in sing-song pidgin English, 'Stool, Madam, small stool! I must need standing *up*.' He raised his hands to make his point. 'Driver is too much high.'

Verity said, 'Too tall, you mean? Madan is too tall? So you need a—' She broke off, looking back into the study, before exclaiming at once, 'Oh! I have just the thing. One moment, I'll be back.' She went inside.

Maddy had turned towards Verity, wanting to ask whether it would be all right to speak normally in front of the barber – as Maddy, rather than as Madan. Surely, of all people, a barber would know that she was not a man! But when the barber had mentioned the problem of height, the opportunity for asking the question was lost.

She glanced now at John, with his strange eyes, her mouth closing and opening, as if gasping for air. And the barber took the initiative.

Tapping the back of the chair, he said, in Hindi. 'Come, come. Sit.' He used a friendly, practised tone, as if speaking to a younger person, a child. 'It's only a haircut, you know! What are you looking so nervous for? It's only a haircut! Not a…' The man's ebony cheeks developed two tight, finely carved creases. The shapely, chiselled lips parted to reveal two matching sets of teeth, as neat and regular as if they had been cut from antique ivory and stained orange with paan. '…not a *snip-snip*!' This last word was said with such an odd combination of menace and amusement that its meaning could not be missed. He clearly believed she was a man.

The blood drained from Maddy's face. She felt a shift in the current of reality.

Turning away from him and towards the chair, she sat down without saying another word. The soles of her feet and the palms of her hands were tingling. She could see the lower part of her face in the mirror, yet she took a few seconds to recognize herself. It was as if the barber, by some form of casual sorcery, had caused her to become what he'd been told she was: a driver, a man.

What she saw was a young man's chin and mouth. His skin was pale and smooth, the mouth pink and vulnerable. He looked terrified, like someone on the threshold of an ordeal. Indeed, that's what it had become, she realized. The barber was her first real encounter between her alternate self and The World. An encounter involving scissors. Severance. The cord that connected her previous life with the life that lay ahead was about to be *snipped*.

The door of the study opened again. She heard approaching voices while, in front of her, the barber had reached around and picked up the blue plastic sheet. The voices belonged to Verity, Chetak and one more person. Beneath the plastic sheet were arrayed the tools of a barber's trade: a bar of soap in a plastic dish, a shaving brush, two combs. Two pairs of scissors, one longer than the other. They were as shiny and wicked looking as daggers. They had circular finger holes rather than the more common elliptical handles.

Behind her, Verity said, 'Here are these little platforms. They're from Bombay, you know, Chit? For John to stand on.'

'Yes,' said the third person, a woman. She had a husky voice, filled with smoke and fire. 'They're called patlas. I've just come from Bombay. I love them too.'

It was Malli's voice.

Maddy wanted to twist around immediately. But the barber had already thrown the plastic sheet around her, swaddling her from the neck down. *Malli!* she wanted to cry out, *You were right! This is happening too fast. I'm not sure… it's the wrong turning…*

But it was already too late. Maddy remained rigidly in place, like a driver newly arrived at his place of work. He would be ignorant of the friends of his new employers. He would feel desperately awkward at being subjected to a mandatory haircut under the gaze of strangers, two of them women.

Maddy heard the sound of the wooden platform being placed on the floor behind her chair. She heard whispering. That would be Verity, speaking to Malli, Malli answering, Chetak adding something. She could not hear what was being said. Her head was filled with a sound that she couldn't identify. A type of roaring. As if her thoughts were thundering across the plains of her mind, like a stampeding herd of... what? She didn't know.

Then Chetak, close at hand and addressing the barber, said, 'Here's the hot water. Towel. Anything else you need?'

John said, 'No, no. This is fine. Just as it is with the sahib.'

He came around, within Maddy's field of vision, holding a small plastic mug. The corner of a yellow hand towel poked up from the mug. With quick, neat movements, the barber wrung it out, folded it so that it made a fat strip, then disappeared behind her once more. To her, he said, 'Open collar.'

Maddy undid the top button of her uniform and spread the two sides of the collar, baring her neck. The barber wrapped the hot towel snugly around it. The damp heat felt wonderful despite the heat of the day. A powerful sense of security enveloped her. The water was scented, and the fragrance of expensive cologne filled her nose.

The barber moved in front once more, adjusting the angle of the mirror. She could see her whole face now and the thick fringe of her hair. Behind her, to her right, the man's polished face appeared and disappeared, eclipsed by her own head as the dance began.

First, he massaged her head with strong, firm fingers that felt less as if they belonged to a human being than to a machine. He did not use any oil. She could see him drawing out the strands of her hair, as if assessing them, gauging their length, their character, their properties.

Then he began to cut. His movements were swift and economical, as if he had a train to catch. For every clip he made, he made two extra clicks in the air with the flashing blades of the scissors. As the hair fell away from the back of her head, Maddy felt the air moving on her scalp, a sensation like gooseflesh in an unfamiliar location.

Up and around the crown of her head his blades danced, snipping, clipping, snipping, clipping, carving away the old persona and replacing it with a bare inch of hair at the very top of her head. All the rest was practically gone. She was as shorn as a chicken on the back and sides, with a thick crest of black spikes on top.

And still, he wasn't done. Once more, he reached for the plastic mug, where a second hand towel awaited him. Wringing it out, he applied it now to her face. With precise strokes, he wiped the whole surface of her face. Then, reaching for the soap dish with one hand, he snatched up the shaving brush with his other hand and began to work up a lather.

Maddy's eyes widened in alarm. She began to struggle, wanting to protest. She saw, in her peripheral vision, Chetak start forward. But she heard the hiss of a whispered command. Someone – Verity? – must have pulled him back. There was clearly no stopping the barber. He had a routine; he could no more be turned off than an electronic timer that has no kill switch.

'Back,' said the barber tersely to Maddy. 'Head back. Like that. Yes.' In swift strokes, he applied the scented foam to Maddy's now flaming cheeks. She felt literally paralysed, with only her eyelids blinking. Tears seeped unbidden from the outer corners of her eyes. She feared that she was panting or sobbing from her open mouth, though she could not hear herself.

She saw the flash of the cut-throat razor, and her eyes closed of their own accord. The man wielded the steel as if it were made of silk. He talked as he worked, making soft, soothing noises, such as might be made to put a child to sleep. She couldn't make out what he was saying. With smooth strokes, he swept the white foam from her cheeks. She heard and felt the blade slipping over her hairless skin, finding no purchase anywhere. The barber's firm fingers shifted her face, first one side, then the other, using the chin as a handle. Then up, as he caressed her defenceless throat with the blade.

Then he was done. He brought her head upright once more, using one hand. With the other, he whipped off the neck towel. Unfolding it, to where its interior retained its heat, he wiped her face again but only the cheeks this time and her throat. He removed every vestige of the fragrant foam.

'Eyes open,' he said to her. 'Look. Look.' He held her head delicately between his fingertips, showing her the view in the mirror. 'See. How handsome you look. Wonderful. A perfect pearl.' He did not wait for her response. Instead, she saw him look behind himself, whereupon Chetak leaned forward, holding his arm out. She could not see what was given, but a moment later, smelled the answer: Aramis.

John splashed it liberally between the palms of both his hands and then, still standing behind her, he applied it with soft, slapping motions to her cheeks. Her skin smarted, twanging and tingling, so that her eyes spilled tears once more. It wasn't pain, exactly, but something else, something completely unknown, drenched through with the steel-and-tobacco reek of the aftershave.

He whipped off the plastic sheet now and stepped back, out of her field of vision in the mirror. To Verity he said in English, a note of triumph and pride in his voice, 'See, I am finish. Driver is complete. He is look handsome fellow now. Super handsome perfect.'

22

Slap me tight!
Or I might bite!

– JINXES, BIG & SMALL

'You're going to need a wig,' said Malli to Maddy. The three of them were in the study, standing in the attitude of people who have not committed to staying or leaving. 'I'll get one for you,' she said. 'I know a place that supplies good ones at short notice. You'll need to have one right away. Don't go anywhere and don't do anything before I return.'

'Really?' said Maddy. She wanted to add, *Does that mean you're okay with all this then?*

Malli read her thoughts. 'Did you give me a choice? No. You jumped into the fire – straight in, headfirst – against my advice. Now my only choice is to jump in after you.'

She looked at Verity. 'I'm sorry, but I'd prefer you to know what I think. It's foolish, what she's doing. Wrong at so many levels. But it's done. I can see that. I'm part of it now. That's what I'm saying. I'm not leaving her alone.' She paused. 'With you.'

Verity nodded uncertainly, saying, 'I... I can understand that...'

Maddy turned to Malli. 'I don't know. About the wig, I mean.'

'Oh, come *on*! You're going to need something to cover your haircut when you're not in uniform,' said Malli in an exasperated tone. 'When you're in your normal clothes! You don't realize it, but from the neck up now, you really do look like a man!' She paused, smiling. 'A young man. Handsome.'

Maddy didn't smile back. She felt jumpy and restless. Caged.

Verity took a half step in her direction. 'Something *has* changed,' she said.

'Meaning what?' asked Maddy, glancing at her.

'I was watching you,' said Verity, nodding towards the veranda. 'Not your face, really, but your shoulders. They were stiff initially. Then a moment came when they relaxed. I saw that but couldn't understand it.' She looked at Malli. 'You know what I mean?'

Malli shrugged. 'I was behind the barber. Don't know if there was just one moment.'

Maddy said nothing, her thoughts whirring in her head.

'Maddy, if you're having doubts, we don't have to go forward.'

'No,' said Maddy with cool finality.

'Change into your clothes and come home with me now,' said Malli. 'You can stay with me for however long you need to.'

'No,' repeated Maddy. 'The time for doubts is over. I want to move forward. Into the next stage. Get to know the car that I'm going to be driving. Get behind the wheel. Get on with what we're doing.'

Verity's forehead puckered. 'Yes, but—' she began.

'You don't understand,' Maddy interrupted her. 'Maybe it's the haircut or maybe it's the uniform. Either way, the person I was yesterday, the one who went to Fabindia and bought women's clothes? That person has stepped into the shadows. This other person has taken over.'

She paused, consolidating her thoughts. 'Maybe it's because I don't have my own home. My own things physically around me. I didn't know that things mattered so much, ordinary objects – like my furniture, my books, my rugs. I mean, are *they* what make me who I am? Is the loss of them what gives me this disconnected feeling? As if the whole of my life before this particular moment was smoke and dreams?'

She shook her head, flexed her shoulders. 'All I can say is that without any physical things to remind me of who I used to be, *this* is all I am now. All my earthly possessions fit inside a single bag – oh, and my car, of course. I still have that. But aside from that? I'm someone in a driver's uniform. Who got a haircut. And a *shave*.'

She looked at the other two, feeling an unfamiliar tension in her cheeks. As if she were trying to smile and frown at once, the conflicting urges warring within the muscles of her face.

'Getting that haircut was strange enough but that... that... *shave*! It was like nothing I'd ever imagined happening before. I mean, why would I have! Obviously, I've never imagined having my face shaved with a cut-throat razor. I can't even understand why that fool, that *idiot* – why did he do it! *WHY*? He must have known,' she said, looking at Verity. 'That I don't have facial hair. He could see it; he could *feel* it! And yet he went ahead and did my face.'

Verity's pupils had widened, becoming black pools. 'I don't know why either. It was … maybe it was just his routine? It's what he always does: cut-shave, cut-shave? It's what he does all day long. You were just one more client. And let's not forget, barbers are people who keep their clients' secrets!' she said, essaying a small joke.

Malli had gone silent, her hands clutched together in front of her.

Maddy rubbed her cheeks. 'I stopped breathing when I saw the razor. Then he began working on my face, and I could feel the steel against my skin, and it was like... I can't describe it. There are no words to contain it. Not even pleasure or pain. The scent of the soap was intoxicating. The motion of the blade was so smooth and... *dangerous*! I was vibrating inside. White hot with fear. I could feel that silky blade slipping smoothly under my skin, slicing it up, making ribbons of my face. My life. I could feel tears pouring sideways out of my eyes. My whole face was screaming, tiny icy fires blazing, as if phantom hair follicles were sprouting everywhere, even as he cut.'

'My god, my god,' whispered Malli.

'And now?' asked Verity.

'Nothing,' said Maddy. 'It's perfectly smooth. Not a cut, not a nick.' She breathed in sharply. 'I don't know what it means. Any of it. At this moment, all I want to do is... move around. I don't know. Do something fast and reckless. Drive hard and wild – going for miles and miles.' She stopped, her breath ragged.

'You're panting,' observed Malli.

'I know,' said Maddy, balling her fists and pressing them to her eyes; then, in the next moment, she broke out, saying, 'The point is, we *can't* stop! Not now. We've got to move on and move forward.

'Malli?' She turned to her friend. 'You're right. I'll need a wig. I'll get showered now and changed, and yes, of course, I *can't* be wearing women's clothes with this haircut.'

To Verity, she said, 'Please, we'll need to sit down together and work this out. There's a lot to talk about, actually. And I'm going to need a lot of your time, I'm sorry... I'm going to need everyone's time.' She glanced at Malli, who was at the door. 'I'll be ready for you whenever you're able to get back.'

Verity was nodding when Maddy turned back to her. She was preparing to leave the room, too. 'You're braver than you think, Maddy,' she said, standing at her desk and picking up a notebook and pencils. 'I'm going to start making my own lists of what each of us needs to do. At the top of my list is settling you in your own room here. That is, *Maddy*'s room, not Madan-the-driver's room.'

She had picked up her phone from where it lay on the desk and was moving forward as she spoke. 'You're two separate people now. You'll be living two separate lives. Madan will stay... somewhere else. We'll have to figure that out. But Maddy will stay here, in this building. As my guest.'

She was level with Maddy, looking up at her now. 'And you will get as much of our time as you need,' she said.

Her pale eyes blazed like searchlights, staring straight into Maddy's own.

'Thank you,' said Maddy.

There were fine lines on Verity's skin that Maddy hadn't noticed before. A bluish tint under the eyes. A moment later, she had turned towards the pressed-glass door, opened it and passed through. A ray of sunlight caught highlights in her hair, giving her a halo.

23

O broken promise
Made of glass!
Let me make thee
Out of grass!

– JINXES, BIG & SMALL

Malli was as good as her word and came back within two hours. Maddy had showered and changed back into 'her' clothes by then.

Malli had brought a wig with her, saying that it was only a stopgap until a better-fitted one was made. This one was short-haired, dark brown and lightly curled whereas Maddy's own hair was dense black, speckled with grey and straight.

Standing in the study's washroom and looking at the mirror above the washbasin, Maddy said, 'I suppose it doesn't really matter that it's not the same as my hair?'

'It's looking good on you,' said Malli, standing at the door. 'You should consider wearing your hair like this!' They both laughed.

It was time for lunch by then. Verity looked in from the mirror lobby to say that it was being laid out upstairs on the side table.

It was a self-serve meal of minestrone soup with chunks of French bread in a basket, a fresh green salad on the side and butter curls in a silver dish that had a compartment underneath it for ice.

Malli agreed to stay, and Chetak had also come in from court.

'I looked into housing Madan in the servants' quarters at the back,' said Chetak. He was sitting in one of the armchairs, holding his bowl of soup with a cloth serviette underneath.

'Yes, I was thinking of that,' said Verity, who was on the sofa.

'Really?' Malli was already starting to frown. 'Wouldn't that be too close?' She, too, was sitting on the sofa and had served herself the salad. She was working through it with obvious relish.

'Too close to what?' Maddy wanted to know. She was sitting in the other armchair, straining the liquid elements in her bowl of minestrone, leaving the solid bits for the last.

'The house,' said Malli. 'If you want to maintain two separate characters, then that's asking for trouble.'

'It wouldn't work anyway,' interposed Chetak. 'I asked. Suresh, that is,' he said looking around at the others.

'The cook,' explained Maddy to Malli. 'He lives there with his wife, Jyoti.'

'She's the reason it won't work,' said Chetak. 'Suresh said he won't have an unattached man living in the quarters above his own.' His expression was quizzical as he turned his attention to the soup.

'Cooks know their worth these days,' said Malli. 'They can make their demands.'

'Did he actually say that?' Verity wanted to know. 'He said no, flat out?' She was nibbling on the bread, adding small pats of butter as she went along.

'His exact words were, "Young men cause trouble."' said Chetak. 'And, "I won't allow it."'

'That's a bit cheeky, wouldn't you say?' remarked Verity. 'Even for our Suresh?'

'It's like Malli said.' Chetak tipped his head towards her. 'Cooks know their worth these days. But Suresh is right, too,' he went on. 'The quarters are small, and he has three children; there's only one bathroom and toilet. From his perspective, a young man so close to his family would be... unacceptable. And from our perspective, too. I mean, surely, they'd start to suspect?'

'Are you joking?' exclaimed Malli. 'Servants are the first to know everything! Believe me, they already know about this one. About Madam Madan.'

'Oh... I don't know,' said Chetak. 'They've not seen enough of him. Suresh caught barely a glimpse of him... er... that is, Madan, in the evening yesterday. When Russi met him.' He glanced over at Verity. 'Suresh opened the door, asking about dinner. Remember? Well, *he* remembers. He said he knew about the new driver for Missy.' He added, for Maddy and Malli's benefit, 'That's what they call her. It's their name for Verity.'

Malli was shaking her head. 'Believe me, they already know everything!'

Verity didn't agree. 'Then why bring up the "young man" excuse? Surely that tells us he believes Madan is a man?'

'They allow us our little illusions,' said Malli. 'It's easier for them, don't you see? They don't want to stir things up. In their opinion, all employers are mad and foolish. But they let us have our way, for the most part.'

Verity turned to Maddy. 'How do *you* feel about all of this?'

Maddy responded slowly and thoughtfully, 'Well, I've barely met Suresh myself. Neither as Madan nor as me. He was behind me that day. My god! Was it just last night? I barely know what he looks like. I've not actually seen Jyoti, though I heard her moving around today. She's not seen me as Maddy or as Madan. But I agree with Malli. I think it would be impossible to keep my identity hidden if I lived here as Madan and also as Maddy. It's absolutely true that if I were living in the servants' quarters, they'd know at once!'

Verity drew in a deep breath. 'Okay then. What are the options?'

'Staying off-site,' said Chetak at once.

'Meaning?' asked Malli. She was immediately on guard.

'A room in one of these workers' lodges,' said Chetak. 'They've come up all over. People scrape together enough money to build themselves two- and three-storey homes with half a dozen single rooms to let out. I've had a couple of peons who did that—'

'What're you saying?' demanded Malli. 'Maddy can't stay in one of those places! One toilet for ten people, no running water, god knows what kind of rat-infested power supply – they won't even accept women in such places—'

'But Madan isn't a woman,' interrupted Maddy. 'Don't you see? In order for this to work, I've got to be a shape-shifter. I've got to live and breathe as Madan. Not just pretend.'

The other three listened silently as she continued.

'For a young driver just starting out, like Madan, a one-room accommodation is the only option. Either that or he sleeps in his rental taxi. He eats all his meals from a dhaba. He uses the bathroom facilities that other cabbies use at their stand or maybe takes his chances up against a friendly roadside wall. What do all the thousands of young men in the city do, after all? They have very little to choose from! I've only been Madan twice, right? Even so, between last night and this morning, I can see the way that being him has affected my actual thoughts—'

'Yes, but you *are* still a woman!' insisted Malli. 'Where will you shower, where will you, you know...' She trailed off.

Maddy chuckled and shrugged. 'I've learnt a few tricks as a woman cabbie, too, you know! Speaking of which, I'm still feeling restless. Ever since this morning. The haircut, the shave.' She looked around at the others. 'Stir crazy. I really want to go out on a drive, you know?'

She turned towards Verity. 'Would you like to come out? For an inaugural?'

But Verity shook her head. 'Thanks but no. I'm feeling a bit tired. Plus, we've got to set up Maddy's room, too, don't we?' She smiled, though it was clear that the discussion had drained her. She was looking paler than usual.

'Come,' said Malli. 'I'll leave my car here and you take me for a jaunt. As Maddy.'

24

The idle mind
Is less unkind
Than a busy brain
That welcomes pain.

– JINXES, BIG & SMALL

Maddy asked Malli whether she cared where they went. When her friend shook her head, Maddy nodded happily and said, 'Okay then! Yamuna Expressway it is!'

It was barely 2 p.m. when they left the villa. They crossed the river at Kalindi Kunj, swung south onto the Noida Expressway and thence onto the recently completed speedway that went straight to Agra and the Taj Mahal.

They were soon flying along at 100 kilometres an hour.

Malli clutched her head. 'Why on earth d'you like this horrible road!' she moaned. 'So surreal, so monotonous!'

By comparison to the usual Indian highways, there was none of the spectacular variety of speeds and shapes of vehicles. A majority of the cars whizzing alongside or by them were foreign brands, air conditioned and sealed up, some of them with tinted glass. Low trees bordered the satin-smooth four-lane speedway. Beyond the trees, the baked yellow earth spread away to a featureless horizon, with only the occasional water tower hinting at future townships to come.

Maddy narrowed her eyes and grinned. 'The speed, the speed. The sheer recklessness of bombing along. Crazy fast and going nowhere!'

Malli said nothing for a few minutes. 'Okay. I get it. You just want to *go*. But I have to tell you, it's making me uncomfortable, okay? Plus, we haven't even brought anything to drink or eat.' She reached into her handbag. 'I'll just have to smoke, I suppose.'

'There should be a bottle of water in the side of the door,' said Maddy.

'Want a smoke?'

'No, thanks. Just let me go like hell for another twenty minutes or so. Then I'll turn back. You go ahead and smoke. I'll join you in a bit. When I've worked off this... whatever it is. This need for speed.'

Malli occupied herself for a few minutes before asking, in a quieter voice, 'Do you know what you're doing, Mads? I'm not talking about the drive now. I'm talking about this... whole... villa situation. These new friends of yours. Or whatever they are. Two days ago, you'd never heard of them, and now, you're joined at the hip.'

Maddy paused before answering. 'I would say, yes, I know what I'm doing. But only in the sense that I don't know at all.'

'Riddles,' said Malli.

'Remember that song, "Walk on the Wild Side"?' asked Maddy. 'Sort of fifties jazz? I don't remember who it was by or anything. It was considered kind of racy. Or something. All I know is the feeling it left me with. A desire to *cut loose*. To be anybody. To be nobody.'

Malli released a long, curling streamer. 'Everyone knows that song. Or used to, anyway. By Lou Reed. It wasn't just racy! It was considered totally X-rated. About living dangerously. Out on the streets.'

'Well, well, I didn't actually know any of that! I just liked the feeling it gave me.'

'So that's what you're feeling right now? That you're out on the streets – in this foreign car you brought back from the West like a sort of dowry to yourself? And now in a villa with god-only-knows-who underwriting that gold-dipped lifestyle?' She gave a dry chuckle. 'Sweetie, really. This is just the rich side pretending to be wild.'

Maddy shrugged. 'Whatever.'

'Sweetie, please. Listen to me. Do they even know, your villa friends – your villain friends – about your life before coming back to India?' She laughed at her own small joke, but her voice was kinder now. 'About... anything?'

Maddy said, 'I told Verity that I was married and that my husband died. But I didn't say how it happened. Or how shocking it was for me. And anyway, why does any of that matter? It's so long ago now.'

'Everything matters,' said Malli. 'They need to understand that you're not some daisy in distress that they've picked up off the streets. That you had a full life and a good career. And that even after your sweet man's death, you could have just continued on there. Instead? You chose to leave that life. You chose to come back.' She tapped her ash into the little silver ashtray.

Maddy smiled. 'Exactly. I came back! To a bitch-vulture landlady who throws me out because she thinks I'm not respectable enough to live on her property!' She leaned back in her seat and stepped on the gas pedal. 'Yes, yes, yes – all of the above. I don't have tidy explanations! I tried the safe, predictable life! And it didn't work for me, did it?'

Malli, alarmed by the sudden spurt of speed, said, 'Slow down, slow down! It makes me nervous, this driving!' She exhaled slowly. 'It makes me wonder if...' She didn't complete her statement.

Maddy reduced her speed. 'Go on. If what?'

'Don't misunderstand me,' said Malli. 'It's not a critique. It's a genuine concern. There's a thing known as survivor syndrome. It's when a person feels—'

'Yes, I know,' said Maddy a little curtly. 'Feels guilty about surviving something when others don't. Like the death of a spouse, for instance.'

'I just worry, that's all,' said Malli. 'That you're punishing yourself.'

Maddy was silent as the car flew along. 'No,' she said presently. 'I don't think so. I didn't come to Delhi imagining that desi ghee and aam panna would heal the scars on my psyche. I know that there's nothing here aside from diesel fumes, murderous rage and filth. But I don't think of it as punishment. I think of it as a wake-up drug. Like Liman dying was a wake-up drug. It punched me awake. Forced me to understand that... that... life *is* unfair. Things *do* fall apart. Horrible clichés. But also true. You know? I came back because I want to stay awake. To never fall asleep again.'

Up ahead, signs indicated an exit where motorists could get off the expressway and turn around, back towards the capital.

Malli finished her cigarette in silence.

Maddy cut her speed way down and began making the turn.

Then they were heading back the way they had come.

At the villa, Malli hugged Maddy and made her promise to stay in touch.

'I will,' said Maddy.

25

Plants and birds
Wind and words
Chocolate creams
And happy dreams!

– JINXES, BIG & SMALL

Maddy stepped out of the lift on the second floor and was momentarily disoriented. In the place of the Moroccan wall hanging that had previously faced the door of the lift, there was now another door.

It was open, and Verity was looking out expectantly, having heard the sound of the lift on its way up. 'Hi!' she said. 'I hoped it was you. Jyoti has done a great clean-up job. Come in and see?'

She stood aside, revealing a room so spacious that even with a four-poster bed taking up the middle of it and a glass-topped desk along the near wall, it still managed to seem a little bare. At its farther end were two more doors, both closed. The wall on the left was taken up with an old-style teakwood almirah. On the right was a bank of windows, fitted with wooden shutters to keep the sunshine at bay. One of these was open, admitting a view of the inner courtyard and a patch of sunlight that blazed on the white marble floor.

'What do you think?' asked Verity. 'Can you see yourself living here?'

Maddy's head was turning this way and that. 'Wow,' was the first thing she said. 'It's absolutely *huge*!'

She turned around and around, unable to take it in. She could see herself in the free-standing full-length mirror that occupied the space between the two doors.

'I love it,' she said in an uncertain, wondering tone.

'Oh, good,' said Verity, smiling. 'I'm so glad to hear that! Come, come, there's more to see. The bathroom, of course, is over there, but let's go...' she walked briskly towards the left-hand door at the end of the room, '...up!' Opening the door, she showed Maddy the beginning of a spiral stairway. 'It goes all the way to the terrace.'

Both women were slightly winded by the time they reached the top of the stairs and the dark, windowless landing there. The small space was as hot and still as an oven, the air trapped behind a solid white door. 'No one's come up this way for ages,' said Verity as she reached for the handle. 'Chit said he'd get someone to oil all the – oh, good, it doesn't need it.'

She pushed the door open, and the dazzling glare flooded in.

'Ready?' she asked, stepping through.

Maddy followed her out and gasped.

An oceanic expanse spread away from the small room, more garden than terrace, open to the sky. Rectangular patches of emerald-green grass were intercut with white porcelain tiles. Mature frangipanis in bronze planters with Chinese dragons swirling on their sides had been placed here and there, providing oases of shade from the blinding light overhead.

'Come,' beckoned Verity. 'Jyoti's made some tea for us,' she said, pointing to a low table and folding chairs some distance away on the other side of the terrace. 'That's my side of the building if you see what I mean. Instead of a landing, I've got a regular-sized room. A proper barsati, with a little pantry and sink.'

She was walking ahead, almost talking to herself. Maddy followed at a slower pace. The unease she'd experienced that very first day in the washroom of Verity's study was prickling within her once more. The sense of being in the presence of some invisible power, some unholy wealth that she couldn't identify. The kind of wealth that she, privileged and well-travelled though she was, had been brought up to think of as *wrong*.

She took her place in one of the folding chairs, facing back the way they had come. The impression of being in a garden was very strong despite the sides of the terrace that she could see forming a boundary. They were solid and broad, the sides, coming up to waist height. She would have had to lean over them to see, on the left, the front garden of the building and on the right, the inner courtyard. Here, on Verity's side of the terrace, the view towards the central well and the entire rear of the house was screened by a forest of tall, waving ferns.

Verity had removed the quilted cosy from a plump white teapot and was pouring the tea into plain white cups with saucers. 'I know it's a little fussy, all this,' she said, indicating the tea tray. 'I don't always do it. Just for fun really. Like playing at being...' she paused to look up and smile, 'grown-up.'

Maddy gave an uncertain smile in return. 'This whole building is the absolute definition of grown-up.'

She was looking around once more, unable to take her eyes away from the terrace. There were very many plants, all potted and neatly grouped. Cactuses in one group, sansevieria in another. 'It's hard to take it in. This... entire... I don't know what to call it! It's not just a building. More like a sort of cruise ship.' She didn't want to sound ungrateful or critical. 'Everyone in it. Me, too, now, I suppose. I'm here now. It's very hard to believe. That I'm suddenly just... here. Part of this. Whatever this is.'

Verity was looking down, stirring in milk, the teaspoon making a musical chink.

'You're right,' she said. 'I try to feel the same way – the way you're feeling now, I mean. I try not to grow used to it.' She handed Maddy her tea. 'Maybe you won't agree with me? I don't know. Perhaps.'

'Agree about what?' asked Maddy.

'That it's easy to grow used to luxury,' said Verity. 'To this. All of this.' She had her teacup in hand. She made a slight gesture with her head, including the building, the property, the entire ethos of the place they were in.

There was a pulse of silence. In the great distance, the grumble of traffic.

'I used to resist it, you know,' Verity said. 'For a long time. The only reason I agreed to stay here was that I couldn't...' She gave a small laugh and stopped. She took in a breath. 'I suppose you could say that I couldn't afford *not* to.'

She looked up at Maddy and then away again, quickly. 'I know that I'm not making much sense. Because there's something I should be telling you, Maddy. And I... I... *will*. Not just now though, please.'

Maddy was taken aback by the change of mood and said, 'Of course.'

'I'd rather we squared away some practical matters first, if that's all right?'

'Of course,' said Maddy again, wondering why she sensed a strain.

'We need to talk about payment,' said Verity. 'Is that okay with you?'

Maddy smiled now, relieved. 'Oh, yes,' she said. 'I'm fine with that.'

Verity looked relieved, too. 'Okay. Because it can be difficult sometimes to talk about money.'

'I got used to it,' explained Maddy, 'with the cab service.'

'Ah,' said Verity. 'That's a good thing. I talked it over with Russi, you know? About what we should pay you. He feels that a combined salary of, shall we say, eighty K? Per month?'

'Eighty... thousand?' asked Maddy. 'That seems rather a lot!'

'Not really. Think of it as compensation for what you lose by not taking your regular clients,' said Verity.

'Hmm,' said Maddy. 'The normal charge for one of my passengers is twenty-five hundred. That's more than double the amount that private taxi operators charge, but we all understand that it's an exclusive service. It's literally *not* a public service.'

'All right then. And in a typical week, how often do you go out?'

'It varies. On average, I'd say… oh… maybe six days a week? But there are weeks when I have fewer than three.'

'Six days! And it's not for the whole day, is it?'

'No, no,' said Maddy. 'Usually not more than a couple of hours. The understanding is a maximum of four hours, but almost none of them keep me for more than two. They're not going shopping or visiting. It's usually just for a drive.'

'Well, so you see what that comes to, right? Fifteen thousand a week. Times four. So that's sixty already.'

Maddy raised her shoulders. 'Yes, but...' She spread her hands out. 'What about, you know, all of *this*? The house. The meals. The lifestyle. None of it is what I can normally afford.'

Verity had finished her tea and was leaning back in her easy chair with a faraway expression on her face. She said, choosing her words carefully, 'The reason you're here, in this house, is because of misfortune. A calamity. It could have happened at any time, but instead, at the very moment your life was being pulled apart, Chit happened to hear your name and... the rest followed.'

She turned towards Maddy. 'Sometimes, terrible things happen. We all know that. But sometimes, good things happen, too. Actually, they happen all the time. Some people are born smart *and* they have parents who can afford to send them to good schools. Some people are born good-looking *and* they're enabled to make use of their good looks. None of us is born with a guarantee of easy passage through life, and yet, some of us get an upgrade to first class. With no strings attached.'

She shaded her eyes from the sun with her hand, and Maddy started to suggest that they should move, but Verity forestalled her.

'No, I'd like to finish my point first. Then I'll need to go inside, and you'll need to get ready for Chetak, right? He's coming for you at seven, I think he said?'

Maddy nodded.

'I just wanted to say, something good came out of your calamity – an opportunity to do something new with your life. A network of new friends, maybe. Or just a quiet place to live while you take stock of your situation. Either way, you suddenly have more options than you had before the calamity. In my opinion, that's a boon. A gift from Fate. It doesn't happen very often. Just... be open to it. That's all I'm saying. Don't push it aside.'

She smiled, once again with that trace of a shadow. 'And talk to Chit. He's always a good sounding board,' she said as she began to get up from her chair.

26

The moon is blue
When you are too.

– JINXES, BIG & SMALL

Back downstairs in her new room, Maddy took stock of what she had in the way of toiletries and vital accessories, such as laundry soap and cleaning supplies. *I'll need stuff for the other place,* she thought, looking around, trying to get used to the idea that this was now hers, complete with bed linen, towels and laundry services.

Chetak had messaged to say he'd located a residence for Madan.

He hadn't had time to say more but suggested that she should be ready to leave the villa as Maddy, then be prepared to change into Madan en route to the new place. It was just after 5.30 p.m. now. She had time for a power nap before dressing for what was bound to be a demanding evening.

At five minutes to seven, there was a double knock on her door. That was the signal for Chetak.

'Come in,' she called to him, picking up a shoulder bag, 'the door's open.' She was wearing one of her tent dresses, dark blue with white patches.

Chetak leaned in. 'Ah, okay. Good. You're still Maddy.'

'Isn't that what we agreed on?' she asked as she exited the room. She pulled the door close behind her. There wasn't much reason to lock it. Her most valuable possessions were her phone and credit cards. They were in her handbag, and she had that with her. 'Don't I have to get past Bahadur?'

The mirror lobby was in partial darkness. Light spilled in from the door to Verity's study and from the windows of the courtyard. Chetak had kept the elevator open with a doorstop so that they could step into it quickly.

'Yes,' said Chetak, 'but I wasn't sure how you'd manage. I was thinking through the alternatives.'

She entered the lift. 'Yeah. It's not comfortable. I suppose I can manage. I keep thinking of Superman!'

'Didn't you ever read Flash Gordon?' said Chetak as he followed her in and pressed the '0' button. 'He didn't even need a telephone booth!'

The lift began its jerky descent.

'There aren't many telephone booths left in the world,' said Maddy. 'Today's superheroes would probably have to make do with public toilets! Can you imagine? Poor guys.'

They were both still smiling as they exited the lift. Bahadur looked up at them, then down again to mark their passage through his tiny domain.

Chetak's car was right by the door. It was pointed towards the gate. Maddy let herself in the passenger side while Chetak went around to the driver's seat.

As soon as they'd driven out of the gate and were in the unlit lane beyond, Maddy reached for the hem of her garment and rolled it up so that it was at chest height. It had a wide, loose neck, making it easy to lift the front over her head. She drew her arms out of the sleeves one at a time, sweeping off the wig as soon as her hands were free.

Underneath, she was fully dressed in Madan's uniform.

By the time Chetak reached the first of the tight corners that would take them out of the back lanes of Hauz Khas and onto Khel Gaon Marg, she had effected the top half of the transformation.

'Wow,' remarked Chetak. 'Neatly done.' He hadn't been looking at her while she changed but took a quick glance now.

'I've still got the lower half to do,' said Maddy. 'I'm going to strap my seat belt in so that I don't go through your windshield if you have to brake suddenly.'

She tugged open the drawstring on her salwar, lifted her hips off the seat and pushed down in a spare and economical motion that suggested she had carried out similar car-seat operations before. She slipped the cuffs from each of her feet. 'There,' she said when the whole garment was off. She balled it up and tossed it onto the back seat. 'Done. Are we at the main intersection yet?'

'No,' said Chetak, 'It's up ahead. There's usually a bit of a jam at this time of day.' He had stopped moving forward. 'You've got plenty of time.'

'Great,' said Maddy. She was already reaching for the bag she'd brought with her, drawing out a pair of men's shoes. They were plain black sneakers with white soles and white laces. 'Thanks for these, by the way,' she said. 'They're a perfect fit. Probably a little posh for Madan, but he's not going to fuss. They feel very comfortable, and that's what matters.'

'They're mine,' said Chetak, 'or *were*, I should say. A little tight for me, so I thought I'd donate them to the cause. I hoped Madan would not be offended that they're not new.'

'He prefers it that way,' said Maddy, with one knee tucked up so that she could do the laces on her left foot. 'He can't afford new things. Speaking of which, he's been wondering. About expenses. When is he – when are *we* going to talk about costs?'

'Very soon,' said Chetak as he eased his car smoothly into the river of vehicles flooding north. 'Maybe even tonight. As soon as we get back from,' he tapped his steering wheel with his fingers facing forward, 'where we're going now.'

'And that is?' asked Maddy as she took out a comb now to straighten out her hair that had been rumpled by the wig.

'Shahpur Jat,' said Chetak.

'Oh,' said Maddy. She froze with the comb still held to her head.

She felt as if she'd been punched in the gut by an invisible fist.

Now they were turning.

'I had a friend who rented space for a print-making studio from one of the original villagers years ago,' Chetak continued as he guided the car back along the divided road that led towards the place where they had first met. A mere three days ago.

'It was cheap in those days, and I remember how glad they were to get such a large space in the middle of Delhi. I sent my guys to ask about monthly rentals for single men. Of course, things have changed since the early days. They had to hunt around quite a bit. Still, there are some places available. So I put some money down today – just for one month—'

He finally noticed her silence. 'Wait. Is something the matter?'

'No,' said Maddy, finding it hard to breathe.

He had taken the first right turn and was approaching a parking area. 'There must be. You've gone silent.'

'I just didn't somehow think it would be *here*,' said Maddy.

'What's the matter with here?'

Maddy wondered if he was being deliberately obtuse.

'It's where...' she began, then had to swallow hard before she could continue, 'where I discovered that my life had been turned inside out,' she finished. She hoped that her voice didn't sound as insubstantial as it felt in her mouth.

They had come to a halt. The parking lot was dim. It had a single cluster of lights powered by a tiny solar panel, perched on top of a sixty-foot pole. It was 7.30 p.m., but there were only two other cars parked there.

It was Chetak's turn to say, 'Oh.'

Maddy didn't wait for him to go further. She heard herself say, 'But it doesn't matter. Come on. We're here now. Let's go see the place.'

Then she opened her door and got out.

Behind her, she heard rather than saw that a parking attendant had materialized next to Chetak's window. Chetak was dealing with him.

It's going to be all right, she thought. *It has to be. It will be. It's an adventure.*

27

Raining cats and snowing dogs
Hailing bats and drizzling frogs.

– JINXES, BIG & SMALL

Chetak and Maddy walked along a narrow, winding lane. There was a power cut in progress, and no street lights were on. The air was thick with heat and sweat as tired shift workers returned to their lodgings even as their replacements were setting out. The majority were men or boys. But a sprinkling of young women was out and about, too, recognizable even in the darkness with their chunnis glittering and their glass bangles flashing.

Diesel generators were roaring. Light spilled fitfully from the tiny windows of residential buildings, crammed tight on either side of the lane. Their miniature front balconies were separated by barely four metres. At ground level, gas fires flared under the broad-mouthed vessels of food stalls, sending up pulsing columns of masala-laden fumes. A wedding was in progress around the next corner. Exploding firecrackers threw jagged shadows onto nearby walls in staccato flashes of blinding light. Tongues of distorted wedding music lashed out from crackling speakers.

'This is it,' yelled Chetak, leaning in towards Maddy to make himself heard, 'next to the hot chips stall!'

He pointed to a patch of blackness punched into a nearby wall, then plunged in.

Maddy entered behind him only to stub her toe on the first step of a stairway. She was relieved when Chetak turned on his phone torch. The stairs were pitched at a steep angle, more ladder than stairs, ending at a door on what must have been the first floor.

There was no landing.

Standing two steps from the top, Chetak banged on the door. Maddy was surprised when it opened, imagining that no one could possibly hear any knocking over the cacophony from the street.

A man's shape blocked the doorway, his face obscured by the shifting blue glare of a TV behind him. 'WHO IS IT?' he shouted, towering over Chetak.

'Tenant,' answered Chetak, brandishing a key in the air.

'NAME?' roared the man, as if he were angry, though it was just his manner. Turning his head to yell over his shoulder, he called to his wife. 'Eh, You—' he called, using the pronoun as a name, 'your new tenant has turned up!'

Turning back to Chetak, he said, 'What's that? *Mada*? Madu? Oh, okay, *Madan Lal Singh.* Say that, na.'

Maddy, standing behind Chetak, listened passively. The heat was like a physical weight, pushing them down, crushing them.

Then they were being allowed in. Chetak stepped up and inside, revealing Maddy behind him. 'It's not for me. For my little brother.' The word could mean anything from nephew to cousin to an actual sibling. 'He's the one who needs the place.'

They were in an airless room lit only by the TV. Two shiny black faux-leather sofas were jammed together in front of the set while a kitchen sprawled open on the right. To their left was an actual ladder, made of iron and fixed in place, leaning up to the next floor.

Now on the same level as the owner, Maddy saw that he was shorter than Chetak and herself. He wore striped pyjamas and a threadbare vest. His black hair stood up in clumps from the top of his head and his coarse-grained skin was shiny with sweat.

The heavy-lidded eyes flicked in her direction, took her in with one glance, then spat her out again. To Chetak, he said, 'Heh. What is he – fifteen? Sixteen? Looks like a plucked chicken. Won't last a week, eh, Mother?' He called again in the direction of the kitchen. 'Come, look at your baby-faced tenant!'

But the woman didn't appear and the man – Maddy's new landlord – told them to go on up and find their own way to the room. 'Last door at the end.' He turned away towards the TV, muttering, 'Plucked chicken.'

Chetak had already started up the ladder with Maddy following him. It clanked and rattled as the two of them climbed. At the top was a lightless corridor, hot as a pizza oven.

'This way,' said Chetak, entering the passage with his phone lighting the way. 'Watch your step.'

There were two doors along the way. One had a line of light underneath while the other did not. The door at the end was padlocked. Maddy had taken out her key fob now and shone the small torch for Chetak as he used the key on the lock, drew back the shrieking bolt and pushed open the door.

'You first,' he said, standing aside.

She entered a space just slightly larger than a train compartment, playing the narrow beam of her torch this way and that. The ceiling was so low that she could stretch up and touch it. A postage-stamp-sized window was centred in the wall opposite the door. The floor and walls were bare cement, untiled and unpainted. The stench of recent construction scraped the inner lining of her nostrils.

A wire hung down from the ceiling with an empty bulb holder at the end of it.

'I brought one,' said Chetak. He'd drawn the bolt shut on the inside of the door and now produced a light bulb that he held out towards Maddy. She hadn't noticed before that he was carrying a small kit bag, slung under his left arm.

'Oh, thank you!' she said, handing her torch to him as she took the bulb, still in its protective sleeve. 'How very resourceful you are...' She stopped. 'I'm sorry, that sounded sarcastic, but I really meant it.'

He shrugged, smiling. 'It's only true after all!'

She reached for the empty socket and push-turned the bulb into place, then jerked back as it lit up in her hand. 'Eesshhh!' she exclaimed, letting go. 'I *hate* when that happens.'

The room's stark squalor sprang into view in the pitiless glare, the naked bulb swinging back and forth. It was a mean-spirited space, created as a form of punishment aimed at that breed of deadbeats who could not afford higher rent. All the corners – where walls met ceiling, floor met walls, walls met wall – were uniform in the sense that they were all equally irregular and crudely finished. Construction filth remained wherever it had accumulated. Red slashes on the walls and floor showed where the departing workers had spat out their paan-laden contempt for the building's owner, the contractor and the world at large.

Maddy turned her head this way and that as rivulets of sweat poured down her back. Then she looked back at Chetak with an odd light in her eyes.

'What?' he asked.

'You know what I see?'

He shook his head, mopping his face with a large white handkerchief.

'A palace,' said Maddy. 'For a young unattached man alone in the big city. An empty room. No relatives, no baggage. Just empty space.' She pointed at the light and the window. 'Electricity. A view. What more can he ask for?'

Chetak inclined his head but in response to her question, asked, 'The so-called window faces a blank wall. And how about a tap? Running water? A *toilet*?'

Maddy's hand went to her mouth. 'Oops. You're right, I forgot—'

'The facilities are downstairs,' cut in Chetak. His air of cool self-possession had worn thin. 'There's a curtained recess by the ladder.

Behind it, a sink and a stall. No in-house bucket or mug. In the stall is an Indian-style toilet and tap. You will be sharing these luxuries with the other tenants, all males.' He sucked in his breath. 'Maddy, I don't have the right to ask you this, but have you lost your mind? Are you bent on destroying yourself?'

'I—' she began, surprised by his tone.

'It's ridiculous. You don't need to live this way. You don't need to expose yourself to a job as a male chauffeur merely to earn your keep. That was never part of the original offer, by the way. You were to stay in the house as Verity's guest and with the *option* of driving her around now and then. She likes you. You can stay as long as you want.'

Maddy shook her head. 'No. That's not what she said. As I understand it, the deal involves driving Russi's car and working for *both* of them. Not just her. And anyway, why would I live with a virtual stranger when I could live with friends? You heard Malli; I can always stay with her. Any time. It's true that I didn't consider that option at the time of the... the eviction. I was too shocked then to think straight. But it was the first thing Malli said to me: *Stay with me. As long as you like.*' She paused. 'I do have choices, real choices. All the same, I choose this.'

She looked around the desolate little room, then back at the lawyer. His face was pouring sweat. 'I'm not entirely crazy. It's not as if I'm imprisoned here. I'll come and go from it. I see it for what it is – a human-sized rabbit hutch. And yet, this experience, to be exposed to this kind of degraded existence...' She checked herself before continuing. 'So, it's degrading, dehumanizing, whatever, but it's how hundreds of millions of people live. It seems wrong to just shudder and look away. To remain forever in that bubble of privilege.'

Chetak shook his head while wiping his face again. 'Look,' he said. 'I'm not going to argue with you. I'm only registering my concern that you're exposing yourself to harm and that I am, to some extent, a party to that harm—'

She cut in, 'Chetak, there's also this other thing. I don't think you can understand, and it probably won't convince you anyway. You simply cannot know what it's like – for me, that is – for me to stand in front of a man like the guy downstairs, the landlord, and to be, for all purposes, *invisible*!' She paused again. 'You simply can't know what it's like!'

'Not being stared at, you mean?' asked Chetak.

'Oh, it's *much* more than that! It's being regarded as... as... *normal.* Because of not being seen as a woman. Because of being accepted as a man. I've had a small taste of that while driving around in my own car. But this? This is something else altogether! This is stepping completely out of my skin and into another level of existence. It's standing directly in front of a man for whom women like me are... you know, whatever... and yet, because of the way I'm dressed and because he's been told to expect a young man, *that's what he sees*! No double take. No narrowed eyes. Nothing.'

Chetak wiped the back of his neck, his gaze thoughtful.

There was a long pause.

'Okay,' he said. 'Well then, Madam Madan Lal Singh the driver, I suppose we have to accept that you've been successfully installed in your luxury suite.' He looked around the room again, then back at her. 'Though not staying the night just yet. Are you ready to go? Oh, wait, one more item.' He got out his phone. 'I need Madan's mugshot to make an Aadhar card and driver's licence.'

'Sure,' said Maddy as she posed.

She didn't ask how he planned to get these items made without requiring her presence.

28

Please don't moan
For the tropic zone
Just lie prone
And mind your own.

– JINXES, BIG & SMALL

'You're awake early,' said Malli approvingly. It was before dawn. 'Are you calling to say that you're ready to return to your senses?'

'No! Only to share the morning,' said Maddy, gazing at the tentative glow in the east. 'I'm up on the terrace. I wish you could be here right now,' she said. 'You would love this fabulous garden in the sky.' She had lit a cigarette before calling and drew on it now.

'Forget it,' said Malli. 'I'm not staying overnight in that place. It reminds me of that horror movie in which the house is some kind of—'

Maddy chuckled. 'Oh, so you're afraid of the *house* now?'

'And the people in it. I'm telling you, they seem all friendly-friendly, but I still don't trust them,' said Malli. 'Give me a rude, plain-speaking fool any day over a polite, smooth-talking genius.'

Maddy had called her the night before and brought her up to date with the events of the day, including the room in Shahpur Jat. 'At least with the fool you can see what he wants and you can decide whether to run or to stay. But with these people? You won't know until they've left you behind in the dust.'

Maddy sighed.

'Just tell me,' continued Malli, 'are you wearing your wig? Because you can't afford to let your guard down, you know. Not for one moment. I've ordered a second one so that you'll never have an excuse not to be wearing it. And that's another thing. How exactly are you going back and forth to that slum joint? This whatever-his-name, Chitty-Chittoo, is he going to be your mobile phone booth for whenever Ms Superman needs to change?'

They both laughed.

'No new developments,' said Maddy. 'I haven't met with Verity yet.'

'You're still treating it like it's one great joke,' said Malli, serious once more. 'That's what bothers me. It's not them – your new friends – it's you.'

'*Stop*,' said Maddy. 'Don't scold me! Just tell me when I can come over.'

But Malli wasn't ready to let go.

'You realize, don't you? That Madan can't come to visit me? You can't be seen with me if you're in Madan mode. It will look too weird. The whole neighbourhood will know that I'm being visited by a tall, handsome driver!'

'I *know* that!' protested Maddy.

'So then how will you come?'

'As Maddy,' said Maddy. 'When I'm Madan, I can either be in Shahpur Jat or I can come back here and get up to my room via the secret stairwell—'

'Hold on! What secret stairwell? How do you enter it?'

'I told you about it. The house is riddled with secret passages. This one is from Russi's library all the way up to the second floor. To that space between the mirrors.'

'You never said there was a stairwell there!'

'Well, I did mention it last night, but you've forgotten. There's a long, thin carpet on the floor of that space. Under it, there's an entrance to a concealed stairwell, and it goes down two floors.'

'Oof! These people have too many secrets,' said Malli, clicking her tongue in disapproval. 'What about the carpet then, on the second floor? How do you open the entrance from underneath if it's covered on top?'

'Last night, I changed back into Maddy in order to re-enter the villa,' said Maddy patiently. 'Then Chetak showed me the access to the secret stairwell. We rolled the carpet up and kept it to one side in anticipation of my future use of it.' She relented, however. 'And yes, I agree, it *is* like something out of a murder mystery!'

Malli pounced on that at once. 'See! What did I tell you?'

'But there's no murder,' said Maddy, laughing. 'Or not yet anyway!'

She had been standing all this while at the front end of the vast terrace, facing east. The faint glimmer had grown in strength, but it was still dark overhead, with a light sprinkling of stars. Leaning on the broad, flat surface of the parapet wall beside the luxuriant bougainvillea frothing out of a huge metal drum, she could see the floor of the veranda outside the study. Directly beneath her was the partition that divided the veranda in two. On the left was the sit-out in front of Verity's bedroom. It was very similar to the one in front of the study, except that it had no bougainvillea screening it.

A light came on now from within Verity's bedroom. Maddy heard the sound of curtains being drawn back and one of the sliding doors being pushed open.

Out of an instinct for privacy – hers and Verity's – she immediately straightened up and took a step back from the wall. She could still hear the cricket-chirp sound of Malli talking, but her attention was caught and held by the sight of a figure emerging from the bedroom.

It was a man's figure, in a dressing gown, moving towards the front of the sit-out.

Russi.

It could only be him. His cap of curly white hair was unmistakable, even in the darkness.

Maddy turned swiftly away from the parapet. In her ear, she heard Malli say, 'What's happened? Are you there?'

'Yes!' said Maddy hurriedly. She spoke in a breathy whisper. 'I... I'm here. I suddenly realized how early it is.'

'And now you're whispering!'

29

Barking mad and
Growling sane.

– JINXES, BIG & SMALL

The scene kept playing in Maddy's mind like an unwanted internet video pop-up.

The implications screamed out at her in giant 3D titles: Russi and Verity were lovers.

He had a wife and grown children in Mumbai.

She was a single woman living in his house.

Granted: he was famously separated from his wife.

But not divorced. Which made Verity his mistress.

Maddy frowned at herself for admitting these cheap and cheapening thoughts, these outdated words, to her consciousness. She had gone back down to her room, still talking to Malli, but her mind refused to delete the video worm in her brain. She said nothing to her friend about what she'd seen, but it was clear that she was distracted. The conversation petered out with nothing resolved about when and how they would meet.

Back in her room, she showered and got ready for her day. The only time she removed her wig was when she was in the shower.

All the while, the carousel of thoughts kept whirling.

It was not a moral objection. She knew that much about herself. Intimacies that jogged alongside a marriage had ceased to be of note to her many years ago. Too many people engaged in marital excursions great and small. Too few people bothered to even regard them as subjects worth mentioning. Sometimes, they resulted in separations and divorce, other times, they did not.

Either way, the issue of morality did not apply. Such words as 'mistress' and 'kept woman' had ceased to be used altogether in Maddy's world. She could not remember the last time, outside of a novel set in the past, that she'd encountered them.

Why, then, were they in her head now?

There was a fold-out ironing board in the bathroom and an iron. She sprinkled water onto the creases of a white-on-white chikankari kurta and allowed the steam-hiss of wrinkles being smoothed out to mesmerize her.

The answer to her question, she told herself, was simply this: it was the implied dependence that bothered her, compounded by a consciously maintained veil of deception.

Maddy knew perfectly well how difficult it often was to disengage emotions from financial arrangements. Many unmarried couples lived together without fuss.

But they did so out in the open, not hidden. Whereas Verity...

Verity proudly claimed the status of brave singlehood while, in fact, being spliced to a man. An extremely powerful and well-connected man. Who just happened to live in a giant house, with 'staff', an apparently limitless budget and all the innumerable perks that go with privilege.

The fact that she genuinely liked Verity only made it that much harder to admit these thoughts to herself. She decided that, at least for the moment, she must concentrate on the task at hand – her ironing – and on the events of the day ahead.

She had mentioned to Verity, when they'd spoken after her return from Shahpur Jat, that she was keen to start doing what she'd been engaged to do, which was to drive Verity around. 'Let's go after breakfast,' she'd said. 'Anywhere. Just so long as I'm back behind the wheel.'

Verity had agreed and said she'd confirm the timing of the outing in the morning.

She also said that it was necessary, now that Maddy was formally installed in a room in the villa, that she be introduced to the others.

'Yes,' said Maddy, 'I'd like to meet them.' Verity had mentioned them to her but with no details.

She had heard the smile in Verity's voice as she answered, 'They call themselves the harem of Hauz Khas!' They were the residents behind the two doors on the first floor. 'They've already noticed your presence. They can see the windows of your room from their rooms. They want to gather you in as the latest member of their exclusive little club.'

At the time of that conversation, Maddy couldn't tell whether or not there was an edge of sarcasm in Verity's voice. It could have been ordinary humour, for instance, with no edge. But in the light of what she now knew about Russi and Verity, she felt sure it was sarcasm.

She wondered who the women were. Why they were in the house. How long they'd been there. What they looked like.

She'd been dressed and ready for an hour with no word from Verity when she heard a light tap on her door. She got up to answer it, to find Jyoti standing just outside.

'Will you come down?' said the woman. She was short and slight, her head and shoulders covered in a pale orange dupatta. Beneath it, she wore a brown embroidered kurta, a matching salwar and sky-blue plastic slippers on her feet. 'I can show you the way.'

She spoke in a low, deferential voice, and her gaze, while directed at Maddy, had the blankness of someone who had acquired the habit of *not-looking* from many years of domestic service. Both eyes were open and looking directly at the person in front of her, yet she might have been looking at a plant or at the horizon. There was no emotional engagement.

'Of course,' replied Maddy. She left the room, pulling the door shut behind her. 'Verity madam is downstairs?' she asked.

Jyoti had crossed over to the door of the lift and was holding it open. 'Madam is not feeling well just now,' she said. 'She said to tell you, *Please call her, after breakfast.*'

'Oh,' said Maddy, discomfited. How odd. It would be a breach of social practice for her to meet the 'others' without anyone to make introductions. Not a major breach but still unexpected in this house of formal practices. 'I...' she began.

Jyoti anticipated the question that wasn't asked. 'Bade sahib will be there,' she said. 'And also Chitti sahib.' She pronounced the name as if she meant to say the word 'letter' in Hindi. Which was funny, though most likely unintentional.

When they reached the ground floor, Jyoti opened the door, stepped out and held it open for Maddy. Then, turning to her right, she pushed on the panelling at right angles to the lift and lo, like magic, a doorway appeared. She hadn't wasted a second's attention on the security guard, who was also present in the cramped space. He sat in his chair in the opposite corner, behind his little table, as immovable as a life-sized brass statue dressed in a khaki costume.

'Please come,' said Jyoti to Maddy, holding the panel open from the inside.

Maddy, glancing at the guard, was disconcerted to see that he was looking up at her. His gaze was as steady and unblinking as if his eyes were made of obsidian beads. In the next moment, a crease appeared on either side of the eyes: he was favouring her with a slight smile of recognition.

She inclined her head at him, and he acknowledged the nod.

Then she passed through the panel door, following Jyoti's lead.

They crossed a hallway, which was similar to the one on the other side of the mansion. The left-hand door opened into the dining room.

It was a high-ceilinged chamber, big enough to contain a twelve-seater table with ease. The door through which Maddy had entered was matched with one on the opposite side. Light from the inner courtyard entered via tall windows, silvery-white with frosted glass. The graceful shadows of a creeper swayed in the breeze on the other side of the windows.

One window was open, however. A woman stood beside it, smoking.

She had shoulder-length black hair and wore a mauve silk caftan. Beside her was a pedestal fan, blowing the smoke outward.

She turned as Maddy entered and said, 'Ah! At last. We get to meet the mystery lady!'

She did not acknowledge Jyoti, who hurried away to the left and vanished through a pair of swing doors into the kitchen.

'I'm Preeti, Preeti Chowdhury, but everyone calls me Pretty. Such a silly name. But that's what people are like. And this...' she turned herself around fully, revealing an African grey parrot perched on her right shoulder, 'this is Monkey. My consort. My best boy. Say hello, sweetie? Say hello?'

The bird bobbed his head and made the sound of an exaggerated sneeze.

Pretty laughed, saying, 'That's because I'm smoking! He hates the smell.'

Maddy advanced into the room, saying, 'How wonderful. A parrot!' To Pretty, she said, 'My name's Madam. But everyone calls me Maddy. Hello, Monkey! Nice to meet you.' She continued moving forward. She understood now that what she'd heard on her second night at the villa was most probably this bird's screech.

Monkey turned his head so that one eye was looking at Maddy. 'Monkey,' he said in a parrot's tinny wind-up-toy voice, 'Monkey! Hello. Hello. Monkey.'

'See?' said Pretty triumphantly, like a proud mama. 'He loves you already.' She was obviously so preoccupied with introducing her pet that she didn't pay attention to Maddy's unusual name.

She was not a young woman: the skin around the eyes was crêpe-thin, and a pair of creases rose up on her forehead. But her cheeks were as smooth and plump as an Alphonso mango. She wore a fine, precise line of dark blue along her upper eyelids. Her brows were plucked high and arched. Her small, crisp lips were touched with a trace of pearly pink. Her hair was black and shiny, a long lock falling over her forehead and trailing towards her chin.

'Come on,' she said, stubbing her cigarette out on the window sill. 'Let's sit down, and you tell me everything about yourself before the others come—' then gave a little gasp. 'Oh! Too late!'

The door on the north side of the room swung open.

Another woman peered around the edge.

'Oh,' she said. 'No Verity? Not down yet?'

'As you can see,' said Pretty in a catty voice, coming forward towards the table.

Five places had been set on the plain white tablecloth. Each place had two plates, a glass bowl and a full complement of breakfast silverware. A water glass, already filled, was on the right of each plate. Beside it stood an empty glass, short-stemmed and squat, intended for juice.

Pretty had pulled back the chair closest to where she stood, right by the head of the table, saying, in a school-girly voice, 'Bags I the place of honour!' She glanced up at Maddy. 'When Verity's not here, seating is free-for-all – and *this* is where *I* like to sit!'

The other woman came in now and claimed the chair opposite Pretty. 'Fine then,' she said, as if settling an argument. 'I'll take this one.' She wore a grey close-fitting blouse with a high collar. Loose black pants conveyed austerity and expensive tailoring both at once. Square-framed glasses matched the broad, flat shape of her face. Her grey hair was drawn back tight and secured in a single braid long enough that the end of it dangled over her left shoulder like a sleeping serpent.

To Maddy, she said, 'I'm Lata Venkatesh, and you must be the new guest.' Then she darted a venomous glance towards Pretty before addressing Maddy once more. 'When Verity's here, *that*'s her usual place. Pretty comes around to where I am now, and I'm usually on the opposite side, as far as possible from the feathered fiend—'

Pretty interrupted in a sing-song voice, 'But it's free-for-all day!' To Maddy, 'Don't pay any attention to Lady Field Marshal, dear! Sit wherever you like.'

Lata pulled back her chair. The corners of her pretty mouth were flexed like someone whose wayward tongue is wriggling ferociously within the cage of its mouth. But the comment burst loose anyway: 'If you want my advice, you'll avoid that creature!' She sat down. 'He bites!'

On cue, Monkey bobbed up and down and sneezed.

'I'll take my chances,' said Maddy, smiling as she drew back her chair. 'My name's Madam.'

The swing doors to the kitchen opened.

'What did you say?' asked Lata. She made the question sound like a rebuke.

Jyoti held the swing door open while Suresh pushed through a trolley laden with breakfast dishes.

Lata asked again, unsmiling. '*Madam*? Is that your *name*?'

Maddy sat down. 'I'm afraid it is,' she said and smiled again.

'But that's not a *name*,' persisted Lata. 'It can't be. It's... it's... not even really a title!'

'Yet it *is* my name,' said Maddy. 'The full name's Madam Sen.' Then, on a mischievous impulse, she added, 'But my married surname was Ahmed.'

In the dead silence that greeted this announcement, the trolley rattled slowly to the head of the table, moving towards Lata.

'It was my late husband's name,' continued Maddy. She glanced towards the rattling as if waiting for it to quieten down. When it didn't, she continued, 'He died eight years ago. In Dubai. I dropped the name when I returned to India. Because, you know...' she shrugged, 'things being what they are.'

Both women were staring at her, as if shocked that anyone should provide so much vital information with no prompting whatsoever. 'I thought it best to get the personal details out of the way at once,' said Maddy.

Suresh had stopped now behind the vacant seat next to Lata.

She was the first to recover. 'Meaning what exactly?'

Suresh began to unload the trolley. A cut-glass bowl of papaya chunks was first.

'Sorry?' asked Maddy as she reached forward to take the bowl and push it towards the head of the table.

A covered glass dish containing golden mounds of scrambled egg followed the fruit.

'What you said just now. About "things being..." you know. Whatever they are.'

The silver butter dish with the concealed ice compartment was next.

'About the country being in a bad state,' continued Lata, 'is what you meant, I suppose.'

A silver toast rack with all four slots loaded was handed over.

'Oh! *Please* don't answer!' exclaimed Pretty, addressing Maddy. She had to bend her head to look around the bird perched on her shoulder. 'It'll just set her off on her favourite rant!'

Now Jyoti leaned over the table, handing a small metal dish containing papaya to Maddy. 'For Monkey,' she said.

At that moment, the bird, turning towards Maddy, seized his chance to grab a curl of her wig that had come invitingly within reach of the black scimitar of his beak.

'Aaaah, watch out!' shrieked Lata.

Jyoti dropped the small dish on the table with a frightened squeak and jumped back.

'Monkey!' cried Pretty as Suresh began berating his wife in furious whispers.

But Maddy's peripheral vision had registered the bird's movement before he made contact and she jerked aside, shielding the side of her head. 'Oh!' she exclaimed. 'Bad boy, Monkey! Bad boy!' She tried not to clutch the wig.

'Watch out, he'll try again. He's a demon!' shrilled Lata.

Maddy stood up. There was no question of sitting next to the bird, she realized. 'No harm done!' she said, just as the north door opened again and Russi came in.

His arms were thrown wide, making him seem somehow twice as tall and wide than he actually was. 'My goodness, what's happening, what's going on?' he cried, the mound of his exuberant white curls shining silver in the blaze of light behind him.

It was like a great gust of air had blown in, clearing away the lines of force that had been threatening to bind the room in invisible knots.

Chetak entered in the wake of the older man.

He took in the situation in an instant. He threw a glance at Maddy as both the other ladies turned their full attention towards their host, each one cooing and helloo-ing their morning greetings.

As smoothly as if they had rehearsed their movements, Chetak came around to where Maddy stood while she moved around the foot of the table and towards the seat beside Lata.

Suresh pushed the trolley to where Russi remained, still standing, behind the throne-like chair at the head of the table.

A fresh round of introductions began as everyone took their seats because, of course, Maddy had not yet met Russi in her present form.

Jyoti practically ran away, back into the kitchen.

The room filled with the sound of convivial clinks and chinks as breakfast got underway.

30

Don't let
The ear worm
Eat the apple
Of your eye.

– JINXES, BIG & SMALL

An hour later, Maddy was describing the scene at the breakfast table to Verity as they raced along the Delhi–Jaipur Highway with three giant trucks roaring and panting alongside them.

Verity sat in front. When Maddy got to the moment, in her description, of when Monkey had almost succeeded in pulling off the wig, Verity said, 'That bird is a menace. Someone should put it out of its misery. *Aaaah*!' She stopped with a soft shriek as one of the giants swerved into their lane before swerving out again. '*Oh* my god, my god! I don't know how you drive in this... this...' She broke off, shaking her head.

Maddy smiled. 'I did warn you,' she said. It had been Verity's idea to leave the house at 10.30 a.m. Peak mayhem hour.

'If you're willing to go, then I am, too,' Verity had said. 'It's your choice entirely.'

This conversation had been on the phone. 'Oh, it's fine for me,' said Maddy. 'I was only concerned about you. It can be stressful.'

'I'll be okay,' Verity had assured her. 'I'd really appreciate a long drive. I've asked Jyoti to pack a picnic lunch for us. And a flask of coffee.' She said they didn't even have to stop anywhere; they could eat in the car. Maddy had agreed easily. The Delhi–Jaipur Highway was one of her customary routes.

Maddy brought her car around to Verity's side of the building just as Verity stepped out. A ray of sunshine enveloped her head. Her pale skin became momentarily translucent, and the fine hair framing her face filled with light. She seemed to be hovering on that front step, insubstantial as a daydream.

In the next instant, she had stepped out of the beam of sunlight. Reaching around to take the picnic basket from Jyoti standing just behind her, she turned towards Maddy, who had remained seated behind the wheel, and said, 'My inaugural drive in your car!'

For the first hour of the drive, Verity had been silent. She gazed out of the window on her left, her fair curls stirring in the airstream from the air conditioner. She had asked if it was all right if they didn't talk, at least not right away.

Maddy had said, 'Of course.' Clients often requested silence. She didn't mind it at all.

Verity was dressed in a plain black T-shirt over jeans. She had a mirror-work waist pouch looped through her jeans and a shawl wrapped around her shoulders. 'Because of the air conditioning,' she said.

They had made slow progress all the way until the West End flyover. It was only as they arrived at the boundary between Delhi and Gurgaon that she stirred, flexing her neck and doing a few shoulder shrugs to loosen up. That was when she had asked about breakfast in the dining room. In particular, she had wanted to hear about Maddy's impressions of the other two women. Then, when the monstrous truck gave her a scare, she was silent for a few minutes before asking Maddy to complete the story.

When she was done, Verity said, 'I wonder what would have happened if the wig had come off?' She was gazing ahead, as if imagining the scene. 'What would you have done?'

Maddy laughed. 'Oh, I would've owned it, of course! Said that it was part of my treatment, you know? I mean, I've already thought about the moment of exposure because, of course, it can always happen. If not today, then some other day. I have a scenario worked out. A script.'

Verity turned towards her. 'What... treatment?'

'Well! You know, radiation. I'd say that I'd had a cancer scare and was recovering. You know? It's not at all uncommon these days. We all have friends who've had encounters with the Big C. I could easily be just one more.'

She glanced at Verity, who was looking out towards the horizon once more. Her face creased in a faint smile. 'Yes,' she said, 'that's true. But tell me... tell me about... I mean, I've been so curious about your decision to be a taxi driver – not just anywhere, I mean, but why *here*, why in *this* city, where traffic conditions are so... what word shall I use? Extreme? Unpredictable?'

'Hostile,' said Maddy. 'Unrelenting. Like being in the midst of a stampeding herd of Pamplona bulls – not that I've ever been to Spain! It's that the other drivers on the road behave as if they have no reason for being on the road *except* to bully everyone around them. As if they don't have actual destinations. They're so furious, so directionless—'

'All right, all right,' Verity cut in, 'which is why I ask, *why* are you willing to engage with it? Why would anyone run with the bulls voluntarily – of course, it *is* voluntary in Pamplona – but no one does it *every day*.'

Maddy shrugged. 'A kind of masochism?' she volunteered. She cast her mind back to the conversation she'd had on the morning of her eviction. 'I was talking to Malli about it just recently. How driving in this city is changing me. Making me into one of *them*.' She inclined her head towards the window. 'One of the bulls. At the time, I didn't think I could possibly miss the aggression. I was saying how much I hated it. But the weird thing is, I sort of *do*. Miss it, I mean. Just a few days of being in... in the villa,' she said, thinking of the word that Malli had used. 'Maybe it's the adrenaline? Or even just the car? I mean, I really do love it. The car itself. The way it wakes up, the way it shuts down. It's a person, really – a person with moods and feelings. And words. He speaks to me when I let him—'

'*He*?' Verity cut in. 'You think of the car as *masculine*?' Then she immediately reconsidered her remark and chuckled. 'Yes, why not! Men have always referred to their cars as female, after all! So you've changed it! I like that. D'you have a name for him?' She turned towards Maddy, her face lighting up with a broad grin. 'Did you give him a naming ceremony?'

Maddy returned the smile, nodding. 'I tried! Not a naming ceremony, just a name. I tried all kinds. They never stick. He just snorts them away. He prefers to be the Nameless One. You know? Like that dragon in *The Dragon Tamers* film?'

'Toothless,' said Verity, correcting her. 'In *How to Train Your Dragon*. Not Nameless, but yes, I understand what you're saying. I loved that movie. The first one. Not so much the second. I thought the romance was a bit forced. Too cutesy-cute. You know?'

Maddy nodded but in her mind, the video worm popped up suddenly. *Russi. Walking out onto Verity's terrace. In his silk dressing gown. His crown of silver hair.* When would Verity get around to mentioning the relationship?

'Oh, I didn't mind the sequel,' she said. 'I liked the way girl Vikings were integrated into the story. Each one was spunky and silly and clever, in the same way as the boys.'

'Really?' said Verity. 'You didn't think they were obviously an afterthought? Women viewers complained about the lack of equal representation, so all right, the producers went ahead and made a second film. And yes, equal representation and all that but also, *of course*, Romance. Capital 'R'. As for the Great Mother... oh *my*.

I detested that bit. Dragged back in from the Void! You know? Happy-endings-ever-after-and-forever?' The edge of bitterness was saw-toothed with viciousness.

'Umm,' said Maddy, taken aback. 'Maybe I was too distracted by the dragons to notice the gender messaging. I... I thought it was rather nice to have the mother back from the Void! I remember reading an article about how, in the Disney universe, mothers were either missing altogether or swapped out as evil stepmothers. Whereas fathers are either absent or else they're woolly-benign! You know? And no evil step*fathers* anywhere!'

They both laughed.

'I think I read the same article,' said Verity. 'It made me smile. And I agree with what it said about mothers. Always the same two stereotypes. The evil stepmother whom we can all hate and the saint-like True Mother, goddess-like and pure.' There was the bitterness again. 'Never any mention of the *other* kinds of mothers.'

'What other kinds?' asked Maddy.

'The real mothers who aren't good at being mothers,' said Verity. 'The lousy ones. Who never get any stories told about themselves because no one wants to acknowledge them. Who aren't smart or... or... even if they are, who hated being mothers. And were incompetent. Never wanted to have children and hated the ones they did have.' A dark pause. 'Mothers who tried to end a pregnancy and didn't succeed.' Another pause. 'They don't make animation films about those mothers.'

There was silence in the car.

Verity had turned towards her window again.

They were flowing along, fast and steady. The flat country blurred past on either side. Now and then there might be, for no apparent reason, a row of rickety boxes propped up on frames on either side of the road, looking like steamer trunks raised on stilts. Tiny stalls, each one. A few of them were open for business. Their wares were arranged on the insides of the doors – plastic slippers, cigarettes, children's toys, pink-faced idols with multiple arms – while the proprietors sat hunched up inside. Human tortoises contained within their tiny tin shells, slow-cooked in the heat.

Verity broke the silence.

'She died two years ago,' she said. 'My mother, I mean. She wrote to me from London, asking me to come. She knew she was dying. She wanted to make her peace with me, she said. And that did happen. In a certain sense.'

Maddy, who hadn't realized she was holding her breath until now, said, 'I... I'm so sorry.' It was hard to avoid sounding absurd. 'That she died, I mean. It must have been especially hard for you if...' And now it was really awkward to go on, but she forced herself, 'if it was an unhappy relationship, to begin with.' Clumsy, clumsy, clumsy. 'If you don't mind my asking, what did she die of?'

As the words left her mouth, she knew what the answer would be.

'Cancer,' said Verity. She turned her head towards Maddy right then. 'Please don't feel bad about it. Please. Sometimes I think – no, in fact, I actually believe – that we put out subliminal messages so that even though it's not actually telepathic or mystical, it has the same effect—' Then she broke off, shaking her head, clicking her tongue in exasperation. 'I'm sorry! I'm going into all this back to front.'

Maddy didn't know what to say.

Verity paused, took a deep breath and started again. 'Look, I wanted us to drive out to talk about something else. Not my mother at all. Something I should have mentioned at the outset when we first met. I didn't have to at all, except that it would have been more honest. It would have maybe explained why... all of this.'

She waved her hands to indicate the car, Maddy and the countryside flying by. 'Wanting my own great black beast to fly around in. Without going to the bother of getting taxis or... or... using someone else's car.'

Maddy was nodding as she listened. She felt sure she knew what Verity was going to say to her. It wasn't an easy confession to make, after all, to tell someone who is not a close friend or family member that one is in a secret relationship with a married man. Not just in a relationship but dependent upon him. Living in his house. A man who is constantly in the public eye, eminent and important. She was looking forward to the relief she would feel once the subject was finally out in the open and she wouldn't have to pretend she didn't know about it.

Which was why it came as a complete shock to her when, after another long pause, Verity said, 'You see, the thing I've been concealing from you is that I, too, have cancer.'

These words entered the tiny speeding space capsule of the car exactly as if Death, like an unwelcome passenger, had crash-landed in through the roof. Grim and implacable.

'And the reality is, I'm... not doing too well. I'm dying, in fact. There, I've said that little, little word now. Dying.'

In that bare instant, that most terrifying of passengers had filled the entire smooth, clean-scented, plush-lined interior of the vehicle with its presence.

'Of course, we don't know that for sure right now, that I'm dying, I mean. The doctors won't say that just yet. But it's the same type as my mother's. Breast cancer. That's why she called me back to London. To tell me. That she knew it was hereditary and that she should have told me about it earlier. If she'd told me early enough, I could have checked for the wayward gene. Taken precautions, maybe. But *of course*, she didn't do any such thing. She had to keep it hidden. Because that was her habit. To hide anything she didn't want to face. She didn't tell me about it right until she'd been told that the end was around the next corner. Two weeks, as it turned out.

'That's when she called me to London. She had to tell me because of... of... you know, the end-of-life duties. All of that. She kept telling me that she didn't want to die without having this "little chat". And to give me this, what she kept calling her "parting gift" to me, this information about my genetic legacy. It became a small joke, which she kept on repeating. Until we both began to laugh when she said it. Really laugh. And then she'd stop and call for the morphine or the bedpan or the whatever.'

Verity's voice was dry.

'The thing about death is that it becomes completely mundane. Humdrum, even. There are routines to follow and procedures, tubes and pills, input–output – and then, one day, it just stops. And that whole vast, glittering, echoing, unimaginably complicated edifice that contained a life just... collapses. Vanishes.' She made a breathy, whistling sound. '*Pfffwhit!* Gone. And all that remains is the small, dry, semi-transparent husk left behind on the hospital bed. Empty. So *very* empty it's almost ridiculous! I remember wanting to laugh. It reminded me of nothing so much as the empty shell of a shrimp.'

She paused. 'You can say something now if you'd like,' she said.

There was a wry smile in her voice.

Maddy said, 'No. I'm all right.' And she was.

'I know it's an awful thing to dump into someone else's lap,' said Verity. 'Not just my mother's story but mine, too, all in one go. I *know* that there's nothing much that can be said to someone in my position. But I did very much want you to know. That's one reason I wanted to say it when we were in your car. Because your attention would be on the road. I can just keep talking, and you don't have to say anything. Perhaps that's a little trick that chauffeurs always have up their sleeves? They drive and they listen.'

Maddy allowed herself a smile. 'You're right,' she said. 'That does happen.'

'I'm going to change the subject now.'

'Of course.'

'Let's have our sandwiches,' said Verity, looking around to see if she could reach the picnic basket that she had placed directly behind them. 'I'm hungry.'

31

A cold shoulder
Is better than
A frozen shoulder.

– JINXES, BIG & SMALL

On their way back to Delhi, Maddy heard the buzz of a muted incoming phone call, then saw the light flashing from inside Verity's waist pouch. She had fallen into a light sleep, her head resting on a travel cushion.

Maddy decided not to wake her. The thought crossed her mind: *Maybe it's not my place? Do regular chauffeurs wake their employers under similar circumstances?* She shook the thought out of her head. It was pointless to entertain such speculations.

They had left the highway and were on the elevated road that would return them to the capital via West End. It was late afternoon. The traffic was postprandial: men returning to work after lunch, women setting out from home for a round of rummy at the club. Working women tended not to be part of this post-lunch crowd. They avoided commuting during the workday. Was it for ideological or practical reasons? Maddy allowed herself a smile. Practical, of course! Women would much rather take a packed lunch or no lunch at all than track back and forth through the traffic.

A moment later, her cell phone rang. It was paired with the car's GPS, so she had muted it, but she saw the number on her car's dash screen. It was Chetak. She clipped her Bluetooth headset on and connected the call.

'Can you talk?' asked Chetak with no preamble. She'd noticed that this had become his manner towards her. A friendly informality. It was his signal that they were both on the same side, employees of the same person, social equals. Even though they weren't, she thought. That was the sham. The soft lie that they were all engaged in maintaining.

'Yes,' she said, keeping her voice low. 'We're halfway home. Verity's taking a nap.' *He must know,* she thought, *about Verity's illness.* And about Russi? *Yes,* she thought, *yes. He must know.*

'Oh, okay,' he said. 'Russi said he'd called her, but she didn't answer.'

'Her phone is on mute,' said Maddy. When, she wondered, had the relationship begun? How long had Chetak known? How many others knew?

'He was calling her to ask about you, actually. He needs to make a sudden trip to Mumbai. Night flight. It's his driver's day off. He wanted to know if you're okay with stepping in? If you won't be too tired that is?'

'Of course,' said Maddy reflexively. 'We'll be back by two-thirty, latest. What time does he want to leave?'

'You sure? Around seven-ish. He prefers getting to the airport early. Checks into the lounge, that sort of thing. Sure you'll be up for it?'

'I'll have plenty of time,' said Maddy. 'But even if I didn't – hey, it's what we do, isn't it? Chauffeurs, I mean. It's part of the job description.'

'Right, right,' said Chetak, his voice thinning out slightly, as if losing reception. 'I'll tell him then. Russi. He'll be happy. He's been looking forward to this—'

'What? A trip to Bombay?'

'His inaugural ride,' said Chetak. She could tell that he was smiling. 'With his own private Amazon *chauffeuse*!'

She laughed at the title. 'Heh. Okay, then! Game on.'

'It'll be in his car, though, if that's all right? His Jag. Have you driven one before?'

'*Oh,* my,' said Maddy. 'Major thrill! Yes, I've driven one, but it's been a while—'

'I could show you if you like,' said Chetak. 'He had it customized to suit his needs. It has a couple of unusual features.'

They agreed to meet in the early evening.

It was 6 p.m. by the time Maddy had changed into Madan and gone down via the secret stairs. Chetak was waiting for her in the library, standing by the hidden panel.

'He'll join us in about half an hour,' said Chetak. 'We don't have much time, but I thought—'

'Absolutely,' said Maddy. 'I mean, *any* driver would want to know the car they were going to be using for the first time.'

He handed her the cards he'd had made as he went towards the door to the library. 'Driver's licence and Aadhar,' he said, then turned to open the door. 'Ready?'

Maddy squared her shoulders and coughed to prepare her voice to maintain the lower register she used for Madan. She settled the peaked cap on her head, then followed Chetak as he opened the door. They passed through the octagonal hall and out the front door. Russi's Jaguar was parked right there.

Chetak handed her the key fob before moving around to the passenger's side. They had glanced at one another for an instant as they emerged from the house, the same thought crossing both their minds at once: *Chetak must not open the door for Madan!* There didn't seem to be anyone who might have seen them, but from the start, they had all – Verity, Chetak, Maddy – agreed to operate under the assumption that anyone *might* be watching at any time.

The interior of the car was upholstered in textured leather, ivory grey in colour, with mirror-polished real wood detailing. A tangy scent that might have been a combination of sandalwood and lemon was perceptible but not overpowering. There were reading lights poised above both sides of the back seat.

Maddy drove out and around the narrow lanes of Hauz Khas, doing the circuit a couple of times. There was nothing so rare or unusual about the car that Maddy needed to familiarize herself with. They were still some distance from the villa when Chetak suggested that they park before returning. 'A couple of things I'd like to discuss,' he said. 'We have forty minutes before your tour of duty officially begins.'

'Sure,' said Maddy. They were close enough to the parking area near Hauz Khas Market for her to begin looking for a spot.

'I thought you might have some questions for me about... you know...' He trailed off.

Maddy glanced towards her passenger and away again as she looked for parking. 'You mean, you have advice for me?'

'Something like that.'

'Not about the car then?'

'About Russi,' said Chetak.

About Russi and Verity? Maddy wondered. 'I'm not sure what you mean,' she said.

Chetak said, 'He's set in his ways. Has his little routines. When he gets in the car, for instance, he always settles into the back first, on the left-hand side. Oh look, there's one.' He pointed towards a spot that Maddy had also just sighted. 'Okay, good. But he also likes, sometimes, to ride in front. He does that with his own driver. What I know for sure is that he'll want to sit in front with you.'

Maddy eased into the spot. The car's glamorous bulk made her self-conscious, like a weight-conscious film star who was known for her generous proportions. Leaving the air conditioning on, she turned to her left, saying, 'Chetak, what exactly are you telling me?'

He was looking away, the faintest suggestion of a frown on his otherwise smooth forehead. 'Just that,' he said, after a pause, 'he gave his driver the evening off. It wasn't by chance. He wanted to have a drive with you. He's been impatient.'

Maddy was inclined to laugh about this. She understood right away what Chetak was trying to warn her about. If she were to tell him that receiving advances from older men was par for the course for young women – even not-so-young women like herself – he would get offended or feel that his good intentions had gone to waste. She nodded, noncommittally. She could see herself in the rear-view mirror. With her peaked cap in place, her face beneath it looked as bland as any driver's face might look. Any male driver. She looked remarkably masculine.

'He's going to be disappointed in that case,' she said. 'I'm going to be as uninteresting as I suppose his regular driver is! Or...' here she grinned, 'maybe that guy's a real party animal?' The unspoken irony, of course, was that it could never be. A chauffeur's job description included being discreet. A nonentity. A presence whose absence of personality was highly valued.

Chetak did not smile back. 'Russi is a... complicated man,' he said. Then he shrugged. 'But that's not the point. That's not what I wanted to talk about. Two things.' Now he turned to look at her. 'One is, he's going to ask you to drop the Madan pose when he's with you. No, wait—' He held his hand up so that he could complete his statement. 'And I would suggest, please *don't* do that. Because it'll make it that much harder for you to maintain your cover on other occasions.'

Maddy said, 'Agreed. I'll say so. I mean, I'll do it deferentially, but I'll insist that I can't stop and start. That it'll be too much for *me*.'

Chetak's mouth twitched in a smile. 'He's not used to taking no for an answer! He wanted to know about the "safe word" concept – of course, he knew the concept, but he wanted to know what the safe word was, for you. He noticed that I said something to you that first time he met you in the library. He's extremely sharp. I said something to you, and it resulted in switching off the little drama of your disguise. He asked me about it the next time we met. He found it thrilling, the idea that you could be turned on and off like that.'

Maddy nodded. 'Supposing I simply... refuse? To turn Madan off?'

'That might irritate him,' said Chetak. 'Like I said, he's not used to being denied.'

'All right,' said Maddy, feeling a prickle of irritation stirring within her. 'But he can't, surely, get his way all the time!'

Chetak shrugged. 'All I'm saying is, be warned. The issue will come up, and I wanted you to be prepared for *something*. A discussion. A request. He won't insist or become unreasonable, but you need to know it will come up. What I'm suggesting is that you should have your reaction and an argument in place. So that's one point. The other point is, well... about you. Maddy. The Asiad Village apartment.' He smiled now, seeing that she was taken aback. 'Remember that? Yes. It's going forward. The case, I mean. Against your landlady. There's going to be a hearing tomorrow.'

'What?' Maddy's voice, which had remained in Madan mode ever since she'd fitted the cap onto her head, now shifted up an octave. 'Really... I mean, why! And *how*? Won't I have to be present?'

'No,' said Chetak, answering only the last of her queries. 'That's what you signed consent over to me for, the first morning at the villa. Remember? I asked for your signatures. That was because I said I would be appearing for you as your counsel. And I have. You've been distraught, after all. The shock of that brutal eviction destroyed your peace of mind, made it impossible for you to earn a livelihood, ruined your social life... oh, yes, indeed! You made a suicide attempt and are, even at this moment, recovering in a friend's house.' He spoke with a perfectly straight face.

Maddy stared. 'You're not joking, right?'

'No,' said Chetak. 'Unlawful evictions are no laughing matter.'

'But I thought court cases dragged on and on forever! Isn't this extremely...' she searched for a forceful word, 'unprecedented?'

'Indeed, it is. Such cases are intended to drag on for eternity. But under certain circumstances, they can be expedited. Particularly when the plaintiff is well-connected. Which, as it happens, you now are.' He paused. 'Even though you're not aware of the fact, are you? Well, that's what I wanted to tell you. That the case is moving forward.'

'Chetak, I don't understand!'

He was looking away once more. 'No. The situation is that you *do* understand but would much rather not.' He waited a moment before continuing, 'Ask yourself: how did your landlady, who appeared in court looking like a pathetic bag of bones dressed in widow's white, succeed in getting you evicted? Instant answer: she bribed her lawyer, who bribed the bailiff, who manufactured documents that would give him the spurious right to seal the property while you're not at home.'

He glanced at her. 'With me so far?' When she nodded, he went on, 'I'll cut to the chase. We whispered in a couple of friendly ears and miraculously got ourselves a court date such that your landlady was unable to attend. And glory be! It turns out that our Mrs Bansal is a conniving vixen who will regret the day that she decided to evict you.'

'Goodness,' said Maddy.

'We didn't have to manufacture evidence. Her own lawyer was so delighted to be of service to us that he handed over evidence to show that she'd already re-leased the apartment to a fresh tenant. Who has paid her three months' advance rent.'

Maddy was silent.

'It's a dirty business,' said Chetak.

'You mean the law?'

'No,' said Chetak. 'Being alive. Being part of an organic continuum. It's hypocritical to be unaware of that reality.'

'So then... what's the difference between you and Mrs Bansal? If she's a – what did you call her? – a conniving bag of bones, then what about you?'

'A *pathetic* bag of bones is what I called her. As for me? Okay then, if you want to be a reductionist, you can say that I'm merely a superior bag of bones. That's all. Which is the reason that you, as a result of your association with me, have vaulted up to this elevation and are no longer underfoot to the likes of Mrs Bansal.'

'I—' Maddy opened her mouth to say something, but Chetak forestalled her.

'No, wait. We don't have time right now for the argument that you want to have. I promise you I'll give you that chance someday. Right now, we need to get back to the villa. You need to put your Madan face back on. You've got a long night ahead.'

Maddy breathed in sharply. 'Okay then,' she said, turning away from him. They both knew that Chetak had used the situation to his advantage. 'Right.'

She pressed the ignition switch. The car thrummed to life.

Nothing more was said on the way back. By the time she had brought the car to a halt in front of the entrance once more, some of the tension had dissipated.

Then, with a start of genuine surprise, Maddy said, 'Wow. Can you believe it? I entirely forgot to have a smoke. Is there time?' She glanced at Chetak as she patted her pockets. Cigarettes were verboten in Russi's presence.

'Yes,' said Chetak, opening his door. 'We'll have to be quick.' He had already told Maddy what the drill was: if she had to smoke, she needed to do it outside the car. She must stand some distance from the car. Once she was done, breath mints or chewing gum were mandatory.

Their feet crunched across the gravel as they walked over to a well-developed frangipani tree growing out of a mosaic-tiled planter along the boundary of the drive. The flowers glowed in the twilight, as if lit from within.

'Here,' said Chetak, offering to light Maddy's cigarette.

She bent her head towards Chetak's cupped hands. She straightened up, closing her eyes to savour the momentary rush as she inhaled. 'Oh,' she said, 'that's *so* good!' After a pause, she added, 'It's really odd. I haven't missed it all day so far.'

'Ha,' said Chetak. 'The villa's having a beneficial effect on you. Interesting. A rare case.'

She laughed.

He released a slow, meandering stream of smoke. She could only see his face in silhouette, a darker solidity against the surrounding scene. 'I remember what I said to you when we first met. On the day of your eviction. What I said to you about the villa. I was trying to make it seem like a worthwhile option for you to consider.' He turned his face towards her now. 'I've often tried to imagine what you think *now*. You've been here – what is it – three days? Four?'

'Four,' she confirmed. But she didn't answer his question.

'I'd really like to know,' he persisted.

You can't force me to say, she thought. *Which is great. Because I really don't know.* Out loud, she said, 'Fair enough. I'll tell you. But not now. I've got to enter Madan mode.' She took another puff from her cigarette, then dropped it and began grinding it under the toe of her new and recently polished shoes. 'Tell me something – anything! – that'll help me transition—'

'Yes, of course. Sorry,' said Chetak. 'Your inaugural ride! My goodness.' He continued to smoke. 'I think... well... who *is* Madan?'

'Good question,' said Maddy. She said the words again, in Madan's voice. 'Good question. Who am I? A young man. Decent. Nothing much more than that.' She glanced at Chetak, widening her eyes.

'Nuts. That won't do. There's got to be more!' she said, though continuing to speak as Madan.

'Do you like to read?' asked Chetak. 'You're educated, after all. Seem like a nice chap. Father in the military?'

'Yes. And I didn't want to join,' said Maddy, improvising. 'Left home.'

Right then, the light came on over the front door.

'And that'll be him now,' said Chetak. 'Quick! Breath mint!' He dropped his cigarette and stubbed it out as both he and Maddy reached into their pockets.

They hurried, almost running towards the car.

Just as they came level with the vehicle, Chetak reached forward and gripped her by the elbow. 'Listen?' he said, then let go of her. 'You'll call me, won't you? If you need anything?'

Maddy, having turned at the touch, saw the expression of concern on his face. She said, 'I will. Thank you. Really.'

Then she squared her shoulders and stepped towards the door.

Ahead of them, it opened. Russi stepped out.

His face beamed as he saw her. 'Ah! Good.' He glanced at Chetak. 'Everything okay? She knows where I'm going?'

'*He*,' said Chetak at once.

'Of course,' said Russi as Maddy stepped forward smoothly, opening the door to the car. It was on the right, she realized, one second too late. '*He*. Right, right,' said Russi absentmindedly as he bent to get in. He seemed not to notice the wrong side.

As Maddy closed the door, in the same absentminded tone, he said, 'Thank you, dear.'

She glanced over at Chetak, who was on the other side of the car. Then she turned, opened her own door and got into her seat.

32

Wrong foot, right feet,
Left boot, right beat.

– JINXES, BIG & SMALL

Russi turned on the reading light and got out a sheaf of papers from the portfolio he had in his hand as soon as he was settled. The rear-view mirror was curved, providing a panoramic view of the back.

He looked up at Maddy. 'Terminal Two, yes?' he asked. 'Chetak must have told you?'

'Yes, sir,' said Maddy as she began to ease the car out, the gravel crackling under the wheels. 'Your flight is at 10.35 p.m. We'll be there well ahead of check-in, sir.'

'Good, good,' he said. He returned to the papers in his hand. 'If you don't mind, huh? I have about a half-hour's work.'

'Sir, of course,' said Maddy. Exhibit C, she thought, in the line-up of missteps made in the effort to maintain her identity as Madan. Surely, no employer would normally ask their chauffeur if he 'minded' anything, least of all when the reason for asking was the employer's need to work!

She shook the thought out of her head, however, and turned her focus to the drive ahead.

It was a familiar pleasure, this shifting of attention from human interactions to that of the powerful machine that contained and surrounded her. She thought of it as a relationship with a form of intelligence that she found intensely attractive. The more sophisticated the model, the more particular the intelligence it displayed. But the type of consciousness remained the same from one vehicle to the next: cool, efficient and respectful. Despite all that the machine could do on its own, it would always defer to her. She loved that deference. The humility of it. The dependability.

In and out of the narrow lanes of the colony, she threaded her way towards Khel Gaon Marg for the second time that evening. At the lights, she turned left. North, towards the city centre rather than away towards the airport. At this hour, it made very little difference: the traffic would be frenzied in either direction. It was just her preference, whenever she went to the airport, to travel along the roads and avenues that she associated with the older and more gracious areas of the city.

She would normally have mentioned this to a first-time passenger. Anyone who lived in New Delhi would have regarded it as an odd move unless it was something that they themselves did. However, Russi had asked for silence, and Maddy decided to defer to that request. He had not looked up from his papers and gave no indication of having noticed the unorthodox route.

She entered into the rhythm of the drive, flowing and halting, watching for the lights, responding to the constant darting aggressions from vehicles on either side. A full twenty minutes passed: past the choke points beside Defence Colony and on towards Lodhi Road, thence alongside the Gardens, towards the onion domes of Safdarjung's Tomb followed by the swerve right towards Racecourse Road. Up ahead would be the roundabout that would lead towards the immense bulk of the Ashoka Hotel rearing up on their right... There it was now, lit up with festive lights for some reason, a wedding, perhaps.

She saw a movement in the rear-view mirror.

Russi had looked up from his papers and turned towards the window beside him. Then he caught her eye in the mirror. 'So!' he said. 'You prefer this route too, huh?'

'Yes, sir,' Maddy replied. 'At this time, it makes no difference which way we go—'

'Verity prefers it too,' cut in Russi. He was smiling fondly. 'She would approve!'

'Yes, sir.'

He looked out again and allowed a moment of silence to pass. Then, he said, 'When you get to the Ring Road, if you don't mind, perhaps we could stop briefly? Will there be time?'

'Yes, sir. There will be time,' said Maddy. She paused very slightly before asking, 'Any particular location, sir? Along the Ring Road?'

'No, no, nothing like that. Anywhere that you can easily park. It won't take a moment.' He glanced outside and then back towards her in the rear-view mirror. 'I like to sit in front. Chetak may have mentioned it to you?' He didn't wait for her to confirm this. 'I mean, that's how I normally prefer to sit, even with my man, Ravi. Good man, Ravi. Good driver. Very steady. Been with me for six years now. No, seven. I'm quite used to him.' He smiled again. 'Not that I can't get used to someone else!' Pause. 'You're good. You're very good.'

Maddy said, 'Thank you, sir.' She inclined her head and allowed herself a smile, but she kept her eyes on the road. She was turning. He would know that she must look away.

She felt his eyes on her for a while. Then he returned to his papers.

They were on Shantipath now, the broad, well-lit avenue with embassies on either side. Moving fast. She slowed again as they crossed Rao Tula Ram Marg and approached the Outer Ring Road.

She was starting to think about where they would halt.

There were more parking spots on this road than on the Ring Road.

She chose one.

'I'll stop here, sir,' she said as she began slowing down. 'Better parking.'

West End was on their right, and a small green zone was coming up on their left.

She was barely moving now. On their left was an overflowing garbage dump, a mess of handcarts, food stalls selling freshly fried snacks, flowers and tobacco products. It was the end of the day, however, and only stragglers remained within the circle of hot light from Petromax lanterns.

Some distance away, a car was pulling out.

'There,' said Russi, gesturing from where he sat. 'Parking.'

'Yes, sir,' said Maddy, turning on her indicators. On their right, another car attempted to butt in ahead to grab the spot. She could sense the frantic energy pouring out of that car, a much smaller breed of machine, yet possessed of that heedless yapping quality that small dogs had. But she was already in place. She was a Great Dane next to a Chihuahua.

She made the turn and parked.

In the sudden silence, Russi's voice boomed. 'We won't be here long,' he said as he rocked forward in his seat, reaching for the handle of his door.

Maddy anticipated him and had already vaulted out to open the door behind hers.

'This way, sir,' she said, hovering protectively around the white-haired man as, behind her, the relentless tide of belching, fuming, roaring beasts went hurtling by. She was at least a foot taller than her employer. 'This way,' she repeated, resisting the urge to take him by his arm to steady him.

'I'll be fine, I'll be fine,' he said, glancing up as if startled that she had been the one to hold open a door and that she was so much taller than him. She could see the confusion on his face, the uncertainty about this change in roles. Then he smiled and shook his head, saying, 'That's all right, dear! I'll get it on my own.' He gestured with his hand, meaning that she should get back in the driver's seat.

Wrong! thought Maddy, *wrong, WRONG! You should allow me to do what your driver would do.*

She said nothing, however, and got back into the car.

It took him a couple of minutes to walk around the rear and to the passenger seat. A moment later, they were both inside once more.

The car was generously proportioned. There was plenty of room for two adults to sit comfortably. Yet now, the luxurious, cushioned interior felt unaccountably cosy. The man in the passenger's seat seemed to overflow his allotted space even though he was not physically broader or taller than average. It was as if his aura had spilled out beyond his body's dimensions. As if he sprawled as he sat in his seat, his arms and legs crossing over into the driver's area, even though, physically, he remained sedately in place.

Maddy, who had strapped herself in automatically as soon as she sat down, had to resist the urge to strain against the strap, to draw away from him. To counteract this instinct, she turned towards her passenger, her hands resting on the steering wheel, her gaze neutral but friendly.

'Sir,' she said. 'Shall we go? Or would you like to wait a few minutes?'

Russi turned towards Maddy, his left arm along the windowsill beside him. 'So,' he said. 'So. I must tell you this is *very* interesting to me. Very interesting.'

Maddy had learned a useful technique many years ago, of being able to look straight at someone without looking into their eyes. It was similar to what Jyoti had done earlier the same day. She employed this technique now. 'Sir,' she said.

'When Verity first told me about you, I couldn't understand what she saw in the idea. Of a woman working as a driver. Why she thought it was such an unusual or even remarkable situation. After all, in the West, there are any number of women taxi drivers. But,' he paused as if about to make a portentous announcement, 'I am starting to understand.'

There was an expression on his face, a combination of indulgence and a heightened, awakened curiosity. 'It's not the abstract situation. It's the individual. It's you. *You* are an unusual person. Somehow, she knew that even before she had ever met you.'

Maddy kept her face very still.

'Sir,' she said, again. Then, after a slight hesitation, said, 'May I say something?'

'Go ahead,' said Russi, 'please.'

'I may seem unusual, but it's only because we are *here*. In India. Actually, more so in Delhi than elsewhere—' She stopped because she could see that he was shaking his head.

'Na, na, na,' he said, slipping into a Parsi-ism, as he sometimes did. He was gesturing with his left hand. 'That's not it. You're not getting my point. Maybe it's because you can't see yourself. It's not just that you are a woman who works as a chauffeur. It's that you are...' Here he used both his hands with their palms up, indicating the whole of her being, her presence. 'It's your complete absorption into this role as a *man*. I mean, it's absolutely remarkable.'

There was nothing that Maddy could reasonably say in response to this, so she merely pursed her lips.

'If I didn't know that you are, in fact, a woman,' said Russi, 'I would not for one minute doubt that you are what you say you are: Madan, the driver. A young man. And a good-looking man at that.' He shook his head in wonderment. 'I mean, it's really an achievement.'

Maddy felt she had to speak. Inclining her head to one side, she said, 'Sir, if I may? Looking like a man was never my intention. Not in any way. I was operating a private taxi service as a woman, and that was all. Not as a man. To pose as a chauffeur was a completely unexpected idea. For me. And it *is* strange. I will admit that. To play this role. I'm not sure that I even like it. But it intrigues me. That's all I can say.'

Russi nodded. 'Good. I'm glad to hear that. Because otherwise, I would wonder what... I mean, it happens, of course. We live in a world where people are changing their, you know, their genders. Their bodies. For people like me, of an older generation, it's a little bit confusing, you know? I mean, I'm a bit old-fashioned, I'll admit to that. I prefer women to be women and men to be men. And at the same time, I have read accounts, I've read legal arguments. I understand that the paradigms *have* shifted. I accept that, too. And yet... I like to think that I...'

He smiled self-deprecatingly. 'I'd like to think that I still know how to distinguish a woman from a man. Even though we're being told now that the entire foundation of such beliefs is wrong. The legal definitions are all shifting. What used to be written in stone is now turning into mist before our very eyes.'

His mood was starting to shift.

'*Kher*,' he said. 'The fact is, I have been wanting to speak to you about another matter. Well, it's related, of course. Nothing to do with gender. But about this driver business.'

He was no longer smiling. His eyes, as they sought to engage Maddy's eyes, were cold behind the large, curving panes of his square-frame spectacles. 'Verity has talked to you, I'm sure, about why she wanted to engage you. As her own personal chauffeur. Or... some other word she likes to use – she's a great one for new words! – chauffeuse. French. Hasn't she? Talked about why she wanted to engage you?'

Maddy was paying close attention. 'Yes, sir,' she said. 'Madam Verity said that it was because—'

Russi cut in. 'Please. No "Madam Verity". We're talking informally now. You don't have to be Madan the driver all the time.'

Maddy shook her head. 'I'm sorry, sir, but I must. It's necessary for *me*. I need to remain in character continuously. Or else I can't manage. It's very strange for me, too, believe me. Please excuse me for saying this.'

'Oh!' said Russi in mild surprise, as if the idea had absolutely not occurred to him. 'Oh, ah. Okay. I understand. Okay. Well. The thing is this. Whatever she told you, Verity, about – you know, whatever she said – about wanting a personal driver because of... She's told you, hasn't she? About her illness? And that's another thing, but no, I want to get this point across now, quickly, because, of course, we have to be on our way… No, no.'

He stopped abruptly and looked away. When he started again, it was as if he had opened a floodgate that had remained closed for a long time.

'What I wanted to say to you is this, and once I say it, please, we don't have to mention it again, all right? I mean, not to anyone. The point is this: the real reason she wanted to install her own driver – and a woman driver at that – is that she wanted someone who would drive me around because...'

He paused again, pressing his lips together by tensing the muscles of his chin. It was clear that he was conflicted about making what appeared to be a confession of some sort.

Looking away, looking out of the windscreen, he said, 'Because... because she doesn't trust me. She thinks that I… when she's away – and she *will* be away now because of her treatment – that I'll run around. *With other women.*'

Now, when he returned his gaze to Maddy, his eyes were a pair of hard, black stones. 'The fact is, I'm sure you must know, I'm sure she's told you, hasn't she? We're together. I mean she's my... she's the love of my life. That's a fact. My soulmate. I would never betray her. That's what she cannot understand. And yet – this is also true, you know? – I will also run around with other women when she is not here.'

And now, to Maddy's astonishment, she saw the man's eyes film over with tears.

'It's not because I even want or need anyone else. It's because I… I can't bear to be alone,' he said. 'And I'm afraid I will be. Because of her illness. She's very sick. She will leave me. I know that, I understand that. At the same time, I also know that I am weak. I don't know why I am telling you this. But I have to tell someone. It's an absolute fact, you see. When she's away in Mumbai, and if… if… an *opportunity* comes my way… I… I… *will take it.*'

He reached in his pocket for a handkerchief and covered his face with it, lifting his spectacles up and using both hands. Then the moment passed, and when he removed the handkerchief, he was composed once more.

'All right,' he said, looking away, breathing in sharply. 'I'm fine now. That's all I wanted to say. We had better get going, huh?' He reached forward to tap the car's playback system even as he re-attached his safety belt. 'Maybe play some music?'

'I can do it from here, sir,' said Maddy, tapping the steering wheel. The car had been on the whole time. She flicked a switch to turn on her indicators. As the mechanical beeping began, she said, 'What would you like to listen to, sir? Classical or jazz?'

'How about Mozart's "A Little Night Music"?' said Russi. He pulled out a small travel pillow from the glove compartment and positioned it between his head and the side of the car. 'Thank you, dear. For hearing me out. I might take a small nap.'

33

Burning bridges falling down
Let them totter, let them drown.

– JINXES, BIG & SMALL

It was just after 11 p.m. when Maddy returned to the villa. She had decided that this would be the night she'd use the bicycle that had been provided for her to stay away for the night in Shahpur Jat.

Chetak had not been in favour of this idea. 'I'll hide the house key in the frangipani planter,' he'd said, 'and you'll enter from this side.' Because on the other side was the security guard.

But even as he said it, he knew that it wouldn't work. It would look utterly bizarre, in case anyone happened to be watching – and there might *always* be someone watching, always; that was the norm for urban India – for a newly employed chauffeur to be rooting about in a planter. Or even re-entering the house when both employers were away.

Maddy said, 'Madan would have no reason to return to the villa. He'd return home to his – wherever he lived.' As a non-resident employee, his off-duty whereabouts would be of no interest to any of the resident workers. 'But what about the car's key fob?' she wanted to know. 'I can't keep it with me.'

'Drop it in through the letter slot on that mailbox thing,' said Chetak. 'You've seen it? By the front door?'

'I've seen it,' Maddy had said at the time of this conversation, which had been on the phone, in the afternoon, after she'd returned from the drive with Verity.

She'd packed an overnight backpack for herself and a change of Madan's clothes for the next day. She'd stashed the bag in the boot of the Jag. When she returned from the airport, she retrieved the bag and pressed the button on the rim of the boot to get it to close itself. She stood, bathed in the red glow of the tail lights as she watched the black lid sink down, swallowing up the lighted interior of the boot with silent inevitability. Then she *beep*ed the key fob, and the regal machine went dark.

The porch light over the front door was off. She looked around for the letterbox, remembering that it was on the left, placed on its own square-base cement pedestal. There it was, a sturdy black metal box with a small padlock on the front. She was about to push the key fob into it when it occurred to her that she had better check to see that she had whatever she needed in her backpack.

And if I don't? she asked herself. But there was no answer to that.

The night was hot and still. Continuous immersion in artificially cooled spaces had already altered her connection to the heat: it now felt like an oppression, an unfair imposition. Mosquitoes were buzzing around her ears, insects chirred and trilled in the garden, accentuating the silence directly around her. In the distance, the murmur of traffic and the lurid glow on the horizon reminded her that she was, after all, in the heart of a giant metropolis.

Propping her foot up on the edge of the mailbox so that she could balance the backpack on her knee, she checked what was in there, using her phone's torch: a change of clothes, a sheet to sleep on, a hand towel, a plastic mug, a comb, a tiny rectangular mirror, toothbrush, toothpaste. What else would she need? The key to the lock on the room, check. Key to the lock on the bicycle, check. A regular-sized torch, check. Two cell phones. Yes, her own was in her pocket, the Nokia was in the backpack. iPad, no. She'd deliberately left it back in the villa.

She was forgetting something. Something vital was missing.

She looked around, wondering what it was, feeling self-conscious. She must not allow her guard to slip, even though she felt as if she were completely alone and the likelihood of any prying eyes was extremely low. She told herself there was surely no point looking around since there wasn't anything of hers that she might expect to see. Still, she looked around as she zipped up the backpack, slung it onto her shoulders and got out the cycle's key in preparation.

And then she remembered what was missing!

The bicycle. She had forgotten to bring it around. It was on the other side of the house. Then one more thing came to mind: the charger for her cell phone. Up in her room, charging the iPad.

Did the cell phone need charging? She didn't need to check. Of course, it did. Wasn't that always the case? Was there ever a cell phone that did *not* need charging when there was no charger available?

She could, she thought, walk around to the other side of the house. She couldn't go around the front because the trellis fence had a locked gate on that side. Which meant going all the way around the back. The property was extensive, and it would take a little while, five minutes at the very least, to walk all the way around to where the cycle was chained to a hook on the side of the house.

But she didn't want to walk around. The rear of the house was terra incognita for her. Aside from the day of her arrival, she hadn't been around to the back. She remembered the sleepless night when she had stepped out onto the wrought-iron catwalk and looked across the interior courtyard to see the phantom presence on the other side. She remembered feeling a sense of complete unreality, as if she were staring through a portal into some other dimension.

She didn't have the energy to face alternative dimensions tonight. She was still thinking about the conversation with Russi.

Which left her with the only other option: to walk to Shahpur Jat.

It wasn't all that far. Not at all.

It was, however, a test of her disguise.

Under normal circumstances, she would never undertake a trek from Hauz Khas to Shahpur Jat at night. She would normally have her car, but quite aside from cars and other modes of transport, she knew, without having to question her reluctance, that she would simply never consider walking around at night. The city's streets and pavements emptied out after a certain time of night, becoming unstable zones for women. Especially along those long, empty stretches without shops or homes, which, even during the day, could feel unnerving. Just the act of being outside, on a pavement, as a woman alone was enough to attract catcalls from passing drivers and raking, insulting stares from any other pedestrians who happened to be on the same side of the road as herself.

Would today really be all that different? she wondered. Did men truly enjoy such an extraordinary advantage? *I will soon find out*, she thought.

She had already made up her mind to go, so now it was only a question of actually setting off. While making up her mind, she had taken out a cigarette and had been standing there, smoking in the semi-darkness by the car.

She stubbed out the cigarette and shouldered the backpack. When she raised her hand to slap away a mosquito on her forehead, she realized she was still wearing the cap. She took it off now as she walked towards the gate, her feet crunching on the gravel. She slung her backpack around to the front so that she could stuff the cap into it, careful not to let it get crushed, before shouldering it once more.

Another decision lay ahead of her now. She needed to pee. The urge had been nagging at her for about an hour now. It had started perhaps halfway home from the airport, just at the turn-off onto the Ring Road.

She was, like most women, fairly good at holding it. But there were two considerations. One, the toilet at the Shahpur Jat accommodation was not exactly inviting. True, she would eventually have to use it, but it was nothing to look forward to. Plus, by the time she got into her room, she would be at bursting point.

Two, however, was that she had never actually peed on the road standing up. It was one of the few assets that men had that she actively and frequently envied. She had a method for achieving that result while wearing pants. She had used it – but only while visiting a ladies' public restroom, while wearing jeans and feeling immensely superior, though hidden from the sight of others in a stall.

This, now, would be her first-ever chance to stand by the side of a road and just... do it.

She had decided that she'd exit the property first, then stand by the gate and pee towards the wall. There were no other gates around the dead end and no structures or lights of any kind visible from the gates. She adopted the stance that she had seen so often, bent her knees slightly and unzipped the fly of her pants.

The device had a catchy name: Peedom. She had bought it in the US, custom fitted and made of flexible silicon. The custom fitting had been expensive, but the device itself was basic and easy to use. It had the general shape of an elongated avocado. It had a generous opening that was made to fit snugly within the exterior folds of her body and came out as a spout at one end. The spout was extendable, though not by much.

Very little prior practice was required to control the flow in such a way that there was a minimum likelihood of spillage. She wore the device whenever she thought she might need it during a journey, and she was careful to keep it washed and sterile. So far, it had not given her any trouble.

She released a steady stream of warm liquid, holding the flexible tube so that the stream went into the slight gap where the wall met the gatepost. She was smiling at herself but trying not to grin. Just in case someone happened to walk up the lane. When she was done, she pushed the end of the tube back into its housing, did the little jig of zipping up and flexing her knees once more, then took out her handkerchief and wiped her hands.

Done.

Still trying not to grin, she now began her walk. First along the quiet lane, then towards the roundabout from which one spoke led towards Khel Gaon Marg. Property walls and hedges bordered both sides, with narrow sentry posts at every second gate. At this time of night, many of these small wooden huts were either lit from within or the occupant was sitting outside on a battered plastic chair, shooting the breeze with a companion sentry from a neighbouring home.

She walked past them in an easy, loping stride. Her shoulders were back, and her arms hung loose on either side though she felt the urge to fiddle with the straps of her backpack. It was difficult to avoid the defensive curving of shoulders that was so much the norm for women.

She did not glance at any of the sentries as she passed them nor at the small knot of figures around the paan-wallah at the corner of one of the side roads. One or two faces might have turned to look at her as she passed. It was idle curiosity, however. She was taller, relative to the average pedestrian. That was enough to cause a slight stirring, as of a larger and healthier predator passing beside another group of lesser entities.

There was not the least frisson of attention of the other kind, the gendered kind. The men on the street registered only that a young man of above-average height, dressed in what looked like a driver's uniform, was walking past them.

If at all any glances came her way, she thought, it was almost certainly because of her light skin. Only now did she understand why Chetak had suggested darkening it. She was fairer than most of the men roaming the streets. It was a simple reality. If any homeowners came out, they were more likely to look like her than the men who made their living around these homes. Her lighter colouring made her stand out as much as her height.

With the idea of seeming preoccupied, she took out her cell phone, dialled up Pandora and held the phone to her ear as the music played softly. This gave her the opportunity to partially cover her face.

In this way, she reached the throbbing artery of Khel Gaon Marg.

She put her phone away and walked briskly now. The avenue was brightly lit, and it was that time of night when the goods and produce trucks came thundering through the city. There were cars and taxis, too, speeding by like bullets while three-wheelers puttered along at their much more sedate pace. A scattering of cyclists, moving like tired gnats between racing behemoths, drifted slowly wherever they could along the open road.

Maddy crossed at the first of three traffic intersections, half jogging between the vehicles that would, at this time of night, not slow down even an instant at the sight of a mere human at a zebra crossing. The lights were orange blinkers, with no greens or reds.

There were more pedestrians on this road. All men, all stragglers of some description. She paid them no heed, neither pausing to look at them nor noticing if they looked at her. She had caught her stride and walked with the swift, confident urgency of someone on a mission. She only slowed down when she reached the first entry point to the village of Shahpur Jat.

She was sweating freely and felt powerfully exhilarated. She had earlier wondered if she'd be able to find her way through the narrow lanes, but the positive energy crackling through her veins gave her superpowers. She navigated as easily as if she'd been following a lighted path.

There were no crowds at this time of night, no crackers or loud sounds. The power was on, and the street lights provided sepia-tinted visibility via dim bulbs strung along cobwebs of electric wire two storeys above the surface of the rutted lane. A lone cow stood in her path just by the Hot Chips stairwell. A stall selling cigarettes and paan masala on the other side of the lanes was still open.

Maddy stopped to buy a pack of tens. She did not expect to find her preferred brand and didn't ask for it. She glanced at the pouched and greasy face of the man who spent most of his day squatting on an elevated platform selling tobacco products and said, 'Open late, huh?'

He said, 'What else? There's always someone needing a smoke.'

She gave a slight chuckle. Then she asked if he knew where she could buy a jharoo. 'Right here,' he said. 'I keep a few things. Soap, tooth powder, Aspro. You never know who's going to want what in the middle of the night.'

She paid for the cigarettes and the jharoo and thanked the man. She crossed the lane and entered the stairwell. The landlord's door was unlocked. A single bulb lit the way up to the second floor. The doors along the narrow corridor were closed. Blue light spilled onto the floor from inside the room right next to hers, and she could hear the muted bonks and boops of an electronic adventure in progress. From one of the other rooms came the contralto boom of a lusty snorer.

Maddy opened the lock on her door, her penlight torch in hand.

Only when she stepped inside the room, playing the narrow beam of her torch around, did she observe that it looked different from when she had first visited it. Cleaner, for one thing. It had been swept and perhaps even swabbed.

A rush mat, rolled up tight like a pale golden rod stood to attention in one corner. Beside it was a diminutive morra, the kind that can be bought at the roadside stalls on the Jaipur Highway. Then she looked up and saw that a simple shade had been fitted on the light fixture.

Flipping the switch at the door, she winced as the tiny dwelling flooded with light, but she was grateful for the shade.

Chetak, she thought as she looked around. Or someone instructed by him.

She smiled as she looked around. What a difference it made to see a clean version of what had earlier seemed the very definition of a slum.

Beside the morra was a lidded plastic bucket, a stack of mosquito coils, a tin plate on which to place a lighted coil and a tube of Odomos. On the morra was a two-tiered stainless steel tiffin box.

Maddy half-filled the bucket from the tap in the toilet downstairs, brought it back up, then locked the door and turned off the overhead light. She propped the standard torch up on its end to make herself an impromptu lantern and unrolled the rush mat. She undressed until she was down to the thin cotton shorts she'd worn instead of panties and the binding across her breasts. She did not remove either of these, but instead, put on a rough cotton kurta, originally dark blue in colour, now a muddy grey. She had purposefully bleached it so that it no longer looked new. She pulled on a pair of plain white pyjamas.

Then she knelt on the mat and reached for the tiffin box.

She had wondered if it would have anything in it, and yes, it did: upma. Cold, of course. But very welcome. She hadn't even thought about food until that very moment. Her stomach gave an appreciative squawk. There was a flat, spoon-like implement that functioned as a locking device, holding the two handles of the tiffin box together.

She smiled as she lifted the top compartment off, then saw that there was a bit of paper – a yellow Post-It, folded over and stuck to the lid of the lower container.

Opening the note, she saw what had to be Chetak's handwriting. *Bet you forgot your charger. Look under the morra.*

She smiled again but felt a familiar shiver of discomfort.

The solicitude bothered her, as it had from the start.

Was it, after all, just another form of bribery? A means to an end? Was she simply being jollied along to keep her compliant? It saddened her to think this way.
But she ate the upma all the same.
And fell into a sound sleep.

34

My fair lady, my fair ground,
My play script, my playground.

– JINXES, BIG & SMALL

Maddy woke to the sound of blood-curdling groans. She shot up, her heart pounding, in the sweat-drenched darkness of her lodgings.

The sound continued unabated.

A moment later, she identified it – a man performing his morning tongue-cleaning ritual.

She giggled weakly to herself. She had slept so soundly that there had been no cushion between the absolute oblivion of deep sleep and this contralto retching.

It was a peculiarly masculine sound. She had heard it for the first time many years ago as a child. She and her parents had been guests in a Mumbai apartment. The bathroom attached to their bedroom shared a ventilation shaft with the bathrooms on the floors above and below the one they were on. When the window was opened, the shaft functioned as a vertical auditorium of sounds from other floors. The Morning Strangler is what she had called the anonymous man then. She had been eleven years old at the time and remembered being terrified by the sound. Her parents had to explain to her that there was nothing wrong with the man. He was not dying or being attacked. He was using a flexible strip of plastic to scrape out the back of his tongue. By reaching far enough back, he was able to trigger his throat's automatic gag reflex, which was what they were l istening to.

How d'you know it's a man? she had asked her parents then. They had laughed, and her mother had said, *Oh, darling, please! Ladies don't make that kind of racket!* Then they had glanced at one another and laughed a little more and changed the topic. It would be several years before Maddy understood the reason for the second laugh.

Now she checked the time on her phone: it was not yet 6 a.m.

Using a washcloth dipped in water from the bucket to clean herself up, she dressed herself in a fresh set of Madan's clothes, reorganized her backpack and left the room. Ten minutes later, she caught an auto and was rocketing along towards Press Enclave, where Malli lived.

Malli was an early riser. When Maddy texted her from the auto, she responded enthusiastically about seeing her friend at home for once.

Maddy got out of the auto some distance from the gate to Press Enclave, paid the driver and walked the rest of the way. When she got to the familiar gate, the security guard on duty glanced at her. His eyes narrowed, and he stood up when it became obvious that she planned to walk through the gate. The two pye dogs asleep at his feet stirred and raised their heads, too, sensing trouble of some sort.

As Maddy drew up, the guard cried out, 'Stop! Where d'you think you're going?'

Maddy didn't dare look directly into the man's eyes. She knew him well, in that she'd seen him many times over. Not that she'd ever known his name or spoken to him. She was familiar to him, too. Or her car was, anyway. Had she been in it, he would have instantly let her through, whatever she looked like.

'G Block,' she mumbled, feeling extremely awkward. 'Number 42.'

The man's face was like a brick wall. He had a narrow head. Shiny brown skin. Thick black hair, oiled and raked tight with a comb. His expression was so hostile it was almost comic. 'What purpose?' he snapped. His eyes, sharp and black, were darting this way and that across Maddy's face, gathering information in quick stabs.

Maddy was unnerved but managed to say, 'I'm... I'm Madam's... new driver.' She remembered to pitch her voice low.

'Madam already has a driver,' said the guard, his voice hard. 'She never mentioned any driver coming to see her. Especially not this early.'

'Please call Madam,' said Maddy. In her texts to Malli, it had not occurred to her to mention that she was in Madan mode. And that was because she'd absolutely forgotten what Malli had said: *Do NOT come to Press Enclave dressed as Madan!*

It was now much too late to send a message.

Maddy's best hope was that Malli would understand what was happening at the gate and perhaps intercede in some way.

The guard stepped up into his guardhouse. It was a more substantial structure than the typical security cubicle. This one had a couple of chairs inside, a table and even a pedestal fan. On the table was a black landline telephone. Usually, there were two men on duty, though perhaps they staggered their shifts through the night.

The man lifted the handset on the phone, then looked down towards Maddy. 'Number?' he barked. Everything about his manner was rude and offensive. He spoke in the belittling tone and form of address that he would never have dreamed of using had he known that she was a woman, even an unfamiliar woman.

Maddy gave him Malli's cell phone number, and he punched in the digits. The instrument was set on speaker, so she could hear it ringing. She knew that her friend was on very cordial terms with the security personnel. She would recognize the number of the incoming call.

A moment later she heard the cricket-voice chirp of Malli's voice responding on the guard's phone. 'Yes?' she said.

'There's a young man to see you,' said the guard, glaring at Maddy as he spoke. 'Says he's your driver. I told him you already have a driver. What should I do? Also, he has a bag. Should I check the bag?'

Maddy held her breath. There was a pause before she heard Malli answering, 'Oh! Yes. Of course. I'm expecting him. Do one thing, please? Just ask what his name is?'

The guard held his hand to the mouthpiece. 'Name?' he snarled at Maddy.

'M-Madan,' she answered, 'Madan Lal Singh.'

'Madam,' said the guard into the phone. 'Says his name is Madan.' Malli told him to send Madan in. A moment later, he was glaring at Maddy once more. All right,' he said to her. His shoulders were no longer tense, but he didn't smile. 'Madam says, you can go in.'

Maddy nodded, allowing her mouth to relax in a very mild expression of gratitude. Just the ghost of a twitch. Not enough to seem like insolence yet enough to express thanks.

There was a flimsy barrier erected across the entrance to the estate. It could be brought down or raised by a heavy cord operated by whoever was on duty. The guard released the barrier, and Maddy walked in.

The main road into the colony at this time of the morning was teeming with morning walkers. Maddy moved off the tarred road and onto the cemented pavement beside it. It was a well-maintained colony with blocks of two- and three-storeyed ivory-yellow apartment buildings, organized to provide privacy despite verandas, sit-outs, tall windows and many variations of brick-work jali.

Maddy kept her eyes down, not wanting to meet anyone's gaze.

It would be inappropriate for a young man dressed in a driver's uniform to be looking around when surrounded by flotillas of the residents of the colony, many of them women, as they paced briskly in their yoga pants and smart jogging shoes. The older women were dressed in kurta-pyjamas belonging to the backs of their closets – slightly faded, very loose, dull colours – while all the younger women wore stretchy skintight outfits in shiny black with slashes and stripes of pungent greens and screaming pinks. Headbands held back their hair and kept their earbuds in place while they listened to music or audiobooks.

There were a few dogs on leashes. At least two of them raised their heads to look at Maddy. But aside from the dogs, no one paid her any attention.

Maddy walked quickly, her stride long and loose. She tried to recover the poise she had felt the night before, but the exchange at the gate had troubled her. She should have anticipated it. Been ready for it. Why had she forgotten that she was not to visit while in Madan mode?

It had been inconsiderate.

More than that, though, it suggested that she was settling into the deception of her assumed identity without paying attention to the range of consequences that followed in its train.

She was very soon at the perimeter of a tiny patch of grass which, in the late afternoons, would be full of young children playing on the swings or climbing the jungle gym. Their cries would be sharp and piercing, like bird calls, while mothers and young female childminders sat nearby giggling between themselves or talking on their phones.

But at this time of day? No. The interior of the colony was much quieter. The only people visible were domestic helpers. Maddy saw two women, who were probably maids, and an older woman who might be a cook. They were all dressed in loose, almost shapeless clothes, salwar-kameezes in pale, faded colours. Only the dupattas moulded to their heads and shoulders were bright and fresh. On their feet, they wore plastic sandals. One of them had a milk container in a striped bag by her side, the stainless-steel handle poking out. All three were sitting on the cement rim that defined the grassy area, talking in low voices.

And, of course, there were drivers.

She saw three of them, each one attending to a car. Two were just starting to wash down their vehicles; the third was polishing his with a small rag. All three cars were white, and all three men were young and wiry, burnt caramel brown in colour. One wore a dark blue T-shirt with the entwined alphabets YSL printed in white, front and back. The other two wore threadbare white banians. All wore greyish-white cotton pyjamas, loose and grimy. All three were barefoot. They each had smart haircuts, however. One of them sported the latest fashion, faded to a crest of dusty black curls at the top of his head.

In the bare minute or so that Maddy took to reach the foot of the stairs leading to Malli's home, each of them turned to look at Maddy.

It was very subtle: just a feather-light lick of interest, expressed by eyes that were expert at concealing the subject of their attention. It would never do for them to actually stare, and yet, it was imperative to be witnesses to whatever happened within range of the homes they were attached to. It was an unspoken, unwritten part of the contract of domestic employment. They were not merely faceless work-producing machines. They were also the all-important eyes and ears of the organic whole that made up the warren of homes and families.

Maddy sensed their uncertainty, even with that briefest of glances towards her. *Could such a person actually be a driver?* they were thinking. *With that height and skin colour? And if not a driver, then what exactly?* She felt the electric ripple of their curiosity and unease prickling up and down her spine, in her nose, in her throat.

Then she was at the stairs.

She climbed them energetically, resisting the urge to run up. That would have been unseemly. She was suddenly desperate to gain the sanctuary of her friend's home, to be enabled to drop the charade of her current existence.

To her surprise, Malli was standing out on the landing at the open front door.

'Ah,' she said. 'Good to see you, Madan. Yes. Come in.'

A spasm of acute pain shot through Maddy's gut.

There was no flicker of recognition in her friend's face.

She might have been looking at a complete stranger.
An anonymous piece of furniture.
An unknown driver.

35

The moon is a river
The sun is the sea
The stars are the wind
The comets are thee.

– JINXES, BIG & SMALL

The moment they were inside, Malli spun around and hissed, 'What were you *thinking*!' while Maddy, leaning with her backpack against the door, covered her face with her hands and began to shake with silent sobs.

'Stop it,' said Malli, though in a friendlier tone. 'Wipe your face. Come on, come on! Be quick about it. We must leave right away.' She hurried to her bedroom as she called over her shoulder, 'Open the door! And stand right there. I'm still getting a few things together.'

Maddy had wiped her face as instructed and now opened the door. She was still recovering from the shock of Malli's impersonal reception out on the landing. 'What—' she began.

But Malli forestalled her, 'Here, take the key, please? I'll be down in a minute. Car number DHX 5760. Red Maruti.' She gave Maddy the fob. 'Shut the door behind you, huh? The mosquitoes are getting in.'

Maddy went back down the stairs. She knew where to find Malli's car. As she returned the way she had come, she could feel the tracking gaze of eyes upon her back, openly staring now that she was retreating. She dangled the key fob ostentatiously in her hand and walked briskly, hoping that the display would be convincing.

She understood what Malli was hoping to do: to suggest that a tall young man had arrived at the gate equipped with the correct address, prospecting for a job. How else to explain the appearance of a 'Madan' on her doorstep? It was typical of her friend's practical, quick-thinking brain to have worked out a method to cover for Maddy's ill-planned early morning visit.

Maddy got to the car, opened it and slung her backpack on the front passenger seat. Then, she found the little rag that Malli kept tucked under the driver's seat and began wiping down the windows. It calmed her to be doing something, even as it helped her to remain in character. She thought of the steps that lay right ahead. Returning to the villa as Madan meant that she'd need to take another auto. Or maybe she should get dropped off far enough away from the address that she could walk back to it without anyone noticing.

She had just begun working on the rear windshield when Malli appeared. She was looking as fresh as if she'd just stepped out of a shower, in an off-white blouse and black skirt. Her hair was caught up in a business-like ponytail with clips on either side to keep stray strands from falling out of place. She wore pale pink open-toed sandals, and her face was lightly made up, as if she didn't intend to stay out for long. On her shoulder and in her hands, she was carrying a couple of cloth bags.

She waved out to a couple of the walkers on the road as she approached the car, then turned her attention to Maddy. Her expression was once more unyieldingly remote.

'Thank you,' she said, 'that's fine.' She was referring to the cleaning 'Let's go then. I'll manage, thanks,' now referring to Maddy's move to open the rear door for her. 'I'll sit on the left side.' She spoke loudly so that anyone within earshot would hear what she said.

Maddy slid into the driver's seat. The moment she sat down, she realized yet again why her height was considered an oddity for a driver: because the average car was sized for shorter people, including men. While her own car and the other two that she'd used recently had all been roomy sedans created for the Western market, most Indians drove more compact models. Malli's Maruti was so dinky that the top of Maddy's hair grazed the ceiling as she settled into the seat. Even if she'd wanted to, she couldn't have worn her cap.

Malli said, now in her normal voice, 'Maybe remove the seat cushion? You'll have to get out again to do it.'

'I'd rather leave it as it is,' said Maddy. She faced forward, frowning slightly, wondering how best to negotiate the road while there were still so many morning walkers.

'Turn left,' said Malli. 'The rear exit gate is right there.'

Within a few minutes, the car was nosing its way out of the maze of streets behind the colony. Malli directed her to go towards Deer Park. Maddy didn't ask what her plan was until they were once more on the Ring Road.

'Please let's change seats,' she said. It was still quite early in the morning. 'I'm really not comfortable driving your car with you behind me!'

'Just follow my instructions, please,' said Malli. Maddy could see her in the rear-view mirror. She was fussing with one of the cloth bags. 'We're not changing seats until we're so far from Press Enclave that we're not even near any of the bus routes. There are enough people returning from night shifts who might see us. I don't want to take that chance.'

'What chance?' asked Maddy.

'Of seeing us switch over. Of you putting on this new wig I got for you.'

'Huh?'

'Eyes on the road. Oh my *god!* Have you completely lost your senses?' Maddy had swerved sharply to avoid a slow cyclist.

'I saw him, I saw him.'

'Just drive quietly please, and don't ask questions. You're the one who wasn't thinking straight, and now I've had to cover your tracks for you!' She wasn't angry. It was just her way of speaking. 'Really, it's just by chance that I'd had my first cup of coffee or, who knows what I'd have said to that guard, what's his name, Balvinder! I can tell you, it took me a great leap of imagination to guess what had happened and why he was calling.'

'I know, I know,' muttered Maddy. 'I am a complete idiot.'

'No doubt you're going to tell me some crazy saga about your night duty, which will explain why you woke up with your head in the clouds!'

'Oh, *god*,' breathed Maddy as her mind flashed back to the events of the previous evening. 'That's certainly true.' They were approaching a break in the road. 'Is this where I can hook right?'

'Further,' said Malli. 'Don't tell me anything just yet. I would prefer that we're stationary. I'm guessing we'll need half a pack of ciggies each just to get through the intro.'

Maddy agreed to this plan, but as she did so, she wondered how much she was going to share. What she'd been told by Russi had been said in confidence. Not just any confidence, as between friends, but the professional confidence between a chauffeur and her employer.

Ten minutes later, they had turned around and were coasting to a halt alongside the dark green shade of Deer Park.

'We're not going in,' said Malli. 'You'll have to be quick. First, as soon as you stop, I'm going to hand you the new wig – don't look around – which I've arranged and got ready for you. The moment you stop, don't even park. Just take the wig from me and settle it onto your head. Don't bother with doing it carefully; just make sure that your head is properly covered, and then, drive on!'

Less than a minute passed as Maddy followed Malli's instructions.

Now wearing the new wig, she slid back onto the Ring Road. Traffic was still light, but what was there thundered by at high speeds. 'Now what?' she asked. 'Where am I going?'

'Ultimately, we'll end up at that café – what's it called? Garden-something? – at Lodhi Gardens.'

'Whaat? No!'

'Just do what I say! Please! I have it all worked out,' said Malli. 'Keep going straight, then you'll take the next left turn. From now on, it's less complicated, believe me. There you go, that turn up ahead.'

Maddy slowed to take the turn onto Aurobindo Marg. Shortly thereafter, following her friend's instructions, she slowed to a complete halt by the side of the road. They were near a bus stop but far enough from it that the car would not be considered a hindrance to an arriving bus.

'Okay,' said Malli, 'now we exchange places. You scoot over to the left. Can you do it? Okay… and I'll get into the driver's seat.'

Maddy shoved her backpack onto the floor of the car and made the transition with a contortionist's skill. A moment later, they were both sitting in front, with Maddy panting from the effort.

'Oh, my,' said Maddy. 'I'm applying to be shorter in my next birth. *That* was a squeeze!'

'Great!' said Malli, 'but you're not done yet! See that green bag at the back?' She talked as she adjusted the seat to suit her own height, buckled herself in and prepared to pull away from the curb. 'Reach around and bring it forward. Inside the bag is a set of clothes for *you*. Meaning, Maddy. Between here and Lodhi Road, you'll transition back to your current self, complete with the wig. But you'll have to do most of it while the car is in motion, and at least the top part will have to be a real striptease at double-fast time!'

Maddy smiled. 'Not a problem for a boarding-school girl,' she said. 'We did that kind of crazy stuff all the time. Sneaking out of the school grounds at night and changing out of uniform in the back of a car!'

Two hours later, both women were seated in the leafy shade of the Garden Café Restaurant. It was open for business earlier than most places because the park was such a walkers' paradise for city residents as well as tourists.

They had both had their breakfasts and were now waiting for their coffees. They were sitting in the open-air section, and each was smoking her own brand of cigarette.

Maddy told Malli much of what had transpired the night before. She shared what Verity had said about her illness and what Russi had said about it. She kept back two items. One was the affair and the other was what Russi had said about being morally weak.

Malli had listened attentively. Now she was looking away, a thoughtful expression on her face. When she turned back to Maddy, she said, 'It sounds to me like they're...' Then she paused, nodded and continued, 'But no, you can't tell me. And I don't want to know.'

Maddy could see a distorted reflection of herself in a nearby plexiglass panel. She'd had time to settle her wig properly into place and now looked closer to her normal self, with dark shoulder-length hair framing her face, wearing a voluminous embroidered silk kurta the colour of sandalwood. Malli said that she'd bought it in anticipation of an incident of this type, choosing a loose tent-like style exactly because of the possibility that clothes might need to be switched around in whatever passed for a phone booth these days.

'I'm very lucky to have you as my friend, Malli,' said Maddy. 'Thank you.'

36

Slice the bread
Make your bed
Blood is red
Don't eat lead.

– JINXES, BIG & SMALL

When Maddy got back to the villa, she received a message asking her to come to Verity's bedroom. Maddy had never actually been in there. She entered warily, wondering why she'd been called in.

Verity was standing at the far end of the room, wearing a pink cotton kimono tied loosely at the waist. She was looking out through a gap between the gauzy white curtains that shielded the interior of the room from direct sunlight.

'Hello... Verity?' said Maddy.

'Hi,' said Verity, not looking around. 'Thanks for coming.' She turned around now. 'Sorry I didn't get in touch after yesterday's ride. I really enjoyed it. It meant a lot to me.'

Her voice was friendly, but she wasn't smiling.

The shaft of white light coming in through the gap in the curtains pierced through Verity's skin and caught in her hair, eyebrows and lashes, turning her translucent. From across the room, Maddy could see the creases, the fine lines and the pain – she was, for the first time since they'd met, noticeably unwell.

'I'm sorry,' she said again. Then she turned, and supporting herself on the wide arm of the cushioned cane chair right by where she stood, lowered herself into it. 'I'm so sorry. But I had a bad night, and now...'

She looked up to where Maddy had continued to stand by the door through which she'd entered. 'Please come in, Maddy. Please. Bring up a chair and...' She didn't complete the request because she needed to lean her forehead on the tips of her hand.

The room was similar in size to the studio on the other side of this floor where Maddy had spent her first night in the villa. It was austere but tasteful, as Maddy had come to expect of Verity. The decor was cream and bamboo, with small personal touches in the way of art and a hand-woven dhurrie on the floor. The single bed was queen-size with its head against the north wall, bookshelves framing it on either side, extending upwards.

The bed was unmade. It gave the impression that the pale cream sheets strewn in graceful disarray, the baby blue blanket that peeked up from underneath and the lace-trimmed pillows lying at jerky angles... all of *these* were aberrations because they would normally never be seen.

Over by the windows was another aberration – a pair of shiny steel cabinets, their upper surfaces covered in glinting, sharp-edged instruments, small glass bottles, and plastic daily-dispenser pillboxes. There was also, as part of this line-up, a ceramic planter from which a tiny patch of bright green grass poked up about five inches high. It drew attention to itself exactly because it was so incongruous, so fresh and insouciant, as it leaned towards the French windows, worshipping the light.

Maddy brought over a chair that was the twin of the one that Verity sat on. The only difference between the two was that this one's padding was covered in a Warli-style print, white on black, while Verity's was unbleached plain.

'Just give me a minute,' said Verity. Her face was turned away.

'Of course,' said Maddy. She wondered what the right thing for her to do was. She was neither a friend nor an employee. No mere guest either; she'd been drawn unwittingly into a very tight inner circle.

'It's the drugs,' said Verity, her head still turned away. 'They make me weak.' Maddy saw that she had reached into the pocket of her kimono and taken out a tissue. She dabbed at her cheeks. Then she turned her head and said, her eyelashes still wet, 'I don't usually cry much, but of late, that's all I seem to do!' The corners of her mouth lifted in the ghost of a smile.

You have every reason to cry, thought Maddy, but out loud she said, 'Everyone needs a good cry now and then, Verity!'

Verity nodded slowly. 'Yes... but this is not a good cry.' She looked up. 'It's an angry, wretched, pointless cry. It doesn't help me. It doesn't ease me in any way. Instead, it just reminds me of everything that's gone wrong – everything that I've *done* wrong and can't set right.'

Her gaze was steady now.

'Maddy, I know that I have no right to treat you as my confidant. And you have no obligation to accept that role either. But...' she took in a deep breath and looked away again, 'now that he's told you... which he *has*, hasn't he? About us?' She turned her pale eyes towards Maddy. They looked like searchlights.

'He told me what he felt about you,' said Maddy guardedly.

'Yes, but did he tell you what he thinks? About why you're here?'

Maddy felt the sands of loyalty shifting under her feet. Who was her employer, Russi or Verity? 'He told me that you are his soulmate. He used that word.'

'Did he tell you,' said Verity, 'that I don't trust him? That he thinks I want you to spy on him for me?'

'Yes,' said Maddy.

There. It was out now. Raw and bleeding, roadkill on the drawing room carpet.

Verity relaxed visibly. 'Okay,' she breathed out. 'Okay. Thank you for being honest with me.'

You're welcome, Maddy thought. *Except that's not all he said.*

'I felt sure he would. Even though I specifically asked him not to. I didn't want you to be dragged in. It's a terrible thing, a secret. It corrodes, it corrupts, it poisons the very thing it's supposed to protect. And this one isn't even yours.'

She stopped and composed herself before saying, 'Please feel free to ask me anything you might want to ask. You have a right to know. Without intending to be, you've become enmeshed. That's not how I wanted it, that's not what I—'

Maddy broke in, 'Verity, *stop*! Please.'

Verity closed her eyes.

'My friend, Malli, begged me to leave,' said Maddy. 'That first night I was here, and after I explained what had happened to my flat, she *ordered* me. To go to her home. To get out of what she believed was an... an... *unnatural* situation, I think was the word she used. But I didn't leave. That was my choice. That's how I see it. That's what I'm sticking with.'

Verity didn't say anything for several moments before wringing a word from herself, as if from a great depth, 'Not unnatural. *Unwholesome*.'

'No,' said Maddy. 'Let's not go down that path.'

Verity was looking away. 'But we must. That's at the heart of everything. Some actions are right, and some are... wrong. We make our choices. And I made mine. And it was the wrong one.'

'What you're doing is a waste of time,' said Maddy.

'No,' said Verity. 'It's the exact opposite. Making moral choices is what we were given brains for.' She paused. 'Are you religious, Maddy? I seem to recall that you said something about your schooling. Did you go to a convent?'

'Yes,' said Maddy. 'We – well, my parents – are Christian. But that doesn't mean that I'm a... I mean, I'm *not* a believer. When my brothers and I were little, we used to go to church, and I went to convent schools. But I stopped believing. A long time ago.'

Verity nodded. 'Yes, I remember now. You said that. I would say the same about myself, too. My father was an atheist, but my mother claimed to have faith. So we went to church and all of that when I was a child. I grew up in a small place, where everyone went to church, but it was social, you know? Faith Lite rather than Faith Xtra Strength. Then I went away to uni and became completely disenchanted with the whole, you know, the whole monstrosity of mass religion. The steam turbines of the Almighty. I hated all of it. Ran away from it. All the way to the East, to get away from it. Only to find it manifested in other forms. And also... also...' her voice faltered, '... to see the indelible stain of it in myself.'

She broke off and shook her head, frowning, tapping her forehead.

'But we were talking about something else. Unwholesomeness. You said "unnatural", and I said "unwholesome". The point I wanted to make is this: Nature is never unwholesome. Can't be. Nature is... *Nature*. Elemental. Beyond our ken. It's *we* who are outside of Nature. We stepped away. We made our own laws. So when we break them, we're only breaking what we made ourselves. Not God. Not Nature.'

'You don't have to...' Maddy tried to interrupt.

'Please, I need to finish my thought. Humans make choices. That's what we do, that's what we're trained to do from earliest childhood. Unlike the tiger that attacks honey gatherers in the forest, unlike the shrike impaling hedge sparrows on thorns, we make moral choices. That's our gift or our curse. I knew that the choice I made was the wrong one. Yet I made it anyway.'

She paused before saying in a clear, steady voice, as if reading from a catechism, 'The world to which I used to belong believed that an affair with a married man is a deep and unforgivable wrong. A sin. I thought that I had left those values and those harsh judgments behind me. But I haven't. I am not strong-minded enough. The poisoned dart of guilt is embedded too deep. And therefore, in my deepest heart, I believed

– and still believe – that it's wrong. For me to be with Russi. To love him and to accept his love. I believe that it's wrong and therefore—'

Maddy broke in again, more firmly this time. 'Verity, please! Punishing yourself isn't right either, don't you see? That's what I'm calling a waste of time. Forgive me for speaking plainly, Verity, but I just can't sit by watching someone whip themselves senseless for... for...' she forced herself to continue, 'for loving someone.'

Verity allowed herself a faint smile. 'Oh, of course, I *shouldn't* punish myself! I don't believe in punishment, and I don't want to punish myself. And yet, it's happened anyway, hasn't it?' She used both hands to indicate herself, her body. 'This disease. This hateful, cruel, wasting disease. Why has it lodged in me? Is it merely genetic roulette? My mother had it, and therefore, so do I? Is that all there is to it? Or is it my own value system turning in on me—'

Maddy exclaimed, 'No! Oh, *please* don't say that. Don't! It's ridiculous, it's so wrong, so pointless—'

'Okay, I'll stop. I'll stop. And anyway, this isn't why I called you in. I just wanted to explain that I... I'm going away. To the Tata Memorial Hospital. In Mumbai. Probably for two weeks.' Verity looked up. She was calm once more. 'And I'd like you to continue here, please. I'd really like that. In particular, I'd like you to be here when I get back.'

Maddy felt Malli's spectral presence tapping her on the shoulder. Heard her voice say, *Here it comes. The soft command. The demand that cannot be denied.*

'Yes, of course,' said Maddy. 'I'll be here.'

'And I want you to know, explicitly, that I do *not* want you to spy on Russi for me. Never mind what he said, what he thinks, what he perhaps fears. That never was my intention. Never. I do not want to hear about whatever might happen in the car or outside it when I am away. I do not fear his indiscretions.' She glanced up at Maddy, a faint smile clinging once more to her lips. 'Because I am indiscretion incarnate.'

37

Please be nice
And break some ice
Cook the rice
And boil it twice.

– JINXES, BIG & SMALL

Verity left for Mumbai the next day. She was accompanied by two close friends. The three of them went to the airport in Chetak's car, with his driver.

The reason it wasn't Maddy who took them was that Russi had a reception to attend at the French Embassy that night. He had asked for Maddy to be his driver, saying that he needed the car at 8.30 p.m.

As before, Chetak let her into the library. This time, he escorted her through to 'her' side of the house, unlocking the gate in the trellis so that she could wheel her bicycle through the garden and bring it around to Russi's entrance.

While they were in the house, Chetak seemed preoccupied, and that suited Maddy. There was too much to say, and some of it couldn't be said.

They shared a cigarette as they waited for Russi to come out, passing it back and forth companionably. It had been Maddy's idea; she said she didn't want to smoke a whole one, and she asked him if he wouldn't mind. Smokers' etiquette gave her the right to ask and him the right to refuse. He chose to accept.

In the stillness of the evening, with mosquitoes pinging in their ears, Chetak said, 'Did Verity say anything about what you should do while she's away?'

'Only that she'd like me to stay.'

Chetak had just taken a drag. He released a narrow stream of smoke before saying, 'Do you have any plans?'

'Well,' said Maddy, 'I was thinking that maybe I should use this time to catch up with some of my former clients. They've been leaving messages and asking for rides.'

He smiled. 'That must feel nice! To be in demand.' He passed the cigarette back to her. 'What have you been telling them?'

'My phone's "away" message says that I'm busy till the middle of the month, but yes,' she smiled in return, 'I'm looking forward to doing something...' she almost said *normal*, 'familiar once more.' She took a drag. The faint wetness on the filter was from his mouth. She was conscious of the intimacy implied by this sharing. She wondered if two men normally shared cigarettes in this way. If it meant anything.

'Change of subject,' said Chetak. 'Your case is coming up. Tomorrow, in fact.'

'Really!' Once again, she was amazed that it was moving along so fast.

'I was wondering if you wanted to come. To court.'

She handed the cigarette back. 'Wow. That's...' She didn't know what to say.

'You don't have to decide right this minute. I'll call you in the morning. It'll be early, of course, and you'll have all the rigmarole of getting here, changing over...'

'I think I can manage that part but...' She reached into her pocket for the breath mints. 'I'll message you tonight – thanks, no, I'm done,' she meant the cigarette, '– depending on how late it'll be tonight.'

'Oh, it'll be late! For sure. He likes to party. I hope you've eaten? Okay, well, see how you feel. The hearing might get cancelled if the other side wants to delay. Oh! Here he comes now.'

The front door opened, and both of them moved forward. Russi was standing in the doorway but had turned away and was talking to someone behind him. Undoubtedly Suresh.

'Remember,' said Chetak as he stubbed out his cigarette underfoot, 'he'll want to sit in front.'

'Should I assume that right away? Or let him choose?' They were both speaking very softly.

'Let him choose,' said Chetak. 'Always let him choose.' They were by the side of the car now, lurking near the rear. Russi was still standing at the open door. His phone had rung, and he glanced over at the two of them before deciding to take the call, waving the lit phone in the air momentarily before pressing it to his ear.

'And, Maddy?' Chetak was frowning and biting his lips but looking away from her and speaking in a conspiratorial whisper now. 'Don't be surprised if he has other passengers in the car with him on the way home.'

'Huh?' said Maddy.

Chetak nodded but continued as if she hadn't spoken, 'Don't let him bully you. Okay, he's done now.'

He raised his head towards Russi, whose face was still lit by the phone's blue glare as he thumbed it off. 'Goodnight, sir!' called Chetak. 'See you in the morning!'

Then he turned and hurried away to his car, which was also parked in the driveway.

38

Full swing
Half swung
Quartering
Done.

– JINXES, BIG & SMALL

Russi sat in the back of the car. Aside from acknowledging Maddy as he got in, he did not exchange any words with her. Nor did he turn on the reading light. Instead, he seemed distracted, searching in his pockets for something. He then found his phone, and when he had it out, began scrolling, his face lit by the screen.

Maddy started towards the gate but looked up in the rear-view mirror to say, 'Where to, sir?'

Russi raised his head with a surprised jerk. 'It's a reception at the French... uh... it's not the embassy… but… Chetak must've told you? Somewhere else… oh, here… the card…' He leaned forward to hand the white envelope to Maddy. 'What does it say there?'

Maddy stopped and turned on the overhead light. The address was along Amrita Shergill Lane. The residence of one of the consular officers. She turned off the light and handed the card back. 'Thank you, sir. I know where that is.'

'Good, good,' said Russi. 'We have plenty of time. Best not to arrive too early.' Then he got on the phone. Ringing. Ringing. Ringing. Then the robotic squawk of a voicemail prompt inviting him to leave a message.

Russi ended the call without responding.

Maddy turned the car north and left, towards Aurobindo Marg, nosing her way through the narrow roads around Hauz Khas Market. It was 8.45 p.m. and a weeknight. The traffic had not yet started to thin out.

Russi asked, his voice tense, 'Has she spoken to you? Since she got to Mumbai?'

'No, sir,' said Maddy. She could have asked for context but decided against it.

'Hasn't called, hasn't sent any message,' muttered Russi. He was looking out of the window at nothing in particular, his eyes magnified by the thick lenses of his spectacles.

Maddy considered saying something comforting but decided against this, too. She did not want to initiate a conversation.

He went silent, alternately staring out of the window and at his phone. Soft beeps and dings signalled incoming messages, but he ignored them after an initial glance.

Half an hour later, they were turning onto Lodhi Road. As they entered the quiet, dimly lit environs of Amrita Shergill Lane, the phone rang.

'Ah!' said Russi. His face lit up like a child receiving his first tricycle at Christmas. Holding up the phone's bright screen in triumph, he said, 'Just in time!'

He tapped the instrument while saying to Maddy in an excited voice, 'Please find some parking, huh? Anywhere, anywhere – it doesn't matter.' Then he was on the phone, speaking in a voice so different, so gentle and hushed, he might have been a teenage girl talking to her first love. 'My darling, where have you been? Are you all right? I've been...'

Fortunately, the lane was wide enough and the properties along one side of it so generously proportioned as to offer plenty of space between entrance gates. There were no other cars present on the road. Maddy came to a quick halt, then leapt out to open the door for her employer. But he had already opened his door and was starting to get out. Glancing at her, he signalled with his free hand that she was to remain in the car.

She got back inside. The cool interior was like a universe apart from the instant sauna outdoors. She listened to the sounds the powerful beast made as it idled – a low purr. After the hurly-burly of the traffic, the lane seemed unnaturally quiet. She had parked in the relative twilight between two street lights. Russi had stepped onto the cemented footpath and was trotting back and forth as he talked, a few steps this way and that, as if he couldn't contain the motion. She could see his hand and the side of his face illuminated by the light from the screen. He was still smiling.

The green hands of the clock on the dashboard read 9.15. Still fairly early by the standards of the capital. A few minutes later, Russi tapped on the window, then briskly opened the door of the car for himself and got inside.

'*Chalo*,' he said, 'let's go.' He was bright with fresh energy, like a lamp with a new bulb. 'I spoke to her. She sounded tired but said she had a good meeting with her doctor. She'll tell me more later.'

'Good to know that, sir,' said Maddy as she left the curb.

Golden light spilled from the marble-fronted building. Maddy followed another car onto the pebbled driveway.

A white-gloved valet awaited them at the steps.

He opened the door to Russi, who got out and immediately tapped on Maddy's window. When she lowered it, he said, 'I'll call you on the phone, huh? Or maybe this nice young man,' he patted the valet on the shoulder, 'will come looking for you. I'll give him the car number. And be sure to eat something, huh? I'm told they put on a nice spread here.'

The next moment, he had turned and jogged up the shallow steps towards the man waiting by the open door of the residence.

Maddy caught a glimpse of the glittering interior as the valet bent to look in at her window. He gestured to her to go forward and then turn right. He looked more like a teenage boy than an adult in his smart all-black uniform, buttoned to the collar. Perhaps the son of one of the live-in staff? He even wore a little cap on his head, stiff and circular, with a thin gold braid defining the rim. Maddy nodded and raised her window.

The pebbled driveway curved back towards the gate, but a stone-flagged path led away at right angles around the outspread wing of the building and on towards the rear. It was a huge property. The parking area was at the far end. As she went towards it, Maddy could see, on her right, that the rear of the residence opened onto a mini courtyard. Trestle tables and folding chairs had been set up under bright overhead lights. A pair of tall swing doors were in constant motion as two waiters bustled in and out of the kitchen.

Maddy followed the red tail lights of the car that had preceded her. Its blue license plate told her that it belonged to an embassy, but she didn't know the codes and couldn't tell which one it was.

There was another valet in the parking area, equally young but not wearing the little cap. He bent to speak to the driver of the car ahead. As that car moved off, he motioned to Maddy to come up to where he stood. Bending towards her window as she lowered it, he barked, 'Car number?' He spoke in a rough, impersonal tone, with an edge of insolence. 'Owner name? Driver name?' In his hand, he had a small notebook into which he was entering the information. She could see, from the movement of his pencil, that he wrote in a hasty scrawl. She wondered how or if he could ever read back his own notations.

She followed the direction of his outstretched arm. Her headlights swept the rear ends of eight or nine other cars plus a couple of drivers, who happened to be standing near their own vehicles, before turning towards a bare patch. The stone-flagged surface gave way to bare earth and grass. The big car lurched this way and that before coming to a halt.

She waited a moment or two before switching off. In the ensuing silence and darkness, she reached down to where she had stowed a few essentials in a detachable pouch that was part of her backpack and got out a tube of Odomos. She began smearing it on her face and ears, thinking about the options ahead of her.

It was cool inside the car, but it would, of course, soon heat up. Glancing around, she could see a scattering of red tail lights. Some of the other drivers were cocooned within their air-conditioned cars. Some employers objected and others didn't care either way. She didn't know what Russi's position was and hadn't thought to ask.

It was a few minutes past 9.30 p.m. She couldn't know what exactly was meant by 'very late'. 12.30? 2 a.m.? She'd brought a sandwich back with her from the Garden Restaurant. She planned to eat that for dinner, plus she had two bottles of water. Of course, if she drank the water, she'd need to pee.

Come to think of it, she wouldn't mind taking a leak right away.

She looked around again. The car closest to her was the one she'd followed out to the parking area. It was to her left, a comfortable metre away. Its tail lights were off; that could mean that the driver was either in the car with the air conditioning off or that he'd left the car and was wandering about. She could see a number of figures silhouetted against the lighted area around the kitchen's back entrance.

Getting out, she stretched, then fished inside her pockets for cigarettes. She waited for the overhead light inside the car to turn itself off. Now she looked around again. The front of the car was close to the boundary hedge of the property, with thin grass underfoot and the branches of tall trees – neem, perhaps? – arching overhead. It was a dark night, with no moon. Insects chirred and droned, and the heat held her tight in its steamy fist.

She didn't really need to pee, but then again, why not get it over with?

She stepped towards the front of the car. She felt the impersonal, mechanical heat pouring out of its front grille. Looking around again, just to confirm that there was no one close by, she put her cigarettes down on the hood, then went into a crouch as she unzipped.

It was the sheer thrill of doing it that had motivated her. Out in the open, under the stars, into the grass of the back lawn of a consular residence! *So cool,* she thought, grinning to herself. *There is some corner of a local field that is forever Maddy's uric salts...*

'And what are we doing down there?' came a deep voice.

The words were like a physical blow. Maddy almost lost her balance.

'Wh-what?' she said, then coughed, remembering to maintain her voice at a lower register. She clung to the grille of the Jag to stop herself from toppling over. She hadn't quite finished peeing. The little pipe had to be shaken to clear it completely. Then she straightened up and looked around.

Leaning over the hood of her car on the driver's side was the dark shape of a tall man. She couldn't see anything of him aside from the silhouette of his shoulders and head. He wore a uniform but no hat.

'There's only two reasons that a man needs to be crouching down in the dark,' said the man. 'One is to take a crap. Which you're not doing because I don't see your bum. So it must be the other reason. Which is...' He didn't complete his remark.

Maddy had recovered her wits. 'I'm doing what everyone's got to do,' she said as she tucked away the pipe and began to stand up, zipping up as she went. An expertly executed manoeuvre, she thought. 'What's it to you?'

The man was standing against the light, so she could not see his face, but there was a flash of white as he grinned. He had good teeth. 'Just checking.'

'On what?' she asked. Her voice was breathy, and her heart was still pounding hard.

'Well,' he said, reaching for the pack of cigarettes she'd left on the hood of the car as he spoke, 'I notice a young fellow get out of his car, stand up and stretch. And then, instead of going towards that heavenly dinner over there, what does he do? He gets in front of his car and... vanishes!'

He opened the pack, held it to his nose and took a deep sniff.

'So I say to myself, this is very strange. Perhaps he has stepped on a scorpion and has fallen down in a faint. After all, even in heaven, there must be a scorpion or two. Perhaps he has had the misfortune of encountering one. Who can say? And what am I to do? So I decide to take a look.'

Now he tapped the packet to encourage a cigarette to emerge.

'That's when I find the young fellow crouching down in the grass. Just like that. As if he has something to hide. But what can it be? After all, if he needs to go to the toilet, there's a fine one back there. Anyone of us here knows where it is. All he has to do is ask.'

The unnamed man put the cigarette in his mouth, and producing a matchbook from the palm of his hand, lit it with a sharp crack. In the sudden flare, Maddy saw his face: sharp-featured, with a thin moustache. Long black eyebrows, a broad, clear brow, tobacco-brown skin.

Handsome, she thought.

39

Bite the bullets
Saw the guns
End the fighting
Have some fun.

– JINXES, BIG & SMALL

They continued to stand in the dark, talking and smoking. His name was Preet, Maddy learned. He was part-owner of a fleet of taxis. He also worked late-night gigs as a driver for the Austrian Embassy.

'Austria!' said Maddy. 'Wow.'

'You even know where that is?' said the man.

Maddy said, 'Of course. It's a big island. On the other side of the world.'

Preet began to laugh. A low, wheezy sound, a smoker's laugh.

'What are you laughing about?'

'I didn't say *Australia*! I said *Austria*! What a dummy. Australia is way over on the other side of the world, as you say. But Austria is much closer. In Europe. Next to Germany and also France.'

Maddy said, 'Oh. Okay, I didn't know that.'

'Never mind,' said Preet as he finished his cigarette, dropped it in the grass and ground it under his heel. 'It doesn't matter. How about getting something to eat? The food's really good, and there's always lots of it. Or maybe you've been here before?'

'No,' said Maddy. She looked towards the oasis of light, where other drivers could be seen milling about. The little courtyard was very well-lit. It would not be smart to expose herself to scrutiny at close quarters. 'I don't know. I brought some food with me.'

'Arré, forget your baby food from home!' he teased. 'Who made it, your mother? Your wife?'

'Huh! Of course not,' began Maddy, then checked herself. 'I'm not living at home. I'm not married.'

'All the more reason, then, to have some real food!' He paused, then said in a consciously provocative voice again, 'Or maybe pretty boys like you don't actually need to eat? Is that the problem?'

Maddy felt a peculiar thump behind her navel. It had been a very long time since anyone had called her pretty. *Stop it!* she told herself, *Stop this now!* But she did not stop. 'Fine,' she heard herself say. 'I'll try it.'

They walked over. Maddy felt as if the more rational, practical person she thought of as 'herself' had separated from her body and was now hovering anxiously a few feet away, wringing her hands. The person she now was, this daring adventuress, walked as if an inch or two off the springy grass underfoot.

Preet walked a little ahead of her. He was the same height as she was, though his hair perhaps gave him an extra inch. His back was ramrod straight. He walked with an easy, cat-like stride, neither energetic nor relaxed. As if he was on continuous high alert.

The lit-up area had been arranged as a small-scale buffet. There were at least a dozen young men present, all wearing uniforms of one sort or another. By the time Maddy and Preet got there, the others had already helped themselves. Most were eating where they stood, with the plastic plates held close to their mouths and an expression of blank concentration on their faces. A couple were seated at one of the trestle tables, hunched over their food.

The kitchen staff was no longer buzzing back and forth but could be seen behind the swing doors, which were half-glazed, moving around in the busy kitchen.

'You've never been to one of these places before?' asked Preet as he headed to where there was a stack of plates.

'Not really,' said Maddy. She didn't want to lie outright. 'Not to this address.'

'You pick up one of these plates, and then you can help yourself to anything from any of those pots.'

He pointed to the steel vessels that had been set out in a row, each with its own giant ladle. Each one bore the logo of the Taj group of hotels. Unlike at a typical buffet in a hotel, there were no chaffing dishes underneath, but there were labels identifying the contents: rice; dal; cauliflower korma; mutton korma; roti; dahi.

The labels were in English. Maddy was fairly sure that no one present spoke much English, except to get by. But maybe it made sense when a good half of all the men present appeared to be from states other than Delhi. Based purely on their build, their smooth cheeks and spiky hair, she thought she identified several of them as being from the hills rather than the North Indian plains.

'Okay,' she said in response to Preet's guidance.

'I hope you're not veg,' he said as he began loading his plate. 'Because their mutton curry is the best. Believe me. I've been here at least six times already this year. And it's always good.'

'Non-veg,' said Maddy, trying not to stare openly at the others around her. She didn't think she could bolt her food in the same concentrated manner as all the other diners present. At the same time, she asked herself, *So what? Why does it matter? Who's going to care, and even if they did, why should it matter to me?* She swatted her thoughts away, trying to remain focused on the present.

Preet had helped himself to a thick wad of parathas, a knobby hillock of mutton curry, an equally knobby hillock of the cauliflower, and then, picking up a stainless-steel cup, he filled it to the brim with dahi. He picked up a flat stainless-steel teaspoon from a plastic tray full of utensils and looked around to see how she was doing.

'I... I'll follow. Just give me a minute,' said Maddy. She took a heaped portion of the rice, poured the mutton gravy over it and then a bit of the dal. She wanted to conceal the fact that she couldn't put away as much food as the others were doing by eating rice rather than solid chunks of meat.

Preet had walked a short distance from the buffet table and was facing away from the courtyard. Holding the plate close to his face with his left hand, he began shovelling the food into his mouth, using his right hand. It was a controlled movement as he delivered each mouthful with a precisely repeated jerk. He would stop briefly to chew on a piece of meat, or to remove a piece of bone or gristle, before continuing with the delivery of one mouthful after the other.

Maddy struggled to follow this approach. She'd had some experience of eating with her hands as a small child, but once she and her family were living in the US, cutlery was the norm. It had been many years since she'd eaten a whole meal with her hands. Certainly never at such speed.

But Preet paid no attention to her. He ended his meal by picking up the cup of dahi and finishing the last dregs of it with a loud slurping sound.

Only now did he look around at her. He saw that her plate was still full and gave a small, amused shake of his head. 'What a slowpoke!'

He didn't wait for her to finish. Going over to a tall blue plastic bin at the end of the buffet table, he slung his plate, the dahi bowl and teaspoon in, then immediately picked up a plastic bottle filled with water. He went over to the side of the courtyard and briskly rinsed his mouth and hands, then ended by drinking what remained of the water.

While his back was turned, Maddy disposed of her plate with whatever was left in it in the blue bin, then followed suit with the hand-washing and mouth-rinsing, though she did not drink the water, guessing that it was ordinary tap water filled into generic plastic bottles.

He looked around to see her wiping her face with her handkerchief, just like him. 'Not bad!' he now said. 'You managed to finish after all!' He belched, then smiled. 'So? What d'you think?' He didn't wait for her to answer. 'Good, huh?'

'Great,' she agreed, glad to be facing away from the light as she answered. 'I don't think I've eaten such a big meal in a long time.' Which was the truth.

'And that's not all,' he said. 'Stay right here. I'll bring you something that I bet you'll like.'

He went back to the buffet tables, and when he came back, she saw that he'd brought two pink plastic bowls, each with a golf-ball-sized gulab jamun in it, swimming in syrup. No spoon, however.

Maddy made big eyes. 'Wah! I've never even seen them that size.' But she pushed it away. 'Please. I can't. I've eaten too much already.'

He made it clear that he thought she was out of her mind. He gave her one of the bowls to hold while he picked up the dark brown sphere with the tips of his fingers, squeezed it and wolfed it down. Then he drank the syrup, reached for the bowl in Maddy's hand and polished that one off, too.

When he'd washed his hands once more, they walked back towards their cars in satisfied silence. The night air was as heavy as an army-issue blanket. Even the mosquitoes seemed to have given up.

The other drivers had scattered. A small knot of men was standing near their cars, identifiable as individuals only by the discrete glow of their cigarettes. Small fireflies of companionship.

'You said you've been to this address many times?' asked Maddy.

'Oh, yes,' said Preet. 'My boss is good friends with the man who lives here. Consulate-wallahs. They have parties where they spend the whole evening playing cards. Not ordinary betting games like we play but something different. One of the bearers from the kitchen let us look inside once. Just from inside the kitchen, through the half-glass. The door of the dining room was wide open, and beyond it, in the big hall, they're all sitting at tables and playing. Four people to a table, everyone dressed up and laughing. In their hands, the cards flashing and glittering. New packs, the bearer told us! They only use new packs at these parties. And ladies, too, playing together with their men. Such a sight!'

They neared their cars.

'Not bad, your car,' said Preet, 'Jaguar. Boss had one before, but he exchanged it for a BMW.' The English alphabets sounded exotic in his mouth. 'Wah.' The reverence in his voice could not be faked. 'What a beauty she is. Driving her is like... you can't imagine. I can't describe it.'

His use of the female pronoun for a car was very natural, thought Maddy with surprise. The word in Hindi was feminine, too.

The air was no longer just heavy. It was becoming difficult to breathe.

It wasn't just the air, Maddy knew.

They had come to a halt. Preet gave his car an electronic tap on its shoulder with his key fob. The cat-like red eyes blinked on with a seductive chirp. He grinned in the cherry light, his teeth turning pink. 'Isn't she sweet? Even her voice is like a bird.'

'Oh, I don't know,' said Maddy, struggling to repress her irregular breathing. It was as if she'd been walking briskly uphill. Her heart was pounding. The top of her head was tingling. 'All these cars are equally special, really. Anyway, that's what I think.'

'Huh,' said Preet. 'You'll change your mind once you sit inside.'

There was a pulse of silence.

'Want to try?' he said.

Maddy heard herself answer, 'I'm sure your boss will not approve.'

Preet responded with, 'Who's going to tell him?'

Then he opened the rear door behind the driver's seat. She folded herself down and slid inside. The air inside the car was still crisp.

He opened the driver's door, leaned in to turn on the air conditioning, then returned to the passenger door and folded himself into the seat. He still had the key fob in his hand, and with another soft musical tone, he turned off all but a single dimple of light low on the control panel in front.

He turned to her.

He reached for her head with both hands, pulled her close and crushed her mouth with his. Maddy parted her teeth, and his tongue entered her mouth. It was thick with spices from the meal, the sweet scent of the gulab jamun and the dark tang of tobacco underlying it all.

Whatever plan he might have had, she had already decided what hers must be.

He held her tight against his chest with his arms around her shoulders. There was a roaring sound in her ears, in her mind. Only her left hand was free. With this, she reached down to his crotch. Found the hard, curving bump there. And rubbed it with a confident upward stroke.

A jolt of lightning shocked through both of them.

He gave a strangled cry.

Then it was over, and his head was on her shoulder, heaving and gasping for breath.

40

Save your bet!
Just get wet!
You're all set!
Have we met?

— JINXES, BIG & SMALL

They both got out, and he walked away quickly, not saying anything. He went towards the lighted courtyard. Maddy assumed that the toilet he'd mentioned must be somewhere there.

He took a while to return.

Maddy went to her car, opened the driver's side door and got out her water. She washed out her mouth, then took a long, grateful draught. It was still cool. She splashed her face and wiped it dry once again with her handkerchief.

Then she went back to where she had been, standing by the Beamer.

She lit a cigarette.

If anyone had asked her what she was thinking or how she felt at that precise moment, she would have had to shake her head mutely, unable to speak. Her throat was clogged tight. She would have liked to cry or scream or even laugh, but there was no question of any of that.

What do I feel, what do I feel! The thoughts went chasing around in her mind, but really, there were no words. The entire exchange, the event, had been entirely of *the body*. Two bodies had experienced a violent storm, and then, just as suddenly, it was over.

She could not have said what had happened to her. It wasn't... she refused to say the word even in the fortress of her mind... it wasn't *that*. But it was something. Nameless. Neither good nor bad. Her body was still in the grip of that bolt of energy, though now powering down, like her car when it ticked down to stillness after she turned it off.

By the time she saw the dark shape of Preet's figure returning, she was almost relaxed. Her skin was no longer burning as if with a fever.

She saw him glance at his phone, which reminded her to look at hers as well.

It was a few minutes past eleven.

As he approached her, Preet said, 'It won't be much longer now.' He cleared his throat, then hawked, turned his head to the side and spat. 'Boss usually likes to start for home around eleven-thirty.' His voice, though noticeably deeper and gruffer than it had been, did not in any other way sound as if anything out of the ordinary had occurred between them.

Maddy said, 'My boss said he would be late, but I don't actually know how late is late for him.' She paused before adding, 'I haven't been with him for very long.'

'Hmmm,' said Preet. He had also lit a cigarette, but it was one of his own now. Not a cigarette at all, but a bidi. Its harsh scent was like a snaggle-toothed blade, carving jagged shapes inside the nasal passages of anyone within range of it. 'Yes, I was thinking that.'

'Really?' said Maddy. She dropped her cigarette in the grass and stepped forward onto its red glow.

'Just the impression I got. It seemed to me that you are uncertain of yourself.'

'I've only been with him a week,' said Maddy.

'It's not the job,' said Preet. 'It's you.'

Maddy's heart began to pound once more. 'What d'you mean?'

'You're not really a driver, are you?'

'I am,' said Maddy, her voice steady. Her heart was so loud, she thought it must surely be audible from five metres away.

Preet turned his head to his right, took a drag, held it, breathed out, then turned back to look at her once more. 'What can I tell you? Something about you is different. I don't know what it is. It's just something I feel.' He tapped his chest. 'I feel it *here*.' Then he tapped the car. 'It's not because of what happened in there. Don't get me wrong. Those things happen. We take what we get. Then we let go. I'm not talking about that.'

'Okay,' said Maddy. She certainly wasn't going to give him any clues.

A furious yapping sound, like a Pomeranian in the final stages of a hysterical meltdown, erupted from the phone in Preet's hand. 'There we go,' he said. 'That's my boss.'

He took the call. 'Hallo?' he said, his voice altered with automatic deference, followed by the contralto growl of the other man's voice. She couldn't hear what he said. 'Ji, sir. Ji,' answered Preet. He reached for the door in the same instant that Maddy moved aside. 'Right now. Yessir, yes. Thank you, sir.'

He slid into the car; the lights came on and the engine hummed. In the final second before he shut the door, he looked straight up at Maddy and said, 'Ninety-eight, twenty-seven, twenty-seven, sixty-four, fifty-eight.'

Then he was gone in a grand churning of tyres and cherry-red light.

Russi called for Maddy twenty minutes later. By the time she had brought the car around to the front steps of the residence, the party had spilled out onto the steps. Shrieking laughter, coloured lights and riffs of music ebbed and flowed as fifteen or twenty people, men and women, stood glittering and jittering out there on the steps. Their chariots drew up one by one to collect them.

She spotted Russi in his midnight blue suit, leaning out, looking for her. Two young women were leaning out with him or else on one another as they teetered together on the steps. They wore identical neon pink stiletto heels. One wore her hair in a curly bush while the other had let hers slide down her back in a silken reddish-brown tide. Shiny black dresses sheathed their slender bodies like cling film and aluminium foil combined.

Russi waved to acknowledge Maddy. The moment she had drawn up and stopped, quick-quick, as if in the greatest hurry to accomplish the task, he nipped around the front of his car and over to the passenger seat even as Maddy leapt out of her side. 'These young girls will come with us, huh?' he cried just before ducking inside. Then from inside, 'We're giving them a lift home.'

Maddy wasn't quick enough, however, to open the door for them. The valet had got there first. Both women were snuffling, giggling and tossing their hair as they got in. The young valet with his ridiculous pillbox hat ogled them openly, particularly as one of them seemed to have trouble retracting the glistening tentacle of one of her limbs. It remained for what seemed like an entire minute, shimmering within its sheer silver stocking, dangling outside the car as if it had a life of its own while its owner struggled to rein it in.

When the valet was finally able to shut the door, he threw a glance up at Maddy, who had remained standing by her own door. An expression of such complicity and mischief had appeared on his face that she could not avoid allowing a tiny smile to flicker across her face.

Maddy slipped into her seat. The instant she was inside, she became a stern, peak-capped drill master whose job it was to interrupt the party in progress between the rear and the front seat. Russi was backed up against his door, turned towards the rear with a happy grin on his broad face. The two girls, both emitting incoherent squeals and exclamations, were squashed together in the space between the two front seats, their arms extending forward and around him as if they had become a single two-headed four-armed entity.

'Where to, sir?' said Maddy, in her drill master's role, as she eased the car forward.

'Come on, girls, come on now, better sit back, huh? Sit back, sit back now.'

'Oh... whyyyyyyy!' both girls chorused like a pair of cartoon mice. 'We're having so much funnnnn!'

'Or-or-or…' stammered Russi in a delighted chortle, 'you'll annoy my… my-my driver!' At this, he turned to glance at Maddy before returning to his guest passengers. 'Please now, come on, come on. He needs to know where to go.'

Maddy had reached the gate by now. She had to make a decision right away, so she turned towards Lodhi Road.

She was wearing her cap and was grateful for the way it shaded the top half of her face. Her cheeks were burning, and the back of her neck was prickling. She was consumed with several different wave fronts of embarrassment, each one clashing and bumping up against the other.

One wave was for being in her position, and specifically, for being a *woman* in her position. For being privy to the kind of behaviour that would normally never take place in her presence. She was embarrassed for the girls, for what they exposed of themselves, for the naked vocabulary of their flirtatious behaviour.

But another wave was for herself. She was judging these young women and their unbridled antics. She was reacting with squirming distaste towards them. And in that very instant, she keenly disapproved of her own distaste. She hated to see it in herself. She couldn't explain it, she couldn't condone it, and yet, *there it was*. Absolute and inexplicable.

There was one more wave front, a final one, on behalf of Verity. Had she been present at the party, none of this would be happening. No question about it. And yet, the fact that it was happening not even a day after her departure told Maddy that this was the norm. This was what had always happened, and always would happen, in her absence.

Did this mean that she, Maddy, really did have a role to play? Not as Verity's spy, because she'd been specifically requested not to do that. But as a kind of full-size Jiminy Cricket, a conscience for a man who had openly confessed to her that he was weak, and that, in effect, he needed saving from himself.

Stop, she told herself. *Stop*.

Needless to say, there was one further item for her to consider, wasn't there? Oh, yes, there was. One more. It wasn't a wave front of anything. Instead, it was something that had managed to slip away from the centre of her thoughts even though it was hugely more urgent than any of these other topics. And of course, much more personal.

What was that thought? Ah, yes, it had a name. Preet. That was its name.

Out loud, she said, 'Sir?' They were approaching the turning where they would have to make a decision about which way to go on Lodhi Road.

Russi, who had somehow managed to wrest control of the situation, now said to Maddy in a steady, sober voice, 'Jor Bagh, dear, Jor Bagh. It's very close by.'

Hoots of laughter sprayed out from the back seat. 'He... he... he calls his driver *dear*!' screamed both girls in unison. 'Oh, my god, if I laugh any more, I'm going to die!' said one.

Maddy had not tried to distinguish between the voices, but the other one now said, 'If *I* laugh any more, I'm going to pee! I swear, I swear, don't make me laugh, don't!'

Fifteen minutes later, both women had been deposited on the sidewalk outside a high-walled residence that the curly-haired one said was her aunt's house, where she was a guest for the week. Maddy had opened the door for them with Russi remaining in place in front.

By the time Maddy got back into the car, Russi had subsided into a silence so complete it was as if he'd fallen into a deep sleep or a faint. But it was neither. He was sitting up, Maddy noticed, his face turned towards the window.

She turned the car onto the main road and aimed it south. She could see the regular twitch of movement as he blinked.

'Home, sir?' she asked, wanting to return to familiar ground.

'Obviously,' he retorted, not turning. 'At this time, where else will I go?'

She couldn't tell if he was joking or irritated.

She turned once again, and in a few moments, they were on Aurobindo Marg.

The giant avenue was virtually empty, except for the trucks that would continue their headlong racing all night long.

In under ten minutes, they were turning into the front entrance of the villa.

No words had passed between Maddy and Russi during the trip.

As soon as they halted, Russi said, as Maddy automatically unclicked her seat belt, 'Just wait a bit, dear? Just wait a bit. If you don't mind.'

Maddy sat back in her seat. Her mind was blank.

'It's very late,' said Russi. 'How are you getting back to... your place? Where is it, that place? Close by?'

'I have my bicycle, sir,' said Maddy. She was looking straight ahead, her hands on the steering wheel.

Russi glanced at her, startled, and said, 'Oh, come on now! You can drop that "sir"!'

She said nothing.

Now he turned away again. In a changed tone, he said, 'All right. You've seen me now. You've seen that side of me.'

Maddy opened her mouth as if she might say something but didn't. She knew he was looking at her and might understand that she was deliberately choosing to remain silent.

'What are you going to tell her?'

'Nothing, sir,' said Maddy at once. She had thought this through.

He looked at her again, this time with a shrewd, measuring expression. She could see him reflected in the windscreen. 'Really. Nothing? You'd tell a lie? For me?'

Then he said, without waiting for her to reply, 'Or is *this* the lie, and you'll tell her the truth?' He had a half-smile on his face. It could have been crooked or mischievous.

Maddy drew in a breath. 'The truth is, sir, there's nothing to say. Nothing happened.' Then she relented and dropped her pose. She turned her face towards him. 'Verity did *not* ask me to be a spy, sir. Truly, she did not. And anyway, if she had, I would have refused to do it. I don't want to be that. Not for her, not for you.'

There was silence as Russi contemplated her. She looked away, maintaining a stony-faced composure.

Finally, he said, 'You're a very interesting woman, you know that?'

She frowned very slightly and shrugged very slightly.

'I don't suppose you'd like to come in for a drink, huh?'

'No, sir, but thank you, sir,' she said.

She saw him smile then.

'Chalo,' he said. 'Good night, dear. And thank you. You're an excellent driver.'

He got out of the car, waved aside her assistance, went into the house, and a moment later, the porch light went off.

41

Hold your horses
Wait a while
Pace yourself
And walk a mile.

– JINXES, BIG & SMALL

The buzzing of her phone woke Maddy up. She turned on her side, registering the dense heat and the blind darkness of her room as she squinted at her phone's screen: 6.15 a.m.

Chetak: *Are you up?*

Maddy: *Not really.*

Chetak: *Meet you in 20 minutes?*

Maddy: *Can it be 30?*

Chetak: *Yes. Parking area.*

She remembered now that he'd mentioned the possibility of an early morning meeting. She continued lying on her side, wincing at the thought of sitting up. Her body didn't approve of the hard floor, the rush mat, the inflatable pillow and the thick air. Especially the air – the way it lay on her skin, the way it pressed her down, reminding her many times over of the bizarre anomaly of her situation and her choices.

But at least no mosquitoes.

She had brought a net with her, which she'd found in the back of the almirah in her room at the villa. It had been patched many times and was old and worn, but for that reason, had lost all its stiffness and fit easily into her backpack. Setting it up had been a struggle. She used her backpack and the morra as north and south termini to drape the two extremities of the net. The result was a sagging, narrow, tube-like space. She had wriggled under the thin protection thus afforded. Then she lay there, exhausted by her efforts but grinning in the dark at the tiny predators pinging and whining in frustration a few inches away from her skin.

Chetak's car was rounding the corner as Maddy hurried towards the rendezvous point. He stopped to let her in, then drove off at once.

'The hearing's been postponed,' he said. 'No surprise.'

'You'd been expecting that,' said Maddy.

'Yes and no,' he said as they paused for the light to change at the end of the narrow lane. 'Yes, I hoped the old bat would just accept the inevitable and accept our terms. But no, they never do.'

'Old bats, you mean?' asked Maddy. If the hearing had been postponed, then there must be some other reason of equal consequence for this meeting.

Chetak shook his head. 'No, everyone. No one ever gives up.'

She waited.

'What've you done with the bicycle?' he asked now.

'In the stairwell,' she said. 'Locked. I suppose it will be safe-ish.'

'Maybe,' he nodded. 'But I'll have my fellows bring it back to the villa.' They were headed south. 'Unless you want it in Shahpur Jat?'

'Not especially,' she said. 'Where are we going now?'

'We need to talk,' he said. 'And I'm not sure what's best. I mean...' He glanced at her. 'So long as you're Madan, we could eat at a roadside joint. You have the day off, am I right?'

'Yes,' said Maddy. 'I can dismiss Madan and change into me.'

'Okay, *good*,' said Chetak, sounding relieved, then immediately adding, 'Though... I'm not sure where—'

'No worries,' said Maddy quickly. 'Just let me into the back seat, will you? Compared to making the switch in Malli's car, yours will be a breeze.'

He stopped by the side of the road while she scrambled into the back. 'Shall we try one of the hotels? Any preference for breakfast?'

Maddy's voice was muffled as she pulled Madan's shirt over her head instead of unbuttoning it. 'How about that tall hotel near the mall in Saket – what's it called? – the ITC?' She wore a light vest under the shirt, and beneath the vest, the chest bandage.

'ITC Saket. Yup,' said Chetak. 'Great. It's close by. Does that give you enough time?'

'Plenty.' Maddy reached for her wig and fitted it on before pulling on a fresh kurta. 'The last time was in the front seat of a Maruti.'

He stopped when she was done to let her into the front seat once more. He smiled as she got in. 'Pretty good! Shoes and all.'

'Flip-flops with silver straps. They go with everything. Compared to Madan's costume – those giant clodhoppers especially – my clothes are so easy.' She fine-tuned the placement of her wig, saying, 'It's also easier because your car's bigger and because fewer people pay attention when the driver's a man.'

Half an hour later, they were seated in the coffee lounge of the ITC Saket, where the breakfast buffet was in progress. They had ordered and were waiting for their masala dosas to arrive. Two cups of South Indian coffee had already been placed in front of them, identical plumes of steam rising from the elongated white coffee cups.

Maddy was looking out at the greenery outside.

'You seem distracted,' remarked Chetak.

'I am.' She turned to look at him. 'What did you want to talk about?'

'About last night,' said Chetak.

'Huh?' asked Maddy, her eyes widening. *He can't know!* she thought. *He can't.*

'Russi,' said Chetak, only mildly surprised that she did not immediately understand what he'd meant.

'Oh.' Maddy shook her head as if to clear it. 'Of course.'

'What did you think I meant?'

'Nothing. I... well. Nothing. Russi was fine. He said he'd be late leaving the party, and he was. But only in the usual sense.' She looked up. 'Why did you ask?'

'I wondered whether he had any companions with him. In the car.' As soon as the words were out of his mouth, he looked as if he wanted to bite them back.

Maddy sucked in her breath. 'Well. Yes. Two cocktail girls needed a ride home.'

'Cocktail girls?' Chetak gave a slight chuckle. 'Is that even a category?'

'Giggly and jiggly,' said Maddy. 'Poured themselves into the car and then poured themselves out again. In Jor Bagh.' She looked away, fingering her coffee cup. She wasn't happy with her choice of words.

'So, there were two of them?'

'What are you getting at?' she asked.

Chetak shrugged. 'It's...'

'You have to explain. I don't understand.'

'I believe he's being targeted,' said Chetak.

'*Targeted*? By whom?'

'He's arguing a case,' said Chetak. 'On behalf of an NGO that speaks for tribal groups all across India. The argument is straightforward: tribals are the original inhabitants of this vast land. They have prior rights to everything – the forests, the minerals, the rivers. Opposing the NGO is a consortium of neo-colonialists. Industrialists from around the world armed with the single most formidable weapon there is – money.'

Maddy nodded.

'These are people who are used to getting their way. Ordinarily, they'd be able to buy out any opposing counsel. But they can hardly buy out a man like Russi! So, they do the next best thing. They target his weakness. The moment Verity is no longer by his side, these girls attach themselves to him—'

'Oh, come on!' cut in Maddy. 'That's just not fair. He's not some witless jellyfish being taken advantage of! He's not innocent. He enjoys the attention.'

'Oh, I don't deny that for one moment,' said Chetak. 'But he doesn't see the difference between – what did you call them? Cocktail girls? – and people hired specifically to harm him.'

'I'm sorry,' said Maddy. 'I should never have used that term. They were in the car for such a short while. I kept thinking that we're all so unfair. Towards young women. They're just being—'

'High-spirited?' cut in Chetak. 'Sowing their version of wild oats?'

'I was going to say, playing the part expected of them,' said Maddy. 'They're invited to such events in order to twinkle under the lights. They know it, everyone knows it. Why pick them apart for doing what's expected of them?'

Chetak gave a slight nod. 'Did they respond to you at all?'

'They barely noticed me. Except when Russi, who was sitting in front, addressed me as "dear".'

'*Oh*, my—' began Chetak, just as their orders arrived.

He and Maddy leaned back in their seats while the two oval platters, each with its slab of reddish-golden dosa reclining in the middle, were placed in front of them by two young women wearing white aprons. When the drama of delivery ended, and the aroma pulsing up from the food enveloped both diners quite completely, Chetak leaned forward once more. 'Go on. What happened next? What did Russi say?'

Maddy picked up her knife and fork, looking down at her dosa, as if trying to decide where to begin cutting into it. 'Chetak, I... I... ' She stopped and looked up. 'I'm not sure it's right for me to repeat what's said in my presence. As a driver, I mean.'

Chetak's naturally impassive face grew a shade more still.

'When I was a kid, my father had a chauffeur who used to take me back and forth to my school. I used to be alone in the car because my brothers went to some other school. That driver used to tell me little stories about his life in the hills and how he used to work for someone in the army. According to him, all good drivers follow a code of silence. Because a driver is privy to all kinds of conversations. If the word gets around that a particular man has been repeating anything that he's heard, that man will lose his job and his reputation...'

Maddy faltered to a halt.

Chetak was shaking his head, very slightly, from side to side.

'I don't know why you're shaking your head.' She could feel her face flushing. 'Are you saying I don't have the *right* to have scruples? Because I'm new? Because I'm untested? I mean, which is it?'

Chetak had begun cutting into his dosa. He looked up between making a series of precise slices. 'No, that's not it. None of those things. There's something else at play that I think you're not taking into consideration. Something that I can't... maybe for the same kinds of reasons that you're struggling to talk to me. To do with loyalty.'

He stopped cutting and looked up. 'It's because of who he is. He's not just any employer. He's also a person with tremendous power.' Chetak looked away, then looked back. 'The kind of power that makes him vulnerable. There. I think that's the closest I can get to it. And he behaves as if he doesn't know it.'

'You're talking about the girls, right?' Maddy had begun tearing into her dosa.

'Yes, the girls – but not necessarily *these* girls.'

'Well, I think it's unfair to brand them, to treat them as generic.'

'You did it yourself a moment ago,' Chetak reminded her. '*Cocktail girls*, you called them.'

'Yes,' said Maddy. She forked a morsel of the dosa and its potato stuffing into her mouth; she immediately realized that it was too hot but chewed and swallowed quickly anyway. Her anger, combined with the heat, temperature, as well as spice, caused her to choke and her eyes to water.

She cleared her throat before speaking. 'Yes, I did. And maybe that's why I'm so annoyed at myself. I was annoyed last night, too, in the car. And the fact is, yes! They were behaving in that idiotic, school-girly way. Yes, I wanted to slap them. Yes, I wanted to tell them to pull up their knickers and behave themselves. But also, I was shocked and saddened by my own reaction. Disgusted. Disappointed.'

A tear popped suddenly from her left eye and rolled down her cheek.

It took her by surprise. It was from the choking, of course, but it seemed emotional too.

She went silent, continuing to work on the still-steaming mass of the dosa on her plate without looking up. The tear trickled down the full length of her face before she wiped it aside with the heel of her hand.

Chetak broke the silence. 'There's still something I need to say.'

'Go ahead.' Maddy nodded. 'I'm fine.'

'It's to do with Russi,' he said.

'Yes,' said Maddy.

'It's what I wanted this morning's meeting to be about.'

'Okay,' said Maddy.

'I feel we've got to take some action to protect him.'

'Such as what?' Maddy looked up from her platter.

Chetak had finished as much of his dosa as he wanted. He folded his cutlery and met her gaze. 'The next time you're on night duty, turn on your phone's voice recorder.'

She took in a deep breath. 'Despite what I've just said!'

'That's right,' said Chetak. 'Despite your objections, I'm asking you to set aside your scruples, your code-of-chauffeur ethics and *record what's said in the car*. For his own sake. And yours, too, maybe.'

'Isn't that illegal? To record someone without their consent?'

'I have his consent,' said Chetak.

Maddy stared at him. 'You've already asked him!'

'Yes.'

'And?'

'He knows what's at stake,' said Chetak. 'He's agreed.'

42

Kill time
Eat lime
Drink a cup of
Starlight wine.

– JINXES, BIG & SMALL

It was still early in the day when Chetak dropped Maddy off at Malli's home. They had talked on the phone, and Malli was expecting her, the scent of freshly brewed coffee emerging from the front door like an embrace.

As soon as their cups were filled, Maddy said to her friend, 'Last night, something happened. Something I can't explain or understand.'

Malli gave her a questioning look. 'Context? Something to do with your Verity?'

'No, no. Not at all. It's something completely out of the... just... outside the range of...' Maddy stopped and shook her head. 'I can't even… I don't have the words.'

'Russi?' began Malli.

'No, no! Neither of them. No one we know. God. I need to *say* it. Somehow.'

Malli shook her head, frowning. 'Come on! Spit it out!'

Maddy looked away, looked at Malli, looked away again. Took a deep breath. 'Last night, in the parking lot, I... I... *God*! This feels so idiotic!' With her eyes shut now, as if inside a confessional booth, she said, 'I got into the back seat of a car with one of the other drivers.' She paused. 'And then we... we... *kissed*. In the back seat of his car. Like a pair of teenagers.'

She opened her eyes.

Malli stared back for a moment.

Then her face flexed into an ironic smile. 'Oh my god!' she said. 'Oh. My. God.'

'I don't know what to think about it,' said Maddy. Her hands were on either side of her face; she was pulling the skin of her cheeks backwards. She wasn't smiling, nor was she frowning or crying. 'I don't know, I don't know.'

'Come,' said Malli. 'On the balcony. Cigarette.'

As they stood lighting their smokes in the mild sunshine under the shade of tall, nodding monstera, Maddy gave Malli a stripped-down description of what had happened. She did not go into detail. When she was done, both women were silent for several minutes.

Malli spoke first. 'You made a note of his number?'

Maddy nodded.

'Meaning, you're going to call him.' It was a statement, not a question.

'I can't. I shouldn't,' said Maddy.

'But you will,' said Malli.

'Why do you say that? If I don't call, I'll simply never see him again.'

'Huh! Already you're so sure? You have no idea how persistent men are?'

'It wasn't like that,' said Maddy. 'He won't try to chase.'

'Oh, please, please!' said Malli. 'Don't give me that guff. What is he, some kind of saint? He'll hunt you down, believe me. Men are like mosquitoes! They never give up until they've had their fill!'

'I'm telling you,' said Maddy, blowing a plume of smoke, watching it pass in and out of the shade and sunlight. 'He wasn't like that.'

'And besides, what makes you think you won't be at another event where the same guy is invited as a guest? The Austrian whatever.'

Maddy inhaled, holding in the smoke, then released it slowly as she spoke. 'Yes. That could happen. But if I don't call him, he won't approach me again. I know it.'

Malli was shaking her head in disbelief. 'Teenager. Total teenager! One kiss, and you're lost to the world as the rest of us know it. Look, you don't even know his name! He could be married a thousand times over! A serial rapist.'

Maddy flicked her ash. 'Don't even go there! I do know his name. It's Preet. There was no *forcing*. Nothing like that. I can't even begin to explain *what* it was. Not like snogging in the back of cars with a boy, with the frantic hands and the panting and the giggling. Not like that at all. Not... funny. Or even fun. More like deadly serious. Like hunger. Like suddenly, with no warning, seeing the pit of hunger that rages inside of another person. And for one moment, becoming the meal that satisfies that hunger.' She stopped. Her own words shocked her.

Malli stared at her. In a softer voice, she said, 'And you. What about you? Weren't you hungry, too?'

Maddy tried to answer the question. 'I don't know. I didn't want anything. It was like being struck by lightning.'

Malli gave a small chuckle. 'Like in *The Godfather*! Michael Corleone says that about the woman who becomes his wife – he calls it the lightning bolt.'

'Malli,' said Maddy, 'no. Really, *no*. In the movie, that was love. This wasn't. There was no question, not even the slightest little itty-bitty element of luuurve.' She exaggerated the sound of the word. 'That's what I'm trying to explain. It was about hunger, and that was all. There was no emotion, at least not of the romantic kind. It was about appeasing hunger. And finding that it's... a kind of power to be able to do that, to offer that.'

Malli groaned aloud. 'Oh, my god.'

'Why are you finding this so hard to understand? I'm trying to explain something that really didn't feel like anything else that's ever happened to me, but you're treating it as if I'm refusing to see that it's completely mundane, just another love story, nothing to see here.'

They had both finished their cigarettes.

Malli said, 'Look, I'm trying to understand, but everything I hear sounds like the dialogue from a 1960's era Barbara Cartland novel. No, wait—' as Maddy started to protest 'something has just occurred to me. I can't tell, from what you've described, whether this man, this Preet – I mean, does he know?'

'What?' asked Maddy.

'That you're a woman!'

Maddy shook her head vehemently, 'Oh, no. NO. I'm sure he doesn't. I think he'd be... I mean... no, of course not. All he said was, he knew in his heart – well, he tapped his chest – that there was something different about me. But that was all.'

Maddy moved to go inside, and Malli followed her. 'All right then. So the question to ask yourself is, when you meet him again, are you going to have that conversation? Would you tell him straightaway?'

'I don't think I can, Malli. It would be too much. I wouldn't want to tell him. Maybe that's why I shouldn't ever see him again.'

'It would be smart of you not to.' She paused before continuing, 'But you're not smart. You're a fool. And you're in love, and you're refusing to see that.'

They were both inside now. They had left their coffee mugs, no longer steaming, on the table. They sat down now on either side, Maddy facing out, Malli facing in.

'I'm not in love, Malli,' said Maddy, reaching for her coffee, 'but I *am* fascinated. Maybe you will say that's the same as love. I don't think it is. And you're right to say that I'm not smart. Because it's not smart to play with another person's feelings when I know that for me, it's a form of research. A kind of intimate tourism. I'm only peripherally attracted to the man *as a man*. It's the situation I'm riveted by. Because it's just so out of the box. Mind you, that's only because we're in India. Because of the rigid structure of society here. The way that there's so little mingling between social classes. For him, so long as I'm just another driver, there's nothing very exceptional about that, is there? Hooking up with another driver must be something that happens now and then. But for a driver to hook up with a woman? Of the employer class? That's...' She shrugged. 'I can't even.'

'He'll be furious,' said Malli. 'Just think about it for a moment. He won't have any model to follow except the usual one. Of being treated like a plaything. A toy.'

Maddy winced. 'I would hate that,' she said, her voice breathy.

'So then, don't do it. Don't call him,' said Malli.

Maddy sipped from her coffee mug, not looking up.

43

A stitch in time
Mends the clocks
Fills the days
And darns the socks.

– JINXES, BIG & SMALL

Maddy returned to the villa in a cab. *Oh, the irony!* she thought. But it didn't bother her. She'd done it often enough in the context of her previous life when she'd needed to get from point A to point B without wanting to be burdened by her large, handsome car.

She got down at the gate and walked up to the entrance on 'her' side. The security guard rose stiffly to his feet, and she realized with momentary unease that she did not know him. He looked similar enough to Bahadur to perhaps be related to him: broad, low-slung and bronzed, giving an impression of dense tautness.

But he knew her. 'Madam,' he said as he extended an envelope towards her with his left hand cupping the right elbow. 'From Rani Mahal,' he added in his husky, accented voice. He was using English words but sounded as if he was speaking in Hindi. 'Please. You go now.'

If it sounded like a command, it was just his manner, not rudeness.

She said, 'Now?'

He bobbed his head. 'Yes, yes. Go now. Madam Simi is there.' He spoke as if it must be obvious to her whom he meant. He gestured towards the door through which she had just entered. 'Go from the back,' said the man, whose name she did not know.

She could have insisted on going up to her room first. She still had Madan's backpack with her. She would have preferred to keep it hidden. But she did not want to compromise the guard's authority. 'All right,' she said, smiling just enough to suggest that she knew it was her choice and not his command.

She stepped out into the heat wishing she had her sunglasses. They were in her car, of course. She'd get them, she told herself, once she'd met with Madam Simi. Whoever that was.

This was the first time she'd retraced the path that Chetak and she had taken when she had arrived at the villa in what seemed like an age ago. She remembered thinking it was so strange for a building to have no windows at all on the ground floor.

Around the halfway mark, the wall beside her changed to the stone latticework. This then was the rear half of the mansion. She touched it as she walked along, confirming that it really was carved stone, the eight-point motif alternating with a rhombus. On the other side of the lattice was a shadowy darkness. She could probably have looked into the space if she'd put her nose to one of the apertures. But she didn't. It was too hot for idle curiosity.

Presently, the lattice turned into a dressed-stone wall, with the pattern present as raised relief, with no apertures. The wall extended for perhaps three metres before ending at a corner shaped like a pilaster. Rounding the corner and looking up, Maddy saw the fantastically decorated façade of the building's rear once more. Two storeys up it went, the formal lacework in pale golden stone, with four pairs of windows per floor and each window ornamented in a different style. In the centre of the ground floor was the marble archway with the double wooden doors.

A woman stood at that point, looking towards Maddy as if waiting. The guard must have spoken to her on the phone.

She was of indeterminate age, thin and tall, with long black hair left open like a smooth velvet hood. She wore a dark chiffon sari covered in writhing magenta paisleys. Silver ornaments in her ears, in her hair and on her neck. Silver bracelets up to her elbows on both arms. In her nose, a diamond flashed. Her skin looked oiled and seamless, olive brown in colour. Her eyes were outlined in black, her mouth painted maroon. Her eyebrows were plucked thin and arched high, as if in constant disdain.

'Hello,' she said, 'Madam Sen. I am Simi.'

'Hello,' said Maddy, who had some distance left to go before she'd be at the entrance. 'I'm sorry, but I—'

'Come inside,' said the woman. 'It's very hot.' She turned and vanished from view.

Moments later, Maddy was stepping through the marble portal into a dimly lit air-cooled hall. The design appeared to have been lifted from the Taj Mahal – white marble from floor to ceiling with small diyas flickering in wall niches. They appeared to be real diyas, made of clay and filled with oil. In Maddy's mind, the immediate thought they conveyed was that someone must be employed not merely to replenish the oil every day but also to clean the black residue of the smoke from all the surfaces that would be affected.

An elderly man dressed in white cotton – kurta, pyjamas, embroidered cap – stood by the door in an attitude of mute deference, his eyes directed downward. She turned towards him as she stepped through, wanting to acknowledge his presence. He closed the double doors behind her, then remained standing there with his hands folded in front of him, not looking up at her or anywhere else.

But Simi was standing at a door on the right and looking impatiently in Maddy's direction. 'This way,' she said, as if there might have been a choice.

A room the size of Maddy's bedroom upstairs was Simi's office. An enormous glass-topped desk was angled such that it took up one entire quarter of the space. Books lined the walls. The floor was tiled in black and white marble. No rugs. Two heavy leather-clad recliner chairs defined the corner to the right of the door with a square glass-topped coffee table between them.

With no preamble, Simi said, 'The Rani Sahiba is interested in you.'

Maddy blinked. 'I'm sorry? Who—'

'She would like to take a ride,' continued Simi, as if Maddy had said nothing, 'in your car.'

'Oh,' said Maddy, gesturing towards the ceiling. 'Do you mean the—'

'Rani Sahiba,' Simi, broke in, speaking severely. Then she relented very slightly. 'You have seen her, I think. One night.'

The second night I was here, thought Maddy.

'Uh... yes... but I hardly knew who or what I saw...'

'It does not matter,' said Simi, 'what you knew. What matters is that Rani Sahiba saw you. On the opposite landing, at 4 a.m., when she sits in her jharoka to meditate. You waved at her. She thought that it was very impertinent of you. Rude. So she made enquiries. She found out that you drive ladies around in your car. For a fee. So she wants to take a drive.' Pause. 'It has been many years since she set one toe outside the palace.'

'I see,' said Maddy. She was nonplussed.

'There will be no payment, however,' said Simi. 'Rani Sahiba does not believe in paying women for their services. It would be too insulting.'

To whom? wondered Maddy. *To the women or to her?* Out loud, she said, 'I see.'

'So... the Rani Sahiba is ready to go right away,' said Simi.

'But wait,' protested Maddy, '*I* might not be ready.'

Simi leaned forward a fraction of an inch. '*There is no question of refusal,*' she said in a theatrical, hissing tone. It was quite extraordinary, how much hostility she packed into this commonplace utterance. '*You* are the interloper here. You and all the... worthless... *usurpers* who live on that side of this palace! Huh. They think that their court orders and bits of paper can hold back the royal will of the true owner of this land! Huh.'

She had spoken so fast and at such length that she was out of breath. Her rigid frame remained still while her thin chest, encased in a tight bodice of mirror-work silk, moved rapidly back and forth.

She continued, 'By noticing you at all, Rani Sahiba has conferred a great honour upon you. The fact that she wants to take a ride in your car is unheard of. Let me be frank. I do not approve of this plan. Yet I have agreed to engage you for this duty.'

She paused once again to catch her breath. 'Be ready in ten minutes. Bring the car to the Marble Door. I will accompany her on the ride. Now... go!'

44

Chase that star
Catch that goose
Hitch your wagon
To a moose.

– JINXES, BIG & SMALL

Maddy sat at the wheel of her car, the engine idling. She had arrived at the entrance within ten minutes as requested. But fifteen minutes had already passed, and the wooden doors remained closed.

How funny it all is, she thought. *These people with their imperious commands. Their belief in themselves as great wielders of power and status. And why? Because they married into wealthy families. Nothing more, nothing less.* Really, just variations of Mrs Bansal in the end.

She could have walked out of Simi's office, she supposed, and gone back to 'her' entrance. Would the guard have refused to let her in? Perhaps. In which case she would have gone around to Russi's side and rung the doorbell.

But it had been easier to agree to the plan. More interesting. She wanted to know where this teacup tyrant of a Rani Sahiba would like to go. What she'd like to see on this, her once-in-a-century expedition. Would she talk, Maddy wondered. Was she curious about the world that she did not engage with? Did she have interests that extended beyond her marble-lined queendom?

Ten minutes later, one of the doors opened.

Simi came out and stood to one side.

Two more women, young girls from the looks of it, wearing white uniforms similar to the old man by the door, came out now. Each was holding what looked like a slender rod, with a flexible arch connecting them at the top. Extending backwards from this flimsy structure and into the darkened interior of the building was a curtain of white gauze embroidered with starry white flowers. It was kept taut to create a diaphanous corridor, perhaps a metre-and-a-half tall and a metre wide, with the nether end out of sight.

Maddy sprang out of the car and went around to open the rear passenger door before Simi could reach it.

The two girls moved forward. The gauzy corridor now extended all the way from the open front door to the open door of the car.

Simi said to Maddy, 'You can get back. I will take care of this.'

'Sorry,' said Maddy, holding Simi's gaze. 'I take care of my car. All right? You take care of your Rani.'

For a moment, Simi's black eyes threw sparks, but in the next instant, she had ducked under the gauze curtain, hurried down the temporary corridor and into the building's interior.

There was a long pause then, during which the two young women looked down at their feet. Maddy gazed at them, her height giving her an advantage. She took in their unadorned young faces, each with a tiny pearl nose ring in the left nostril, each wearing identical silver ear studs, plain spherical blobs. What did they know of the world, wondered Maddy. What did they think of their lives in the so-called palace? Were they allowed to have thoughts of any kind at all?

There was a swishing sound as Simi appeared once more, walking within the makeshift corridor, stooping because it was too low for her. Beside her, half-supported on her arm, was the Rani Sahiba. However insubstantial the curtain corridor was, it did a surprisingly good job of concealing its occupants. The best that Maddy could make out was a slight figure, clad all in white, approaching the car. She held herself erect, moving with a slow but deliberate step. The head and shoulders were swaddled in what appeared to be a mist speckled with twinkling points, pulled forward to shield the face. Beneath this covering was a flowing garment, or perhaps two garments, of which the lower one was a richly pleated skirt.

Maddy suppressed a smile and looked away as the final part of this journey to the car was completed. Considerable fussing and unladylike grunts ensued. When the Rani was finally inside the car and facing forward, Simi popped out from under the gauze curtain wide-eyed and panting like a wild bird released from a cloud net.

'Okay,' she gasped, dismissing the two curtain maidens with a single flick of her wrist, causing them to retreat backwards as if on springs. Turning towards Maddy, she said, 'Come on! What're you waiting for?'

'To shut the door,' said Maddy as she did so. Then she stepped back and opened the front passenger door for Simi. 'Madam?' she said, and the other woman, while sending poison-dart glances her way, had no choice but to get inside, swivel forward and meekly accept the door being closed for her.

The Rani communicated with Simi via a cell phone that she held to her mouth. Maddy could see this in her rear-view mirror. The sound she made was like the fluttering of a moth's wings outside a mosquito net.

Simi, however, felt free to snarl these commands out to Maddy, as if channelling her employer's tone of thought, if not voice. 'Rani Sahiba says we will not go far,' she said. 'We will see gardens and trees. No people and no other cars.'

Maddy answered Simi while keeping her gaze trained upon the reflection in her rear-view mirror, 'Please tell the Rani Sahiba that we will see people and cars until we reach the Lodhi Gardens. There will be people and cars there, too, but with trees overhead.'

The figure in the back seat clearly heard this because she raised her head and stared up at the mirror. The cloud-like odhani fell away from her head, revealing an ancient face that looked as if it had been carved in ivory.

Simi repeated Maddy's statement in a soft, respectful voice and in Hindi into her own phone.

The face was coloured in the most delicate shades of mauve and rose: the eyelids, the sides of the nose, the mouth. The eyes were enormous globes and the irises dark. They were staring directly at Maddy in the mirror. There was a small, sharp nose like the beak of a dainty raptor, a shrike, perhaps. There was a downturned mouth that must once have been full-lipped. A high, bony forehead. Thick, wavy hair, white not silver, was combed back tight, with no parting.

The cell phone she was using was like a piece of jewellery, either gold-dipped or gold-encased. Jewels winked along its edges. She whispered into it now.

Her head and shoulders were contained within the fine, crisp folds of white organza, sprinkled with minute sequins that twinkled with each breath she took. Beneath it, she wore a white bodice thickly embellished with mirror-work. It was tight, and the frame beneath it was that of a sparrow.

Simi listened to the whispered words, then barked them out to Maddy. 'We will go to the Lodhi Gardens. We will shut our eyes from here to there. Start the car.'

Maddy gave a slight nod. A moment later, they began to move. When she looked up to check, she saw in the mirror that the Rani Sahiba's eyes were indeed closed.

She chose the Aurobindo Marg route.

Silence reigned in the car. Maddy maintained a steady pace, doing her best to avoid swerving or unnecessarily speeding up. She slowed as they drew close to the traffic intersection at AIIMS.

There was a stirring from behind. She heard the chirp of the cell phone beside her. Simi listened, then said, 'Have we arrived?'

Maddy, glancing at Simi, wondered why she didn't answer of her own accord. She must surely know the answer. Nevertheless, Maddy said, 'No. It will be another twenty minutes at least.'

Pat came the reply, 'That is too long.'

Maddy said nothing. There was no response possible.

After a pause, Simi said, on behalf of the Rani, 'We will go back now.'

Maddy inclined her chin. She was only the driver. She would do as requested. Looking straight ahead to where the traffic had started to move, she said, 'All right.'

'How long will it take?'

'Fifteen minutes if we're lucky,' said Maddy, starting to move. From the position they were in, it was still just possible to make a U-turn without having to go through the intersection.

'That is too long.'

'It cannot be helped.'

'Then we will get down here and walk.'

'No,' said Maddy.

'*No*?' said Simi, as if in shock, speaking on her own behalf. 'What does that mean, *no*? Who are you to say—'

'The doors are locked,' cut in Maddy as she leaned into the U-turn.

There was a long pause, during which some chirping ensued on the phone.

Then, from Simi, 'Either we return faster or...' She stopped.

'Or what?'

'Or we will make potty in your car.' Simi's voice was hoarse.

Maddy glanced up at the mirror. The Rani's eyes were still closed.

'As you wish,' said Maddy.

On her left, in her peripheral vision, she could see that Simi was also staring ahead. Her hand was held to her mouth. Maybe she was imagining the storms of fury that she would face back at the palace. Maybe she was feeling ill.

There was a protracted silence until they approached the Green Park intersection. As Maddy slowed to another halt, there came a fresh query. 'Have we reached?'

'No,' said Maddy. 'Another five minutes at least.'

Now from the back seat came a string of words spoken in a soft, hissing monotone. They were curse words. Maddy understood only a couple of them: *Whore. Cunt. Pig's...* She switched her mind off. Simi did not repeat these words, either in their original Hindustani or in English.

When they were at the final intersection and turning towards the home stretch, there was another question. 'Ask her why she does this job.'

Maddy glanced at Simi but saw that she was looking straight ahead, as if suffering. 'Because I like it,' said Maddy. 'I like to drive.'

'It is a dirty job,' said Simi in the Sahiba's tone. 'Only men must do such jobs.' Pause. 'Tell her she must stop. She is spitting in the face of all women by doing this dirty work.'

Maddy drew in a deep breath. 'Another minute,' she said. Then added, 'I will not stop.'

'Tell her she must stop,' repeated the Rani through Simi. 'It is wrong, it is immoral for women to have desires. They must do what they are told. By their husband. By their father. By their brother.'

The gate was in sight.

'Men are gods. Women are slaves.'

The car's tyres hissed on the gravel.

'Why is she not married? Unmarried women are a curse on humanity. Tell her she must get married. To anyone. Anything. It does not matter. Some women get married to a dog. There are many dogs in the street. Tell her—'

But they had arrived.

Maddy turned the engine off and swivelled around in her seat. She was facing Simi, but the Sahiba was in her field of vision. 'I am a widow,' she said. 'I am happy with my life. I enjoy driving. Now get out of my car.'

Then she got up, got out and went around to open the doors.

45

Eager beaver
Pudding and pie
Kissed the trees
And made them sigh.

– JINXES, BIG & SMALL

Instead of returning to the villa, Maddy went straight out again, aiming her car towards Aurobindo Marg and thence to the Lodhi Gardens. She went to the Garden Café, sat there and ate an entire primavera pizza all by herself.

Anger flickered on and off in her brain, like LED fairy lights outside a wedding venue.

It was a directionless anger. She refused to blame herself. It wasn't her fault that she was trusting. That she didn't assume the worst of others.

She looked around at the green space with its tall trees arching over glass-topped tables. The waiters in white, circulating with their trays and their carafes of fresh-brewed coffee. The patrons sitting at their places, locked in conversation, laughing, animated.

Everyone so unaware of the hidden lines of force pulsing around them. Social contracts that made it possible for a living corpse like the Rani Sahiba to maintain a private army of caretakers in virtual imprisonment on one side of a building while, on the other side of the same building, lived four unattached women, each following her own independent life path.

She was feeling sick now with the sheer volume of pizza plugging up the middle of her gut. The coffee she had asked for had been delivered. The heat from the cup radiated upward and mingled with the curling smoke from her cigarette.

I must leave, she thought. *That ghastly building is getting to me. Chetak tried to warn me that time in the car... or did he?* Had his warning really been a lure?

She'd been staring idly towards the entrance of the eatery, noticing the slow trickle of people entering and leaving, when a figure caught her attention. A man, discreetly well-dressed, above average height, with a shapely head and dense black hair.

Chetak.

He was scanning the restaurant, looking around with a raptor's high-focused concentration until he caught sight of her. Only when he raised his hand did she nod and raise one of hers back.

He wasn't quite smiling at her, and she wasn't smiling back at him at all.

'Ah,' he said when he drew close enough to speak. 'I should have guessed you'd be in the smokers' section!'

'Where else,' she said, making it a statement.

'May I join you?' he asked. He was carrying the familiar stack of files with him, suggesting that he had come directly from court.

'You came looking for me,' she said. 'You expected to find me.'

He settled into place before answering, 'Yes.'

She looked down, not meeting his gaze. 'I had forgotten. How you tracked me that very first time. I noticed it then but forgot about it in the crush of events that followed.'

'It's just an app,' he said. 'Not some James Bondian tracking device attached to your car.'

'Seems pretty James Bondian to me.'

'I have your phone number,' he said. 'The app allows me to see the number's location on a map. Like the Uber app.'

'Is it legal?'

'It's not illegal,' said Chetak, the corners of his eyes creasing in the beginning of a smile without going there. 'What's happened? Has something happened?'

'Yes. Something has happened.' She paused. 'I'm starting to snap.' Now she looked at him. 'This morning, at the villa, I got a summons. From the west side.'

Chetak bobbed his head at once. 'Ah, yes. The lunatic wing.'

Maddy raised her eyebrows. 'Why did no one say *that* to me before today?'

'What happened?'

Maddy gave him a brief description of the morning's incident.

Chetak asked, 'So, did she do it?'

'What?' asked Maddy.

'Potty,' said Chetak, deadpan.

Maddy gave a breathy snort. 'No, thank goodness. I'm guessing that she'd never risk messing up the beautiful whiteness of her... whatever that kind of skirt is called.' She paused. 'But it's not funny. Living like that. How many staff does she have in there? Are they all contained within the building?'

'So far as I know, yes. They're not permitted to leave. There are deliveries of supplies to and from. They have their own well.' He shrugged. 'Until recently, they had their own cow. Then it died, and there was a great to-do about how its carcass would be got rid of.' He shrugged again. 'Some people live their whole lives like that. Not many here in Delhi, of course. But elsewhere? Sure. In Delhi, it requires a great deal of string-pulling. Maintaining the old witch in her marble-lined coffin probably takes up one entire wall of files in the Delhi administration offices. I can't believe that she actually agreed to come out of the building!'

'Insisted,' said Maddy. 'That Simi woman told me she tried to dissuade her but didn't succeed.'

'I can bet she didn't try hard enough,' said Chetak. 'She's a smart one, that Simi. But never mind the old bat and her cynical sidekick. There's a reason I came searching for you. I have some news.'

Maddy looked at him questioningly.

He patted the files that he had placed on the table. 'The case. Dragon Lady Bansal. She's agreed to settle. On our terms.'

'What?'

'Wrong question,' said Chetak. 'Right question: For how much? And I can tell you: a lot.' Now he was veering towards a smirk. 'Even by my standards. I was impressed. I mean, it's what I asked for, but I expected there'd be some considerable arm-wrestling.'

Maddy was staring at him. 'Chetak, what're you saying?'

'I'm saying that Mrs Bansal has agreed to pay you two crores.'

'No!' Maddy's mouth fell open. 'I can't believe it – I can't! She'd never!'

'But. She. Has.'

'I don't understand,' said Maddy. She wasn't smiling. 'I really don't understand why she would do that. I can't.'

'That's because you haven't allowed yourself to recognize the fragility of the common tyrant. Someone like Mrs Bansal? She'll threaten and torment her tenants with every kind of legal bombshell while conducting her own affairs like a sewer rat. And unlike the Rani, she has no strings to pull. She gets away with her dirty business by choosing her victims with care – people who don't know how to call her bluff.'

'No,' said Maddy, shaking her head. 'No. That's *not* the whole story.' She gave him a searching look. 'You gave me a hint, early in this game. You said – I forget your words – that to be associated with... the world of the villa... gives me an advantage.'

'Yes, that is correct.'

'It's not something I asked for, looked for, understood. This "advantage" has come my way for reasons that I can't... that I don't—'

'But I've told you what it is,' cut in Chetak.

'What?'

'A combination of your own uniqueness combined with two other unusual individuals. Verity. And Russi.' He paused. 'Okay, so Russi is a powerful man in a world full of powerful men. But Verity is different. Her specialness is of a different order. I could tell you what it is but I'm not at liberty to.'

Maddy stared across the table at him.

'This is your decision,' he said. He met her gaze without flinching. 'You don't have to stay in the game.' He patted the files again. 'Especially not now. You can take the money and *go*. It'll be a clean transfer. I will ensure that. You'll always have access to my counsel if you need it.'

A waiter wandered up. He had a coffee carafe in his hand and looked enquiringly at Chetak.

'One cup, please,' said Chetak to the waiter, immediately turning back towards Maddy. 'You're at that point when you're distrusting everything – me, Verity, Russi... everything. I don't blame you. But the money releases you. That's what money can do. It can have that effect.'

'*You* did that,' said Maddy. 'You created an escape route for me.'

'In a way,' said Chetak. 'Yes. I couldn't have known that she'd settle quite like this. I'm flabbergasted, to be honest. She must be sitting on a secret so disgusting that she's grateful she has enough money to settle. To be sure, if she can pay two C now, it only means that she considers it a bargain. But,' he shrugged, 'not our problem. You have the money. You can forget about her.'

Maddy bit her lip. 'You make it sound easy.'

'It is. It can be.' The coffee arrived, and he dealt with it with a couple of nods and hand gestures, leaving him with a brimming cup of fragrant blackness.

Maddy watched him pour milk in. Stir it. Pick up the cup and take a preliminary sip before looking up at her. 'Don't make any decisions now. Think about it. Talk to someone else. Your friend Malli.'

'I know what I can or can't do,' said Maddy. 'Please.'

'Okay, then,' said Chetak. 'Say what's at the top of your mind.'

Embarrassed, Maddy looked away.

'What is it?' asked Chetak. 'Did I hit the submarine?' He laughed and said, 'Sorry! It's from that game, you know.'

'Yes, yes, I know – Battleships.' She blinked hard. 'It's... I... well. There's another way to think of this money, isn't there?' She paused, frowning. 'By calling it a... a...'

He wasn't going to help her.

He was holding his coffee cup in both hands and taking small sips.

'It's a kind of bribe, isn't it?' she said. 'To keep me in the game?'

He was silent for a beat. 'If that's how you want to see it, I won't argue with you. Anything I say can be used as evidence against me.' He smiled now. 'That, too, is your decision.'

A phone rang. For a moment, both of them looked around, not sure whose it was.

Then Chetak said, 'Mine.' He reached for it in his pocket. He looked at the lit screen, and his expression sobered. Then he put the phone away again.

'From Russi,' he said to Maddy. 'He's asking me to find out whether you're available this evening.'

Maddy shook her head as if in mock wonder. 'Oh, my. Talk about timing.'

Chetak shrugged and took another sip of his coffee. His mood had changed.

'Where will it be?' asked Maddy.

Chetak raised an eyebrow. 'Why does it matter?'

'Just... wondering.' If it was at another consulate, she might run into Preet again.

He frowned uncertainly. 'I feel there's something else bothering you...'

'No!' said Maddy. She was suddenly irritated. 'I'll do it. Wherever it is. I'm a taxi driver by profession. I go where the client wants to go. That's what taxi drivers do.' She turned and waved to a waiter, making the bill-paying hand gesture in the air.

She pursed her lips. 'Chetak, thank you for the money. You're right. It's a game changer. The game is changing already. I really can't wrap my head around it.'

He nodded. 'You're welcome, Maddy,' he said, but the frown had not left his face.

46

Over the rainbow
Under the sun
Over the moon
Under your thumb.

– JINXES, BIG & SMALL

The evening began early. Russi was in the car at 8 p.m. He sat at the back, with the reading light on, and remained immersed in his papers until they were at the Taj Mansingh. It was only as he was getting out of the car that he looked up at Maddy holding the door open to him, as if suddenly remembering that it was she rather than his regular driver.

'Thank you,' he said, biting back the 'dear' with a visible effort. 'I'll... I'll call you, hanh? On the phone. I might be quite late, so go on and have dinner.' He seemed distracted and tense. 'Probably around eleven. But you never know.' Then he turned and ran up the steps with a youthful energy that belied his years.

Maddy had decided in advance to park away from the hotel. She had brought a sandwich dinner with her and a flask of coffee. Drinking the coffee meant taking the risk that she'd need to let it out again before her tour of duty was over. Just thinking about it was causing a faint whine in the bladder department.

She drove aimlessly for a short while. First to Connaught Place, where she amused herself wheeling around and around the central roundabout several times. It felt like a real-life version of the Mock Turtle Race from *Alice in Wonderland*. All the other smaller vehicles, including three-wheelers, motorcyclists and scooters, were tooting and parping around her. In Russi's Jag, she felt like a whale shark surrounded by guppies and goldfish.

She returned via Raj Path, where she stopped to buy ice cream from one of the itinerant vendors. He came up to her window to take her money and returned with a Nutty Buddy cone. She drove away with it nestled in the cup holder beside her and parked on Pandara Road to eat it. She stayed inside the car as she bit down into the frozen layers of chocolate and ice cream, peeling away the paper sleeve to keep pace with her nibbling.

As she sat there, she realized she could go to one of the restaurants in Pandara Market to have a proper meal, rather than her sandwiches. Dilli-Dilli's had once been a great favourite. They used to provide an entire hundred grams packet of 'extra' butter on demand for those patrons who felt they weren't getting enough cholesterol from the butter chicken and dal makhani.

She parked outside and strolled into the market on foot, knowing that she'd never find parking near the restaurant around dinner time. There was bedlam inside the popular joint, now considerably spruced up compared to what it used to be like. The only table available was a single-seater right by the kitchen door. She took it, guessing that it was the kind of space reserved for the occasional chauffeur who might be offered dinner at the same time as his employers, but not at the same table.

When her meal arrived, she tucked her cloth napkin into the collar of her uniform to avoid food dripping onto it. Then she bent over the plate and shovelled the food into her mouth in the way that she recalled the other drivers eating.

When she was done, she wiped her hands on the napkin and got up, signalling the nearest waiter that she wanted the bill. Then, turning to locate the men's room, she went towards it.

It had been her intention all along to use the facilities in the restaurant. It was one of the reasons that she had decided to eat there, rather than in the car. But she had never actually stepped into a men's restroom before. Her heart began pounding as she pushed open the swing door. *What's there to fear?* she asked herself. Pat came the answer: *As a woman, you're afraid of entering an all-male domain. To be exposed as a fraud here would be...* She didn't have time to complete the thought.

The stench in the small room reminded her of the tigers' cage at the zoo, pungent and brassy. There were four urinals against one wall. Each was taken when she stepped in, by older men of differing heights, facing away from her. One had a full head of grey hair. The other three were partially bald, and all seemed to wear dark baggy trousers and pale bush shirts. It was remarkable, how similar they looked from behind, as if they had reached a certain stage of life when it was no longer necessary to make an effort with their appearance.

There were two stalls. A tall man stepped out of one of them, dressed in a dark blue Afghan suit, his black hair and beard contrasting sharply with the almond pink of his skin. He glanced at her, then away again, quickly, as if the initial glance had been a mistake.

She moved towards that stall, stepped in, closed the door, unzipped, did her business and stepped out again. She blocked all the sensations of sight and smell that assailed her in order to act as the others in the room, as if completely unconscious of their surroundings.

Three of the four men who had been at the urinals were each walking away now, variously bent at the knee, arranging their tackle while zipping up, but moving briskly, not looking to either side. For her, the pressure to leave was like a physical force, propelling her outside before she could even wash her hands. She felt an absolute sense of wrongness for having observed others in a space where they did not expect to be observed as *others*. It was like spying on blameless civilians for no reason other than being a spy.

She picked up her bill from where it had been left on her single-occupant table, in a saucer under a glass bowl half-full of saunf. Taking it over to the cash desk to pay, she completed the transaction mutely, throwing down the cash and not waiting for the change.

She practically ran out of the eatery. A churning sensation in her gut told her that she was about to throw up – a delayed response to the smell of the men's room. She was in the back lane just as her mouth filled with saliva and the first heave began.

But she held it down.

Down! she commanded herself. *DOWN! We will NOT throw up. Not.*

Gaining the sanctuary of the car, she sat still, swallowing hard, swallowing down the plug of lava that was doing its best to erupt out of her gullet. The only argument she had against it was: *It's not food poisoning. There's nothing physically wrong inside. It's only a sense of disgust. And that's not reason enough to throw up. That's weak, that's childish. We can stop it. We must stop it.*

She was breathing hard, as if she'd actually run all the way. The heaving stopped.

She bent towards the nearest air-conditioning vent, closing her eyes to the calming stream of cooled air.

When there was a sharp tap on her window, she jerked back as if she'd been stung, her heart racing all over again. But it was only the sleepy parking attendant, a thin rake of a boy wearing a dirty string vest, holding out a ticket. She gave him a hundred rupee note and left without taking the ticket from him. If he had brightened at the sudden windfall, she did not wait long enough to see that either.

She drove away slowly, refusing to give in to the urge to race off, brakes shrieking, sparks flying, like a bank robber at the getaway moment. She would not allow the fact of almost unravelling in public to overwhelm her. She willed her mind to concentrate on the smooth movements of the Jag.

We can do this, she said to herself. *Yes. We can.*

47

Fee-fie-fo-fum
What a handsome panjandrum!

– JINXES, BIG & SMALL

Maddy drove towards Shanti Path and did a full circuit of each avenue before wending her way back towards Mansingh. It was 10.45 p.m. She had checked the Nokia a couple of times in case she had in some way missed hearing an incoming call, but no, she hadn't.

She parked near the hotel. At this time of night, it wasn't a problem.

She turned on Russi's music selection, but when a contralto voice soared out of the speakers, she turned it off. She didn't have an ear for opera. Her own phone was not with her. Madan's small Nokia played music from Hindi language stations, and she wasn't in the mood for it. She returned it to the place Chetak had suggested to her – in one of the car's cup holders.

She sat in silence, thinking about the panic she had felt while in the men's room. It was entirely self-generated, she decided. The one man who'd noticed her was almost certainly drawn to the colour of her skin, which was close to his own, and nothing else. It had been, she believed, an automatic flickering towards something familiar, not even rising to the level of an attraction. If he'd had suspicions about her gender, he would have given her that hard, unblinking stare that was so unnerving in this part of the world.

No, her panic had arisen out of the conviction baked into her psyche that for a woman to enter the men's room was deeply taboo. Even now, distanced in time and space from that washroom, her skin rippled with unease and a desire to wipe herself clean of the experience.

As a child, travelling with her mother and brothers while their father was away, it had sometimes happened that the boys had needed to come into the ladies'. When they were too young to use public facilities on their own, that was considered the norm. But never the other way around.

'Why does it matter so much?' she wondered out loud to the car's quiet interior. There was no reply, of course.

She had grown up in the company of her brothers and their friends. She had seen their dangly bits, and they had seen hers. It had all seemed natural and unremarkable. When and how had that changed? She couldn't remember.

The Nokia buzzed in the cup holder. It was 11.55 p.m. She answered the call, saying 'Yes, sir. Of course, sir. I'm very close by. It'll take me three minutes to get there.'

She reached for her flask of coffee and took a deep swig without bothering to pour it into the lid that doubled as a mug. Then she was off.

There were two cars ahead of hers on the approach ramp that led to the hotel's front steps. Another two cars were parked alongside the one that was actually at the steps. The bright lights spilling from the foyer mingled with the tail lights of the cars and the swirling exhaust fumes to create a bright tableau. The hotel doormen, all of whom seemed to be at least seven feet tall, with the fanned plumes of their turbans adding another foot of height, cast dramatic shadows even as the equally plumed and silk-clad guests descended towards their waiting chariots.

Maddy searched for Russi's pale face, cap of white curls and the dark suit he had been wearing among the throng of glittering figures coming forward.

Yes, there he was. And yes, he had a woman on his arm.

Maddy had ample time to observe the pair of them as she waited her turn to be waved forward by the towering doormen.

The woman was an inch taller than Russi as she teetered on scarlet needlepoint heels. She wore a dress to match the heels, so skintight that it might have been painted on, flaring to a glorious frothy skirt at the hips. Iridescent black stockings. Her hair was braided in tiny strands that dripped over her face and onto her shoulders and back. She wore shiny bracelets on her bare arms with which she clung to her escort, as if unable to stand unsupported.

By the time Maddy swept forward, Russi had seen his car and was starting down the stairs. He and the girl both seemed to be tottering slightly. Maddy sprang out to get the passenger door behind her while one of the doormen, who was already on the other side of the car, reached down from his great height to open the left-side back seat door.

Russi helped the girl into her seat and moved around the back of the car, his face blazing red and orange as he passed behind the tail lights. Maddy shut the door on the girl and then glanced up to ensure that Russi was being taken care of on his side. At that moment, he looked up, too. She had a split second in which to register that he looked odd, almost as if he were in pain. Then he had ducked out of sight into the car.

Maddy slipped into her seat, buckled up, quickly shifted the car forward and out of the hive of activity at the hotel's steps. In a moment, they were gliding down the exit slope. Only when they had passed well clear of the gates and were headed towards the semicircular roundabout behind Khan Market did she look up at the rear-view mirror and say, 'Sir? Which way, sir?'

'Just a minute,' said Russi in a muffled voice while the girl held the side of his face, forcing him to remain turned towards her. She was covering his mouth with hers, but he seemed to be resisting this in order to speak. 'One minute, dear,' he said, now to the girl. 'I need to tell my driver where to go.'

He was holding her hand away from his face to turn towards the front to speak to Maddy. 'I'm so sorry, Madan – this... this young lady would like to go to... to...'

Maddy coasted to a halt. 'That's all right, sir. I'll wait.'

The girl was now attempting to swarm over the older man. She had covered his face with her own, making soft, moaning sounds while her left arm slithered around the back of his neck. Now she began to slide bodily over him, her right hand roaming free and her right leg shifting between both of his.

With an energetic jerk, Russi broke loose. He sat up and moved forward, his voice suddenly loud and commanding. 'Now see here, miss, that's quite enough. Stop this, stop at once.'

He spoke to Maddy. 'Come on, we'll go to Defence Colony. That's where she lives – that's what you said, dear? No, no, now come on, come on.' He was no longer leaning back in his seat but was actually holding her down by both her wrists, her arms folded up at the elbows. 'What's your address? You mentioned it to me earlier – C Block, you said? D? Come on now.'

Maddy started moving once more, deciding to take the route that went past the Nehru Stadium, then on down to the Ring Road, where she took a left. By that time, the girl had sulkily yielded up her address. It was in C Block, she said, but as the big car glided along, she wheedled, 'You can come in, sir. Why not? Why not! I'll show you a good time, I promise you.' She continued wheedling and cajoling long past the moment when it must have been clear to her that she would not succeed.

Russi was facing the front, his expression tense as he struggled to maintain his grip on the girl. He said to Maddy, 'You know the way? Because these lanes can be very confusing.'

'I know the way, sir,' said Maddy. One of her regular clients lived on the street parallel to the one they were going to.

They drew up at an address with a security guard hut at the gate. The property he was guarding had the appearance of a company guest house. It was severely white on the outside, with a ten-foot-high compound wall and a brass plaque set into the gateposts.

The girl was coaxed out of the car with difficulty. Maddy helped her get out of the car, realizing as she did that the young woman was completely wasted. She was swaying on her heels and in tears now. 'You hurt me, oh, oh! You hurt me,' she said to Russi, clutching her arms. The whining quality in her voice reminded Maddy of someone. 'You have made marks on my skin...'

Russi remained inside the car, leaning across the seat and looking out at Maddy through the open door as he said, 'If you don't mind, please take her up to the gate, haanh? I had better not get out.'

Maddy half-supported, half-carried the wretchedly sobbing creature to where the guard was now standing outside his hut, looking on uncertainly.

'You better tell him you live here,' said Maddy to the woman, wondering what would happen next, in case the guard refused her entry.

At this, the as-yet-unnamed party girl straightened up and said, her voice suddenly full of thorns, 'Get your hands off me, you stupid fuck! Who d'you think you are to put your dirty paws on me? Get away, get away.' And then, to the guard, she said, 'What're you waiting for, you donkey? Don't you recognize me? Open the gate!'

At that moment, Maddy recognized the girl and the voice: it was the same person who, barely a week earlier, had run out of Maddy's car without paying.

The drive home to the villa was conducted in sober silence. Russi sat in front, as if to distance himself from the recent scenes in the back seat.

It was past 12.30 a.m. by the time they drew up to the front door.

Russi sat without moving, and so did Maddy. Together, they sat in silence, listening to the ticking sounds the car made as it cooled down from its night's exertions.

Presently, the white-haired man turned towards Maddy and said, 'I don't know about you, dear, but I need a drink. I would really appreciate it if you would just come inside and sit with me. Just for a few minutes, that's all.'

Maddy took a second before saying, 'All right, sir.' Then she drew in a breath and said, 'But if you don't mind, sir, I'll remain as... as Madan, sir.'

Russi gave a tired smile and nodded. 'As you wish, dear. Chalo. Let's go in.'

Maddy made sure to remove her personal effects from the car.

They went into the library. Russi loosened his tie, threw off his jacket and went across to where the decanter and glasses were kept. Maddy dropped her backpack to the floor and put the Nokia in her pocket before sitting down in one of the winged armchairs.

Russi half-turned towards her, lifting an empty whisky glass. She shook her head. 'Thank you, no,' she said, then added, 'sir,' as an afterthought.

Russi added ice to his glass, brought it over and settled into the other chair.

'So,' said Russi presently. 'Is it that you never drink or... only not with me?'

Maddy said, 'Sir, may I explain something?'

He was looking at her with an expression of relaxed and engaged friendliness. 'Please, of course.' He sat up straighter in his chair.

'This job is not something that I would have ever sought on my own.' She was still managing to speak as Madan, but the words belonged to Maddy. 'I don't regret it. I've seen things I could never have known or understood in any other way. But I think we both know it must come to an end.'

He nodded. His expression was neither glad nor sad.

'Until that time, when I am no longer Madan, I cannot have a drink with you, sir. Because, yes, I do drink now and then. But so long as I remain in this uniform and in this position, what you're seeing is a mask. It's a role that I'm playing. You're not seeing me at all.'

He twinkled at this. 'You forget! I've seen you at breakfast, too. Right? With the other members of the "harem"!' He chuckled. 'Yes, yes, I know what everyone calls them. The simple fact is, I love being surrounded by women. I do! And I count myself as immeasurably lucky to also have the love of a superlative being. Verity. What a mind she has. What a sterling personality. She understands me, you know? More than anyone else I have known.'

Maddy wondered where he was going with this.

'She's also extremely modest,' said Russi. 'Never talks about herself. She's got a remarkable story. I don't know whether you know what it is?'

Maddy shook her head.

'For instance, do you realize that we are all *her* tenants?'

'I'm sorry, sir,' said Maddy, completely taken aback. 'What?'

'No, she wouldn't have told you. It's not her way,' said Russi.

Maddy had absolutely no idea what he was talking about.

'But we were speaking about you.'

'No, sir,' said Maddy, deciding that he was starting to ramble, 'I think we need to discuss the girl. Tonight's girl. Did you know that she is a...' Maddy wasn't sure how best to proceed, 'professional?'

The change in Russi's expression was like a light being switched off. His face went dim. 'Oh my god! Yes. I knew what she was. Of course, I knew.' His voice dropped to a whisper.

Maddy's face may have shown that she was perplexed. 'So... if you knew...'

Russi shook his head. 'Chalo,' he said. 'Maybe someday I'll be able to explain such things.' He rubbed his eyes. 'But not tonight.'

The audience was over, Maddy realized. She got to her feet. 'All right then, sir.' She had decided that she'd stay in the villa overnight. 'If you don't mind, I'll go up now.' She had to cross the room to get to the secret panel.

'Yes, yes, of course,' said Russi. 'And I'm off to Mumbai tomorrow. Good night, dear, good night. And,' he looked up at her from where he sat, 'thank you. If not for you, I don't know how I would have got her out of the car.'

48

Candle wicks
And fiddle heads
Walking sticks
And pencil leads.

– JINXES, BIG & SMALL

The next morning, Maddy woke up savouring the pleasure of a clean bed and cool room. She had set the alarm for 9 a.m., which meant that she'd miss the formal breakfast downstairs.

When she stepped outside the room, she found a small package waiting for her, placed on the table by the door. It had been delivered that morning and was from Verity.

She stepped back into her room before opening the parcel. Inside, she found a book and a handwritten letter.

The book was a very famous one called *Jinxes, Big and Small*. It was a collection of whimsical poems written for children and had, since its first publication in the late sixties, been a huge success. Maddy had never read it, but she realized now that she'd seen a copy in Verity's study.

She was mildly puzzled by the gift but opened the letter first.

Dear Maddy,

It's hard to explain what exactly I'm thanking you for. Maybe I'll find a way to explain some other time. For the moment, however, please do accept my sincere thanks – and this little book.

I don't know if you've ever read it? Something tells me that you may not have.

Anyway, I am feeling awful, but my doctors here tell me that they're very pleased with my progress. I'm finding it hard to believe that any part of the word 'progress' can be attached to me, but what do I know? I'm only the silly, wrong-headed patient who whines about the horrible taste in her mouth and lives in terror of the bedsores she does not yet have.

I'm being very unfair, and I know that, too.

Plus, Russi calls all the time, and he cheers me up no end. He's a humorous person, is our Russi, when he's not hunting down human scum.

He thinks very highly of you, by the way. He's told me so several times over. He calls you his Amazon Driver and wishes only that he could parade you in public in that role. As you may have noticed, despite all his brilliance, he loves to show off. He can be altogether childish at times.

It makes me glad that he approves so heartily of you. But I feel guilty, my dear. Really, deeply guilty. It was Russi's idea, but I should not have allowed him to convince me. We're not living in Shakespearean times, where men and women could exchange roles as lightly as changing their clothes. Chetak has told me that he advised you against accepting the position. I see, now, that he was right.

You may think that your acceptance was made in full possession of your faculties and of all the facts. But that's not true. In the first place, you were in shock at the time that I asked you. You may have chosen very differently if your circumstances had been different. In the second place, as you now surely know, you were <u>not</u> in full possession of all the facts. And for that, I hold myself solely responsible.

You must not feel that you have to continue as Madan. Please discuss this with Chetak. If you want to stop, he will support your position. Even if you don't want to stop, please do consider talking to him. We are all capable of making choices that are deeply harmful to ourselves. My worry is that this might be harmful to you.

Chetak has a wonderfully clear mind. He can help you find the best path forward.

Whatever you choose, I would be very happy if you continued to live at the villa. For however long it suits you.

With warm good wishes,

Verity

PS: I'm told I'll be discharged in a day or two. But I wanted to send this anyway.

Maddy read the letter twice through.

She felt a buzzing sensation inside her.

It was something she associated with strong, high emotions, such as anger or fear.

Right now? Her face was hot. It was anger.

She moved towards the bathroom to wash, but when she entered, she found herself confronted by her reflection in the mirror that filled the wall behind the basin.

She moved forward and washed her face, still looking up at herself. It was idiotic, really. Like being an adolescent again, staring for hours at the mirror, trying to penetrate the mystery of the Self. Treating the reflection as if it were indeed a stranger living on the other side of reality.

She used to talk to her reflection, half-hoping that by some magic chance, the image would talk back, with its own voice and its own insights.

Now, though, she could not make herself speak at all.

After a few minutes, she could no longer look herself in the eye.

She turned away, embarrassed.

It didn't matter that Verity was telling her that she should remain at the villa. The underlying message was: *If you continue as Madan, you can't blame me if things go wrong. Because I am telling you that you should stop. At the same time, I'm not commanding you to stop. That is your decision. Your grave to dig.*

She remembered what Malli had said: *When they're done with you, they'll just kick you aside.* Was that what this was? The most genteel and courteous way of being kicked aside?

She returned to the room. It was cool, of course, as it always was. The fan was not on. It was also always in darkness, even in daylight, unless she opened the shutters. Right now, with only the bright edges along the joints of the shutters of the windows on either side, she walked slowly up and down.

Think, think, think, she commanded herself. *What is the right path? What is the path that I want to take? Are they the same thing?*

But the answers did not come.

49

Apples and oranges
Peaches and cream
Fruit salad fit for a
Midsummer dream.

– JINXES, BIG & SMALL

Maddy showered and dressed carefully, first as Madan. Instead of putting on his driver's uniform, she took out the two shirts that Chetak had bought as 'casual wear'. No one had anticipated any particular reason when the driver might need to be seen in them, but it made sense to have the option.

Both were loose and long-sleeved. One was black with streaks and splotches of white spattered randomly onto the cloth. It was a print but cleverly done. The other had a faux-camouflage pattern in shades of purple, black and brown. Both were effective for keeping her shape concealed.

Choosing the black shirt, she wore it with a pair of old baggy jeans that Chetak said he'd picked up in Lajpat Nagar. Then she chose a tent dress with white magnolias scattered over a burnt magenta field and put it on over Madan's clothes. She fitted her wig onto her head, shouldered the backpack and left the room as Maddy.

It was late in the morning. Chetak would be at court. Russi was away in Mumbai.

Maddy crossed over to the mirror wall and entered the tween space. Once inside, she removed the wig and changed out of the tent, stowing them both in the backpack. She was wearing Madan's sneakers, rather than his clodhoppers.

She proceeded down two floors.

At the panel that opened into the library, she paused, listening.

If there were to be any awkward encounters, this was where they'd take place. Suresh might be in the library, or Jyoti. Maybe even someone else. Maddy had never had any reason to know much about the domestic arrangements in Russi's apartments.

Hearing no movement, she opened the panel and gave a strangled shriek: Chetak was standing right behind it.

'Ah!' exclaimed Maddy. 'Omigosh—'

'What—'

'I thought you'd be at court!' said Maddy, almost in accusation.

'I was... but... you! What're you *doing*? Or maybe I should say, *Madan*?'

'Oh my god!' said Maddy, clutching her face. 'OH my god!' She caught her breath before speaking again. 'I suppose I should be grateful it was you and not—'

'Suresh,' said Chetak, drily. 'Yes. That would've been a bit of a disaster.'

'Is he around?' she asked. 'How careful do we need to be?'

'Careful,' said Chetak. 'He's in the dining room at this time. Jyoti's doing her dusting.' He glanced around. 'Let's at least leave the building. We can go to my car. Unless...' He gave her a questioning look as he moved to the door, gesturing to her to go ahead. 'You must have had some other plans?'

She said in a low voice, 'No, you go ahead... remember? I'm—'

'Oh, right,' said Chetak as he hurried through, with Maddy following.

When they were both outside, she said to him, 'I didn't know how else to get out of the house as Madan. I wanted to go for a ride. On the cycle.'

Chetak was standing by his car. Squinting against the harsh sunlight, he cocked his head to the side. '*Cycle*?' Then immediately reconsidered his remark and said, 'Well, I suppose, why not.' He looked away now. 'Frankly, I was about to call. To ask if you'd like to talk about... you know...' He was clearly uncomfortable. 'Last night,' he said finally.

Maddy was standing aloof. She couldn't decide how much of her posture was because she was in Madan mode versus the feelings brought on since reading Verity's message in the morning.

'Well,' she said, 'of course we need to talk. I mean, last night was...' She ran her hand through her short hair, wrinkling her nose. 'Bad. Really bad.' Then she patted the Nokia in her pocket and added, 'But I think we're in business.'

His face relaxed. 'Oh! Okay, good. Great. You're sure you wouldn't rather talk about it right away?'

She glanced around, not expecting to see anyone but had that crawling sense of eyes scraping the back of her neck. 'It's hard to maintain a long conversation in Madan's voice. Plus, I need to...' she flexed her shoulders, 'I need to sort out my head. There's a lot going on.'

'Yes,' said Chetak. 'I'll bet there is.'

'Verity sent me a letter,' said Maddy, changing tack. 'Did she write to you, too?'

'No,' said Chetak. 'How is she doing? What was it about?'

'She says she's better. But said I should talk to you—' Maddy broke off. 'No. Wait. I really need to get away. I'll go off now, but let's meet later today? Because I really need to. Be on my own, I mean. Get away.' She swung her head around to where she hoped to see the cycle, then pointed as she saw it. 'Okay, yes, the cycle *is* back.' Courtesy Chetak's tireless elves. 'I need the exercise. I'll go off now. I'll catch lunch somewhere. Then I'll get back to you? And we can talk. When I'm back here.'

Chetak nodded uncertainly. 'Okay, but surely, you'll have the same sort of problem getting back into the villa? As Madan?'

'Oh, damn!' said Maddy.

'How about you tell me where you'll be at a particular time, and I'll meet you there?' he suggested. 'Somewhere far enough away from here that we won't be seen stowing the cycle in the back of my car. Then you can change back into Maddy.'

They agreed that this was the best way forward.

Chetak went back into the villa while Maddy wheeled the cycle out from behind the bushes, slung her leg over and sailed out.

She didn't have a specific destination in mind. She joined the fleet of other men on bicycles who were, at this time of day, returning for lunch from their places of work. They occupied the left-most lanes of all the roads.

Some of them had small children in school uniforms riding pillion behind them. Some had one child riding behind while another child was balanced precariously in front, on the top bar. Maddy tried to coax a smile out of one of the tiny tots sitting at the back. He stared back, his enormous round eyes stained with kajal, his hair oiled and slicked back, grave and unsmiling. It was the same with all the children she tried. Like attempting to coax a smile out of an oyster. She gave up after a while.

She had started her ride on the Outer Ring Road travelling east, then doubled back, then doubled back again at Africa Avenue. She remembered a small café in the SDA shopping complex a short distance from the IIT Metro station. There were several small cafés there, she discovered; she hadn't realized there would be a choice. She settled on the one that seemed the most modest, called the Corner Joint. It had the kind of decor that would have made 'no-frills' look baroque: stainless-steel tube tables with matching stainless-steel tube chairs.

She ordered a hot coffee. Then, as she waited, she picked up Madan's phone from her pocket and returned to the message she'd written to herself the night before last.

Preet's number.

She waited till the coffee was served. It was as stripped down as the décor, in a plain white ceramic coffee mug, with the milk already mixed in. On the table was a steel-wire condiment caddy containing sachets of salt, pepper, sugar and a stand of black plastic cutlery.

She gazed at the number, thought about all the reasons why she should not call this man. She stirred two packets of sugar into the coffee and took a sip and was surprised to find that it was quite good. She took another sip. She finished the whole mug and placed an order for another one.

Just when she thought she had successfully resisted the urge to call, she picked up the phone again and dialled the number.

Ring-ring... Ring-ring... Ring-ring... Ring-ring...

Ten times before disconnecting.

She smiled at herself. *Of course,* it would not connect. Nothing had changed in the two decades since her late teens. It might as well be one of Newton's First Laws of Phonodynamics: A Called Man Will Not Answer.

There's a second law, however: On Rare Occasions, He Will Call Back.

Her phone rang, flashing an unfamiliar number. She answered it anyway.

A man's voice, grainy with an edge of slate: 'Hollow.' No question mark.

It was Preet.

Shifting her voice to Madan's register, Maddy said, 'Uh... hello?'

'Jaguar,' he said. 'DHX 7990.'

'Yes,' she said.

There was a pause. 'Where are you?'

She told him.

'All right,' he said. 'I'll come there.'

Then disconnected.

50

Alas, poor Yorick!
Who needs him?
I prefer poor little
Tiny Tim.

– JINXES, BIG & SMALL

Maddy left her coffee untouched to forestall the need to visit another men's room. She ordered a grilled cheese sandwich, then cancelled the order in favour of a kathi kabab roll.

As she waited, she contemplated the multi-layered folly of her decision to call.

She could not justify this action in anyway. The word 'relationship' could not even get its toe in the door. There was no question of any continuance. This was a man who thought she was a man. Who would not appreciate her reasons for faking her gender. Who did not think in English and would not be interested in the same books and movies she had grown up with.

Who would never share her social world and would never want to.

It was pure, unadulterated, directionless mischief.

If she had revealed the whole story to Chetak, he would have given her one of his pitying looks. There could be no sympathy. The only advice would be to stay away.

And here was Preet now.

She saw him some distance away. She had seen a white Maruti Suzuki WagonR poking its snub nose into the parking area along the service lane between the SDA market and the Ring Road. The green stripe along its side and the yellow license plate declared the car's status as a private taxi. When he got out of the car, she saw that he was not wearing the grey-on-grey uniform adopted by many a taxi driver, but instead, was in a red and black striped shirt with black trousers.

He stood beside the car for a moment to take out a pair of sunglasses from his breast pocket and put them on. Then, standing still, he carefully scanned the scene in front of him until his eye lit upon her. He did not appear to have any doubts. He locked the car and strode through the mass of parked two-wheelers to get to the open area where she sat.

She wished she'd had sunglasses on, too.

'Hollow,' he said as he got to her table. He pulled back one of the steel-tube chairs and flopped down, in the odd, graceless manner of someone who does not often sit in steel-tube chairs. He draped his arms out over the backs of two other chairs, appearing at that moment to be like a giant cormorant drying its black wings after a dive.

'Hullo,' said Maddy in Madan's low voice.

She wanted to look Preet in the face but found it too difficult.

There was a terrible silence.

In the background, the traffic honked and growled. Closer at hand, a large group of college students dressed in fluorescent T-shirts was squealing and chortling as their cell phones made farting sounds at one another.

'So,' said Preet. 'This is coffee.' He asked the question as a statement.

'Yes,' said Maddy. 'It's... I've already had one cup.'

'Okay,' he said, reaching for the mug. 'What have you ordered?'

'Kathi kabab roll.'

'Good,' said Preet. He took a sip of the coffee and stopped at once. 'This is shit. No sugar.' He put down the mug and reached for the sugar with hands that seemed unaccustomed to anything so refined as opening dainty paper packets. He tore into three of them at once, holding them over the coffee as he did so.

He took another sip after stirring, then breathed out with a throaty hiss to signal approval. 'Better. That's better.' Tipping his head back, he now poured the hot coffee down his throat in one continuous stream, emptying the mug without putting the rim to his mouth.

'That was good,' he said, putting down the mug. He patted his chest, belched and cleared his throat.

He removed the sunglasses and squeezed his eyes shut, rubbing them while screwing up his face as he did so.

'All right,' he said, his eyes still shut, 'Why did you call me?'

Maddy stared across the small table at this man about whom she knew almost nothing. Her mind was blank. 'I don't know,' she said. 'I had to.'

He opened his eyes now and blinked like someone who has not had much sleep.

'No,' he said, turning his face towards her. 'You do know. Or you would not do it. Not after two days to think about it.'

Maddy noticed for the first time that his eyes were a glassy grey colour. Unusual. She hadn't seen that on the night they met. She remembered the barber, John, and thought about the unlikelihood of encountering two unrelated Indian men with light eyes in quick succession.

'What's the matter?' he asked. 'Why are you staring?'

'You have light eyes,' she said.

He gave a short laugh. 'Yes. My son has them, too.'

'Oh...' said Maddy, nonplussed. 'You have a son?'

'Two. Two small boys. One has these eyes,' said Preet.

The kathi kabab roll arrived just then. It was a fat brown tube, almost as long as her forearm, and freckled with darker brown spots. Its contents oozed out on either side as it luxuriated on a bed of shredded cabbage. The waiter, a young northeastern man, had automatically brought two white ceramic plates. He set them down, one each in front of Preet and Maddy respectively. The kabab roll was on a plain white platter he had placed between them.

'Anything else?' he asked Maddy and hurried away almost before he'd registered the negative answer.

Preet sat forward and reached for the roll with both hands, but Maddy said, 'Wait.'

Taking up a knife from the wire caddy, she held the roll with her left hand and cut down decisively, creating two plump sections. She deposited one on his plate and one on hers.

'Huh,' said Preet. 'I was going to do the same thing.'

'It's neater this way,' said Maddy.

'What's the need?' observed Preet. 'It all goes down into the same place.' Picking up his portion of the roll, he held it with both hands and began stuffing the cut end into his mouth.

They ate in silence, looking nowhere in particular. Preet finished before Maddy. He ate with gusto, gulping and swallowing with firm jerks.

When he was done, he fished out a handkerchief the size of a hand towel and wiped his mouth and face with it. Then he turned his pale eyes towards her, to watch her as she ate. She was overwhelmed with self-consciousness. She tried lunging at her kabab roll as he had but failed miserably. She began to sweat with the effort and also because she'd bitten into a chilli. All she could manage were medium-sized nibbles, each one resulting in the contents squishing out from both ends.

Preet looked around for the waiter and signalled for water by pointing his thumb towards his mouth.

He turned back towards her. She still had half of her section of roll left but had given up and put it down on her plate. She grabbed a paper napkin and wiped her mouth with it.

Glancing up, she asked, 'Will you... do you want to finish it?'

His pale eyes were like searchlights.

She realized, too late, that he would consider the idea disgusting.

She remembered from her school days in Delhi how her young friends had shrieked with horror at the very idea of sharing food that had been bitten into by someone else. They informed her that it was forbidden to eat anything that had been polluted by another person's mouth. They assured her that it was her misfortune to have grown up in backward regions of the world, such as the USA, where white-skinned savages indulged in these vomit-inducing practices.

When she protested to them that it was racist to speak of 'white-skinned savages', they teased her all the more. 'You've become one of them!' they roared, 'you poor, unfortunate savage!'

The waiter brought two glasses of water and left them on the table.

'You can't finish?' said Preet.

'It's too much for me,' said Maddy.

She had become acutely aware that whatever they said was charged with innuendo. Was that the lurid bent of her mind? Or could it possibly be the same for him? She couldn't guess whether innuendo worked in different ways when a person's thought base was not English.

'Okay,' he said and reached across the table for the remnants of her roll.

She was sure, as he did this, that he was breaking a deep-seated taboo. It could not be for the first time. But maybe this was the kind of barrier that never went away. Maybe he found himself having to force his way through it every time.

Maybe, she wondered, he enjoyed breaking that barrier.

He looked up at her now as he began stuffing the roll into his mouth.

Once again, she felt her cheeks and neck redden.

He was working at it slowly and thoughtfully now, with less dispatch than with his portion. He took smaller bites, eating with his mouth closed but his eyes open.

Maddy wanted to look away but could not. A flush of heat travelled down her throat. Looking at him, looking into those eyes, she saw that he knew perfectly well what he was doing. The pupils of his eyes had become black pools. The corners of his eyes were crinkled. He was laughing silently with the food still in his mouth.

As he stuffed the final section of the roll into his mouth, he looked away reflexively, his neck jutting forward, flexing his mouth to clear food from the sides of his teeth. To finish, he threw his head back and emptied the glass down his throat.

When he was done, he looked at her. There was an air of triumph on his face.

Maddy felt as completely out of her depth as she had at the time of making her call. She had not managed to take control of the situation. She could not put words to any part of this. She could only stare back, her scalp tingling.

But he was entirely at ease. Reaching forward, he clasped both her hands as they lay on the tabletop on either side of her plate. He brought her hands together inside his and held them tight. 'That was good,' he said. His eyes were filled with light. 'We will meet again.'

Then he stood up, turned and was gone, striding through the parked two-wheelers and towards his car without a backward glance.

51

Helping hand,
Rock and sand,
Building castles,
On the strand.

– JINXES, BIG & SMALL

Chetak collected Maddy from near the Deer Park. They folded the cycle into the trunk and were quiet on the way back to the villa. Chetak called for tea when they were upstairs in the mirror lobby, and Maddy said she needed to wash up after her sweaty ride.

She shied away from looking herself in the eye in the bathroom mirror. She removed Madan's clothes from under her tent. Adding loose white pyjamas and flip-flops, she left the room. On her way out, she picked up the letter she'd received from Verity that morning.

Handing it to Chetak, she asked, 'Please, before I talk about last night, could we discuss this?' When he looked up, she explained, 'Verity's letter.'

He read it with no change of expression. When he was done, he said, 'Well?' And shrugged. 'You already know what I think.'

There was an odd edge to his voice, which acted as a goad to Maddy.

'No,' she said. She remained standing. 'That won't do.' She removed the flip-flops and was now barefoot. 'I'm sorry, that just... *won't do*! I was quite furious when I read it this morning.'

Chetak's forehead creased. 'I'm sorry, too. Because I can't see what there is in that letter to be furious about.'

Maddy clicked her tongue in irritation aimed at herself. 'Oh! I wish I had spoken to you this morning. It was very clear to me then. But now I... I...'

She began to pace, placing her feet deliberately on the pattern of tiles to walk only on the black ones. 'Chetak,' she said, 'this morning, I was very sure that the point of Verity's letter was, "Run along, dear, because I'm worried that you're going to hurt yourself – unless, of course, you *want* to harm yourself... in which case... GO AHEAD! But don't blame it on me, will you?"'

She raised her head. 'Can you understand why I read it like that? Do you see how it could seem extremely callous? I mean... it's *too late*, don't you see? It's too late for me to pull out now. I'm involved. I'm committed.'

'Wait, wait, wait.' Chetak got to his feet. 'There are two separate issues here—'

'Please don't go all lawyerly on me!'

'On the one hand, you feel Verity's telling you to leave, and on the other hand, you're annoyed at yourself for not wanting to leave?'

'No,' said Maddy. 'That's not what I said.'

'I know for a fact that she feels she's led you astray. And that's all she's saying—'

'Not at all,' cut in Maddy. 'It's in the tone of the letter. Very friendly and self-deprecating but letting herself off the hook.'

'Look,' said Chetak, 'it's very simple: if you feel you can't continue, then you shouldn't. There's no obligation. That's all she's saying to you. Really, that's all. And at the same time, if you want to continue, then you should—'

'Isn't that the same as telling me that it's just a matter of my whim?' Maddy was finding it difficult to prevent her voice from growing shrill. 'And... and it's *not*! Not since breakfast at the ITC hotel. Not since the Garden Café. And *especially* not since last night, Chetak! I mean that girl...'

There was a clanking thump, signalling that the lift had come up.

'The tea,' said Chetak. He went towards the lift.

He opened both doors and held them as Jyoti emerged, trundling a cylindrical three-tier trolley with tea things on each of its circular stages in front of her. In her usual manner, with her head slightly bent, she went towards the side table and completed her task of delivering the items from the trolley to the table. Teapot, creamer, sugar bowl; cups, saucers, teaspoons; plate of freshly made paneer pakoras, glass bottle of Kissan tomato ketchup. She returned to the lift without interacting directly with either of the two in the room. Chetak had remained where he was until she was back in the lift. Then he released both doors and turned towards Maddy once more.

'I apologize for my tone,' he said. 'I honestly don't want to seem unsympathetic. It's just that I'm not seeing a problem with Verity's letter.'

Maddy sat down. She contemplated her toes. Speaking slowly, as if to space her thoughts out coherently, she said, 'It's like... telling someone... that they're free to leave... as a way of... of getting them to stay.' She paused. 'Maybe I come across as a contrary person. The sort who, when I'm given a clear command *not* to do something, will break my neck to do it. But I'm not irrational. And I don't think I'm harming myself.'

'All right then,' said Chetak. 'Let's come right out and ask the question: What DO you want to do?' He immediately continued, 'And don't, please, say you don't know. Because I believe you do—'

Maddy cut in, thinking of what Preet had said, 'Why do people keep telling me that?'

Chetak shook the remark aside with an irritated jerk of his head. It was only now that Maddy realized that he was angry. Not just moody.

There was silence.

Maddy said, 'Okay then. What I want is to see it through.' She looked up at Chetak. 'The thing we talked about, when was it, two days ago? The plan to help Russi avoid entrapment. Remember?'

'Obviously,' said Chetak.

'I want to be part of it. I've been in a fog all this while. But I'm not now.'

'Oh?' Chetak was standing still.

'It's because of what you told me, just yesterday, at the café.'

He said nothing.

'My presence in the villa was the result of an emergency. But that's come to an end. Overnight, staying here has become a choice. A real choice.' She was staring up at him. 'I checked my account. This morning. The money's in there. And that changes everything. As you knew it would.'

Chetak inclined his head, acknowledging her remark but not necessarily agreeing with it. 'I went ahead and made the transfer. I'll recover the funds from Mrs Bansal in good time. I figured you needed to see the sum in your books before you'd believe it.'

Maddy gave a short bark of laughter. 'Oh, yes, I believe it. And yes, in the same stroke, it makes me all the more suspicious of *everything*. Large sums of money have that effect. Just like you said. Whatever title they're given, it's hard not to find words like "bribe" or "coercion" flashing like neon signs in my head.'

Chetak turned away.

'This sum is so very large – for me, anyway – that I would be a fool not to wonder all over again: is it a set-up? What am I being conned into doing? You do see that, don't you? And then there's the timing. Barely have you finished telling me that I've received an enormous windfall, but – *ding-ding!* – here comes the quid pro quo.'

Chetak turned towards the tea things. 'Yes,' he said. 'I see how it might look.'

She couldn't see his expression as he poured tea for both of them. His voice was low. 'You can think what you like about the progression of events. But when the hoped-for rewards are sufficiently enormous, they take on gravitational mass. They begin to distort reality.'

'Are you talking about me,' asked Maddy, 'or—'

'I'm talking about the case,' he said, forestalling her while handing her a cup. 'I'm talking about a hoped-for reward in which millions of historically oppressed communities all across India will be guaranteed legal protection. And I'm talking about the plutocrats who oppose that outcome. Because of the fortunes they stand to lose.'

He picked up his cup and moved to the other chair. 'That's when the distortion begins.' He took a sip. 'When we spoke this morning, I said that I was keen to know what happened last night. Since then, however, I've been given an account. And it's grotesquely ugly.'

'What?'

'It's a complete fabrication. It has to be. But if it appears in the press, it's what the world will believe. Because of the distortion. Because of the hallucinations that giant sums of money can create.'

Chetak wore a tense, hunted expression. 'Let's back up to Verity for a moment. The letter you got was written yesterday, during the day. It was delivered by overnight courier and reached you this morning. What I'd like you to understand is, she knew nothing at the time she wrote the letter about the events of last night. She doesn't know what I'm about to tell you. If she was worried for you, it was in the abstract. She had no idea that there might be a real threat of any sort.'

Maddy shrugged.

'As you may have guessed by now, we've heard from the other side,' said Chetak. 'They're a global alliance of industrialists so powerful as a group that they become, almost by default, a criminal organization.'

'They reached out with what?' asked Maddy.

'A serious complaint,' said Chetak. 'From a young woman called Sherry. Claims that Russi offered her a lift home from the function at the Taj Mansingh. According to her, during the course of the drive, he attempted to rape her. When she resisted, the car came to a halt, whereupon he *and his driver* roughed her up. Photographs of the damage show her looking a bloody mess. Her handlers must have really worked her over. Cuts and bruises all over.'

'Oh my god!' said Maddy.

'Plus, they have the sworn testimony of the nightwatchman. He describes the driver as a tall young man, very fair, very abusive, who deposited the woman at the gate. She was sobbing and dishevelled, claiming that the driver and his employer both messed with her.'

Maddy was silent.

'The counsel representing the woman,' continued Chetak, 'is from the same firm that represents the alliance. That's deliberate. They want us to know that they're willing to blow this bogus assault into a media circus. Unless we're willing to let the tribal lands matter slide.'

'They've not actually said that, surely?'

'Oh no, no, no! Nothing so crude and obvious. They've demanded a closed-door hearing right away in order to secure justice for this young woman,' said Chetak. 'They want Russi to be present, naturally enough. But they also want Madan to be the star witness. They're so confident he'll confess that they're already speaking as if Russi's professional life is over.'

'They don't mention the tribal lands?'

'Not at all. To do so would be to expose their motive for bringing Russi down.'

'What makes them so confident Madan will succumb?'

'The distortion field,' said Chetak. His voice was bleak. 'They'll bribe him.'

Maddy's eyes narrowed. 'The timing couldn't be worse.'

Chetak said nothing.

'I don't suppose there's any way they can possibly know that a certain giant sum of money has very recently been deposited in Madan's account.'

Chetak clicked his tongue. 'Your account. Not Madan's.'

'Wouldn't that make it all the more interesting? The fact that "Madan" gets paid in an exquisitely invisible way?'

'Don't joke about this, Maddy!' said Chetak suddenly. He put down his cup on the side table. 'I'm trying to tell you that there's a target on Madan's back! Which means, obviously, on *your* back. If they can't buy him out, it's not a problem. People like Madan are easily erased, rewritten and edited to suit the public narrative.'

Maddy sat forward, her teacup still in her hand, untouched, 'And I'm trying to tell you that the money you've paid me has already changed me. Instantly. However suspicious I might feel about it, well... there it is! A mountain of fairy gold. It frees me to make my own choices. That's what I've been trying to tell you: however twisted and manipulative you may or may not have been, the effect is that you've convinced me. *I'm in*. All the way. And believe it or not, I may even have a workable plan—'

'Oh, stop!' Chetak jumped to his feet. 'You shouldn't have to do any of this, Maddy. This whole situation started out as something light-hearted. *Driving Miss Daisy*, modern-day India edition. Then, before any of us could pull the brakes, the car plunged into the abyss. I did *not* plan to set you up to take the fall for everyone. But that's where it's gone anyway.'

'What about the insurance scheme?'

'What insurance scheme?'

She patted her hip where there would be a pocket if she'd been wearing jeans. 'Madan's phone. I told you this morning that the recording came through all right. Won't that be evidence enough?'

'Not if they murder you and destroy the phone before anyone gets to hear it. I don't understand why you're smiling. There's absolutely nothing to smile about. Your life is in danger.'

'You didn't hear what I said just now,' said Maddy. 'I think I have a plan.'

52

Girls and boys,
Games and toys,
Make the best and
Brightest noise.

– JINXES, BIG & SMALL

Later that evening, Maddy left the villa as Madan and spent the night in Shahpur Jat. In the morning, she returned and parked the bike in its usual place. Then she brought the Jaguar around to the front and began cleaning it with a wet cloth.

At 9 a.m., a couple of men came through the gate on a beat-up blue Bajaj. The pillion dismounted, removing his helmet as he approached and asked for Madan Lal Singh.

'Yes,' said Maddy.

'Phone number?'

She told him.

Whereupon the man, dressed in a black hoodie and grey sweats, with the narrow, large-eyed face of a whippet, handed her an envelope without saying a word. Clambering back onto the scooter, he and the rider left immediately.

It was a summons to the hearing, scheduled for 10 a.m. the next day.

Ravi, the regular driver, was due to fetch Russi from the airport at noon. Maddy spent the rest of the day away from the villa. She loafed about in Hauz Khas market, ate lunch at a busy dhaba and smoked by the side of the road. It was hot, sweaty and tedious, with plenty of time to contemplate what lay in store for her during the next twenty-four hours.

She had used outdoor facilities twice by the late afternoon, choosing walls that bore the stains and smells of recent use by others. No one glanced in her direction.

Towards evening, when the air overhead was sullen with fumes and dust, she returned to the villa, picked up the cycle and rode back to Shahpur Jat. The phone in her pocket trilled twice as she entered the lane. Both times blank messages from an unfamiliar number.

Her heart began to bump softly against the bars of its cage.

She put the phone away and wheeled the bike into the stairwell leading to her abode. She chained it to its place beneath the stairs and climbed the stairs.

It was after 7 p.m. The landlord's place was streaming with noise and light as Maddy passed through their front room on her way up to the second floor.

One flight up, the corridor was in total darkness except for the line of blue light from under the door of the techie neighbour. She turned on the penlight torch, taken from her key fob, and kept it pointed towards the floor as she made her way to her door.

She had sensed the presence that was crouched at the head of the stairs.

Her phone trilled again. Three times now. It would be another blank message to confirm that she was the correct target. She took the little gadget out of her pants pocket, glanced at the lit screen, then put it back in the pocket of her jeans.

It amused her to note the clumsiness with which the assailant began to creep up. With apparently no light of his own, he had only her torch to guide him. She heard his shuffling footsteps and even his panting breath as she stood at her door, tense, and braced for impact while pretending to fumble the lock.

She had just removed the padlock when—

WHAM! A body slammed into her from behind and held her pinned against the door, her face flat against it. She had turned her head to the right at the last moment, or else her nose might have been broken.

The man's forearm was jammed against the back of her head. But he was an inch or two shorter than her, breathing as if he had just run up both flights of stairs. He had to drag her down so that he could speak softly into her ear. 'Not a sound,' he hissed. His body odour was intense, his mouth spraying spittle. 'Ten lakhs for you. Tomorrow. If you say the right thing. Understand?' When she didn't respond, his arm jogged hard again. '*Understand?*'

'Un-un-derstood!' rasped Maddy, tasting the surface of the door, against her mouth. 'Understood!' With her hands, she tugged at the bolt, hauling it partially out of its socket.

'The old man did the girl. You saw him. You helped him. *Say it*!' As he spoke, he felt along the right side of her leg with his free hand. Easily found the pocket. Plunged his hand in. Extracted the small phone.

'D-did the girl!' The left side of Maddy's face was on fire. She was gasping, panting with pain. 'Helped him!'

'Remember. Ten lakhs. Cash. Tomorrow.'

Then, with another vicious shove, he was gone.

The bolt shot free of its housing. The door burst open. Maddy pitched forward into her room, arms flailing wide, unable to break her fall. But she had anticipated this moment. Earlier that day, she had positioned the rush mat and pillow so that she'd fall onto them rather than the bare cement floor.

She lay there, stunned, in the thick darkness. Her little torch had gone blind, perhaps fallen somewhere. Tweeting chirps were sounding inside her head, just like in a cartoon, and she could see flashing blips of light at the inner edge of her vision.

There was a wet taste in her mouth. *Blood,* she thought dreamily.

There was no motivation to move, to stir her limbs, to sit up.

She was afraid she might have broken something.

She passed out briefly.

The next thing she knew, a wash of blue light had entered the room through her door. Another person had come in. Was standing beside her, was kneeling beside her. The bright ellipse from a fresh torch was dabbing here and there, its beam slanting through the dusty air. Careful to avoid her face.

Then a hand was on her shoulder and back. An unfamiliar voice addressed her. 'Hello?' It was a young man's voice. 'Madan?' Clearly, it was someone who knew who Madan was. He was speaking softly, solicitously. 'Madan... Madan Lal. Sir, can you hear me?'

53

Sugar, pepper, salt and spice,
Help me cook up something nice.

– JINXES, BIG & SMALL

The techie said his name was Raqs. She didn't ask what it was short for. She understood now that he was one amongst the mini-army of minions that Chetak apparently had command over. Or maybe it was just one minion, stationed right by her. She didn't care. He had come in when he was needed, helped her to her feet, had not asked questions and settled her in for the night. Then he left.

In the morning, the front of Maddy's body felt like a train crash. But nothing was broken. Or if it was, she couldn't feel it. The faceless assailant had removed a cell phone from her pocket, but it was a dupe. Its number was what she'd given to the two men who served her with the notice, and it had a copy of the recording on it. Her own Samsung and Madan's little Nokia were both still with her.

Using her Samsung as a selfie mirror, she saw that she'd been transformed into a technicolour gargoyle. The left side of her face was scraped red and raw and had swollen up. Her jaw had turned yellow and green. Her mouth had ballooned out where her teeth had cut her lips. Purple bruises were darkening around her left eye, and the brow above it was a bloody smear.

She smiled at herself, wincing as she did so. There was no faking such injuries.

She had to use the first-floor toilet, however. She managed to squat, but it was exquisite agony, every joint screaming in protest. She couldn't face a bucket bath, but she did what she could using a hand towel and mug of water.

She wore a fresh uniform to get to the meeting in the morning. Raqs's parting suggestion at night had been that she should take an auto to the villa, not the bicycle. She understood the advice in the morning, her body whining with every breath. She swallowed a handful of ibuprofen. Next, she removed three tablets of Calmpose from their foil packaging, placed them in her handkerchief and folded the handkerchief carefully into her right pant pocket.

She tried Malli's number, but the call went to voicemail. Maddy left a brief message. 'Don't ring me when you get this message, please. I'm sending you Chetak's number. This phone will be off, but he'll give you information.' She tucked both the Nokia and the Samsung into her left-hand pocket. Then she deposited her backpack with Raqs next door and departed for the hearing.

She wore a black hoodie over Madan's uniform to avoid frightening passers-by on the street with the wounds on her face.

The venue was Russi's official chambers, on the first floor of the villa.

Half a dozen shiny black vehicles were parked like an impromptu showroom of luxury brands in the lane leading up to the villa's main entrance.

She got down some yards from the gate and paid the auto driver. Then she removed the hoodie and limped painfully towards the throng of drivers in grey safari suits who were standing just at the open doorway. There was no one she recognized except Russi's driver, Ravi, who was doing double duty as doorman.

The crowd parted as she approached. She displayed her face, enjoying the effect the swellings and bruises were having. Ravi gave her a puzzled look for a moment before recognition kicked in, and he stood aside. He had, of course, been instructed to expect Madan and to let him in.

Maddy crossed through the octagonal entrance hall and the drawing room, then the hall on the other side and through the panel door, to the tiny lift lobby. Bahadur was on duty there and rose to his feet at the sight of someone he had never seen before: Madan. He gave no indication of noticing the bruising on Maddy's face, but he had a list in his hand with names checked off. He tapped the list and said, 'ID proof?'

Maddy pulled out Madan's Aadhar card and showed it to the guard. He ticked the name off from his list, then pointed to the hoodie Maddy held rolled up in her hands.

'Bag not allowed,' he said curtly. Meekly, she handed it over to him.

On his table was a plaited-grass basket in which glinted several phones.

'Phone?' demanded Bahadur. Maddy placed her Samsung in there, next to Chetak's iPhone.

Then the guard indicated the lift door with his hand and said, 'First floor.'

One floor up, the lift landing was a tiny anteroom to Russi's chambers. Suresh and Jyoti both stood there beside a table of empty glasses and sealed bottles of Bisleri water, ready to carry them inside when needed.

As Maddy stepped out of the lift, their eyes bulged in shock. They said nothing, however. It was clear that their shock was aimed at the condition of 'Madan's' face. When she flashed the Aadhar card once more, Suresh pointedly mutely towards the door that Madan was to go through.

Maddy pushed open the door and stepped into the room.

Seven people were already present: Russi and Chetak; the judge; opposing counsel; the court stenographer; the woman who now called herself Sherry and a shrivelled prawn in human form. This person was the nightwatchman from two nights ago. He was so diminished without his uniform and so convulsed with the shame of his lies that he appeared to have caved in upon himself.

The furniture in the room had been arranged to simulate a court.

The judge sat in a well-padded black executive throne behind Russi's immense Burma teak double-pedestal desk that dominated the entire east side of the room. Two smaller desks had been placed at right angles to this monstrosity. Sherry, the nightwatchman and the sleek, penguin-shaped opposing counsel, Mr Mishra, sat with their backs to the entrance door while Russi and Chetak sat on the other side of the room.

When Maddy made her entrance, Russi gave an audible gasp. His normally ruddy face became chalk white. He raised a hand to cover his mouth, his eyes enormous behind his glasses. Maddy did not dare look at Chetak, sitting right by Russi, but she was conscious of the other faces turning to stare at the young driver with the misshapen face.

Inclining her head towards the judge, Maddy crossed the room, moving slowly and painfully. When she sat down, she had a chance to look at the complainant.

The young woman was dressed in a long-sleeved, high-collared salwar suit, dark green in colour and embroidered in white at the edges. A white chiffon scarf was looped around her neck and draped so that it veiled her shoulders and arms. Her hair was drawn back in a severe plait. She wore impenetrably dark sunglasses, with no jewellery except for a bracelet watch on her left wrist and three silver bangles on her right. In her hands, she held a white cotton handkerchief with which she dabbed her cheeks every minute or two.

All the chairs in the room other than the one on which the judge sat were of the same design: polished rosewood with semi-circular back supports and dark leather padded seats. One of these had been placed in the centre of the room, simulating a witness box.

Maddy maintained the disinterested demeanour of a driver who was yet to understand why he had been called to the hearing.

Introductory statements were made, during which Chetak, next to whom 'Madan' was seated, turned towards 'him', ostensibly translating what was being said into Hindi. It was only when the opposing counsel began to read the charges, and Chetak translated, that Maddy's body jerked as if she'd been electrocuted.

'What—' she began, her voice reduced to a low croak by her injuries.

Chetak put out a restraining hand.

In the next moment, as she heard her name – that is, Madan's name – mentioned in the charges, and understanding what they meant, she struggled to get to her feet.

'No!' she called out in a hoarse voice, 'NO! This is wrong! False! ALL FALSE!'

Whereupon a fit of ferocious coughing overtook her.

'Order!' cried the judge. 'Order!'

Russi leaned forward, pushing a glass of water towards her. Chetak picked it up and held it in readiness.

Under the ruse of overcoming the coughing fit, Maddy removed her folded handkerchief from her pocket and delivered a tablet of Calmpose to her mouth. She had forgotten, however, to separate them while she'd been in the auto. It was too late now. Instead of one, she swallowed all three. Grabbing the glass that Chetak was holding, she took a long draft of the water, then fell back in her chair, panting and overwrought.

'My Lord,' said Chetak, rising to his feet to address the judge, 'as we can all see, our witness is in no condition to give evidence. May I respectfully suggest that this session be adjourned—'

Mr Mishra leapt to his feet. 'My Lord, anyone can see that the witness has been coached! My opponents are creating a distraction to prevent my client from narrating the full extent of the heinous crimes that were perpetrated against her.'

But Maddy had staggered upright. Her eyes were beginning to roll up in her head. This was no charade: the pills had always had a strong effect on her, and this was three times the normal dose. She was terrified that she'd pass out or throw up before completing her task. Launching herself towards the chair in the middle of the room, she pulled Madan's little Nokia out of her pocket. Holding the tiny device aloft in her left hand, she pressed play.

'... I'll show you a good time, sir...' came Sherry's voice, tinny yet distinct.

Maddy crumpled forward into the chair before sliding off altogether, sprawling in a dead faint with her arms thrown wide. The phone skittered across the floor towards Chetak as the sounds from two nights ago continued to unspool, unchecked, into the room.

Fifteen minutes later, Maddy's inert form was bundled into the back seat of a white Maruti Suzuki WagonR that had been parked all morning beside the lift entrance.

Chetak spoke to the driver of the car while looking worriedly at the unconscious figure inside. He handed the heavy backpack containing Maddy's things over to the driver and also a plain white envelope. On an impulse, he leaned inside and took a photograph of Maddy's face with his iPhone.

Then the car sped away from the villa, heading south.

54

Piercing shriek
And shattering cry,
Broke some glass
And made us sigh!

– JINXES, BIG & SMALL

A warm breeze fanned Maddy's face as she gradually emerged from the nothingness of drug-induced sleep. She couldn't make out what the breeze might be from. It felt like hot feathers. Which didn't make sense. Or a friendly blast from a jet engine. That didn't work at all. There were no friendly jet engines. An oven? That would produce steady heat but no breeze.

She woke to find a solemn-eyed little boy, a thatch of black curls above a pair of ripe brown cheeks, standing right by her, fanning her face with a bamboo hand fan on a parrot-green wooden handle. He gave a startled cry, dropped the fan and sprang back two paces. The heat from the overhead sun burned hot despite the stippled shade of the scrawny tree that she lay under.

She shut her eyes once more, deciding that she wasn't quite ready to move just yet. She couldn't recognize anything of her current circumstances except that she was lying on her side, her right side, under a tree in the open air.

A moment later, the fanning began anew. A smile developed in her mind. *How sweet!* she thought. *My eyes are an on-off switch!*

She didn't wait too long to open her eyes again, however, out of concern for the young attendant. He stopped again but did not cry out or drop the fan. Instead, he just gazed at her with a worried frown creased between his brows, surveying her face with minute attention, as if memorizing it. Then abruptly, he turned.

'He's awake!' he called in a bird-like, piping voice.

To which there was an immediate answer in a deeper register, 'Oh? Really? Are you sure?'

The child turned back to confirm. 'Yes,' he called. 'Sure.'

There was a stirring then a short distance away.

Maddy had not yet moved her head. From her vantage point, what she could make out behind the child's short body clad in a pink T-shirt one size too small was a stretch of bare earth, then a stubbly field and then a stand of very straight, very spindly tree trunks. Beyond that, nonspecific greenery.

There were sounds, too, but she had not yet got around to sorting them into specifics.

Various parts of her were reporting pain but in a muted form. She knew that would change the moment she attempted to get up. Which she'd have to do soon enough.

A pair of tree trunks clad in white pyjama legs entered her field of vision. A hand reached down and held the little boy's head, the brown fingers sinking into the black curls, turning the head gently sideways as Preet's voice said, 'Go on now. Find your brother. Go.'

The boy turned without resistance in the direction he'd been shown. A moment later, Preet lowered himself right down, sitting easily on his haunches, his face where the boy's head had been. He wore a dark blue kurta made of thick plain cotton.

'Wah,' he said, surveying Maddy. 'You look terrible.'

Her face twitched as she attempted a smile. 'I feel terrible. But it's only scrapes and bumps. Nothing deep.' Her voice was still hoarse.

'Still,' said Preet, 'you need to see a doctor.'

'No,' said Maddy firmly. 'It's really not serious.'

He was not convinced but said nothing.

'This is your farm?' asked Maddy, thinking that the answer had to be yes.

'Father's,' said Preet. 'I come and go. Brothers live here, wife lives here, children are here. But I come and go.' He shifted his position so that he was angled away from her face. A packet of bidis materialized in his hand. He extracted one, lit it, then sat with his forearms dangling down, the upper arms resting on the tops of his knees.

The sharp scent stung her eyes. She blinked a couple of times, hard. 'I suppose I have to get up someday,' she said.

'How did this happen?' he asked. 'The face.'

'Guy came behind me, slammed me into the door of my room,' said Maddy.

'Who?'

'No idea. He offered me money to shut me up.'

Preet puffed on his bidi. 'How much?'

Maddy considered lying but said instead, 'Ten lakhs.'

Preet gave a snort. 'I would have taken it first, then made khichdi out of him!'

There was a short silence while this remark was processed. They both knew that she had offered him half that amount on the phone the day before as payment for today's unorthodox taxi services. The reason the sum was so large, she had explained then, was the need for discretion and the possibility that she might be slightly groggy.

'How come you brought me here?' asked Maddy. 'When I spoke to you, I said I wanted to be dropped off at a hotel.'

'You said only that you might be a bit unsteady. You never said you'd be a corpse. Hotels don't allow corpses to check in. That's what I said to the vakil who brought you to the car. He took a photo of your face. Said he was very concerned, but he had to get back to the hearing. I told him, "Don't worry. I'll bring the body straight to my father's farm and bury him in the sugarcane field."'

'Heh,' said Maddy, finding the conversation hysterically funny. It was impossible to laugh, however. 'I took too many pills. Three instead of one.'

'You've been asleep six hours. I made you walk from the car, but you have been dead ever since. Better get up. If you don't move soon, you'll be a corpse forever,' he said. He levered himself to his feet, holding the side of the cot she was lying on. He held out a hand to help her get up, but she waved it aside, saying that she'd manage on her own, slowly.

Maddy cursed and winced under her breath but eventually got herself upright. She'd been lying on a charpoy made of multi-coloured nylon rope stretched onto a wooden frame. Her shoes had been removed and were placed nearby.

'Oooch,' she said repeatedly, trying to stop herself from cursing in English.

'Biwi is asking if you want some tea,' said Preet.

Maddy said yes to the tea while thinking to herself that this stay was going to be a test of everything she knew about social behaviour in rural India.

She guessed that the concept of a house guest who was neither a family member nor of the same community would be rare in Preet's world. Even otherwise, though, she had no experience of acceptable behaviours in the context of an Indian farmer's family. It shocked her to acknowledge this. Yet it was an utterly mundane and unremarkable truth. Urban courtesies of the 'please' and 'thank you' kind might seem outlandish to them. Or maybe not? Maybe television and the internet had wrought deep changes?

She did not know.

All this while, Maddy had been facing the fields and the far horizon. But when she stood up and turned in the direction Preet was facing, she understood that they had been in the backyard all this while. Now they were facing a single-storey home built of white-washed brick. Its design was rudimentary, with several separate elements. The main building was a cube, with a flight of uncovered stairs zigzagging up one wall to the open terrace on top. A couple of sub-cubes had been built a short distance from the main house. Square windows without panes punctuated all the walls that she could see.

Off to one side was a grass-roofed enclosure with a buffalo penned inside, stolidly chewing its afternoon cud. An area directly outside the back of the house had been marked out with a low brick wall. Within that area, the earth had been tamped down smooth and flat. A standpipe jutted out onto a brick-red platform, on which stood a yellow bucket.

Leading from this area into the house was an open doorway. Standing in that doorway, framed by the dark interior, was a young woman. She wore a neon orange kurta with a cobalt blue salwar beneath it and a lime green dupatta, spangled with embroidery, covering her head and shoulders. Her face was partially obscured by the dupatta, but even at this distance, Maddy could see a slash of blood-red lipstick across her mouth. She was looking towards Preet and beckoning to him with her hand.

He had already started moving towards her.

The sight of the young woman, undoubtedly Preet's wife, caused Maddy pangs of deep discomfort. She was fairly sure that the reason the woman's face was covered was on account of her presence – an unfamiliar man – in their midst. Maybe even the lipstick. Or maybe she always dressed like this? Maybe it was in honour of Preet, who spent most of the month away in the city? She would never be told and would certainly not be able to ask.

She turned away again, fretting about the limited choices open to her in this situation.

Presently, Preet came back bearing two white cups, each brimming over with scalding hot tea. He handed one to her, saying, 'Biwi wants to know what you will have for food. I said, "Make the same as you make every day." But she insisted I must ask.'

Maddy gave a lopsided smile. 'Please.' She said the word in English. 'Your wife must not trouble herself.'

'At home, we only eat veg,' said Preet.

'Of course,' said Maddy. 'Also... please... I'll eat here. Outside.'

'No need for that—' began Preet.

'Your wife will be uncomfortable,' said Maddy. 'I know how it is.'

'No, no, nothing like that; she'll serve us first – father, brothers, you, me—'

Maddy cut in, 'But there's also the problem that it hurts me too much to fold my legs. I can't sit down.'

'Oh,' said Preet, recognizing now that this was indeed a problem. The family sat on the floor to eat. 'Okay, then. I'll tell her.' He seemed relieved, too.

It was past 4 p.m. by this time, and the day was winding down. Maddy asked to get her backpack from the car so that she could have her medications. She was also amazed and delighted to discover that the lipstick-wearing wife had aspired to own a proper toilet, just for her own use. Maddy understood from this that Preet's chauffeuring job had afforded him an upwardly mobile wife. So there was a western-style toilet just for the lady's use in one of the smaller cube-shaped structures farthest from the main building.

Madan was given leave to use it, too. On account of his injuries.

Maddy was grateful to be left alone to her own devices.

Preet did not attempt to draw the outsider into the family circle.

When it was time for the night meal, he brought a stainless steel thaal with food piled high on it: parathas, two veggies and a katori of dal. Maddy now sat on a form-moulded plastic chair from inside. There was already a matka of water and a steel tumbler for her use and a hissing hurricane lantern for light. A flying carousel of insects bumped and flittered around the blazing cylinder.

As he handed Maddy the thaal, he said, gazing down at her, 'The swelling is less, but you still look like shit.'

Maddy gave a lopsided smile and laughed. 'Oh, thank you,' she said. 'Good to know!'

But Preet did not smile back. 'It's not right. They have left their stamp on your... your pretty face.' He said the words diffidently.

Maddy now gave an embarrassed laugh. 'Heh...' was all she could manage.

'You know I cannot be with you tonight, na?' said Preet suddenly, in a lowered tone.

'Of *course*, I know,' said Maddy, shocked. The reference to that other dimension had come out of the blue. 'I did not expect it.'

'I will go back now,' he said. 'Or Biwi will ask too many questions.'

'Yes, please go,' said Maddy. 'Already you have done too much for me.'

Preet gave a mild snort. 'Why? The vakil gave me full payment! Plus, I have not completed the job. Tomorrow, early morning, I will deliver the package to the hotel.'

Maddy glanced up and said, 'The package thanks you in advance.'

He gave another snort and turned to leave. 'I'll come back later for your plate.'

55

Tick-tock!
Goldilocks!
Ate a clock!
And lost her socks!

– JINXES, BIG & SMALL

They left the next morning before the sky began to lighten in the east. The sound of the car starting up was deafening in the silence. They did not see anyone on their way out, the WagonR bumping and swaying on the uneven mud of the lane that led towards the highway.

Maddy was dressed in Madan's black shirt and jeans. She had changed into these under cover of darkness. She hadn't bathed or attempted to change out of her underclothes, however. The sweat-soaked breast binding was chafing her skin and was undoubtedly adding to the marks down her front caused by being slammed into the door. She hadn't seen her face since the day before but knew just from the easing of pain that the lumpy appearance was probably less conspicuous.

She was sitting in front, with her backpack at her feet. She was wearing sneakers now and had, without discussion, left Madan's shoes back at the farm. Preet wouldn't have noticed them in the dark. She hoped that they would simply be absorbed by the family, one way or another – by the unseen brothers and father or perhaps even Preet himself.

It had been part of her plan all along that Madan would now disappear altogether. She hadn't said so to Preet. She wondered how much he understood. How much he guessed. What his speculations were.

'Did you sleep okay?' he asked. He was wearing his work clothes once more, a freshly laundered striped shirt and khaki pants.

'I took a pill,' said Maddy. 'It helps with the pain as well.'

'Oh,' he said. Then after a pause, 'Why won't you see a doctor?'

'Because I don't have to.'

'Is that the only reason?'

'No,' she said. 'Boss doesn't want questions.'

'Yes, your vakil was very afraid. He seemed to think... I don't know... some people might still come after us. You.'

Maddy reached into her backpack and fished out her packet of cigarettes. Then she looked up to where there was a NO SMOKING decal pasted on the windscreen, just above the dashboard. She tapped it and said, 'Is it okay?'

Preet said, 'That's for back seat only. Front seat is for smokers only.'

She laughed and lit up. It had been almost two days since she'd had a smoke. The first inhale made her head swim. She opened her window.

She answered Preet's remark. 'The boss is fighting a case against big people.' She gave him a stripped-down version of events, of the scene in the car with Sherry and what she later claimed had happened. 'That's what the guy was threatening me about when he offered me the money to shut up.'

She offered him a drag, but Preet shook his head and reached into his shirt pocket for bidis.

'He was sent to frighten me into agreeing with what that woman said.'

'Women!' said Preet. His voice dripped scorn. 'They'll say anything if they're paid enough.'

'So will anyone,' said Maddy at once. 'Women get blamed for the wrong that men do.'

'Huh,' said Preet. 'Why're *you* supporting the bitch? She threw you under the same bus as your boss.' He lit his bidi one-handed with a disposable lighter and opened his window.

'She's just fighting to stay alive,' said Maddy, struggling to maintain a realistic 'Madan' perspective. 'Just like every one of us.'

Preet clicked his tongue dismissively. 'Well. I have no time for them.'

Maddy wanted to ask, *All women? Or only those who earn society's contempt?*

They sped along in silence. Trucks rumbled by infrequently.

It was still relatively dark outside.

'Okay,' said Preet, presently. 'There's something I've been wanting to do.' He decreased his speed, closed both the windows and brought the car to a gradual halt. He had chosen the shelter of an old and sprawling banyan, the kind that used to be common along the sides of main highways but no longer was.

Maddy thought he meant to take a leak. He didn't leave the car, however. He sat a moment or two. Not looking anywhere in particular, he said, 'How much is your face hurting?'

'Not much,' said Maddy. Her heart began to thump.

He turned towards her now, held her face with the same gentleness with which he had placed his hand on his son's small head and leaned down towards her. It was a very different embrace from that first time. For a long moment, there was nothing to think about. Then the wounds on Maddy's mouth began to assert themselves and she flinched.

He drew away.

'Pain,' he said in a whisper, leaning his forehead upon hers. 'I can taste the blood.'

Preet told Maddy that 'the vakil' had made a booking at the Maurya Sheraton. 'But it is not in your name. He said you would know what that means.' It was originally made for the same day as the hearing, but he said he'd re-book for the next day when the program was changed.

Maddy nodded. 'It means I have to dress up as someone else. Madan has to disappear. At least for some time.'

'Wah,' said Preet. 'What do you mean, "dress up"?'

'Become someone else. Look completely different.'

'Huh! I never heard of such a thing. Maybe in a film. Not in real life.'

'It's not common,' Maddy assured him. 'Boss had this idea. And I...' she could feel the fabric of truth stretching thin, 'was available.'

'For me, this is very strange.' He paused. 'What will you dress up as?'

'As a woman,' said Maddy. She held her breath.

Preet was silent for several minutes. 'Are you making fun of me?'

'No,' said Maddy. She waited, wanting the reality of the situation to sink in. 'It's the only way to completely disappear.'

Preet processed this information. 'That's true, I suppose.' Then, 'But where will you change? Where is your costume?'

'In my bag,' she said, leaning down to unzip her backpack. 'I've done it two or three times already. It has to be in a car, you see. I can't go into a men's toilet as a man and come out as a woman!'

Preet smiled a little uncertainly at this.

'It's easier than you think,' said Maddy as she pulled out the dark tent dress she had with her to match the jeans.

'This is One,' she said as she pulled the dress on over Madan's black shirt.

Next, she drew out the wig. 'This is Two,' she said as she placed it on her head. 'At some point, I will look at your rear-view mirror and arrange the hair a little more neatly.'

'And this is Three.' She removed the sneakers and exchanged them for the silver flip-flops. 'Ta-daaa. Transformation complete.'

Preet had been glancing sideways as she made the transition.

She could not tell what he was thinking. His expression was blank.

Finally, she had to ask. 'Well? Does it work?'

He shifted his shoulders in a half-shrug, then shook his head in denial. 'If I hadn't seen it in front of my eyes, I would never have believed it.'

He stopped to consider his next words carefully before continuing. 'You want to know a strange thing? Biwi only saw you from a distance. That time when you were standing up and she was offering tea. But at night, when no one is listening, she says to me, "I don't like him. Your friend." I ask her why. And she says, "He looks like a girl."

'I thought she was just, you know, being like that. Maybe she suspected something, I don't know. But now...'

He trailed off. 'Now it seems she saw something that I myself did not see.'

The knife of truth twisted within Maddy's gut.

'Women have eyes in their hearts,' she said. 'It gives them the power to look under the hood of reality.'

Preet glanced at her, then away, saying nothing.

56

Zebras, aardvarks, kinkajou,
Glory be to all of you!

– JINXES, BIG & SMALL

When they were nearing the hotel, Maddy asked Preet if he would like to come in. 'Why don't you take the day off?'

'And do what?' he asked. 'Sit in the hotel lobby eating chips?' He had told her that his Austrian boss had treated him to meals at some of the fanciest hotels. He used to be afraid of these places, he said, until he'd seen for himself that the people there were just like anyone else, only fatter.

'No,' said Maddy. 'I'll have a big room to myself. My boss is paying for everything. You can eat three lunches and three dinners if you want.'

'Smoking or non-smoking?' he asked, and they both laughed. But he shook his head. 'No. That's all right. I'll go to my stand.'

Maddy said, 'I'll send you the room number by text when I've checked in.'

He flicked a glance towards her. 'Really?'

She could feel her face colouring. 'Really. But it'll be from a different number. I have to switch off the... my number.'

They were just entering the gates of the hotel.

He inclined his head. 'Okay. Maybe I will call you.'

'Only maybe?' said Maddy, wondering when she had become so daring, so coquettish.

Preet gave a slight snort. 'Yah.'

Then they had drawn up to the hotel's front steps, and the ubiquitous seven-foot-tall doormen with their starched cockscomb turbans were coming forward to open the door for her.

She grabbed her backpack by its top handle, hauled it out of the car and closed the door before the doorkeeper could do it for her.

Bending down to the open window and conscious of the bustle of cars arriving and departing at the hotel's entrance, she said, 'I'll see you.'

Though he nodded, she saw that the pressure to leave was upon him. He sped away without any parting words as soon as she straightened up.

Maddy visited the hotel's shopping arcade to pick up fresh clothes and toiletries for herself before going up to her room to have a hot shower after two days of doing without. There was a wall-width mirror in the bathroom, and she was shocked by what she saw when she removed her underclothes.

She knew that it must have improved: where once there had been misshapen lumps, now there were purple and green bruises with only mild swelling. Even so, the damage to her skin was extensive. And not merely from the assault. The breast-binding had left angry red stripes across her chest and back. She touched herself gingerly. The skin was tender and puckered, especially where the edges of the bandage had cut in.

Showering was refined torture. She yodelled softly in pain as the water singed her skin. She soaped carefully and patted herself dry without wiping. The tiny container of body lotion in the hotel's self-care kit was hilariously inadequate. But even the thick white cream from the giant bottle of Nivea body lotion that she'd bought from the chemist downstairs was merely soothing, rather than healing. She was going to need more than that eventually.

She wrapped herself in the hotel's white terry-cloth robe and stepped back into the room. It was immense. A single-room suite: there was a king-size bed, a sofa, a table for two and a view of the hotel's garden, as well as the forested expanse of the ridge on the other side of the road.

She was only mildly bemused by this extravagance. She understood what it was: an apology and a reward for all that she had endured. She loved staying in hotels, and this was, she knew, one of the best. She was delighted with it.

Yet, as she looked around, she was wondering how it would strike Preet. He would perhaps find it grotesque. In her mind's eye, she could see him moving around, sneering at the wall-to-wall carpeting, the windows that could not be opened, the heavy curtains and the double bed.

The bed, especially. Would he even be able to sleep in it? The charpoy she had lain on the night before had been just one stage up from a bed of nails for her. If that was what he was used to, then the memory-foam mattress and its box springs might well be a bed of nails for him. Maybe he'd insist on sleeping on the carpet. Maybe even that would be unpleasant for him.

She called room service and ordered coffee and croissants. Only then, three hours after checking in, did she dig into her backpack to get out her phones. Chetak had remembered to pick up her Samsung from the basket on Bahadur's desk and had also returned Madan's phone to her. She had checked for them at the farm. But both gadgets had been turned off all this while.

There was only one call to Madan's number, and that was from Chetak. She turned the Nokia off once more.

When she looked at her Samsung, she saw that he'd called that number, too, at close to the same time. Malli had also called. Perhaps an hour ago. Verity had messaged to say she was coming back to Delhi three days hence. Eleven other calls had been registered, all from her lady clients. Some had left messages, too. Missing her, they all said.

She didn't call Malli but instead left a voice message. 'Malli! I'm at the Maurya. Feeling great. Come and have room service with me? Come.'

She knew she should call Chetak but was resisting it.

She sent a text message to Preet with the room number.

Then her Samsung rang, and it was Malli.

'Maddy,' she said. 'My god. Have you seen the paper today?'

Of course not.

'Better take a look – no wait, I'll send a screen grab to you.'

A moment later, on WhatsApp, an incoming photograph showed a pale, battered face with the eyes half-open, the mouth cut and bleeding. The caption read: DRIVER SUCCUMBS TO WOUNDS. Beneath it, the first few lines read: 'Madan Lal Singh, 24, savagely beaten for resisting an entrapment attempt, has reportedly succumbed to his wounds...'

Maddy stared at the face, barely recognizing herself. 'Wow,' she said to Malli. 'I look a mess, huh.'

'Totally,' said Malli. 'Can you imagine what I thought when I saw that? I mean, I knew you were all right because of what Chetak told me. But your face! Is that make-up or what?'

Maddy laughed. 'Come and see for yourself! I'm fine.'

Now she called Chetak. 'You've seen it?' he asked.

'Yes,' she said. 'It was a bit of a shock...'

'We didn't get a chance to discuss it.'

'No, obviously. I'd passed out!'

'That was bizarre. But highly effective. Did you know the pills would have that effect?'

'No!' said Maddy. 'I'd brought three tabs with me thinking I'd need them to get through the night, wherever I was. But I forgot to separate them. Just one would have been enough to make me stagger a bit but not pass out.'

'Well, it was certainly convincing. We were shocked out of our wits. There was no faking any of it. And the recording droning on and on! It was total chaos. I managed to get you out with Suresh and Jyoti's help and stuffed you into your friendly cab driver's WagonR. That's when he made this sort of joke – I think he meant it as a joke – about hotels and corpses. And it was true. You looked very... convincing. So I took that picture. And used it a day later.'

He paused.

'Maddy, can you ever forgive me?'

'Huh?' she said, surprised.

'I just parcelled you off. With an unknown man.'

'Oh!' she said. 'Oh. It never even occurred to me to think of that.' Of course, it didn't. She had a reason for trusting the 'unknown man' that Chetak knew nothing of. 'Besides, if you recall, he believed *I* was a man.'

'And that makes it all right somehow?' asked Chetak. 'When *I* knew you aren't?'

'Anyway, look. It's behind us. Really.'

'If it's any consolation, I hope you realized that I was still able to track you. I had his number as well. I knew exactly where you were. All the time. Even this morning. I knew you'd made it to the Maurya—'

'It's really *okay*,' cut in Maddy. 'Please, for heaven's sake, tell me what happened at the hearing! Has the other side gone silent?'

'Oh, yes,' said Chetak. 'We followed your lead about the woman's address. My chaps broke into her place while the hearing was in progress. Grabbed evidence. Dangled it strategically. And miraculously, the complaint was withdrawn. All hushed up, moving along. Needless to say, the other matter grinds on. But at least Russi is still in there, fighting.'

'What about Sherry?'

'Probably in the Bahamas by now. Or maybe Indonesia. Wherever ladies of the night go when they need daylight.'

Malli, looking as cool as a tall glass of frosted lemonade in a white-on-white eyelet-lace skirt and blouse, had brought herbal gels for Maddy. She helped apply them to Maddy's back as they talked. Maddy gave her a blow-by-blow account of the planning that went into creating the scene at the hearing, followed by the almost-disaster of the pills, and the aftermath at the farm.

They spent the afternoon luxuriating in the room.

Only as her visit was drawing to a close did Malli say, treading as carefully as a cat walking on eggshells, 'By the way, I notice that you've said very little about the grey-eyed charioteer.'

Maddy smiled and shrugged. 'Well. Nothing to say, really.' Then she relented. 'Except that I...' She could not bite her lips, so she settled for sighing. 'Okay, then. I sent him my room number.'

'Oh,' said Malli, not smiling. 'So you *are* a fool after all. A silly, thoughtless—'

Maddy cut in, 'Malli, how can I just let go? As if nothing happened?'

'Because *nothing* happens all the time. A butterfly lands on your finger, you admire it, you wish it luck and then you let it go. It can be that simple.'

'Supposing the butterfly is still on my finger? Being admired?'

'Because you glued him down there. With your invitation.'

'No! He's a free agent. He has a wife—'

'And you? You'd be what? His bum-boy – who's not really a boy at all – for a night?'

'That's such a disgusting term.'

'Does he even know? That you're not a boy?'

'I feel,' said Maddy, 'that the least I owe him is to be honest about that one thing.'

'So that you can watch the light fade in his eyes? So that you can enjoy trampling on his feelings?'

'No!'

'Or do you imagine that you, and you alone, will be his female saviour?'

'Oh, Malli, no! Of course not! I wouldn't... I don't...'

'Then please try and understand that what you've done is wrong by inviting him here. Send him another text message. Tell him not to come.'

Maddy looked down at her hands. After a long pause, she said, 'I can force myself to say *yes* to you, but I can't make myself do it.' She sighed. 'You know what I'm like.'

Malli gave a wry smile. 'Yes, dear, I know. You're mad and you're cruel, but either way, you're my friend. I love you all the same.'

She got up to leave, saying, 'There's nothing left for me to do but to wish you a happy butterfly.'

Maddy slept, woke, had a baked Alaska at teatime and watched reruns of *Friends* on the TV. It wasn't until 7 p.m. that she began to think that maybe Preet wasn't going to come.

At 9 p.m., she ordered a double portion of spaghetti Bolognese for dinner, with a bottle of red wine and two servings of vanilla ice cream. She felt fairly sure that he wasn't coming but thought it best to be safe.

At ten, bloated with pasta, wine and both servings of ice cream, she reapplied Malli's gel and went to sleep.

At 1 a.m., her phone dinged with an incoming text.

It was from Preet.

It was in the form of a graphic that took a few seconds to download. When it did, she saw it was a news item taken from the Hindi language papers, showing Madan's dead face.

Accompanying the graphic was a line of text in English: *Sad news. Sorry for your loss. Goodbye.*

57

Let's be merry,
Let's have fun,
Let's laugh often,
Leap and run.

– JINXES, BIG & SMALL

Maddy returned by taxi to the villa late the next morning. The entire length of the approach lane to her side of the building was strewn with marigolds.

She wondered about it enough to ask Prem, who was indeed Bahadur's brother and was on duty that day, why there were flowers on the driveway. He glanced away a couple of times as if embarrassed to have to answer such a basic question before saying, 'There's been a death.'

'Oh, no,' said Maddy, gripped by a moment's awful foreboding. 'Who...?'

'There was that Rani?' said Prem. 'It was her.'

'Oh!' said Maddy again as she stepped into the lift.

Back in her room, Maddy stood for long minutes with her arms wrapped around herself, looking around. How weird and ordinary life could be. She had been to the edge of reality with her overdose, but here she was, returned to this room once more. This space that was her current definition of home.

So many decisions to take. She remembered her last evening here, when she had been angry with Verity about that letter and when Chetak had come close to yelling at her.

The little book that Verity had sent her was still lying on the bed, where she'd left it. She picked it up now and riffled through its pages. It was a decidedly odd choice as a gift, she thought, considering that it was supposedly aimed at children. Though not especially child-appropriate. The verses were mildly amusing. There were several on every page, each with its own sketch, rendered in a loose, airy style. Edward Lear-ish, without being quite madcap enough.

The book had been famous in its day, but Maddy was surprised to learn, from the back-cover blurb, that it was still extremely popular. Translated into dozens of languages. The author's name was Anne O. Nim. She sounded faintly Scottish. There were no other biographical details or a photograph.

Maddy turned the book over again to look at the front cover, which showed a collection of the airy sketches rendered in colour. Then she opened it to see if there was a dedication.

Yes. There was. In Verity's clear and slightly olde worlde handwriting.

Dear Maddy,
Amongst the many things I should
have shared with you from the start,
there's this little book.
With very warm good wishes,
Anne

Epilogue

Epilogue
Sun and fog,
Dusk and dawn,
Moving on.

— JINXES, BIG & SMALL

Some days later, Maddy and Verity were on the terrace, enjoying a late-morning tea.

Verity's head was wrapped in a grey silk scarf. She had lost all her hair, and her face looked a little pinched, but there was a rosy bloom on her skin. She was in the same pink kimono she'd been wearing when they had last met. Maddy saw now that it was printed with a pattern of white orchids alternating with tiny white dragons.

'It's very odd,' she said, 'to be fully prepared to blast off to eternity with my fears and regrets stacked around me, my tears ready to shed, only to be told by my doctors that the flight's been cancelled!' She turned her head, smiling. 'Almost a nuisance!'

'Don't say that,' said Maddy, also smiling. She was wearing her white chikankari tent dress and was reclining in the easy chair, which had fold-out extensions.

'I'm only saying it to you, my dear, no one else,' said Verity, reclining as well. 'I believe that the conversation we had just before I left really helped me. I don't know if a single friendly chat can actually save anyone's life or even if I believe in these theories about positivity and health outcomes. But I'm grateful, whatever the reason.'

'That's wonderful,' said Maddy.

'I suppose you know that I'm waiting feverishly to hear about your adventures? Chit gave me an extremely unsatisfactory account.' She paused. 'I'm guessing that you have some questions for me, too.'

Maddy had heard, via Pretty and Lata, whom she'd met over meals in the dining room, that the Rani's death had opened the way to unifying the entire building. That Verity was indeed the owner of the front half. That she had owned it for many years and that she used it as a way to help out friends in need. She had only moved in recently, on account of her ill health. And that, yes, she was a world-famous author who had changed her nationality in order to live out her life, incognito, in India.

Maddy stretched lazily in the heat. 'Not really,' she said. 'I'm good.'

'That's one of the Americanisms I detest,' complained Verity. 'Maybe because I don't quite understand what it means.'

'It means that I'm happy in this moment,' said Maddy.

She wanted to add that she understood how fleeting such moments were. That she wasn't sure, yet, whether or not to remain in the villa. Or even in the country. That she was keeping her options open.

'And I'm awake,' she said. 'I'm awake.'

Acknowledgements

With warm thanks, always, to Thomas Abraham, Publisher Extraordinaire, willing to take on odd books with a tolerant smile.

With gladness and gratitude to Sonali Jindal, for her insights, her patience and her thoughtful editing.

To my friends Ketaki Sheth (Presentation Convent, Kodaikanal) and Ayesha Kagal (1970s Times of India) and especially Revati Laul, whom I have only met through late night phone conversations. This book began as the merest shadow of an idea, in the mid-1990s. All three of you, in very different ways, triggered the main mass of it into existence, through the middle and end of 2022.

To Poulomi Chatterjee, my editor of many years, who saw two and a half chapters of this book shortly after we first met, maybe in 2009. She gave it a friendly nod despite its complete lack of substance! And that allowed me to keep the idea alive for literally two decades after the character of Maddy first appeared in my head.

And finally, with warm remembrance of Ram Pyare, the Embassy chauffeur in Bangkok, Thailand. For three years, starting from when I was a lonely, nerdy little girl of eleven, he drove me back and forth to school in our shiny black Chrysler. He told me about his life as a truck driver in India before emigrating to Thailand and settling down with a Thai wife. He bought me ice creams, on the way home from school. But when I left my parents to fly back to India and to boarding school, I forgot to thank him. Maybe that long-standing guilt is why I remember him so clearly.